My
BROTHER'S
KEEPER

My

BROTHER'S KEEPER

E-Book Available

www.davidblackauthor.com

My
BROTHER'S
KEEPER

DAVID BLACK

DAISA & CO

First published in Great Britain in 2019 by Daisa & Co

Copyright © 2019 by DAVID BLACK

The moral right of the Author has been asserted.

A CIP catalogue record for this book is available from the British Library.
ISBN 978-1-9997894-9-7

Book typeset by:
DAISA & CO
Westfield Lakes, Far Ings Road, Barton upon Humber
North Lincolnshire, DN18 5RG, England
www.daisa-co.com

Printed in England

Daisa & Co is committed to a sustainable future for our business, our readers and our planet.
This book in your hands is made from paper certified by the forest stewardship council.

DEDICATION

Dedicated to my wife Joanne and daughters, Georgia and Hannah who have accompanied me on my long running journey to deliver this story to you.

Also, to my parents Alan and Rosie who have long worried that my education had gone to waste.

CHAPTER 1

William Brown worked damned hard for his money and wasn't embarrassed to show it. Woodside, the farm he inherited from his father who in turn had taken over from his father before him, was set between the Firth of Forth and Haddington, close to Edinburgh. It was a vast sprawling estate with a large, stone built Victorian farmhouse that easily swallowed up its seven occupants.

It was his first farm, the land was good but the weather was often lousy and unforgiving. William enjoyed the trappings of wealth and was considered by all a 'country gentleman' in post war Britain.

Now aged 37, he was already the proud owner of one of the first Mk VI Bentley Continentals in Scotland. It was a monster of a car in classic British Racing Green which he enjoyed driving to its full potential. The powerful sound of the inline-six-cylinder engine with its twin SU carburetors sounded like thunder, as it echoed off the solid granite buildings that lined the Edinburgh Streets.

William's wife Florence looked after their four children. James and Nick who were 7 and 5, Jack aged 3 years and Elizabeth who had just turned 1 year old, were ably assisted by Susan the hired help.

William had run the farm since his father George had died suddenly from a heart attack at 53 years of age. He'd only been 18 years old at the time and had no choice but to take the reins.

Each morning whatever the weather, William was up by 5:30am helping with the dairy herd of 150 Ayrshires that needed to be milked. This lifestyle had shaped him over the years into the man he'd now become.

Standing at 6ft. 2" he was wide across the shoulders and although he weighed over 15 stone, he didn't look overweight. His dark hair was straight and thin and fell naturally to the right side of his head.

The deep-set wrinkles around his eyes and weather-beaten skin bore testimony to the struggles he'd already had to overcome. His worn and callous marked hands were so big that the cigars he continuously smoked looked like miniatures as he rolled them between his fingers. William was a staunch and stern character who didn't suffer fools gladly.

After the milking was complete and the cows had been herded back to the fields, he would gather his twelve workhands together and brief them on their tasks for the day.

'Organization was the key to success', he would preach in his strong Scottish accent.

The men were left in no doubt that they would face William's fiery temper if their allocated duties were not completed, something they did their best to avoid.

As the home's mainstay, Florence would dutifully have the evening meal promptly on the table for 5 p.m. after which work would carry on, often lasting well into the night, by which time William was ready to relax with a glass of single malt, mixed 50/50 with tap water… nothing more.

The farm had provided William's predecessors with a reasonable standard of living, however with the introduction of new farming methods and the attention to detail that William showed, he had transformed this into a highly profitable enterprise, despite the great depression in the 1930's that destroyed many areas of the manufacturing industry.

Even though the farm had done reasonably well, the country had struggled to recover from the outbreak of World War II. In 1942, due partly to the success of Woodside and partly the poor fortune of his neighbours, William had managed to acquire Coates Farm and Tanners Farm that bordered his, increasing his share of the East Lothian countryside to over fifteen hundred acres.

Farming had been kind to William, as it had to the previous generations of the Brown family. Throughout the war years the farms had pushed their levels of production as high as possible to help feed the country during those days of hardship.

With Conscription being reintroduced in September 1939, all men aged 18 to 41 years of age were called up for military service, making the hunt for strong male workers nigh on impossible.

William, and Bill his farm manager, had been exempt from conscription as their jobs were considered essential to the war effort, whilst William's wife Florence had taken on the role of managing the replacement female workers. She did it well but constantly longed to be back in her home county of Norfolk, where she spent her childhood enjoying long days of warm sunshine as opposed to the never ending fog and drizzle to which she had now become accustomed.

William felt the war had brought people together and given them a real reason to fight to survive; some felt these were actually the best days of their lives. The war felt like it would go on forever but now it had ended Florence had nagged William daily until he'd finally agreed to let her organize a family holiday.

Most people were still scraping by on 'rations' and the best the masses could hope for was a British seaside outing to coastal resorts like Scarborough and Skegness. These were popular choices with plenty of cheap entertainment, aimed at diverting one's mind from the general misery of day to day life. Holidays abroad were a very rare luxury and out of reach for many families. Money however was not an issue for the Browns and even William agreed that a foreign trip would be an interesting adventure; after all he had worked hard for nearly a decade with days off being few and far between.

Having skillfully brought William round to her way of thinking, tickets for a trip around the Mediterranean had duly been purchased and he had grown used to the idea and was now looking forward to the trip. Even so, he'd spent the weeks before becoming ever more agitated about leaving the business to run in his absence, something he had never done before. William wasn't very good at abdicating responsibility. He'd tried delegating before but liked to have his eye on what was going on. Ultimately, he just had to accept that he was going and his men would have to manage without him.

It was a pleasant, if somewhat chilly May morning when the family made its way to the Port of Leith located to the North Eastern side of Edinburgh. The small privately hired bus had more than enough seats for the family along with one extra passenger, Susan Tully, the live-in nanny.

Florence had been adamant in no uncertain terms that she would be having a rest consequently Susan would be needed to look after the four children during the voyage. She had been working for the Brown family since James was born and was now 27 years of age. Having been brought up in the suburbs of Edinburgh, Susan had a strong local accent and always wore a smile. Her pink complexion gave her a permanent look of naivety and embarrassment which added to her youth and charm.

With a good number of bags and suitcases filling up the back row of seats, they were soon on their way to meet the RMS Orcades, a prestigious liner operated by the Orient Line which was to be their home over the next month.

She was a 28,000 tonne two class ship, providing accommodation for 773 1st Class and 772 Tourist Class passengers. The 1st Class restaurant was beautifully finished in oak panels and had brass lamps with salmon pink shades on each table. Neatly arranged gilt chairs with burgundy upholstery and gold studs purveyed a sense of grandeur.

There were three bars for use by the 'upper class' passengers, each stocked with a range of the finest quality wines, beers and spirits, their glittering displays easily enticing their customers to investigate further.

The ship was well equipped for the sports-minded with a swimming pool, gymnasium and racket courts along with shower and bathrooms for massage treatments.

On 'A' deck there was the 1st Class smoke room which had been modelled after the house of El Greco, the Spanish painter. The room also contained an authentic American bar, while the 1st Class Lounge area was furnished and decorated to represent the period of King William of Orange.

On the Boat Deck there were thirty lifeboats and two motor launches. Following the Titanic's tragedy, all liners now carried an ample quota in case they were ever unfortunate enough to meet the same fate.

As the family made their way on board, two Porters struggled with various trunks and cases that were packed with anything and everything needed for a month-long excursion on a modern cruise liner. Florence wasn't one for travelling light. She had outfits for every occasion with shoes and accessories to match.

"We're not moving house woman," William moaned loudly as they made their way over the adjoining gangway.

"It's alright for you William, you only need a suit and dinner jacket. You wouldn't want people seeing me in the same outfit night after night, would you? Don't you want me to look my best?"

William muttered something unintelligible under his breath and pushed forward. The 1st. Class cabins were indeed luxurious. William and Florence had their own private balcony complete with a couple of expensive Teak sun loungers which Florence eyed with delight!

In order for the children to be watched over whilst the parents were dining at night, special arrangements had been made for their room to be adjacent to the Nanny's room with an interconnecting door. Susan was very impressed with these Nanny quarters. The walls were lined in fine wood panelling and the doors adorned with brass furniture. The portholes in her quarters weren't large, but big enough to give a nice view over the sea, which splashed against the side of the ship some fifty feet below. The bed looked inviting with its clean, gold edged sheets and enormous swollen pillows. Even though she was on duty, when left alone for a few moments, she could almost imagine herself as a real lady being waited on hand and foot.

After a couple of hours, the ship's horn gave off a long steady blast and almost undiscernibly, the ship drifted from the quayside. The weather was quite good for the time of year and the water relatively calm as the large ship headed down the Firth of Forth towards the open waters of the North Sea.

The family had joined hundreds of other fellow passengers on deck to wave goodbye to the crowds milling on the dockside below. As the Brown family leant on the railings trying to identify their farm up above Longniddry, Captain Glenn peered through his binoculars surveying the estuary ahead. Satisfied that the route was clear, he signalled his Chief Engineer to notch up the engines. None of the family had been on a cruise before and as they headed out towards the open sea, they quickly had to get used to the ship rolling slowly from side to side, it was almost unnoticeable unless you looked towards the horizon.

The Estuary gradually widened as they passed North Berwick and the Bass Rock which standing just over a mile off shore, soared over 350ft. into the air. Other than the lighthouse keeper, only a few thousand Gannets called this barren volcanic rock 'home'.

The North Sea was quite calm as they slowly headed further down the east coast passing Berwick upon Tweed and later, the Tyne Estuary as it flowed from the heavily industrial areas around Newcastle out to sea.

After two full days of sailing, the ship finally entered the busy waters of the English Channel. Things were quite relaxing until they headed across the open waters of the Bay of Biscay towards the northern coast of Spain.

Passengers not used to sailing were soon awakened to this new sensation as the ship rose, fell and rocked in the now choppy sea. Even though the ship was relatively large, once in wide open water there was no hiding from the fact you were at sea. There were some greenish complexions amongst the passengers, a few of whom were hanging onto the ship's railings with clenched white knuckles, staring towards the horizon. Others seemed completely immune and were quite happy sipping on cocktails or strolling around the decks watching their fellow passengers with amusement.

William was one of these latter groups whereas Florence and the nanny took a couple of days to find their 'sea legs'. Susan had the hardest time. She was extremely sea sick for the first two days and hadn't thought she could survive a month of this and unlike

Florence, who was a lady of leisure, she couldn't retire to her bed, she had no option but to fulfil her work duties.

The family soon acclimatized to life on board. William had found his way to the 1st. class smoke room with its long mahogany bar almost before the ship had left its dock. Here he'd met a fellow farmer from the Carlisle area who'd reserved himself a regular seat.

Peter Binnington was a few years older and wore a rather scruffy unkempt beard which made up for the shortfall of hair he now carried on his head. Like William, he too was also taking his first holiday in many years.

They'd talk for hours about 'farming through the war years' and 'when food rationing may finally end,' amongst other topics.

Florence was happy to position herself on the starboard upper deck where rows of neatly arranged deck chairs offered a welcome vantage point. She could be miles away reading or just looking out to sea watching anything that happened to pass, such as the occasional navy vessel and a couple of smaller cruise ships.

The children were taken each day to the crèche by Susan where all manner of games and entertainment were laid on for those less than 14 years of age. The parents all thought this a marvellous idea, enjoying their time together without worrying about the children getting into mischief.

The ship was due to stop at various ports around the Mediterranean, with excursions laid on for the passengers to sample the sights and sounds of various historic European cities and towns.

The trips weren't compulsory, and many passengers were quite happy to spend the entire journey on-board. Others like Florence, William and the family were keen to see some of the sights and welcomed the brief feeling of being back on 'Terra Firma'.

Once Susan had got used to being at sea, she was quite happy to stay on board and look after Elizabeth, the baby of the family where she could also enjoy a few hours of *not* being at Florence's 'beck and call'.

The first port of call for the passengers was Gibraltar, a small British outpost sitting at the tip of the Iberian Peninsula. A solitary mountain, the Rock of Gibraltar looked out over the entrance to the Mediterranean.

During the war most residents had been evacuated and its defences had been bolstered, all due to its strategic location making it an important Royal Naval base. They'd now returned and the military presence had been scaled back to pre-war levels. Although covering a mere 2.6 square miles, the fact that Spain couldn't gain control over this rock had long been a bone of contention.

Dozens of passengers flooded ashore for a look around and to see the Barbary Apes and visit the Gibraltar museum. After five days at sea, the walk down the gang plank onto the quayside felt quite odd; their legs having known nothing but dry land for all those years had now become accustomed to the sensation of living on water.

After this, the ship sailed onwards to the Spanish Island of Mallorca, the largest of the Balearic Islands where they'd docked within walking distance of Palma's historic Old Town. A guided tour had been organised to The Castell de Bellver. This was built in the 14th century for King James II of Aragon and used as a military prison during the 18th and 19th centuries. Now it was one of the main tourist attractions of the island having been turned into a museum in 1932. William and Florence decided to take the two eldest children, James and Nick ashore whilst Susan watched the youngsters.

Two rickety old buses took turns to ferry any interested parties up through the pine woods to the top of the hill. Looking perfectly maintained, it was hard to believe that this round building with its central courtyard had stood here for nearly 700 years.

Once at the summit, there were amazing views to be had over Palma. The majestic Orcades could be seen in the distance moored in the bay. Next stop was Marseille, France's largest commercial port and the biggest French city on the Mediterranean coast. The ship had arranged to take on some extra supplies here. On this occasion, only William could be bothered to go ashore.

After only a few hours they were underway again, heading for the upmarket town of St Tropez on the French Riviera.

They laid anchor at around 11am and were advised to be back at the quayside by 5 o'clock, or the ship would sail without them.

"That won't give us much time shopping," said Florence with a huff.

"Is that all you think about woman? Another town with an interesting historic past to explore, and all you can think about is dresses," William moaned.

Much to William's delight, as the Brown family wandered around the old harbour district they came across some interesting ancient fortifications. The most magnificent of these was the 16th century Citadel, a well preserved fortress that soared above the port; this was also home to the Naval Museum.

"This is what we've come to see," William announced pompously.

"Really!" Florence groaned under her breath. The children followed quietly behind trying hard not to laugh.

William could spend all day viewing these historic buildings and architectural gems, whereas Florence felt she'd already had more than enough culture for one day. She took the lead and headed towards the 'Place aux Herbes,' a bustling square that seemed to be the place where the locals did their everyday shopping.

The central square, 'Place des Lices' seemed too big for a village the size of St Tropez, appealing shops and open air cafes were everywhere. Beneath the shade of the overhanging trees, retired old men played boules. The children weren't really that bothered about any of it, they were more concerned about getting back to the ship and exploring the decks for another game of hide and seek.

Finding the shelter of a branch-laden tree, William and Florence sat down at a table outside one of the many outdoor cafes and took afternoon tea, content to just watch the people go about their business. Florence loved it!

"Why don't we pack up and move here?" she sighed, in the way holidaymakers have done on nearly every vacation taken before or since.

CHAPTER 2

T he beautiful Sardinian town of Cagliari, had followed and then on to Messina in Sicily, a city that had suffered badly from bombing during the Second World War. Scars could still be seen across many of the buildings and reconstruction work looked like it would be going on for a considerable time to come.

In days past the cruise ships used to travel right across the Mediterranean to the ancient port city of Jaffa, however as there was unrest in the region, this was no longer possible.

Following World War II there had been tens of thousands of displaced people with nowhere to go. The British were in the process of trying to establish a new Palestinian state to be split between the Arab and the Jewish communities. In 1946 there had been a joint attempt by Britain and the United States to agree on a policy regarding the admission of Jews to Palestine.

In April of that year, the Committee reported that its members had arrived at a unanimous decision, approving the American recommendation of the immediate acceptance of 100,000 Jewish refugees from Europe into Palestine.

It also recommended that there be no Arab, and no Jewish State. The Committee stated that, *'In order to dispose, once and for all, of the exclusive claims of Jews and Arabs to Palestine, we regard it as essential that a clear statement of principle should be made that Jews shall not dominate Arab and Arab shall not dominate Jew in Palestine.'*

This created many problems, with the Arabs who were determined to fight back. Needless to say, the port of Jaffa, in the midst of the troubles, was not a suitable tourist destination... certainly not for the time being.

The cruise ship would now make its furthest stop at Limassol in Southern Cyprus, a large island lying off the coasts of Turkey and

Syria where the British had ruled since 1925. They were continually trying to find a solution to the ongoing arguments between the Greek and Turkish Cypriots who both wanted the place for themselves.

Having arrived off the coast of Cyprus in the middle of the night, the first the Brown family saw of the island that now lay off their portside was when they drew back their curtains the following day. The sun was reflecting brightly off the water and the sky was blue, highlighted by wisps of white cloud. The island, a few hundred yards away looked very inviting.

At around 10:30am the passengers wanting to go ashore were advised to head to the disembarking points on the lower deck. In what seemed like a very familiar routine to the passengers of RMS Orcades, a small flotilla of boats ferried the day trippers across the calm waters of Akrotiri Bay. Some of the elderly had to be lifted on and off these Tenders; one had slipped and nearly gone overboard which had sent the children into a fit of giggles.

"Don't laugh children, that's very rude," scorned Florence, secretly wanting to laugh herself.

Once ashore the group generally split up and ambled round the old narrow streets, browsing the artefacts that were being sold from crowded market stalls.

Small purchases were made but only after the seemingly mandatory process of haggling had been completed. The Brown family took a pleasant walk along the harbour front and the adjacent colourfully planted avenues with their fine palm trees and clumps of Oleanders. William dragged them up to Kolossi Castle repeating that it was important to learn a little about the history of the places they visited

"Apparently, in the 14th century the Knights Templar had been in situ," declared William.

"I'm sure we could give these ruins a miss, after all they do all look the same," protested Florence.

"How can you say that? It's important; you may never get a chance to see these things again. You can go shopping anytime," reiterated William, ignoring the protests.

Florence soon stopped her moaning she knew William would get his way. Had he more time, he would have taken them to Berengaria Castle, the place where Richard the Lionheart allegedly married Berengaria, but, to the relief of Florence and the children they were spared.

After stopping for a bite to eat and a much needed cool drink the family headed into a local thriving market. The place was packed. Florence went off to look at some rolls of fancy coloured materials.

Nick and Jack were tagging along, their attention captured by the amazing level of noise that filled the air and the strange sights of the locals haggling.

William, who with James had headed in the opposite direction, pushed their way through the buzzing crowds stopping to look at anything vaguely interesting from hand carved figures to leather bags.

As they emerged at the northern side of the square, William caught sight of Florence to his right and headed to meet her. It was then that they realised Jack, their three year old son, wasn't with them.

"I thought he was with *you*..." said Florence in a panicked tone. For a moment she wasn't sure what was happening, but within a few seconds the colour had drained from her face and she felt sick to the pit of her stomach.

"He's got to be nearby, he was here a minute ago," said William anxiously. "Come on, don't just stand there, let's go and find him!"

The family fought their way back round the crowded market shouting for Jack. The locals looked on but didn't really understand why these tourists were pushing their way through and shouting.

Ten minutes had now passed. Florence was in a state of dire panic, even William who was usually calm and composed, was thinking the worst, his face struggling to hide his inner fears.

'God, what do we do?' he thought. 'There's no use us splitting up again, we'll all get lost, and we need to get some help.'

William knew he had to remain calm and in control but his mind was a jumble with thoughts and images flashing through in the way an old cine film flashes on a screen. He wasn't sure of the best course of action to take. They kept pushing and shoving their way back through the market stopping to ask different locals if they'd seen a little boy.

They got many blank looks and those that did understand just shrugged their shoulders and said, 'sygnomi' (sorry).

Eventually William spotted a couple of men in what he assumed were police uniforms and tried to explain the problem to them. With much use of hand gestures and simple English they eventually got the message across.

Even though these British tourists were clearly distressed, the two policemen didn't seem to be moved into action.

"Are you sure they understand? Why the hell don't they do something?" bleated Florence.

"Calm down dear," said William. "It's just the way they do things in these foreign places."

Sure enough, shortly after, a search of the whole town was underway. More police officers arrived and a message that one of the passengers was missing had got back to the ship's Captain who had ordered his Boson to send twenty of the ship's crew ashore, to help with the hunt.

By 7 p.m. it was starting to get dark, it had been four long hours since Jack had disappeared, and the town was now much quieter. People had drifted away and the market was all but deserted. The various search parties had by now covered most of the surrounding area.

William managed to get hold of the Governor of Cyprus, a British politician, Robert Fletcher by phone. He was based at the Government House in Nicosia about fifty miles to the North East. The honourable Mr Fletcher had agreed to send one of his assistants to Limassol the following day to liaise with the local police.

A superior looking police officer whom the Browns assumed was in charge approached them.

"The search will have to be called off until the morning." William had tried to protest but knew deep down that the man was right, although this wouldn't stop him spending the next few hours walking around the town's now dark and deserted streets and alleyways looking for his son.

By 1 a.m. the crewman who had remained ashore with William persuaded him to return to the Orcades which was still moored in the harbour. Florence was already aboard being comforted by Nanny Susan, and at the same time trying to keep the two older boys from finding out just how serious a situation they were now in.

Many tears were shed that night, and not just by Florence. The couple had tried to be positive with each other about the chances of Jack being found the following day. Surely someone would know where he was, maybe he'd just reappear, and it would just be a matter of time before they were reunited.

Neither of the parents slept and as the sun rose, the pair were helped back into a small boat to return to the town. By 8am they were back on land. God this place was hot, even at this hour. On shore there was a pair of police men waiting to take them to the main police station where they were to be formally interviewed.

The taller of the two had indicated that this was just normal procedure, and everyone's movements and observations had to be accounted for. It seemed reasonable enough, the Browns were just anxious that things got moving and were happy to co-operate. There was no translator, one of the officers had only a rough grasp of the English language and the communications were slow and frustrating.

William had started to get irritable when the officer questioning him had kept pushing suggestions that maybe he and Florence had done something to the boy and created this 'vanishing' to create the perfect alibi.

Finally, he had snapped and unsurprisingly lost his temper He made it clear that there wasn't any reason to 'get rid' of their son, nor was there any way they could have done so.

The police agreed to end the interview and William had headed back into the towns streets to continue the hunt. Florence joined him and together they tagged along as more doors were knocked on and locals quizzed, but still there was no sign.

It was as though Jack had disappeared into thin air!

At the end of the second day the Captain was forced to broach the subject of the ship's departure with these two very upset parents. He explained that he had a schedule to keep and he was already two days behind. Much as he would have liked to, he couldn't keep hundreds of other passengers stranded on a vessel with finite resources this far from home. So on the seventeenth night of their voyage the ship had set sail without William, Florence and of course Jack.

It had been agreed that it would be for the best if James, Nick and Elizabeth also left the ship and returned to Scotland with Nanny Susan. Following some swift arrangements by the Orient Line, Susan and the three remaining children boarded another liner that was heading back to Scotland via France.

William had tried to get Florence to go home with them but she was a strong willed woman and swore she wouldn't leave Limassol without Jack, and that was that!

On 7th June, three days after Jack had vanished, William booked accommodation for them both in one of Limassol's best hotels, The Curium Palace, not that this made them feel any better.

As the days began to drift into weeks the daily searches seemed to be more and more pointless, with the ever dwindling number of participants lacking enthusiasm or initiative. The pictures of Jack in the local newspapers no longer peered out at them each morning. William and Florence had started to grow numb to the pain of reality. Confusion and imagination having now merged into a haze without answers and with no real direction left to travel.

William had stood by Florence in her determination to stay until Jack was found but both of them knew that at some point, at least for the sake of the other three children they would have to leave. They couldn't spend the rest of their lives in a hotel room praying for their little boy to walk through the door.

Leaving Cyprus without one of their children was the hardest decision the pair would ever have to make. Neither would ever believe that Jack had gone forever unless they were presented with proper evidence to that effect.

On the 23rd July the couple packed their cases and despondently left the resort. They couldn't face another voyage by sea and instead had arranged to fly home. They both sat quietly as the taxi wound its way across the dry landscape towards the northern town of Nicosia, home of the International Airport. Each couldn't help but study any passing vehicle or pedestrians for any sign of Jack, but unsurprisingly they didn't see him.

They had to wait for an hour for the first leg of their flight which would take them from Cyprus to Greece before they headed home. On arriving in Scotland, the terrible story of the little boy that had gone missing on his first holiday had been in all the papers. The whole family had been plastered over the front pages and they were now unwilling celebrities in an event they wished to have no part in. Even as they had descended the gang plank in Edinburgh, an explosion of flash bulbs had blinded and infuriated the pair.

"We just want to be left alone," cried Florence. In the scrummage William had knocked one of the tabloid photographers to the ground.

"Sorry, I just need to get home. Please let us get out of here," he shouted, trying to push them all away.

They jostled their way through and climbed into their waiting car, which immediately whisked them back to the safety of Woodside.

Florence thought the old house with its grey pebble dashed walls looked strangely welcoming as it sat under a matching grey sky. Never before had they been so pleased to see their remaining three children standing on the front steps waiting for them, Nanny Susan holding little Liz in her arms.

The family relatives had grouped together to help William, Florence and the children get through the next few weeks. The couple had made up their minds that Jack must have been abducted and it would just be a matter of time before someone shed light on his whereabouts.

By the time the couple had arrived back in Scotland the search in Cyprus had all but faded.

The authorities had done their best. House to house searches and much publicity had revealed nothing.

"I'm not letting this rest Florence. Tomorrow I'm going to Edinburgh to see a man who I think may be able to help us," declared William.

Staying true to his intentions, William was sitting opposite a private investigator in a murky first floor office, one of many nestled in a large granite faced terrace that stood on Market Street, close to Edinburgh's Waverley train station. The room was small yet well organised. Neatly labelled files stood in groups of matching colours stretching the full width of the floor to ceiling bookshelves behind John Clark's leather topped desk.

John stood up and turned, throwing the smouldering butt of his cigarette onto the large pile that already lay in the black open fire grate.

"Are you telling me you want me to move to Cyprus? Are you serious?"

"Never been more so. My son's missing and I want him found. I need a man there now," replied William.

"That's not going to be cheap Mr Brown."

"Don't worry about the money the cost's not an issue. Can you do it or not? If you can't, I'm sure there'll be someone else willing." William however wanted John Clark he had a reputation for getting results.

"Now I didn't say I wouldn't do it, I just want to... you know... be clear on what the score is," John replied.

An hour later the details and expenses had been decided. William wanted his man on the ground as soon as possible so John agreed to leave in two days' time.

Two days later, John had checked himself in for his BAE flight to London's new Heathrow Airport. The first leg of his long journey. The plane headed out onto the tarmac with the rear tail wheel dragging across the less than smooth runway beneath. With a short tug, John checked his seatbelt was fastened and leant back in his deep padded seat.

The two Pratt & Whitney engines built to a scream as they brought the propellers to full speed, hauling the old plane towards its take-off speed. It rattled so much that John was convinced it was about to self-destruct.

John clung tightly to his armrests and peered out over the wing through the small, almost square window on his left. This was his first flight and although he was excited, he also found the whole experience quite disturbing. To his relief he felt his stomach go light as the plane parted company with the ground and began its steep climb.

'Was it always like that?' he wondered.

A couple of hours later the plane was emerging from low clouds over the suburbs of Hounslow on its final bumpy approach onto the main runway at Heathrow.

When the plane finally came to a halt, the 28 passengers were lead from the runway over wooden duckboards to protect their footwear from the rain soaked muddy airfield.

A large tented village formed from military marquees made up the passenger Terminal. It was very primitive but quite comfortable.

John had a very tedious 8 hour wait for his connecting flight to Athens. Luckily the armchair he'd procured made sleeping quite easy.

Following his first experience of flying in the well-travelled DC-3, the silver Lockheed Constellation L-749 that now stood on the tarmac waiting for its 76 passengers was much more impressive. The passengers were led around to the rear of the wing where a set of steps had been wheeled into place to allow them to board. They were soon airborne, the plane banking left as it turned towards the south coast. The flight was scheduled to take around four and a half hours.

An hour into the flight, John was pleased to see an attractive air hostess working her way down the plane delivering meals to the passengers. Served on fine bone china plates, the roast chicken breast, vegetables and gravy tasted surprisingly good all the better for the glass of white Burgundy wine to wash it down with.

Feeling satisfied after eating his meal, the drone of the aircraft's four Wright radial engines, proved strangely hypnotising and John dosed off to its monotonous whine.

The crackly announcement from the Captain sounded over the drone. "We will shortly be beginning our descent into Athens Ellinikon International Airport where the weather is a sunny 85 degrees Fahrenheit."

The plane cruised in low over the sea and hit the runway with a firm thud. As the engines fought to slow the plane down the volume level increased rapidly. The luggage racks shook in protest and added to the general cacophony that filled the cabin. As John stepped down onto the tarmac, the desert-like heat hit him like a blast furnace. He was still well wrapped up from the London air and suddenly found himself wishing he could trade his woolly jumper and thick trousers for a pair of shorts and a tee-shirt.

CHAPTER 3

After a two hour wait, John was heading back out to be greeted by the familiar sight of another DC-3 Dakota wearing the orange nose and tail colours of Hellenic Airlines. This would be his third and final flight in 24 hours, finally depositing him in Nicosia Airport.

On leaving the Terminal, John didn't head straight to Limassol. Instead, William had arranged for a car to drive him to Nicosia where the following morning he was to go to the British Embassy to meet the Governor's representatives.

Here he could get an update on what had been done and any information that may help his search. The driver took him straight to the newly opened Ledra Palace Hotel where a room had been booked for him.

"Is this it?" John asked the driver

"Yes. Ledra Palace Hotel," he replied, in his best attempt at English.

The imposing building stood five storeys high with its sand coloured stone gleaming in the bright sun. The car pulled through the large dressed arch and stopped under the front canopy where a smartly dressed Porter stepped forward and almost before it had stopped, opened his door.

John had soon checked in and along with his suitcase, was now safely deposited in his second floor bedroom that had the latest modern embellishments, including hot and cold running water and a telephone.

The hotel boasted two restaurants, two bars and a cafe. John had endured a long, tiring journey but still found room for a light evening meal and a couple of drinks to help him relax before the work began the next day. That night, lying on top of the clean white sheets, John stared at the large ornate ceiling fan as it wobbled unnervingly on its axis above him whilst contemplating the assignment he'd just taken on. How on earth was he going to find one little boy on such a big island?

At 9:55 a.m. the following morning, he was outside the gates of the British Embassy as per his instructions. A guard on the gate checked his passport before allowing him to make his way up the path that lay between neat avenues of palm trees.

Having been shown into the marble clad entrance he waited in a large hallway that had an array of paintings and statues that would have looked equally at home in an English stately home.

"This way please Mr Clark, the Governor will see you now," exclaimed a tall uniformed Aide.

John was a bit taken back, he'd been told that a member of staff was to brief him on the progress, or lack of it, he wasn't expecting an audience with the 'main man'. He was pleased he'd put on a decent suit and that the hotel had polished his shoes for him, something he hadn't bothered with since school days.

"Good morning Mr Clark, I'm Robert Fletcher. Mr Brown wanted me to keep an eye on things over here. He was quite adamant that I should meet with you before you head down to Limassol. What he thinks you'll find I really don't know?"

"He wants me to try," said John. "And to be fair who can blame him? If any of us lost one of our children we'd do everything in our power," replied John.

"I'm sure you're right, but let's face it, it's like looking for a needle in a hay stack. There's more people come and go from this island than you could believe, especially since our government set up the internment camps," said the Governor.

"I know, I suppose I'll just have to get down there and start looking... I've got to start somewhere. Now, can you tell me if anything's been done since Mr and Mrs Brown went home?" John asked.

"I haven't been down to Limassol myself, but Martin Stokes, one of my top men has. He's spent quite some time there keeping the local police on the case. It's not easy though, they have their own way of doing things that isn't, how can I put it…British?"

"Have they found any trace of the boy?" asked John.

"Not a dickie bird. It's as though he just vanished into thin air." The Governor removed a bulging file from his desk drawer and thumped it down in front of John.

"Everything that's been done is detailed in here," he said tapping his finger on the flap.

"All the interviews that have been done, translations, and lists of all addresses checked since the disappearance are in here. You can have it but we'll need it back before you leave the island." He pushed it across the desk in John's direction.

"Not much more I can tell you. Sorry."

They stood up and shook hands.

"Good luck with your search," the Governor said in a half-hearted manner.

"I'm going to need it," John replied, as he headed off with the file under his arm.

Back at the hotel John packed and got ready for his journey to Limassol. Outside the front entrance, the same driver was waiting. The roads were reasonable other than the occasional pot hole that the driver seemed to take aim at and manage to hit every time. The journey took just over an hour through some quite dusty and austere countryside.

John was booked in to the Athena Hotel, a small 3* hotel close to the market square where Jack had vanished exactly two months earlier on the 4th June. This place was a far cry from the luxurious Ledra Palace.

His new room was simply furnished with a single metal framed bed, free standing wardrobe and a small dressing table. A frayed rectangular rug covered a large proportion of the terracotta tiled floor…the facilities were functional rather than fancy.

The file he'd acquired in Nicosia was stuffed full of notes which John proceeded to spread out across the bed and dressing table. There were all sorts of information in there, luckily most had been translated into English. John quickly separated the remaining documents that were in Greek and piled them to one side. He then began to plough his way through, sorting everything into categories from interviews taken at the time in the market place. Those taken later from hoteliers and cafe owners through to notes made by the police at the time were put in a separate pile. At around 6 p.m. there was a knock at the door. John gave strict instructions to the maid that he wouldn't need his bed turning down or his room cleaning for the next couple of days, she seemed to understand and promised to leave him clean towels every morning but would happily leave everything else alone.

The following morning John decided to retrace the steps taken by the Brown family that June day when Jack disappeared. It was Sunday and the place was all but deserted. There were a few locals milling around and a couple of men were sweeping the paving. John found it hard to believe that someone could lose a child in this place, but apparently that's what had happened. He had a small notebook in which he'd highlighted notes from the initial reports, detailing the movements and positions of people according to their statements and interviews at the time.

The sun was already bearing down relentlessly. John's remaining thin hair offered little resistance and he could feel his head burning. He cursed himself for not bringing a hat, a mistake he wouldn't make again.

He slowly made his way round the square and added peoples' reported positions to the small map he'd prepared the night before. Not wanting to stay in the burning sun for longer than necessary, he walked the short distance to the port where the family had initially disembarked to get a proper feel for the sequence of events.

Now, having looked around the town and got his bearings, once back in his hotel room, John sought comfort from a cold wet towel he put over his burning scalp...cool relief! He began to read through some of the reports again, which made more sense second time round.

The following morning John experienced the square differently. It was now strained under the weight of market stalls and shoppers. The noise level was incredible and the atmosphere alight, it was hard for John to believe this was the same serene place he'd meandered round the day before.

For the first time he understood how easy it would be to get separated from one another, the crowd was overwhelming and very disorientating. He now had a sense of what the Browns must have experienced on that June morning. It was clear that if you lost someone there, they'd take some finding.

John had been given the name of a young interpreter who would work with him whenever needed. William had told him to get help from anyone he deemed necessary and not to worry about the cost, he would make sure they were amply compensated for their time.

The interpreter was a 23 year old student who fancied a career beyond his island of birth. Neoklis thought speaking a couple of extra languages would be his ticket out, but, for now he was more than happy to accept this well-paid holiday job. The following weeks were a challenge. John did his best to methodically talk to all the market stall holders. This wasn't easy, as even with Neoklis translating every sentence, it was hard to get reliable information from these locals. Most remembered the day that Jack had gone missing, but none seemed to remember any useful details.

Over the next gruelling weeks, the pair almost became a fixture in the square. John, who'd looked conspicuous at first with his Trilby hat and tartan waistcoats, was now hardly noticed as he meandered along with his young Cypriot colleague in tow. The couple had eventually moved further afield following various leads that they'd picked up during their interrogations… all had led to dead ends. Questioning the police had proved even harder, they didn't like their investigating techniques being brought into question and were frankly as prohibitive as possible.

With the locals relying on tourism, John's continual stirring up of the situation wasn't proving popular. The number of visitors had certainly dropped off after the incident, certain cruise liners, including the Orcades wouldn't be stopping on route again. The British Governor had tried to encourage the police to keep looking, but even he felt it was a lost cause now and he didn't want to alienate the Cypriots he had to work with.

The weeks dragged into months and John, for his best efforts, was getting nowhere. Back home, the story had drifted from the media and even William and Florence began to lose hope. John had tried every trick in the book to find Jack, but again and again he'd run into a brick wall. He'd well and truly vanished and no one remembered seeing a thing.

John Clark had stayed in Cyprus for a full year, costing William a small fortune. He'd investigated all possible outcomes and, with Neoklis, interviewed hundreds of the local residents. He'd heard rumours of orphans being sold to those that couldn't have their own children and thought this could be a possibility, but with no evidence to go on, there was little else to be done.

In his final report to William he said that he believed Jack could have been abducted and sold but could just as easily be dead, sadly the answer may never be known. John had headed back to Nicosia to return the Governor's file before flying back to Scotland. Although the hunt was laid to rest, the family would never forget.

There wasn't a day went by that William and Florence didn't think about Jack. Following John's return, the Browns never returned to Cyprus. The marriage had survived the next difficult years even though at times the relationship had become quite strained. They'd always loved each other but deep down neither could avoid laying a portion of blame on the other's shoulders. Both knew that really it was no one's fault, it was just unlucky that they had ended up in the wrong place at the wrong time.

Jack's brothers had been hit badly by the departure of their younger brother, even though they didn't really understand that he may never come home. James, being a bit older seemed to think about it more and often woke with nightmares which also seemed to bring on bouts of sleep walking.

Both boys always expected Jack to return at any moment – sometimes one would hear a car approach on the gravelled drive and imagine for just a moment that Jack may be brought in through the open door. He never appeared.

Their sister, Elizabeth, was still too young to remember Jack but one day she would be told the story of the brother she never really knew.

CHAPTER 4

During the investigation, William had tried to distract himself by getting back into his other great love – horse racing. Known as the sport of kings for obvious reasons, owning race horses was a sure-fire way to spend money like it was going out of fashion.

William had three horses in training with Mick Hancock, a trainer who'd produced over 500 winners over the previous 38 years, including one in the Derby and another in the 1,000 Guineas.

Mick had become a wealthy man, some said he'd made all his money by betting on the 'osses' as he called them. Others thought it was through the land and property he'd invested in but no one knew for sure. He was a larger than life character easily recognisable by the flat cap that rarely left his head. Working out the optimum number of furlongs and the 'going' were all pastimes of William. Sadly, he rarely had a winner. His best horse, 'Blessing-in-Disguise' had a good couple of years but had now been laid out to stud.

The atmosphere of the races was quite addictive and William would make the short trip to Edinburgh Racecourse at Musselburgh whenever there was a meeting, whether he had a runner or not. As an annual member he could sit in the comfort of the 'owners and trainers' bar which had an excellent view over the finish line along with the nine-hole golf course that lay in the centre of the track.

The races were extremely popular with the common working man as well as the landed gentry. They were the only place to go at this time, where legal betting was allowed.

William certainly wasn't shy about gambling and often put large bets on horses that Mick told him were 'laid out' for a particular race. Sometimes he'd win, more often he'd lose. Strangely he could always remember the winners when recalling his days out, but the losers slipped his mind.

It was much later that he realised the truth. A certain stables may have prepared a horse for a sure-fire win in a particular race, but so too had a few others, there was no such thing as a certainty. Somehow Mick managed to win a fortune over the years, he always knew when to bet heavy.

Florence rarely went racing. She didn't mind mingling in the 'owners and trainers' bar or sipping 'Mumm Champagne' in the posh champagne marquee, but she was the first to admit that the business of horse racing did little for her.

She wasn't a fan of Mick either, his personal habits left much to be desired. Constantly cursing and spitting, those that didn't know him could have mistaken him for a 'down and out', ironic really as he was worth more than nearly all the other owners and trainers combined. William always said, "He might come across as a bit rough and ready but he's a great fellow once you know him."

Back on the farms, work carried on as ever. Production subsidies were introduced in the UK through the 1947 Agriculture Act to persuade farmers to boost their yields and thus ensure that the food supply, badly needed by the country, was high enough. Farmers would receive a guaranteed price for their produce and were encouraged to make more land available for food production.

They were encouraged to plough up waste land and pastures, drain wetlands and reclaim moorland wherever possible. These subsidies had certainly increased the Brown's income. Ironically, if these subsidies had been introduced back in 1942, the opportunity to buy Coates or Tanners Farm would probably never have arisen.

A year after they returned from the ill-fated holiday, life had carried on and James had started boarding at Aberlour House, Gordonstoun's Junior School This was a public school that was for boys only and had gained a reputation for turning them from happy-go-lucky children into well rounded gentlemen.

Their motto was:

Plus est en vous' - 'there is more in you than you think.'

And their mission was to extract every last bit of it. After a further two years of attending their local primary school Nick had then joined James.

James didn't enjoy his education as much as Nick did. He didn't care a lot for any of the subjects he had to endure and had a strong dislike for the strict discipline now being brought upon him. He liked most forms of sport and outdoor activities. Whereas in lessons, he liked to position himself as near the back as possible and close to the window from where he spent most of his time day-dreaming, looking out over the open countryside that surrounded the school.

In his first couple of years he'd done okay, but as he progressed he constantly had reports that said, 'could have tried harder' and 'has an outgoing personality' which really meant, *is a distraction to the rest of the class and talks too much'*.

Nick, on the other hand, was always keen on outperforming his fellow classmates. He liked the feeling of coming first, be it in Maths, English, Science or Languages. He wanted to show his parents that he was 'top of the class' and worked hard to complete his assignments quicker and to a higher standard than required.

His main strengths were in Biology, Chemistry and Physics. His early grasp of the science curriculum was exemplary. He wasn't quite the sportsman that James was becoming, but he was reasonably talented. The school sports of choice were Rugby and Cricket through the summer along with swimming most of the year.

Nick had grown tall quite quickly and his narrow frame looked fairly scrawny in shorts and a rugby shirt. He was built for speed rather than brute force. He played as a 'full back' and made the school's First 15 rugby squad. At cross country running he was chosen for the school team and often won in races at home and away.

Getting involved with an 'interesting' group of boys led James into a fair amount of trouble. He'd always made it his mission to be as rebellious as possible and smoking had become one of his favourite pastimes. When caught for the third time in his fourth year, James was dragged before the head, 'slippered' and put on detention for a month.

His father was very unimpressed when he received the headmaster's letter. James wasn't bothered, he didn't want to conform and had no intention of doing so, although he told his father exactly the opposite. Being caught in the local free house at the age of 16, with a pint of Guinness in one hand and a cigarette smouldering in the other, was enough to finally ensure he got a week's suspension. On returning home his father went berserk and warned him that he was close to being thrown out once and for all. James had something of an attitude and wanted to argue every point which didn't really help his cause.

His week at home was made a total misery and by the eighth day he was unusually pleased to be returning to school. By the time the summer holidays came around the incident had all but been forgotten, well, it wasn't mentioned again at any rate.

The boys were now both teenagers and loved helping out on the farm. Liz had ponies, the boys had tractors. They'd both been taught by their father to drive tractors as soon as they could reach the pedals. James had been only 12 years old when he was first let loose on the grey 'Ferggie'.

William had purchased a 'Fordson Major', one of the newest tractors available. Built in Dagenham by The Ford Motor Company, unmistakable in its blue paint with orange wheels, the boys were allowed to take turns on her for cutting hay.

These two extra helpers were a welcome addition for the labourers who had to work for long hours to ensure there was enough hay for the animals in winter. The cut grass was dried and stacked into small ricks before being incorporated into larger stacks.

In addition to the fun tasks they also had to endure some hard work hoeing or pulling wild oats, both of which involved walking the fields all day long. This wasn't too bad if the sun was shining but on a grey rainy day it was less than entertaining.

James managed to get a reasonable handful of 'O levels' and would have left school at the age of 16 having completed these exams but his father wasn't having it.

"You're staying to do your HSC's and that's that. We didn't bring you into this world to show this family up. I won't have people saying I've got a numbskull for a son."

It didn't enter James' head to argue with his father on this topic, from past experience he knew it would be pointless.

He made it through the next couple of years and left after acquiring two 'C' graded HSCs, one in Biology and the other in History.

William had realised he would be wasting his time sending James away to University, not that there was much chance of him being granted a place with his low grades. James would have actually been pleased to go, an open invitation to three years drinking and partying.

Instead, his father agreed to let him get on with his chosen career in farming. So now aged 19, James moved from the family home Woodside, to Tanners, the farm alongside, that had been waiting for him. The two houses were only a few hundred yards apart and could be seen through the gaps in a narrow stretch of Scots pine trees that lay in between.

The house at Tanners had been lived in by various farm labourers since being left by its previous owner some eighteen years before when William had bought it. The place was designed for 'purpose' not for architectural beauty. Already over 150 years old, the house showed its age and was generally damp from being unused.

There wasn't a straight wall or level floor in the place. The lounge and kitchen ceilings were supported by large oak beams that still bore vicious looking hooks that had once hung meat and game. The floors upstairs followed the beam contours and were very uneven, creaking under any feet that crossed them. The roof above was tiled in grey slate and sagged badly along the centre ridge but James didn't care; he had been cut free from his mother's apron strings and living alone now could do pretty much as he liked.

He was a strong young man who enjoyed knocking things about. The house was his now and his father had told him he could do what he liked with it, as long as he didn't demolish it.

James knocked the walls through from the ancient kitchen to the small dining room to give him a bit more space. The level of dust created during his renovation was unbelievable. It took several weeks, between farming duties, to strip the yellow stained wallpaper from nearly every wall. As soon as he peeled it away he found chunks of lime plaster crumbling away from the walls.

Once the filler and magnolia paint had been applied, he had the place freshened up in no time. It wouldn't have won any design awards, but James wasn't bothered, he just wanted somewhere a bachelor could enjoy himself and look after with the minimum of fuss.

Each Saturday he would make his way to Recreation Park, North Berwick where he played as 'prop forward' for the local rugby team. He'd been a keen sportsman at school and had wanted to keep playing now he was home. He liked the game and taking part in the socialising was a big part of the package.

Not having a car of his own, he'd jump into the farm Land Rover which having been used and abused around the farm - stank. The canvas covered back was often half full of straw and the roof leaked if there was more than a light shower.

The ventilation system consisted of two lift up flaps on the dash board that let the wind howl right on in. James being a fairly large man couldn't get the seat far enough back to be comfortable. He often wondered why, after all these years, they still produced such a primitive vehicle.

With a top speed of about 60mph and tired leaf springs for suspension, he'd rattle his way down the coast road to North Berwick, much to the amusement of his fellow players.

The club had been founded in 1952. It didn't have its own changing rooms and the lads had to get ready in the old school house about half a mile away. The team consisted of a good cross section of the local community, from farmers like James to a junior bank manager from the local branch. As well as the matches, the boys were quite keen on letting their hair down. The local pubs were used to their boisterous antics and, due to the quantity of beer they consumed, let them get on with it.

Although well built, James was a surprisingly quick runner, even though he liked a beer and had smoked about twenty cigarettes a day since he was 16 years old.

Nick was quite different to James. Yes, he still liked sport. Not being as heavily built as James he was better at speed rather than brute force - more of a runner and swimmer. He didn't mind rugby, however he fared much better at athletic events, being a frequent winner in the 100 and 200 metre sprints.

Nick was an ideal candidate for being 'Captain of House' in his upper sixth form year. He enjoyed this role which helped develop his natural instinct to be a leader amongst his fellow students with whom he was surprisingly popular. Nick gained 3 HSCs with two 'As' and a 'B' in English, Mathematics and Chemistry respectively, which made his mother and father very proud.

CHAPTER 5

It was 1956, eleven years had now passed since Jack had vanished from the market square in Limassol and the whole family had reluctantly grown used to him not being around. William and Florence had both agreed they would never give up hope. The subject was rarely mentioned but little things would often remind each of them of the boy they'd lost.

A letter from their solicitor had re-awakened their painful memories by informing them that they could now legally declare that Jack was dead.

There was a short discussion as to whether they should hold a funeral. Florence was having none of it, she was adamant that he was alive.

She was cross that the subject was even up for discussion and it was soon decided that there would be no such thing until there was firm evidence that Jack was dead, no matter how long that would take.

William made it quite clear that the subject would never be raised again.

Although they would have liked closure on the situation, the whole family would hold out hope that one day he would be found and returned to Scotland. Deep down William was sure Jack was long gone but for Florence's sake, he stood by her.

Having done rather well at school, Nick was going to study further and secured a place at the Harper Adams University College to study agriculture and crop management.

This was a three-year course at the Shropshire College and covered everything to do with arable and livestock farming methods, crop rotations and soil nutrition.

The halls of residence were clean and functional with most modern conveniences within easy reach including cafes and bars for socialising. Nick stayed there for the whole of each term as the thought of travelling back to Scotland for weekends didn't appeal, by the time he'd got home it would be time to turn around and head back.

Nick fell in with a mixed crowd from across the country. His best friend at college was a boy called Alan who hailed from Northallerton in North Yorkshire. He had long blonde hair, and you would be forgiven for thinking he was a pretty girl when he had his back to you but when he turned around, you'd know he wasn't – far from it.

His big love was Rock 'n' Roll and he particularly liked Elvis. His father had told him that it was his duty to carry on the family tradition of farming whereas he'd have much rather tried to make it as a pop star.

Alan wasn't particularly keen on studying, he'd been forced to attend the college and really had no interest in the prospect of living his future life in the countryside, there was so much more 'out there'.

Nick insisted on working hard but was happy to hang about with Alan in his spare time. They made a strange partnership. After the first couple of terms, Alan gave up trying to persuade Nick to skip lectures for jaunts into town – his nagging fell on deaf ears.

The college's motto of *'work hard - play hard,'* was fine for Nick, whereas Alan only recognised the 'play hard' part.

Nick had a small bed-sit on the ground floor, only around 12ft square with its own bathroom. It had a large plain wood sash window which proved very useful for getting out unnoticed if ever required to do so. Other than a small side chair, a simple desk was the only other furniture.

An Anglepoise lamp helped Nick focus on his work which he always tried to complete to the best of his ability before going out to enjoy himself.

The one bad habit Nick had picked up from Alan was smoking. He'd tried it one night after a couple too many drinks and found he quite enjoyed it, – therefore it became a habit he would soon be stuck with.

Whilst the boys were away being educated, life on the farm went on day after day in a never ending cycle as each season replaced the one before.

William had always enjoyed his country pursuits including a bit of hunting, coarse fishing and game shooting. One particular cold, damp Wednesday in the September of 1954 a party of seven Guns, and four Beaters with dogs and an old tractor that pulled a covered trailer had set off onto the grouse moors.

They sat on old straw bales that had become improvised seating as the trailer bumped through the pot holes on the rough track that led into the deserted countryside.

Up on the moors the shooters took comfort from a shot of warming single malt whiskey whilst the Beaters had headed into the heather to drive out any birds that may have taken cover. The shoot had gone well until William had carelessly stumbled trying to get over a stile using his loaded shotgun to steady himself. In a flash it discharged itself.

For a moment William hadn't realised what he'd done. As the gentleman to his right looked towards him he looked pale and shocked, it was then that William noticed blood on his own right hand. As he looked harder he realised his index finger was gone!

Instantly his hand began to throb. A couple of the other men had helped him bandage his hand up in a tartan scarf and given him more whiskey to help him numb the pain.

Amazingly his recently severed finger was found only a few yards away, more or less intact.

William was a brave man and almost shrugged off the accident, more concerned that he'd just lost his trigger finger.

"Bugger, that's not going to help my aim," he exclaimed.

Although he knew he would never be able to get it sewn back on he picked it up. The others took him back to the farm and called for the local doctor to attend.

On arriving at the door William had taken off his flat cap and held it out to Florence, displaying the gruesome remains of his finger now lying in its centre.

Florence fainted and needed smelling salts to bring her back round. She never did see the amusing side to the incident which was recounted every time someone asked about his missing digit.

By the age of 15, their daughter Elizabeth, always known as Liz, was at a girls-only boarding school, which she hated. Back on the farm she had a pony called 'Tom Thumb' and couldn't wait for the holidays for the chance to 'hack out' as often as possible.

Florence had always loved horses. She'd ridden until her early twenties and encouraged her daughter with her riding, joining in frequent outings with the local pony club and a packed summer competing in the Sunday shows kept them both busy.

William's opinion was that Florence took it all too seriously, she didn't just want her daughter to win, she insisted on it.

Getting ready for these shows was an operation in itself. The days before saw Florence getting the tack spotless. Hers being more of a 'supervisory role' as she stood and watched as one of the stable hands applied saddle soap and then polished the leather to a gleaming finish.

Liz's jodhpurs and jacket were cleaned and checked, picnics were prepared and Tom Thumb had his hooves oiled until they shone.

William would take time off from the farm to drive their Bedford TK horsebox to the shows and then head to the beer tent where he could spend the afternoon catching up with his farmer friends who'd been roped into the same job.

On arriving at the event, Tom Thumb would be led from his box ready for a final manicure. He would have his mane brushed and a stencil laid across his croup. By brushing his hair in different directions, a diamond pattern would create the finishing touch before he was paraded in public.

When they won, it may have been just one more Rosette to William, but to the girls it was all that mattered at the time. Back in the farmhouse more than a hundred of these coloured prizes were pinned around the Aga mantel as an ever-growing shrine to their success.

They won again and again and got quite a reputation around the local shows. Liz had contemplated a future involving horses, maybe riding or training, whatever it was to be, she couldn't imagine a life without her equestrian friends.

CHAPTER 6

When the boys had reached 18 years of age, William had signed the two smaller farms over to them. James had settled in to his new life as a full time farmer at Tanners. Nick had been expected to follow suit once he'd finished his exams and take over Coates Farm.

James was still a young man but having been brought up in a farming community he knew how things worked. Needless to say, his father would keep a close watch over him to ensure he did things the right way – his way.

James knew he was lucky to have inherited a farm at such a young age, but there were strings attached. He was on call to his father 24 hours a day, 7 days a week and one thing you could be sure of – with three farms running side by side, there was always a new problem that needed sorting.

Some nights James would just manage to get his boots off and sit down when he'd see his father approaching. At times like this he often wished he lived in a little cottage, miles away.

December 1963 turned out to be a very difficult time for farming, it was one of the worst winters for years in the UK. Temperatures hadn't dropped as low for such a long duration since 1947.

James had been at Tanners for a couple of years and the winters had been typically Scottish. Certainly quite tough but nothing like the one that was about to hit.

Everything was going just fine until late on Boxing Day when around four inches of snow fell. At first everyone thought this was great – a White Christmas with the trees outside looking beautiful.

Then on the night of December 29th bitter Siberian easterly winds delivered another ten inches of drifting powdery snow. This was a seriously large amount and caused many problems on the farm.

Luckily, having tractors with front loaders left them at something of an advantage. Even with their heavy equipment, it took quite an effort to dig some of the locals out who were stranded behind massive snow drifts – some over seven feet deep.

James found the farmhouse cold and draughty, he had an old wood burning stove that when fully stoked, was like an inferno. It pumped tons of heat out but consumed logs at an alarming rate. At least the lounge was always warm and cosy. James enjoyed sitting in front of his fire with a cigarette, always 'Benson and Hedge's Gold' along with a glass of malt whiskey – Glenmorangie with ice.

The cold spell dragged on for a couple of months, with power cuts and food shortages becoming the norm. The cattle had to be kept indoors for weeks, which wasn't ideal for them or the farmers.

In June 1965, Nick left University with a Degree in Agriculture, having decided to make a move that would shock his father and the whole family for that matter. He didn't want to stay at the family's home in Scotland but would head down into England and try to make it on his own.

Although life was comfortable, having already had a farm handed to him on a plate, Nick wasn't ready to settle down and toe the line, he felt he had to 'prove' himself. Whilst he'd been living away he'd been thinking about his future – what he wanted to do and where.

He was strong willed and didn't like being seen with a proverbial 'silver spoon' hanging from his mouth. No. There was no alternative in his mind, he had to show he could make it on his own and earn the respect of his father.

Nick rolled the thoughts round in his mind for many days before summoning up the courage to approach his father to tell him what he wanted to do.

William was a strong-willed man himself and generally laid down the law for the rest of the family. He was however fair, a gentleman, as his friends would describe him. He had hoped the boys would in time take over the running of all three farms and in turn, produce some heirs to continue the family tradition.

Now, Nick was going to rock the boat. William wasn't at all pleased. Nick would need to become a farm tenant, he'd have to rent a farm on a long lease as there was no way he could afford to buy one. William couldn't really see the point when he had a farm lined up for him all bought and paid for. Following a lengthy discussion, a compromise that everyone could live with was drawn up.

Nick would head south to find a farm of his own and whilst he was gone, his brother James would look after both the smaller farms on the estate, Tanners and Cotes. In time, Nick could travel back and take 'his' farm back when he was ready.

And so began a new era for the whole Brown family. Nick and James finalised arrangements for the managing of Coates farm and both promised to stay in touch with the other should Nick succeed in finding a farm in England, which he was determined to do.

It was Tuesday 15th March 1966 when Nick began his first journey south to try and find a suitable farm in England. During the preceding weeks he had studied various newspaper and magazine adverts looking for something suitable.

He'd decided to head to Norfolk, where his mother had grown up, she had told him how fertile the soil was there and how much better the weather was!

In the past she'd told the boys that she'd seen men pulling foot long carrots from the ground and that the farmers in that part of the country were generally well off. Arable crops such as sugar beet, wheat and barley were particularly successful.

Nick said his goodbyes to his mother and younger brother. His sister Liz was out riding, as usual. His father William then drove him to Edinburgh Waverley train station in his latest car, a Bentley T series in his favourite traditional British Racing Green livery.

William harboured mixed emotions. On the outside he was keen to encourage his son to stand on his own two feet. He was immensely proud that he was prepared to give up his safe existence farming on the family estate when he hadn't needed to go. On the inside though he was saddened, he knew that if Nick found what he was looking for, the next time he left it may be for good.

William accompanied him to the gateway that led to the platform where they said their goodbyes.

"Now, take care Nick, don't rush things and remember to keep in touch with your Mother."

With a firm handshake, William turned and went.

The British Rail Class 55 Deltic locomotive destined for London's Kings Cross was now sitting in wait on platform 2, her carriages with doors open, ready to welcome her passengers. Nick climbed into coach C and worked his way down the corridor looking for his compartment and seat.

He opened the door to find he was sharing a compartment with a middle-aged couple, a bearded gentleman puffing away on a cigar and another old man who lowered his Times Newspaper to peer over his half-moon glasses.

The bearded gentleman gave a grunt towards Nick along with an extra puff of smoke, then carried on reading.

Another man across to his right bore the hallmarks of a solicitor or banker with his dark grey suit and short, business like haircut. He inhaled from a freshly lit cigarette but didn't acknowledge the compartments newest occupant.

The early morning sun cut interesting lines through the smoke. Nick took out a cigarette. *'If you can't beat them, join them,'* he thought.

The couple opposite looked like seasoned travellers, showing no interest in the goings on of the train or its surroundings. They seemed to be discussing their son's schooling and his poor reports, it reminded Nick of overhearing his parents ranting over James' performance.

He smiled to himself.

The journey would take around three hours to get to York where there would be a short stop before carrying on to Peterborough. Initially the train headed along the Firth of Forth and then south alongside the east coast. The scenery was stunning. It was a clear day and Nick could see for miles out over the North Sea. A couple of large Tankers looked stationary on the horizon.

The clattering of the wheels on the tracks, strangely hypnotic, was only broken by the occasional howl of the train's whistle. The guard had come to inspect the tickets and a lady pushing a large hot water earn on a stainless steel trolley had brought them some strong coffee.

Other than that nothing disturbed the compartment's occupants. Nick had been deep in thought as he puffed smoke rings into the stale air of the carriage, 'what would he find in Norfolk and what would his farm be like'?

If he could find himself one...

On arriving in York railway station, the loud speaker system announced a twenty-minute wait and invited passengers to disembark if they wished. Nick thought a quick stretch of his legs wouldn't go amiss.

York station was an impressive building set under a large curved glass and iron roof. When it had opened in 1877 with 13 platforms it was heralded as the largest station in the world.

Nick walked up onto the footbridge and admired the train he'd just got off now standing beneath him. A cold wind blew through the station which sent a shiver down his back. He thought he might stop for a look around this historic city if he came back this way.

After purchasing an 'over-done' bacon sandwich on slightly dry white bread, he headed back to his carriage. The whistle blew, doors were slammed shut and the train heaved back into life, heading south.

This stretch of England was a flat place, the land stretched out on either side of the train as far as the eye could see. Just over an hour later the train was pulling into Peterborough station. This was the end of the first part of Nick's journey, the train would carry on to London, but Nick had to change trains to get himself out into the Norfolk countryside.

There was a train at 3:15 p.m. via Thetford, which looked to be his best choice. Nick now had a couple of hours to kill before he moved on. He opted for a short walk around Peterborough. He did a bit of window shopping and took coffee in a small cafe before heading back to the station. The modest two carriage train he boarded was a sorry sight after the grandeur of the east coast main line train.

With a figure of eight wave from the Station Masters flag and short blow on his whistle, they left on time and trundled out towards Norwich.

There were only a dozen or so passengers travelling with him including a young couple with a baby that seemed to cry incessantly. The parents seemed oblivious to the noise, but Nick was cursing within, he was starting to envisage ways he'd like to gag the baby, anything to mute the sound. Obviously, he didn't show it, he was well educated and showed no emotion.

He stared out of the window and turned his mind to the job in hand…finding himself a farm he could make a success.

As images flashed through his mind, the constant noise drifted into the distance of his consciousness. Nick pulled his last cigarette out of the packet and lit it, leaving the now screwed up packet on the table in front of him.

The lady opposite frowned but Nick just looked away and fell back deep into his thoughts. This part of the journey seemed to take an eternity as the small train rattled relentlessly on, across what seemed to be very uneven tracks.

Every wood panel and door in the carriage seemed to creak and groan in protest at the train's progress. Nick was amazed that the luggage actually remained in place on the racks over-head.

He must have nodded off for a while as he woke to the sound of screeching brakes as they ground to a halt in Norwich Thorpe station.

The passengers alighted and headed, in single file through the gates at the end of the platform. A rather miserable guard with a tangled grey beard passed a cursory glance at tickets as they were waved in his general direction.

If someone had waved a cigarette card he would have been none the wiser. The station was an impressive building from the outside, very neat and tidy with rows of neatly attended flower beds to both sides.

Nick finally made it out to the street beyond and headed on past the taxi rank, then followed a small wrought iron sign that indicated the city centre was across the river.

He headed across the bridge and along the Prince of Wales Road taking in the sights around him. It was now 7 p.m. and the sun was low in the sky.

Nick was booked in at The Old Bear on Cattle Market Street which he guessed would be near the cattle market. '*All that education hadn't been wasted*', he thought.

Sure enough, as he headed around the edge of the empty cattle pens he could see a large black bear hanging from the front of a stone faced three storey building. This old coaching inn was to be his home for the next couple of days.

The hotel was more of a large pub with bedrooms and looked closed. Nick tried the door which thankfully was open. He rang the bell on the edge of the reception desk, which was actually a hatch that looked into the bar. A grey haired old lady appeared.

"Can I help you?" she asked.

"Yes, hello, I've booked a room for a few nights." Nick replied.

"You must be Mr Brown. We don't get many people stay more than one night, not these days," she answered.

The lady, who looked to be wider than she was tall, rummaged around in the drawer below the hatch extracting a key attached to a large chunk of wood, after which she then showed Nick to his room on the first floor.

It was at the top of the stairs right opposite a heavy self-closing fire door. This was always a good place for a room if you needed to exit in a hurry, however if you wanted a good night's sleep, Nick knew the constant banging of the door as late returning guests staggered back to their rooms could prove irritating.

"Here we are," she said, pushing the door open. "This should be alright for you."

The room was more like a large cupboard, indeed it seemed a great engineering feat to have managed to shoehorn a bed, bedside table and wardrobe into such a tight space.

The only decorative objects were one antique table lamp and a vase with some slightly wilted daisies that had seen better days. Another door led to a small en-suite shower room. Nevertheless, the sheets were clean and the room was warm which was all that Nick needed.

The medium rare steak he enjoyed that evening washed down with a fine Châteauneuf-du-Pape, had made him feel very content and relaxed, by 11 p.m. he was tucked up and asleep almost at once.

Around 7:30 a.m. the following morning a loud bang from the fire door made him wake with a start. He looked around and got his bearings.

He swiftly got up, showered and headed downstairs for a quick breakfast of bacon, eggs, and tomatoes, politely declining the regulatory chunk of black pudding. After a glass of grapefruit juice and a couple of mugs of black coffee, Nick was feeling a hundred percent and ready for the day! By 9 a.m. he was already strolling down the main street towards the office of Duncan Lawson Estate Agent, to meet the senior partner Mr Graves, with whom he'd made an appointment.

Nick soon came across the office which stood next door to one of those hardware stores that seems to display more products on the outside than in. Ladders, buckets, brushes and many other odds and ends that Nick classed as 'tat'.

Mr Graves, a portly man with his hair combed over the bald part of his head, greeted Nick with a slightly odd, inquisitive look.

"Good morning. Mr Brown?"

"Yes Sir, good morning to you," replied Nick smiling.

"You sounded much older on the phone. How was your journey from Scotland? OK I hope?" He asked, not waiting for an answer.

"I've lined up three farms for you to see, two today and another one tomorrow. They're all tenanted at present but sound like the sort of thing you're looking for. Shall we go?"

He didn't hang about. Nick had barely got a word in.

"Yes, right. Very good." replied Nick.

Mr Graves led Nick round to the back of the office building where he had a functional looking, grey, Rover P5 which seemed to match the man's solemn grey suit perfectly.

The inside was tidy other than the ashtray in the central console, which was overflowing with old cigar butts and a small mountain of ash. Nick could soon see why as the car quickly filled with smoke.

"Do you mind if I put my window down a bit?" said Nick, trying to see where they were going.

"No problem," said Mr Graves. "We're getting done up like a couple of kippers in here," he chuckled.

As the fog was slowly drawn from the car's interior Nick's visibility began to return.

Mr Graves drove them out into the surrounding countryside, heading north towards Aylsham.

The first farm stood on the edge of the small village of Marsham, a typical village farm, named uninspiringly, 'Village Farm'.

The farm was around 200 acres given over to wheat, barley and sugar beet with livestock consisting of a small dairy herd and a good number of large British Saddleback pigs.

The farmyard showed its age with an assortment of rusty farm implements from an earlier age protruding from the long grass that was slowly strangling them.

Amongst old bales, worn tractor tyres, empty rusty oil drums and the odd hen pecking, there was barely an uncluttered patch of ground in sight. In short - a mess!

Nick was given a quick tour of the fold yard and piggery by the current tenant, a Mr Isaacs. Nick knew the minute he'd driven in that this wasn't for him.

Out of politeness he paddled around the muddy yard thankful he'd brought his wellington boots with him. Nick liked things neat and tidy. Organised, nothing like this. He couldn't even imagine how someone lived in this chaos.

The farmhouse had a stable door with the top half hooked open. Looking over the top into the kitchen Nick could see a pine kitchen table that looked gnawed around the edges, three sheep dogs and a fairly high pile of filthy crockery.

Having politely declined the offer of a cup of coffee Nick and Mr Graves climbed back into the Rover and headed off. The agent could see that Nick wasn't impressed and apologised for wasting his time.

"I'm sure the next property will be more suitable for you, much more in line with modern farming practice."

About forty-five minutes later the couple turned off the narrow country lane and headed down an even narrower private road that led to Squire's Farm. The track was a good mile long.

As they bumped along the track the car's suspension struggled to cope with the deep potholes caused by heavy farm traffic. More than once Nick felt his neck crick as the car's tyres fought their way back into line.

This farm was very different from the previous one. A large central farmyard with modern asbestos clad steel framed buildings buzzed with action.

In one corner a tractor fitted with a front loader was scooping up large helpings of potatoes and loading them into a smart burgundy tipper truck. Two farm hands were throwing bales of straw from one to another then stacking them neatly under a slate covered Dutch barn.

The farmer, a Mr Ford of about 60 years in age, appeared from one of the sheds and headed across the stack yard towards them.

"Good morning gentlemen," he said in a local sounding accent. 'I assume you're the fellow's that's here to see the farm?"

Nick nodded.

"Do you want to look round the buildings first?' he asked.

"That would be great," said Nick.

As they walked around, the three men passed chit-chat about how long Mr Ford had been on the farm, how many acres there were and why Nick wanted to move to the area and so on…

"It feels like I've been here all my life," reminisced Mr Ford.

"I'd stay here till the end, but my daughter seems to think she's in charge. She wants me to take it easy, whatever that means." he chuckled.

Like many people close to retirement, he couldn't quite picture himself with nothing to do all day.

Mr Ford was clearly proud of the business he'd built up at Squire's over the last few decades. The buildings were well organised with everything designated a place and the structures well maintained.

The operation here certainly appeared to be well run. Mr Ford then invited the men to take a ride round the fields in his Land Rover. All three squeezed into the front, with Nick having to sit uncomfortably astride the gear lever.

As the vehicle rocked from side to side they were thrown together like three men in a boat. A black Labrador rode in the back but seemed uninterested in the goings on up front. For all the positive signs Nick had witnessed, the land was not very good.

There were many acres that were either water logged or showed signs that they had been. On closer questioning, Mr Ford had to admit that it was a problem in this area and although well run, the farm struggled with flooding.

Mr Ford's son, Nick, had decided to venture further afield and pursue a career as a Chartered Surveyor.

The pair thanked Mr Ford for his time and headed back towards Norwich. Nick agreed to meet Mr Graves the following morning at 10 o'clock, to view one final farm.

As Nick sat in his bedroom that night, he mulled the day's events over in his mind. He was a bit disillusioned but felt hopeful tomorrow would bring more luck.

The firm of Duncan Lawson was well known amongst farmers and land owners in this part of England. Since 1891 they had been marketing property as well as holding auction sales for furniture and other household clearance. In addition the firm were Management Agents for some major landowners including the Church Commissioners.

It was this area of the business that Mr Graves looked after, the letting of farms to tenants on behalf of their owners. He had narrowed down the list of farms that Nick had a chance of taking over to three - now there was only one more to see.

The following morning at 9:45 a.m. Nick headed back to the agent's offices and began another short car journey heading north east towards the famous Norfolk Broads.

The roads were quiet, and the journey only took about twenty-five minutes. This last farm on Nick's viewing list was the biggest of the three at around 450 acres.

The tenant was an old widower in his early seventies and after five decades of working the land was ready to hang up his boots. He'd realised this was a young man's game and his strength was all but gone.

From first pulling in through the gate Nick could see that again, this farm suffered from very wet ground. The men had a good look round the old fashioned yard and walked across a ten acre field behind the house. Nick declined walking further as he'd already decided this wasn't for him.

They said their goodbyes and headed back to town.

On their ride back, Nick thanked the agent for his time but had decided none of these farms were right for him.

"Let me know if anymore become available," he said, before bidding Mr Graves farewell.

The next morning Nick was back on board the train rattling across the countryside back towards Peterborough. He wasn't sure what to do next. It had all been so clear and simple in his plans. Go to East Anglia, take on a farm and prove he could make it on his own. Now, in less than a week his dreams seemed to have collapsed and he was heading north with his tail between his legs.

Nick caught the London to Edinburgh train at Peterborough. This was scheduled to stop at Doncaster, York and Newcastle.

The train was much busier than on his journey down, his compartment had no free seats and he found himself sitting next to a pretty blonde girl. She sat with her legs crossed and held a smart blue leather handbag on her knee. As Nick took his seat she smiled politely.

"Hello. Are you going to Edinburgh?" asked Nick, keen to start a conversation.

"No, I live in York. I've been to visit my brother in London. I assume you're Scottish? By your accent I mean," she added with a slight blush.

"Yes, Edinburgh. I like the look of York though. It's a beautiful place. I've been thinking of visiting. I had a quick look round the station on my way down but that's about it," he said smiling.

"Well you should, there's plenty to see. My name's Sarah by the way, Sarah Turner. And you are?" she said, holding out her hand to Nick.

"Sorry, I'm Nick Brown," he replied as they lightly shook hands.

Nick went on to explain why he'd been on his farm hunt in Norfolk and Sarah told him about her brother's London lifestyle. The pair chatted happily away as the train headed through the flat English countryside. Nick was pleased he'd found someone to talk to, it certainly helped pass the time.

As the train pulled away from Doncaster, Nick made up his mind to get off at York. He'd thought about it on his journey down and now he wasn't ready to go back to Scotland having got no further on than when he'd left only a few days before.

He told Sarah of his new found plan and hoped she wouldn't think he was stalking her. She seemed to understand and told him she thought it was a good idea. It was her that then suggested they might meet up for a drink.

The train came to a halt with a loud screeching of wheels and quite a judder as the carriages concertinaed and then eased apart again.

An elderly man who had stood up a couple of minutes before the train slowed down almost landed in Nick's lap as he stumbled whilst trying to retrieve a case from the overhead luggage rack. Sarah tried to muffle a short laugh under her scarf. A lady announced in good Queen's English that, *the train now arriving on platform 9 was the 7:25 p.m. train to Edinburgh Waverley, calling at Newcastle only.*

The message echoed around the massive arched roof.

Nick had his old suitcase in one hand and helped Sarah with her case with the other. The passengers jostled for space as they made their way up the stairs to cross the central tracks and head for the station's front concourse and exit.

Sarah accompanied Nick over the footbridge and down past the large signal box that stood overlooking the main tracks. At the foot of the stairs a scruffy man with an ill-fitting rain coat squawked "Press, Press," and waved the local evening paper in their direction.

Nick handed the man a coin and tucked the paper under his arm. As the couple emerged into the street Nick thanked Sarah for her company.

"Maybe we could have that drink tonight?" he asked, thinking that it was unlikely she would actually want to.

"I would like that, but I can't tonight, I've got to work," she replied.

Pulling a pen from her bag, Sarah scribbled her phone number onto the top corner of Nick's paper.

"Call me tomorrow," she said smiling.

Nick shook her hand, slightly awkwardly, he'd thought about kissing her but then thought the better of it, as he'd only known her for just over an hour!

The two then headed in different directions. Nick towards the city and Sarah towards the nearby taxi rank.

In his heart he doubted they'd lay eyes on each other again. Nick hadn't visited York before and he had little knowledge of where to stay.

He took the easiest option of heading straight up the steps of the neighbouring Station Hotel to try and secure a bed for the night.

CHAPTER 7

The hotel was a grand looking building, five storeys high with 120 bedrooms, built of stone coloured Scarborough bricks. Since its completion in 1878 the hotel had held many balls and functions and was a well-known place to be seen in the city.

The hotel purveyed a grand old-world charm. The entrance was manned by an elderly door man fully adorned in a long grey overcoat and matching top hat with gold braided piping. He looked as though he'd probably been there as long as the hotel.

The reception was located just below a massive mahogany staircase that rose in the centre of the building. A lady with her hair tied in a large bun to the top of her head politely enquired, "Good afternoon. May I help you?"

The Porter showed him to room 217 on the second floor overlooking the well-tended gardens to the front of the hotel. Beyond the city's ancient walls Nick had an excellent view of York Minster beyond, floodlit in a warm orange glow.

York Minster, the largest Gothic Cathedral in northern Europe, dominated the skyline and dwarfed everything else within view. After a quick freshen up, Nick made his way back down and headed out for a wander round this historic city.

He didn't fancy sitting in the large hotel dining room alone, he pictured walking in and the waiter looking him up and down... 'Table for one is it sir?' No thanks, that wasn't for him.

He decided to go and find a pub or small bistro where he might feel a bit less out of place. He wished Sarah had been there to show him around.

Nick pulled his coat on and headed out - a slight stomach ache was niggling him, but not bad enough to stop him wanting his dinner. The Royal Station Hotel stood just a few hundred yards outside the city's walls. He made his way through a group of large open arches that allowed the roads and pavements to pass through the ancient city walls.

He headed over Lendal Bridge which gracefully spanned the River Ouse below. The road led towards the famous Minster. Nick crossed the river and then took a right turn, he didn't really know where to go but wasn't concerned, he just wanted to find some sign of life.

Heading towards the city centre there was something of a buzz as gangs of students mixed amongst young couples laughing and stumbling from one pub to another.

Nick stumbled upon an old, paved street called Stonegate.

He could see a large wooden hoarding proclaiming 'Ye Old Star Inne - Fine Ales and Food served all day'. This looked like a nice place for a single man in need of sustenance.

"Good evening," smiled the barmaid.

"Hello. Are you serving food tonight?" inquired Nick.

"We certainly are young man, until nine o'clock. We don't have a printed menu, everything's listed on that blackboard."

"That's fine," said Nick surveying the board. "I'll have a steak and kidney pie with chips please and a pint of Magnet."

Nick was soon sitting in front of a traditional thick crusted pie along with a pint of the dark hand pulled beer. He was enjoying it but kept feeling a niggling pain in his stomach. He'd first noticed it on the train.

He managed half his meal and finished off his drink. He felt annoyed that he wasn't feeling a hundred percent – he wanted to take a longer walk but didn't really feel up to it.

"Damn," he mumbled to himself as he decided to head back for an early night.

Back in his room Nick fell into his bed and shut his eyes. He lay there thinking about the day's events and the nice girl he'd met on the train. Would he ever get to see her again? *Yes*, he thought, he would definitely ring her tomorrow. It was all too easy to let an opportunity slip by.

What seemed like five minutes later but was actually about 3 o'clock in the morning, Nick woke in a very hot sweat.

He felt sick and made a run to the bathroom where he was…violently. He had a searing pain to the side of his stomach that bent him double.

He remained there for some time before realising he needed help. He got to the hotel phone and called reception explaining he needed a doctor.

Within fifteen minutes he was opening his bedroom door to the banging on the outside. Clad in just his dressing gown he was looking pale and a shade grey, sweat was dripping down his temples as he stumbled back to his bed.

"Well you're not looking too healthy young man," said the doctor.

"No, not feeling too good. I was okay yesterday though," said Nick.

"My stomach ached a bit before bed but nothing more."

"Have you been drinking much?" asked the doctor.

"Not enough," he said, trying to muster a smile. "No, just one pint last night, I don't think it was that," he said trying to appear light hearted.

The doctor listened to his chest, took his pulse and poked and prodded. As he poked his finger against the right side of his stomach Nick howled in pain.

"Looks like appendicitis to me, you're going to need to get to hospital right away," said the doctor.

He instantly picked up the bedside phone and called Reception. "Can you call an ambulance please for Mr Brown? Room 217… quick as you can."

It wasn't long before the ambulance was arriving at the Accident and Emergency department at the City Hospital. This was a large brick built Victorian building only about a mile from the hotel, in Monkgate just to the other side of York Minster.

Nick was wheeled onto the night admissions ward where a team of nurses undertook a strict regime of temperature and blood pressure observations, filled in various forms and check lists before another doctor appeared.

He supervised the removal of a blood sample which was whisked away.

The doctor indicated that Nick would need to go into surgery within the hour as he was in danger of his appendix bursting.

"I see you've been eating and drinking," he said as he read the notes on the clipboard.

"We'll operate anyway, not ideal but we'll have a go.

'Great,' thought Nick *'how reassuring!'*

He felt drowsy and particularly unwell, he wasn't really worried about having an operation, he just wanted the burning, stabbing pain to go away.

He was wheeled into a lift but couldn't really tell if he went up or down. A couple of hospital porters passed short, well-rehearsed words of encouragement in between their idle chit chat that seemed to centre around their fellow hospital staff and how many hours were left on their current shift.

The last thing he remembered was lying in a small ante room where a general anaesthetic was administered into his right arm. As the cold feeling swept down his arm he began counting down from ten as instructed. He just about got to 'four' and the world blacked out.

In what felt like an instant he became aware of a nurse shaking his arm. Nick was still waiting to hear the count of three...

"It's OK Nick, all over, you can wake up now," she said.

He was worried that the surgeon would start and he was still awake.

"No, don't start I'm not asleep yet," he mumbled.

"Start? It's all done. All over. You're ok, you've had your operation," she replied.

As he started to come around he thought he was dreaming. His eyes were blurred and he wasn't really sure what was happening - there looking down on him was the girl from the train... Sarah.

"Well I did say I would like to see you again but I didn't think you'd be this keen," she smiled.

Nick was still having trouble deciding if he was awake or asleep, it all seemed very confusing.

"What time is it?" he asked.

"It's 6 o'clock in the morning. You had your operation forty-five minutes ago. You'll be OK now. We'll watch over you for a while then you'll be moved to the night admissions ward," she replied.

"I'm glad I'm in safe hands," he smiled.

"Now hush," she said. "You need to get some rest."

When he woke around lunch time, he felt quite good, until he tried to move. It took him a few minutes to work out how to get up from the lying down position.

He needed to pull himself up by the metal bars of the headboard. He was worried that he would pull his stitches apart and ended up lying at a strange angle; the bars of the bed were very uncomfortable as they dug into his head.

He was pleased to be manoeuvred into a more comfortable position by a couple of nurses busy doing more checks on the patients. The next week was spent lying about in bed and gazing out of the window.

Time passed slowly with the now well-known routines of the day; woken early, pills, blood pressure and temperature checks, breakfast, unappetising lunch, more checks, evening meal and eventually more sleep.

Nick never had much time for book reading, now he had plenty of time. The hospital had a small library which he would walk down to. His abdomen seemed very swollen and every movement seemed to pull on his insides; moving around Nick looked like a man in his eighties. He'd try and find something interesting and head back to his bed.

Nick looked forward to the occasional visits from Sarah who worked elsewhere in the building. She promised to let him take her for that meal when he got out of hospital which had cheered him up. Nick's family had been told of his predicament but hadn't felt the need to travel down to see him. This hadn't bothered him particularly, they had never been a 'cuddly' family.

On the eighth day Nick was told he could leave. The ward sister insisted he was taken down to the main entrance in a wheelchair.

"But I've been walking for days," Nick protested. He didn't like being pushed about in a wheelchair.

"I'm not interested," she said. "You have to go in a wheelchair, that's the rules."

She smiled at him. "Once you're out of the front doors, you can please yourself," she added.

Nick thanked her and was pleased to see Sarah arrive with the wheelchair. She found it quite amusing having to push him into the lift and down the corridors.

"I could get used to being pushed around by you," Nick smiled.

"Any more cheek and I'll tip you out on the front steps," came back the reply.

Sarah had organised a taxi to ferry him back to The Royal Station Hotel and agreed that she would come and have dinner with him that night.

The hotel, knowing his predicament, had kindly kept his room for him whilst he'd been laid up in hospital. That evening Sarah came around and made her way up to his room.

Nick was dressed in a smart suit, the top button of his trousers remained open. He'd struggled to fasten it because of his still bloated middle,

"Why don't we stay in and order Room Service?" Sarah said, not wanting to put any pressure on Nick.

"No, I'm very capable of making it down to the A la Carte dining room," he replied.

Although he was better, he still felt under the weather and steadily nibbled away at the edges of his meal as his appetite hadn't really returned. They seemed quite relaxed in each other's company and chattered away about all sorts of things. Sarah told of her nursing and Nick talked about his life on the farm in Scotland.

Sarah was a little sad to hear that he'd decided to get the train back to Edinburgh the next day as he needed to recuperate and couldn't afford to spend a month in an expensive hotel. Besides, back home he would have his mother to run round after him!

Sarah suggested he could stay at her house in the city, but Nick felt that would be a bit much, not really knowing each other. He didn't want to impose on her having only met a week before.

"Why don't you try and find a farm round here?" said Sarah tossing the food around her plate.

"I mean, you didn't find what you were looking for in Norfolk. There must be farms around here you could…well… farm. And you'd be closer to Edinburgh." (*And me,* she thought to herself).

"You're right." Nick's face looked like a little light bulb had clicked on in his mind.

"I think I might like being in Yorkshire, the girls aren't bad either," he laughed.

Sarah thumped him on the arm. "Oi, you'd better be talking about me," she said laughing.

By the end of the evening Nick had agreed to come back to York when he was better and take a closer look around.

The following morning Nick left the hotel by the back door which opened directly onto the station.

After telephoning his parents to advise of his imminent return, he headed out onto the platform to wait for the 10:05 a.m. train to Edinburgh.

A couple of hours later, William sent his driver to Waverley station to collect his son.

Nick was pleased to see the gleaming Bentley waiting right outside the exit to the station, it would have been hard to miss. By lunchtime Nick was already back at Woodside.

His mother was pleased to see him and was soon brewing him tea and listening to his stories from the past couple of weeks. It felt as though he'd been gone for a month!

Nick was feeling quite sore for a couple of weeks after the operation, but slowly he was regaining his strength. The next few weeks seemed to drag by. Nick was pretty much stuck at Woodside whilst he was keen to be out pursuing his dream of finding a farm he could really make his own in Yorkshire; and to see Sarah again.

He would take long walks through the local countryside believing the fresh air would aide his recovery. He watched daily as his scar began to fade; oddly, he quite liked it. It would be there forever staring back at him whenever he looked in a mirror to remind him of his trip to York Hospital and Sarah's smile as he'd woken up there that first night.

William had hoped that Nick's failed last trip would encourage him to stay in Scotland and take over the farm he'd got waiting for him. But no, Nick was a single minded individual; he'd made up his mind and was resolute in his decision to go it alone.

He had spoken to Sarah every week by phone; he couldn't stop thinking about her. He wanted to go back to York and see whether there was a farming opportunity there.

By early May he was fully fit and ready to return.

"This is it," he told his parents.

"I know you want what's best for me but I've got to find my own way. I *will* find myself a farm and make it work. I need to prove myself, if not to you, to me."

They hoped he would soon be back but deep down they knew that he truly wanted it and he would succeed. As he would say, 'Failing is not an option… All I see in front of me is success.'

And so, on 11th May 1966 Nick set off again. No trains this time. He'd recently purchased a Triumph TR6, a lovely convertible in gloss black with red and black leather seats. With only one previous owner it was certainly a smart machine.

Nick had the boot full of clothes and a few assorted homely bits and pieces. He pushed an Adam Faith tape into the eight track player, hiked up the volume and with a quick spin of wheels on the gravel and a new sense of adventure, he was on his way.

It was a sunny day and he had the top down. The wind blew through his hair and the world seemed to offer a million possibilities. The roads weren't busy and Nick enjoyed the drive, especially when he could give the inline six-cylinder engine a kick and blast past any slower cars that stood in his way. He pushed on until he got to the outskirts of Morpeth where he stopped at a run-down service station for a black coffee and a rather stale cheese and pickle sandwich.

He filled his petrol tank with another helping of 4 star and was soon off again. He passed Newcastle and then headed east across to the A19. An hour later he was cutting through the smog that hung in the air over Middlesbrough, billowing from hundreds of chimneys that towered over this industrial stronghold.

You could actually taste the fumes as you breathed. Nick couldn't imagine that living there could be good for your health. Emerging on the other side he could see the North Yorkshire Moors clearly towering up on his left as he continued down into North Yorkshire. Around Thirsk the A19 veered off to the left and headed down towards York.

CHAPTER 8

Nick had arranged to rent a small cottage in Skelton, a village that stood aside the A19 on the northern outskirts of York. He picked the key up from the post office as instructed in his correspondence and drove the last two hundred yards.

He soon found 'Rose Cottage,' a small mid-terraced house painted white with a slate roof and windows in need of a fresh coat of paint.

He couldn't get the key to open the door. He 'faffed' about with it for a few moments then thought he might have the back door key. He walked round the row of terraces and cut through to the back garden.

No, that was a completely different size. Cursing under his breath he headed back round to the front and tried again. With a sharp turn and a heavy push on the door it sprang open!

As he got the first of his belongings from the car and walked up the path, he couldn't help noticing the distinct lack of roses at Rose Cottage. *Perhaps there used to be,* he thought.

Inside, the house was clean and tidy, small but functional. Nick wasn't really bothered what it was like, he had no intention of staying there for long. This would be a bolt-hole while he explored.

Once he'd got himself unpacked, his next job was to tell Sarah he was back; he hoped she would still want to see him. There was a worry in his mind, perhaps he'd read more into it than there was; after all, when added up, they'd probably spent less than a day in each other's company.

He needn't have worried. That night as they sat together in a corner booth at the Lord Collingwood pub it felt perfectly normal. Nick had arrived early on purpose. He didn't want Sarah to be left standing around in a pub on her own.

Sarah arrived about half an hour later. She'd got one of her friends to drop her off; the pub was in the small village of Poppleton on the outskirts of York.

They had a short hug and kissed.

"It's good to see you Sarah, how are you?" Nick asked politely.

"I'm well, thanks, how about you, are you feeling better? Sarah replied. You're not going to disappear off into hospital again are you?" she laughed.

"I'll try not to, I don't want to do that again in a hurry," he replied. "Although, they do have some very nice nurses there."

"I know, but I'm not sure we're meant to take our work home with us," she joked.

"Shall we eat?" Nick reached for a leather bound menu from the end of the bar, "I'm starving."

He opened up the menu in front of them.

"I could manage something, maybe one of these roast chicken platters," she said pointing.

"I think I'll try the steak pie," said Nick as he passed the menu back to the bar lady.

"Isn't that what caused all the trouble last time you were down? We don't want a repeat of that," said Sarah concerned.

"I don't think it was the pie to blame, and you needn't worry, I'm as fit as a butcher's dog now," Nick answered back.

"How do you manage, living alone? I mean a single man having to cook for himself?" asked Sarah.

"I get by, nothing fancy. What I need is someone to look after me, and then I won't have to live on pub meals," he grinned.

After they'd eaten and had coffee, Nick drove Sarah back to the city. Before taking her home, they decided to park in the centre and take a walk round some of the estate agent's windows, so Nick could get an idea of where to begin his property search.

He'd only been back in York for a few hours and was already thinking of his next move.

The city was nice at night. Being a Sunday the streets were much quieter than on his last visit. A gaggle of tourists were being led round by a man dressed like a Victorian with black tail coat and top hat.

"What's that all about?' inquired Nick "There must be a fancy dress do on."

"That's a ghost walk," laughed Sarah. "They happen every night. The people get shown all the famous 'haunted' places around the city mixed up with a bit of local history. There's meant to be a ghost in the Theatre Royal, a grey lady."

"How exciting," laughed Nick.

"You don't need all their theatrics, I'll show you around," she said as she squeezed his hand.

As they carried on, Nick made a mental note of the various different agents he planned to visit the next morning, although he couldn't see much that matched his criteria in any of the windows. Nick gave Sarah a ride home but declined her offer of another coffee.

Sarah shared her rented house with two other nurses; one male and one female. Nick didn't want to start meeting people at that time of night, besides he didn't think he should be inviting himself in just yet!

He gave her a gentle kiss on the cheek and walked back to his car. He headed back to his rented cottage. It took quite a while as he got lost twice. He hadn't paid enough attention to where he was earlier with his mind wrapped in other things.

Nick woke in the morning to the sound of a milk float rattling its cargo outside his part opened window. He was soon dressed and downstairs, finishing off a couple of slices of wholemeal toast washed down with a mug of coffee; the only two consumable items in the house.

He set-to with purpose, he was getting going and nothing would hold him back. By 9:00 a.m. he'd found his way back into the centre of York and was already waiting outside the first estate agents he'd seen.

Stapleton's was a family business with a couple of offices in the city. They specialized in farms, land and livestock sales.

The gentleman that unlocked the front door was surprised to find someone standing there waiting.

"We don't normally get an early morning rush," he joked.

Mr Lightfoot listened as Nick explained how he couldn't afford to buy but wanted to take over the tenancy of a farm as soon as possible.

The gentleman explained that he would struggle to find much at the present time although he did have a couple on his books.

So began a month of visiting agents and seeing various farms on offer... Nick occasionally grew disillusioned but Sarah always managed to raise his spirits and push him forward.

It was a clear, Wednesday morning in June when Nick first drove up the long gravel drive to Chestnut Farm. Close to the village of Stillington, about 11 miles from the centre of York. The farmer, a Mr Johnson had just reached the age of 80 and felt he wouldn't manage another year, his retirement was well overdue. For over sixty years he'd been up at 5:00 a.m. each and every morning and to be fair he'd had his fill.

He was building himself a bungalow in the village and would be vacating the farm within the next six weeks.

From the moment he saw Chestnut Farm, Nick liked it.

The farm covered some 270 acres including one lake about an acre in size. The house was nothing fancy but nicely set against one side of a small wood with the northern side lying next to the village graveyard. The church was on the higher ground and a row of Chestnut trees lined its avenue to the road. The land was flat and slightly sandy but looked good and well drained.

Nick stood in the corner of a field and watched men pulling carrots from the ground, he couldn't believe the size of them, they were massive. '*If I can't make money here – I can't make it anywhere,*' he thought.

Mr Johnson later confirmed that he had done well over the years with good yields of corn, potatoes and carrots.

Back in the office Nick had negotiated with Mr Lightfoot who in turn had negotiated with the landlords, who once again were the Church Commissioners, representatives of the Church of England.

So much for, 'he who has nothing shall be first at the gates of heaven,' thought Nick. The Church were mighty land owners who owned a major share of the English countryside.

A further two weeks went past, and Nick was feeling pessimistic; surely he would have heard by now. He debated ringing the agent for the third time in two days but felt he was becoming a nuisance.

Finally two and a half weeks after his visit, Mr Lightfoot phoned with the news he'd been waiting for. The Commissioners had agreed to give Nick the tenancy. He was understandably excited but at the same time had a feeling of trepidation, what if he made a real pig's ear of it? He knew there was no going back now.

On July 3rd, Nick had moved from the rented cottage in Skelton into the recently vacated farmhouse. Three of the existing farm workers had wanted to keep working there as they lived in the village and Nick was happy to give them employment. They knew the local area and could offer valuable advice on what worked and what didn't.

Within weeks of moving in, Nick had learnt how things had worked in the past. He soon realized that one of the men, Steve Hartoft, was one thing that didn't work. He was more interested in taking as many breaks as he could in the hay loft. Nick, although still young, wasn't one to be treated like a fool; he soon got the measure of Steve and swiftly issued the man with his marching orders. The other two men took Nick more seriously after Steve's dismissal and seemed to work somewhat faster after this incident. Nick's Scottish accent amused them and there were times when they could have done with a translator for some of his instructions.

CHAPTER 9

Following his move from Rose Cottage, this old farm house felt big and empty. On his own he rattled around in it and longed for company. He knew what he wanted. For the last month Nick had seen Sarah four or five times a week. They'd been for dinner in town, had two trips to the seaside. Once to Whitby and once to Scarborough where it had rained all day. They hadn't minded as they enjoyed a fish and chip tea overlooking the harbour.

Nick had now got to know a few of Sarah's friends, who were getting a group together for the Evening Press Charity Ball being held at York Racecourse. Nick said he liked the idea and Sarah added their names to the list making up the table of ten.

It was a grand affair, black tie for the men and new dresses seemed a mandatory requirement for the ladies. Sarah had always enjoyed getting dressed up, after spending all day in nurse's uniform it was nice to swap the starchy clothes for something more glamorous.

The group had come in separate taxis and most seemed to look forward to a good party. One of these was Tim, (the boyfriend of Jill, Sarah's best friend). He seemed to enjoy a good grumble. He was a real 'glass is half empty' type and didn't seem to see the funny side in anything, least of all Nick's sarcastic sense of humour. Nick sat with Sarah on his left and Simon on his right. Simon was a local butcher with a unique accent; he was of solid build with rosy cheeks, indeed the quintessential butcher.

He was very entertaining with humorous tales of awkward customers and stories of the day-to-day life in a butcher's shop. The trouble you could have dealing with animal carcasses and sausages, he had the table roaring with laughter for much of the evening.

Through his trade Simon knew many of the local farmers and he and Nick seemed to get on well from the off; they felt they had something of a common purpose.

Earlier the same day England had managed to beat Germany in the football World Cup at Wembley which was a main topic of conversation for many of the men present. Nick wasn't a football fan but was quite patriotic. Even though his true allegiance lay with Scotland, the sight of England beating Germany 4-2 was great.

The meal was okay. Some sort of pate on toast followed by lukewarm chicken with cream sauce and vegetables. It was edible and the party seemed more interested in finishing off as many bottles of wine as they could.

Following a short array of speeches in which a ratty faced local lawyer encouraged the audience to 'dig deeply' in aid of the local children's charity which was being commended for its hard work, the band took to the stage and the dance floor began to fill up.

Everyone seemed to have lost their inhibitions and participated, with varying degrees of success, in the recent craze of 'doing the twist' along with other strange named dances.

It was a good night all round. As the last dance came to an end, Nick and Sarah held each other in a slow dance, Nick made his mind up to ask Sarah to go home with him.

He wasn't enjoying being alone in this big, empty house. Sarah was quick to accept the invitation.

· "I'd love to," she squealed with delight!

The next morning Nick's alarm woke him at 6:00 a.m., which having gone to bed at half past three felt like he'd shut his eyes about two minutes ago.

He looked across to see Sarah lying there asleep, her hair half covering her face. He smiled as he thought about the intimacy of the night before.

But this morning, he had an awful taste in his mouth and his head was throbbing. He cursed himself for being talked into the last couple of whiskeys sold to him as a 'night cap'.

In the world of farming a heavy hangover didn't stop the livestock from their endless demands on their keepers, Nick had to get on. He gave Sarah a gentle kiss and quietly headed for the bathroom to dress.

After an hour and a half's work in the fresh air he'd got over the worst of the drink's legacy and headed back to the house for some strong coffee. He was pleased to find Sarah in the kitchen with the kettle just about at boiling point.

"I wondered where you'd got to," smiled Sarah.

"Yes, sorry, I didn't want to wake you" Nick replied.

This night was a stepping stone for the couple and as the weeks became months they spent more and more time together with Sarah frequently staying at Chestnut Farm.

It was June 1967 when Nick finally got around to asking Sarah to move in with him permanently. It wasn't planned. The couple had been for dinner at a local pub. At some point during the evening talk had moved onto the subject of Sarah staying down at the farm and Nick's friend Matt had asked bluntly, "I don't know why you don't just move in. It seems a bit pointless all this coming and going."

"Yes, I don't know why you don't just move in," Nick added, looking over to Sarah.

"Is that an invitation?" she asked.

"Probably the best you'll get," Nick grinned, and that was that!

Within a couple of weeks Sarah was packed and moving from her small rented town house to this large old farmhouse overlooking open countryside.

One of Nick's acquaintances had a Luton van and was happy to help with the move, not that Sarah had much in the way of furnishings. It took one journey and even then, the van was only half full at best.

Nick was a keen farmer but his skills in home decor and furnishings left a bit to be desired. He'd been spending a lot of time sorting out the farming practices and preparing for the seasons ahead. Sarah had moved from room to room and realised the entire house needed gutting.

Some of the rooms hadn't been lived in for years and were stuffed full of old furniture. One room was full of long since abandoned wooden bar stools, quite where they'd come from no one was sure.

There was junk heaped up where ever you looked.

Old Mr Johnson seemed to have just packed his suitcase and walked out and Sarah found it hard to believe Nick had lived in the house for a couple of months and hadn't even started tidying up. He had been using one bedroom and the live-in kitchen. This seemed to be all he needed. Sarah wasn't going to live in this mess!

"If you want me to stay here there's going to have to be some changes round here, I can't live like this," she told Nick. He didn't really see the problem, he just seemed to look right past the decor.

He was more than happy though to let Sarah do pretty much as she wanted, he'd got enough on his plate building the business.

"You do what you like love. Just let me know if you need me to do anything. Maybe I could go out and buy some paint or wallpaper?" he asked.

"I don't think so!" said Sarah firmly. "God knows what you'd come back with."

"I'll leave you to it then," Nick said pulling his wellies back on.

Within the first fortnight she'd roped in a gang of her friends to rid the house of its accumulated junk and strip it from top to bottom.

Mandy and Claire worked away at stripping the thick woodchip wallpaper that covered a multitude of previous decorating disasters, only to be revealed as the concealing layers were removed. Meanwhile Nick had parked a trailer alongside the house which the others threw rubbish into. The upstairs stuff was just thrown from a bedroom window, straight into it. When it got full, Nick towed it down the field and tipped it ready for burning.

"Are you sure half that stuff will burn?" Matt asked concerned.

"Anything will burn if you get it hot enough," laughed Nick.

Some walls seemed to be held together by the paper and chunks crumbled away as the gang hacked away with their scrapers. Two bedroom ceilings all but collapsed as the paper was pulled off. Sarah and her four volunteers looked like ghosts covered in grey dust from head to toe, but no one minded; it was quite satisfying ripping the old fabric from the building.

As the morning progressed, a Victorian fireplace was found buried behind some old plaster board. As it was ripped away, they were met by the dusty skeletons of at least three long dead crows. Nevertheless, Sarah was very pleased with the old fireplace and thought it would look very nice if cleaned and painted.

Various rotten floor boards had to be taken out and it became clear there was more to do than first met the eye. That first weekend they got two rooms ready for redecorating.

On the Saturday evening Sarah made a large pot of chilli which had simmered all day in the bottom oven of the old oil-fired Aga and served it with hot crusty bread and plenty of French red wine.

Mandy, Matt, Andrew and Claire had decided to bunk down for the night in the lounge in front of the large log burning stove which kept the entire house cosy and warm. They all talked and drank far too much and it was well into the early hours before anyone caught any sleep.

The next day it was hard to get the troops ready for action, many were still strewn across the lounge floor and were feeling the after effects of a night's heavy drinking.

Nick tried to stir them towards consciousness but was met with varying degrees of groaning from under their blankets.

Nick needed to coax them with mounds of bacon sandwiches and mugs of strong coffee to bribe them back to work.

In the coming weeks Sarah roped a couple of the farm workers into helping redecorate the house and soon it was all looking much better. Sarah and Nick were feeling right at home in their farmhouse, along with their cat, Tigger.

Living in the countryside after life in a city was a big change for Sarah. Without realising, those that inhabit cities become immune to the sounds of cars and the never ending background noise generated by people going about their business.

Away from this, the silence can be deafening. Lying in bed at night and hearing the sounds of foxes and owls was unnerving. Sarah was getting used to the quiet and found herself becoming slowly 'countrified'.

She had carried on travelling into York each day to work in the hospital but soon found the journey arduous, although she had enjoyed nursing, she now felt she would be better off helping on the farm.

Nick agreed, he found being his own master was hard work and knew that just having Sarah around would be a help. She made the decision to hand her notice in but carried on working for a couple more months.

Routines developed and Nick began to get the farm running in a modern and efficient way. The autumn was fast approaching and the first crop of sugar beet would soon be ready for harvesting. Having laid out a large proportion of his savings, Nick was in need of a decent return as soon as possible.

When taking over the farm, Nick had done a deal with old Mr Johnson to buy all the existing tractors and farm machinery, which in reality were well past their best. Much of it looked like it had been in use since the last war and it became clear that it wouldn't be up to the task of coping with the increase in production Nick wanted.

The introduction of the Ferguson tractors with their three point linkage and power take-offs had quickly put the old shire horses out to grass, but now, in the swinging sixties these cutting-edge machines were being replaced themselves by the more powerful Massey Ferguson MF 35X Multi-power Diesels, Allis-Chalmers and David Brown 850's.

New tractors and implements were a priority for Nick but finding a way to finance this on top of all the renovation work that needed doing on the old farm house, would be a challenge.

When Nick first found the farm, he'd been to see John Blake his new bank manager in York, a portly gentleman in his early forties, dark haired and of good humour. He didn't fit the mould of the traditional bank manager but still had to follow all the rules laid down by his bank, the 'Trustees Savings Bank'.

Nick had produced a well prepared Business Plan and even though John hardly knew him, once he'd listened to Nick's proposals, had been pleased to finance the venture.

This was back in the days when a bank manager could make his own decisions.

He'd got a reference from the Brown's family bankers in Edinburgh and weighing up the farm's potential and the family's social standing, had organised a loan for £2,000. Most of these funds had already been assigned to secure the lease on the farm and provide working capital for the first two years farming.

Nick was a bit reluctant to call Mr Blake again only a few months after moving in, however, he hadn't realised quite what condition some of this farm machinery was in. He reluctantly made another appointment at the bank and took his figures with him. Mr Blake did sums on an A4 lined notepad before nodding in approval.

He was surprisingly agreeable to Nick's request and a further £1000 was made available for Nick's modernisation program.

John Blake had suggested any future meetings could be undertaken over a pub lunch, he preferred the more relaxed approach. Nick soon learnt that once John had been bought a good lunch and a couple of pints, he could pretty much ask for any amount he needed and found his bank very amenable.

It was 1971 when Nick finally got around to asking Sarah to marry him. The initial proposal had been no grand moment, he'd finally just said, "Well, I suppose it would be a good idea to get married?"

Sarah had agreed, on the condition that she was asked properly, in the traditional fashion, on one knee and with the offering of a nice engagement ring.

They'd often talked about marriage but had just never quite found the right time. Nick visited Sarah's father, Ken, to ask his permission to take Sarah's hand in marriage. He'd always got on well with Nick, they chatted freely and occasionally enjoyed a glass of single malt together.

Ken, had been a shopkeeper and had spent his working life getting up early, finishing late and rarely seeing an entire weekend.

Although the farming lifestyle was somewhat alien to him, he'd lived most of his life in the centre of York.

He liked Nick and could see that he was a hard worker. He seemed to have good honest values and would surely make a good Son in

Law. Sarah's mother and father had grown quite fond of Nick and were quite happy to see them tying the knot.

The wedding was planned for 12th June 1971. This was to be a small church wedding at the local church with a reception at The Royal Station Hotel in York where Nick had first stayed when he came to York a few years before.

Nick's parents, William and Florence along with his brother and sister, James and Elizabeth and about half a dozen others from the Scottish clan had made the journey down from Edinburgh.

Most had met Sarah a few times before. The couple had travelled to Scotland on a few occasions over the preceding 5 years.

Sarah's brother, Steve had made his way up from London and Sarah had chosen three of her former nursing colleagues to perform the more important roles at the wedding.

Sue and Charlotte were to be her bridesmaids and Michelle would be her maid of honour. When Sarah looked out over her father's garden, having stayed there the night before, she wasn't pleased to see rain pouring down. Luckily by 10:30 a.m. the sky had cleared and things had brightened up considerably.

A beautiful, sky blue, 1964 Rolls Royce Silver Cloud III had arrived and was now waiting in the small driveway for its occupants who would shortly set off on the twenty five minute journey to Stillington.

Ken had organized the car and seemed more excited about riding in it than Sarah; she was enjoying the moment, but her mind was focused on things to come.

They were soon at the church, the bridesmaids and Sarah's mother had followed in another car behind the Rolls Royce.

The church looked deserted, Sarah worried for a moment that no one may have turned up; maybe Nick wouldn't be there. As they made their way to the open porch they saw the vicar come out to greet them.

"You look beautiful, absolutely beautiful, all of you," he said with a wide smile.

"Is anyone here?" asked Sarah still looking slightly nervous.

"Anyone?" repeated the vicar. "Everyone's here, they're just waiting for you my dear. Are you ready?"

"I think so," she said, turning to her mother for encouragement.

Through the large oak door they could hear the slightly muffled sound of Wagner's 'Here Comes the Bride.'

The traditional music was emanating from the pipe organ, played by an elderly organist who lived in the village.

"Let's go everybody," said the vicar.

Ken was the proudest man alive as he led Sarah down the aisle to 'give her away' to Nick who had now turned to see his future wife gliding towards the front of the church. He always thought she was beautiful but today in that dress, in that light, she looked stunning.

From starting the walk down the aisle alongside her father to standing outside with confetti floating from the sky seemed to take no time at all. It was all done and dusted in the blink of an eye.

Following a few photographs, Nick and Sarah were waved off and cheered as the Rolls pulled away from the church. The crowd slowly dispersed to their own cars and an unorganised convoy formed behind, all heading for the wedding breakfast at The Royal Station Hotel.

That afternoon there was a marvellous meal followed by a great party where the Scottish and English contingents mixed well and drank plenty.

Nick and Sarah hadn't far to go, at around midnight they were cheered on their way… Up two flights of stairs to the honeymoon suite that overlooked the front garden.

The next day, after a hearty fried breakfast, Nick and Sarah boarded a train and headed to London. They happily chatted about their memories of meeting on a similar train five years earlier. A lot of water had passed under the bridge since then. From Kings Cross they took the tube to London Heathrow. The Piccadilly line ran directly from the main line station out to Heathrow.

They flew the same afternoon to the island of Tenerife for ten days, on their honeymoon, a holiday they both needed. Sarah spent most of the time on her deck chair.

Nick wasn't as good at sitting still so wandered up and down the nearby beach a lot. He liked the sunshine but was quite keen to get back to his farming, although he daren't say so to Sarah.

Once back home, Nick worked hard against the underlying economic problems to build Chestnut Farm into a profitable business.

By constantly striving to keep his costs at a minimum and increasing productivity with the latest farming techniques, the farm managed to keep increasing profits when many other businesses were struggling to keep trading.

A bout of morning sickness in February 1972 was the first indication that there would soon be a new member added to the ranks of the Brown family.

Nick and Sarah were both very excited, Nick was keen for a son to follow in his footsteps Sarah however wanted a girl to do the things girls do. Whatever the outcome was to be, they both agreed they would love whatever turned up.

Sarah had got her mind set on converting a small corner bedroom into a nursery, one of the rooms that had been relatively untouched since they'd moved in.

Between them they soon had it cleaned up and repainted in magnolia for the time being. When the baby arrived it could soon be decorated in more suitable colours.

As the pregnancy progressed, Sarah, like all expectant mothers made occasional trips to the local hospital to be checked out.

Sarah had worked as a nurse at the City hospital in York, however, the maternity department was located about 4 miles away at Naburn alongside the local psychiatric hospital, formerly known as the York City Asylum.

The Olympic Games were being played out in Munich when on Sunday 3rd September 1972, their child was born.

On the Saturday morning Sarah had started to feel something happening and thought the baby was on its way. Nick had driven them to hospital at speed, unaware that they would then have to wait a further six hours before Sarah's waters broke.

Even then it was well after midnight before the baby decided it was time to make an appearance.

Nick had been in and out of the hospital for a cigarette and was resigned to the fact he'd be up all night. He'd been outside when one of the junior nurses had run down to find him...

"I think you'd better get back upstairs quickly," she bleated.

Once finally underway, the birth went smoothly with Sarah managing on gas and air. The severe looking forceps held by the midwife were laid back onto the equipment trolley thankfully unused.

At 7lbs 4oz Georgia was a pretty baby, who according to those around, looked just like her father. Sarah wasn't so sure! She was sure she could see a tiny version of herself staring back.

Sarah had to stay in hospital for another day after Georgia was born, *just to be safe,*' the midwife said.

Nick turned up around 9:00 a.m. on Monday morning to ferry them both home. Family life changed drastically with this new addition. Things were generally quite hectic living on a farm with hens, a cat, and two dogs, not to mention 64 cattle that needed feeding daily. Having little Georgia around made them feel like a proper family.

Initially Sarah found it hard to cope with late nights, little sleep and early mornings. For a while she felt quite helpless and it's fair to say, depressed.

With Nick running the farm she would have to manage on her own. Nick hadn't really noticed, he helped where he could but to him, life moved along like an express train with the days drifting into weeks and a never ending mountain of jobs to get through.

Luckily Sarah's mother, Pat had been very excited about the arrival of her first grandchild and was always keen to help. Without her mother's help Sarah would have struggled to get through those first few months.

The income generated by the farm still wasn't enough. Nick was building it up but the prices they received just weren't high enough;

were it not for government subsidies paid to maintain reasonable crop prices they wouldn't have made it through those first few years.

Due to the financial strain that the country was under, along with political uncertainty, the seventies were to prove no better. On 1st January 1973, the news in Nick's Times newspaper read; *The United Kingdom has become a fully-fledged member of the European Economic Community. Ireland and Denmark also joined Britain in becoming the newest members of the community, bringing the total number of member states to nine.*

At midnight last night a Union Jack flag was raised at the EEC's headquarters in Brussels to mark the occasion.'

Membership applications by the UK to join the EEC were refused in 1963 and 1967 because the French President of the time Charles de Gaulle said that he doubted the UK's political will.

It was believed however, his real fear was that 'English' would suddenly become the common language of the community. Admission to the EEC produced significant changes in the nature of the agricultural subsidy, as Britain became part to the Community's Common Agricultural Policy (CAP).

Under the old British system, the subsidy was calculated as the difference between the market price for the produce and the price farmers needed to maintain a reasonable standard of living.

Under the CAP, individual commodities were allocated a price across all of the member states. These prices were maintained by intervention (the buying and storing of products when the price fell below a certain level).

The CAP also used import tariffs to prevent cheap imports. It was criticised for sustaining inefficient farming methods and resulted in the excessive storing of surpluses, most famously in the 'Butter and Grain Mountains, along with the intriguing 'wine lake'.

CHAPTER 10

Nick struggled through the early years of the 1970s but had a determination that couldn't be beaten. He had come to Yorkshire to show his father that he could make it and that's exactly what he intended to do.

Whatever adversity he faced, Nick believed a firm focus would see him overcome it. In the middle of January 1974 Nick had a call from his father back in Scotland. Things were quite grim that winter and they were suffering rain like they'd never seen before.

On 17th January they recorded the highest daily rainfall ever in the UK at 24 cm. on the west coast. Farmers were used to working outdoors however, as their lower fields were under two feet of water it became impossible to get anything done.

Nick relayed the fact that they too were also suffering an extremely wet January.

"Soon the tractors will be no use, we'll need a bloody boat," he'd told his father.

As spring came around things were looking brighter and work on the farms resumed in earnest.

April 18th the same year, saw the arrival of Nick and Sarah's second child, a boy who would be called Alan William Brown. The birth had been much quicker than that of their first child. It was all over and done within two hours, much to the relief of Nick, and of course Sarah.

They were both very happy, Nick particularly, having always wanted a son to follow in his footsteps. Like all couples, they'd wondered how little Georgia would take to having a little brother. She loved it, having a baby brother to play with was great fun.

Alan was a quiet baby, rarely crying and generally easier to deal with than Georgia had been. From about two months old he'd slept right through the night. The second child is often easier for the parents, they know what to expect and perhaps don't panic as quickly when problems arise. Alan grew fast and soon had his fingers into anything and everything that didn't concern him.

To say he was a handful was an understatement. Living on a farm could be a dangerous place. Nick and Sarah were well aware of this and took a great deal of care to ensure the children didn't get in to any undue danger. There were strict rules about where they were allowed to go and where not.

Over the years, Nick and Sarah had remained friends with the same group they'd hung around with ever since they'd moved in together; they'd all been Sarah's friends.

Nick had some friends of his own from college in Shropshire, his school in Scotland and a few from around the home he'd lived in as a boy, but not many from Yorkshire. He'd fitted in with Sarah's circle from the moment he'd arrived and now considered them just as much his friends.

Most were now married, some were starting families around the same time and some had slightly older children. They'd often end up round at one or other's houses on a Friday or Saturday night.

The kids would play together, the adults would open a few bottles of wine and chat away about anything and everything.

This particular Saturday night Simon the butcher was coming around. He'd eventually married his long-term girlfriend, Michaela. The couple had a son and daughter of similar age to Georgia and Alan and even at these young ages they played well together.

Being another hot evening they all decided a barbecue would be fun. As was often the case, Simon had turned up with more steaks and sausages than they could realistically eat in a week. The girls had got a salad ready and boiled up a few new potatoes grown there on the farm.

There seemed to be more drinking than cooking going on as the sound of 'Fernando' by Abba drifted through the open windows.

The men were in charge of the cooking, something that only ever happened when the barbecue was rolled out. They enjoyed the ritual of getting the charcoal burning whilst consuming tins of John Smiths bitter.

Saturday night was the only time Simon could really let his hair down and have a few drinks, Friday nights were no good as he had to be in his butcher's shop at some ungodly hour, somewhere before 5am and never fancied arriving with a heavy head. Nick used to joke that he'd stick to farming as he got an extra hour in bed.

With the barbecue still throwing the odd flame from the charcoal, Simon would start tossing the meat on it. He didn't want to wait; as the fat from the sausages dripped, more flames erupted.

The finished item was generally cremated rather than cooked, not that anyone ever seemed to mind, '*better over done than under*,' Simon would say.

Odd for a butcher who you'd think would eat everything medium or rare. He always cooked far more than was needed which was good news for the dogs, they hovered around waiting for any scraps going.

The heat on one particular summer evening was amazing, it just didn't seem to die away, even at 10 o'clock at night they were still sitting on the patio wearing tee-shirts and shorts.

There was a slight breeze, but it didn't do much to ease the uncomfortable, muggy heat; it felt more like the hot air from a hairdryer wafting over them. Other than being harassed by the occasional angry wasp, they had a very relaxed evening.

The heat wave had started as fun but was now proving quite stifling. There was no escape. Even in bed at night the temperature remained high and most people were finding it hard to sleep.

During this long hot summer crops suffered, not from the usual waterlogged ground, now it was just too dry. With reservoirs and rivers virtually dry, there were hosepipe bans across the country. 'SAVE WATER ~ BATH WITH A FRIEND,' was used as a slogan to try and cut the wastage of precious water reserves. Nick frequently pointed this out to Sarah saying that they should do their bit for Britain… She wasn't as keen!

To make matters worse, across the moors there were countless grass fires breaking out, which with the lack of water were hard to control.

The countryside in general looked brown and burnt, with the exception of the trees, there wasn't much green to be seen. Like most farms, the animals at Chestnut Farm struggled and took a great deal of extra looking after but most of them other than being underweight, were fine.

That year, the Agriculture (Miscellaneous Provisions) Act was passed allowing for succession of agricultural tenancies, so on a farmer's death, a relative with relevant skills or experience and no holding of his own could inherit the farm tenancy. This was limited to two generations of tenant.

This was good news for Nick as, if his son Alan (when old enough) decided to continue the family tradition of farming, which Nick hoped he would, he would be able to take over Chestnut Farm as if it was his own.

Nick had always planned to return to Scotland but had grown to like living in Yorkshire. Deep down he knew that he would be unlikely to ever return to Coates, the farm he owned but had never inhabited.

Nick's sister Elizabeth, or Liz as she preferred to be known, had left school and been granted a place at the University of Leeds. She'd changed her mind over what to do many times.

First, she wanted to be a professional equestrian rider and later considered horse racing, although this was just not considered a suitable career for a girl.

Most people in life have grand ideas of what they're going to do or be when they're small; anything from a pop star to an astronaut. As things turn out 90% of the population end up in some 'run of the mill' job they would never have dreamt of.

Liz had dreamed of working with horses, left college with a degree in 'event management' and then not really been sure quite what direction to go in.

On leaving university she'd originally intended to go back to Scotland but then decided to look for a job in Leeds. She soon got her first job, working in a restaurant for a year looking after the front of house, bookings and seating arrangements.

The small bistro in the city centre was quite busy but she soon grew weary of this and moved on to a job in one of the larger hotels where she helped organise events, weddings and business meetings.

She had grown to quite like the job however, she wasn't that keen on Leeds; it all seemed so grey. She was sure there had to be more to life. The one benefit was being only an hour away from Nick's farm in York.

This northern city was lagging behind London in the mid 70's, that's where she thought the action was.

Some of her friends had already moved to London. They'd call her and say, "What do you want to stay up there for? You're missing all the fun."

They were living the high life in the Capital and Liz soon made the decision to join them.

After making a few applications for interviews, she received a letter from a well-known London party planning company, Harper Jones, inviting her to an interview.

She was very excited and determined to get the job. The appointment was set for 11:00 a.m. on August 9th at their office in St John Street, close to the famous Smithfield Market from where restaurants and hotels had been purchasing their fresh meat for years.

Liz had booked herself a day's holiday and caught the train, leaving Leeds at 8am for Kings Cross. Having queued for twenty minutes, she'd taken a taxi from the station to their offices which luckily weren't too far away.

The office was above a hairdresser and accessed by a separate front door with private staircase. Once inside, there was a corner furnished with two burgundy leather chesterfield sofas and a couple of armchairs, and a mahogany table with glass top on which sat an ornate display of oriental orchids.

The area was used both as a general waiting area and a place where clients met to discuss their forthcoming events.

She flicked through a copy of the firm's brochure while waiting for the business owner. A glamorous girl called Francesca had started the company in the late 60's and built up quite a reputation for creating memorable parties in London and through the home counties.

Liz stood up as Francesca came in and was somewhat surprised at how tall she was.

Standing at 6ft, Francesca had long flowing auburn hair and wore large glitzy earrings and clothes from the top London fashion designers. She avoided stiletto shoes as she didn't like the thought of looking down on her clients any more than she already did.

The interview went well and Liz was offered a full time job with a two month probationary period - if things worked out well, she would stay on after that. She'd start work at the beginning of September.

"That's great," Liz thanked Francesca. "I'll see you in a month's time."

Liz had a couple of hours to kill before her train would carry her back up north. She decided to have a walk round the shops at Covent Garden before heading back to the station. As she meandered along soaking up the atmosphere, she knew this was where she wanted to be.

Once back in Leeds she had the task of handing her notice in. She thought the manager would be upset at her decision to leave. He couldn't have cared less.

"Don't worry about it darlin'," he'd said. "There's plenty more where you came from."

He was dismissive but not nasty. It just made Liz feel all the happier that she'd made the decision to go.

Her father, William, thought this seemed like an easy way to get out of doing any 'real work', he couldn't see the point.

He'd told her, "surely a party was a party, a few drinks, a bit of music - what the hell did anyone need a party planner for?"

Florence was, as ever, entirely supportive of her only daughter and being keen herself on things like flower arranging and design, thought this would be a very interesting occupation.

"You'll be able to arrange us the most splendid parties back at Woodside," she'd enthused.

"Oh God, that's all we need," had been Williams only response. Moving to London was a real eye-opener for this 28 year old girl from a farm in the quiet corner of East Lothian. Having lived in Leeds for a few years was a good stepping stone, however London was in a different league altogether. Leeds was a large city but didn't have the same atmosphere as London.

Three other girls named Siobhan, Helena and Victoria, worked in the office. They were all in their late twenties and early thirties.

Siobhan had been brought up near Oxford before moving to London some five years earlier, she loved it and had no intentions of moving back. On the first day she'd asked Liz where she lived.

"I'm staying in a guest house in Gloucester Road for the time being, the room's small but it'll do until I find somewhere."

"I've got a spare room to rent, I had a History student staying but he's flunked out of college and disappeared back to Wales, which is probably for the best. He was a bit odd and never paid his rent. Why don't you move in with me? I have two rooms that I rent, one to a young barrister named Archie, he's just finished his pupillage at Gray's Inn, the other one is empty now," explained Siobhan.

"That's very kind, but are you sure? You don't even know me," replied Liz.

"After spotty Harry and his History homework, I think I could cope with you," she laughed.

"My house is quite nearby, it's in Sekforde Street, Clerkenwell."

Well I wouldn't know where that was but it sounds great, would you mind if I came and took a look?" Liz asked politely.

"Of course not, we'll do it after work," Siobhan replied.

After her first day she was more than happy to go with Siobhan and Helena to a nice bar around the corner for a couple of glasses of wine. After an hour or so Helena left and Siobhan led Liz round to her house.

"There it is," she pointed. "My flat is Number 20."

Across the road was a grand white fronted building with 'FINSBURY BANK FOR SAVINGS' carved in the stonework.

"I hope it passes your inspection," joked Siobhan feeling she would get on quite well with Liz; they seemed quite alike.

Number 20 stood a couple of doors to the right. The street looked like something from a Sherlock Holmes novel with rows of terraced houses and old style black Victorian street lights that may once have run on gas but were now fitted with electric light bulbs.

The house itself had a black front door with black railings, and an arched front window that matched those on either side making the property look quite grand.

"It looks lovely," said Liz.

Once inside, a quick guided tour followed. From the entrance hall with its black, red and white mosaic tiled floor, there was a lounge. Not large but snug, with soft furnishings and a gas fire that stood in a big fireplace that once housed an old coal fire.

The kitchen was at the back of the house, a room decorated in bright pink and orange stripes with pine coloured kitchen cupboards and a very small utility room beyond. The two floors above both had two bedrooms and a bathroom.

Siobhan's bedroom was on the first floor at the front. The room at the back would be Liz's if she wanted it. Archie had the room on the second floor that overlooked the street and the other room was Siobhan's spare room/walk in wardrobe.

"What do you think? You'd have to share this bathroom with me; Archie's got one to himself," said Siobhan. "I'd have to charge you £60 a month, could you live with that?"

"Yes, I think it's great. I'd love to stay here," replied Liz.

She knew she would be paying her own way, however William would subsidise her if necessary; he didn't want his daughter living in squalor. He would rather contribute and know she was somewhere safe. She was sure he'd like this place if he saw it.

A couple of days later Liz had made her excuses to the lady at the guest house, apologising for leaving early as she'd booked in for a month.

The weeks rent she'd paid in advance wasn't going to be refunded and the landlady was still grumbling about her being 'out of order' as she'd closed the door behind her.

Liz took her bags to work with her… She didn't fancy tackling the tube with two heavy suitcases and hailed herself a cab.

As the working day came to a close at 5:30 p.m. she shared a taxi with Siobhan back to Clerkenwell. That night she lay in bed feeling quite content with the way things had worked out.

She found it difficult to sleep, partly because her brain wouldn't slow down and partly due to the incessant noise emanating from the streets outside.

Even in Leeds things quietened down after midnight, here the noise was relentless. The sound of police cars and dustbin trucks gelled together into an unruly symphony which she hoped she'd eventually become immune to.

She must have fallen asleep in the end as the next thing she was aware of was the sun bursting through a two inch gap in the curtains accompanied by the loud ringing of her alarm clock broadcasting the arrival of 7:00 a.m.

Although she'd got into this party planning lark somewhat by chance, she quickly grew to like it and fitted in well with the rest of the team. She seemed to have a natural understanding of what made a party work, what looked good and what didn't, maybe because she'd spent the last two or three years going to as many as she could.

Some of her early ideas were shelved due to budget constraints. She soon learnt how much things cost and came up with good, innovative ideas that were affordable.

They had a portfolio of clients who wanted parties for a range of things, from birthdays to weddings, corporate functions to Bar Mitzvahs.

The job involved meeting clients, either at their own office in St John Street or at their client's home, discussing their requirements, finding suitable venues and arranging sub-contractors for furniture, catering and entertainment.

The list went on and on. Coming up with exciting new ideas for themes and types of food along with interesting colour themes was what separated a good party planner from an average one.

Each girl would deal with individual clients for smaller private parties and weddings. For larger events, such a Christmas parties with hundreds of guests they all worked as a team, each handling different areas of the planning.

It was October when Liz had started work on her first really big event. The whole team were involved.

Every year, Harper Jones took over the Lawrence Hall, one of the Royal Horticultural Halls in Greycoat Street for over a month.

Located about half way between Buckingham Palace and the River Thames, almost every night through December they would host Christmas parties for large companies, anywhere from 400 to 600 guests would sit down to fine food and be entertained into the early hours of the morning.

The venue, constructed in the late 1920's had an interesting Art Deco interior with high vaulted ceilings formed from tall parabolic arches.

Built as an exhibition centre, a use it still had, the hall had seen plenty of grand banquets over the years.

Each of the girls at Harper Jones looked after a particular area of the events with Francesca having overall say in everything that happened. Siobhan was in charge of the catering arrangements.

A well-known catering firm, Goldman's, would look after the food and drink which would be consumed in copious quantities. Siobhan had worked with their catering manager to create some exciting menus, to keep things simple they would use three menus that would be rotated every third day. If guests happened to visit on more than one night, there was at least a chance they'd get something different.

By running the same menu for three days straight it cut down on wastage, many of the ingredients would be fine if left over from the first couple of nights. Liz had the job of organizing the furniture and drawing the table plans for each event.

The numbers were different every day and depending on the entertainment, the stage and dance floor sizes would also alter.

Helena was responsible for the booking of bands and DJs whilst Victoria sorted out all the decorations, from table centre pieces and Christmas trees through to lights and steamers.

As soon as the dust had settled from the Christmas parties the year before, bookings for the current year had been rolling in.

Throughout the summer the girls had been doing their best to sell any remaining covers they had left, where there were smaller groups booking for a certain night they would try and find suitable customers to share the evening.

Sometimes there could be up to twenty office parties all happening at the same time.

Throughout October Liz worked on the table plans for all the different events, she had files in date order and had to work out what would be needed where and when.

There were a couple of important customers who booked the entire place for their exclusive parties. These people spent so much money they could pretty well demand whatever they wanted.

One was a large insurance firm from the City who always had the Lawrence Hall on the last Friday before Christmas. Their liaison with Harper Jones was a terrible woman called Debbie Leethan whose attitude drove all the girls mad.

She would come to the office to discuss her requirements, not that she understood the concept of a 'discussion', she just made demands!

Nothing was ever how she wanted it, although Francesca kept reminding her staff that they should grin and bear it; after all, the customer was always right.

Liz had organised 600 gilt Cheltenham chairs with burgundy padded seats for the duration of the events; these would be delivered at the start and then moved around by the group of stage hands that were hired to set everything up daily.

Most days there would be a bit of rearrangement, a few extra tables added or some removed, each table would be checked for the number of guests that would be seated there. Unfortunately, Debbie Leethan didn't want her gilt chairs with burgundy seat pads, she wanted green.

"Sweetheart," she always called the girls 'sweetheart' or 'darling'. "I can't possibly have red seats."

"They're actually burgundy," replied Liz.

"Burgundy, Red - it's all the same," snapped Debbie. "So this year I need Green, 'Bottle Green' *darling*."

This was her firm's corporate colour. Francesca tapped her foot under the table against Liz's leg.

"I'm sure Liz can sort that out for you, can't you Liz?" smiled Francesca.

Liz went off to ring the furniture hire company who told her it wasn't a problem, but they would need about five hours and help from five extra men to remove all 600 seat pads and replace them, not forgetting they'd need to repeat the exercise the morning after.

This would of course incur extra charges. Debbie didn't care what it cost, she wanted green seats. The menu wasn't quite right either.

Liz, somewhat relieved, called Siobhan to take over. Liz handed over to Siobhan and walked away, in the background she could hear the discussion continuing.

"We can't possibly have Turkey! We need something far more exciting, Turkey's just dry chicken…"

Liz smiled to herself and headed back to her desk in the next room.

As the month progressed the team had got things pretty much sorted out. There'd been half a dozen meetings on site to decide how things would work in reality, along with further meetings with some key customers, including the ghastly Debbie Leetham.

The work load for a party planner was very up and down, they worked like hell for months getting these Christmas parties sorted. Come January work pretty much ground to a halt, there was only office work and a few phone enquiries. This was ideal as all the girls needed a couple of weeks to recover from the Christmas festivities.

There were a few parties in spring, loads of weddings and events in summer, then come October they'd be back into planning Christmas.

Liz had had a couple of boyfriends whilst at college and a slightly longer relationship whilst she worked in Leeds with a guy who served behind the bar in the same hotel but nothing serious. She'd worked with him during the day and gone out with him at night; by the end, she was bored with him and that life.

It had helped her in her decision to move. He'd suggested coming too but she'd had to break it to him that she'd rather go alone.

After a year and a half in London, Liz now 29 years of age, had really settled in. She liked the lifestyle and wanted more adventure. It was now the spring of 1977, the party season was over and she began to date a 32 year old man who ran an artist's management company in the east end of London.

Bernie Roberts was a good looking man, in the eyes of Liz at least, with dark, wavy hair and an unmistakable London accent.

He wasn't quite a true cockney, but he wasn't far off. He looked after various bands and singers, most of them striving to make it on the London circuit, most with dreams of being discovered and becoming famous.

Liz had come across Bernie when finding artists to perform at some of her client's parties. He lived in Pedley Street, across the road from Shoreditch underground station and only five minutes' walk from his offices in Brick Lane. As is often the case, an invitation for a drink after work had led to a dinner date which led to more, and then a full-blown relationship.

CHAPTER 11

Bernie and Liz both liked the night life. They made an interesting couple. Liz, who'd been brought up in a wealthy family spoke with a polite Scottish accent whereas Bernie had come from a family that struggled to make ends meet.

He'd spent most of his teenage years hanging around with a fairly undesirable crowd; he'd started drinking at a young age and had dabbled in soft drugs.

Something had clicked in his mind and he'd decided that he didn't want to be stuck in a life of poverty and made the conscious decision to climb out.

At school, a place that he'd detested when he wasn't bunking off, he'd spent his time with a group of mates who thought they'd make it as rock stars. Bernie had learnt to play the bass guitar (of a fashion) he didn't really understand the technicalities but could pluck the strings and looked the part.

When he came to leave school he finally accepted that, much as he desired it, he wasn't really rock star material.

He loved the idea of being in a band and although he couldn't play, was reluctant to walk away from his dream. He hoped music could provide him with a way out. His friends were determined to carry on playing and wanted to find themselves an agent. That's when Bernie came up with the idea, he'd be that man. The band that Bernie had been a part of soon split, it was clear they weren't getting anywhere, however, he went on to build up a good book of clients, some more successful than others.

Most nights Bernie was attending one of his band's gigs which took place in a range of venues, everywhere from east end local pubs through to the Hammersmith Odeon.

Along with these outings he attended many parties with his 'artistes', which is where he'd met Liz. Sometimes she would take Bernie back to Sekforde Street, the only problem being there wasn't much privacy there.

Archie, the trainee barrister was always hanging around in the lounge and couldn't take a hint when Liz tried her best to move him along. He was okay but a bit boring, usually with his head stuck in some large Law book searching for some slither of information.

Bernie couldn't figure him out, why the hell didn't he want to get out there and party? One typical Friday night Bernie and Liz were planning their evening's entertainment.

"Are you coming down the West End Archie? We're clubbing tonight. It'll be a rave," said Bernie.

"Not really my scene Bernie, I think I'm better off here," replied Archie.

"Well suit yourself, but don't say you're never invited anywhere." Archie shrugged his shoulders and stuck his nose back into his book.

"Shall we go Liz?" Bernie gestured as he opened the front door.

"Not like this," she said looking at her clothes.

"I'll need to get glammed up, I can't go out like this, I mean look at me," Liz snapped.

"You look fine to me. Why is it that you girls always take so long to get ready?" Bernie quipped.

"We just want to look nice. It wouldn't do you any harm to change once in a while; those wretched cowboy boots could certainly do with replacing," Liz said as she closed her bedroom door.

"I love these boots! It's called fashion… You just don't understand," he said jokingly.

Liz and Bernie decided to go to The Roxy in Covent Garden.

It was a small club with a bar at street level after which you went downstairs where there was a small stage, bar and crowded dance floor.

A new punk band performed that night, they couldn't remember the name but both decided that it wasn't their cup of tea.

After twenty minutes of being pushed and shoved around to a most unholy din, Liz had signalled that she'd rather leave.

They were soon up the stairs and pleased to be back in the relative sanity of the street.

They decided to head to a large nightclub that was joining in the craze for disco fever. With the film 'Saturday Night Fever' having recently been a major success in the US and the UK, there were a flood of young men who wanted to step in John Travolta's shoes and strut their stuff.

They both agreed this was much more fun, good dance music and a great atmosphere.

By 2am Liz's head was spinning and she wasn't feeling too good, she'd drunk too much. Bernie had probably drunk more, but it didn't seem to have much effect on him, he'd carry on all night if he had half the chance.

As she was led through the door, half supported by Bernie, she lost one of her stilettos, the heal snagging in a grate in the pavement.

"I think we'd best get you home," said Bernie. "It's past your bedtime."

Liz dated Bernie for a couple of years before she finally decided that she wanted to move on. She'd enjoyed her phase with him but as time had gone on he'd started trying drugs, smoking marijuana and taking acid.

This was a step too far for Liz, she didn't want any part of it and as 1979 drew to a close, so did their relationship.

Liz had become well known in the London party planning scene and had built up a group of her own clients at Harper Jones. It's fair to say that Francesca had been pleased with her work and had given her more responsibility as time had gone on.

As Bernie had gone his own way, Liz decided she was ready to leave Siobhan's rented room she'd been in since her first move to London. The two girls still got on well but they both needed a bit of space.

Siobhan had a more serious boyfriend who came back to Clerkenwell most nights; Liz felt she was becoming a nuisance.

As 1980 began, Liz had found herself a flat of her own to rent, not far away on Amwell Street, closer to the Angel Islington, but still within walking distance of her friend Siobhan's house.

It was also handy for King's Cross, whenever she headed back to Scotland for one of her flying visits she was close enough to walk to the station.

The flat was in the basement of a large three storey terraced house, accessed by a set of stone steps that led down from some black metal street railings.

In essence it was purely a smart cellar. It was clean and tidy inside with a front living room, small kitchenette, bedroom and bathroom.

A very nice family with two young boys lived upstairs. Luckily these old houses were well built and Liz couldn't hear much sound of their life upstairs.

It was whilst organising a party for a large finance company that Liz met Mike Aldrich. Mike was a partner in the business that specialized in organizing the lease of assets to companies that wanted to expand whilst maintaining their cash for day to day operations.

They were clearly a successful operation with around 80 staff housed in their glass fronted Euston Road offices. Mike had taken it upon himself to organise a party for all the staff and their partners to celebrate their turnover hitting the magical £10 million mark.

Mike had rung Harper Jones where Francesca had assigned Liz to the job. From the moment Liz first met Mike in his sleek air-conditioned office, she felt there was some spark between them.

Mike was well built and stood 6ft tall. His dark brown hair cut in a traditional short back and sides highlighted his strong, angular jaw.

The organization of a large party took quite a few meetings which gave the two an opportunity to become better acquainted. At the end of their third meeting, Mike had asked Liz if she fancied going out for a bite to eat, an offer she'd jumped at. One date quickly led to the next.

This was the start of a relationship that soon blossomed into something far more serious. Mike was five years older than Liz and had been married before but sadly it hadn't worked out. He'd split from his former wife some three years previously and enjoyed life as a single man in the interim.

He had built up a very successful business and enjoyed his hobby of motor racing. He loved to follow the Formula 1 races and kept a Porsche 911 as a track day car. Every other weekend he'd be either watching motorsport or driving his own car round whichever circuit he'd booked in at.

This wasn't something Liz knew anything about, the only sport she'd ever known was 'showing' her beloved pony when she was a girl. She soon grew to quite like it though.

She wasn't as keen on the high speeds but she liked the glamour that went with it.

Mike lived in a fantastic four storey, white stone clad house on the Bayswater Road, just above Hyde Park. The views from the upper floors were incredible, you could see right across the vast open parkland.

If you didn't know better you could believe you were in the heart of the English countryside, not the centre of London. Within a year, Mike had asked Liz to marry him. She didn't need asking twice. Liz was now 34 and felt it was the right time to settle down.

She'd left her basement flat and moved in with Mike after their six months relationship. Having been brought up in a large house, she felt quite at home in this enormous terraced house.

The wedding was a quiet civil ceremony held in the registry office at Marylebone Road, close to Regent's Park. Liz's parents along with James and his wife Jill had made the journey from Scotland, Nick and Sarah coming down separately from York.

Mike's mother and sister had been present, sadly his father had passed away a year earlier. After the brief ceremony, they'd all been joined by around twenty of the pair's closest friends for a dinner at the Dorchester Hotel.

Mike had then whisked Liz away to the Maldives for a fortnight in the sun, something she wished she could have dragged out for another couple of months.

On return, Mike suggested Liz become 'a lady of leisure' but Liz insisted in carrying on with the job she'd grown to love.

CHAPTER 12

By the early eighties, the supermarkets were beginning to push the prices paid to farmers lower and lower. The farmers got little sympathy from the public. They wanted cheaper prices and they couldn't believe any farmer, with all their land and new Range Rovers, could ever be hard up.

Supermarkets had been evolving in the United States since the 1920s but had proved much slower to catch on in Britain.

It was the 1960s before supermarkets had really begun to appear, some stocked mainly food whereas a few were starting to stock other convenience items. Straight away it became clear that these new-fangled stores were going to be popular, it was just easier to get all your shopping done under one roof.

Like any business, everything depended on supply and demand. The supermarkets were starting to appear in ever bigger numbers, and their massive retail outlets demanded plenty of turnover to pay their way. The main tool used to drag customers through the door was of course cheaper and cheaper prices.

Yes, they could market their produce on quality, but, the majority of the buying public were interested in one thing and one thing only, *price*. Clearly, there were only a certain number of customers and the battle for their family allowance was being fought for with vigour. The bigger each chain got, the more determined they became to be number one, and so the real price wars began with each stacking the products higher and selling them ever cheaper.

The farmers obviously needed to sell and there seemed to be fewer and fewer buyers. The supermarkets were beginning to force the smaller shops to close, one by one, leaving the farmers with little choice but to do a deal with one of these ever-growing market giants or to sell up.

Admittedly, a few farmers were keen to start their own farm shops and concentrate on the home grown market, which, to be honest, wasn't that large at that time.

Some people would pay a premium for local, home grown produce but most weren't that interested in whether their food had been grown organically or mass produced.

Back in Scotland, Nick's brother James had found the last couple of years a real struggle.

He had often called Nick for advice but didn't often act on it. In a strange way he always knew what he really should be doing but it seemed too much like hard work and besides, he was busy enough already.

He invariably ended up returning to doing whatever it was that was leading him down the wrong road.

"You've got to get out of your comfort zone," Nick used to say, which irritated James.

"What bloody comfort?" he retorted.

James had been farming since he left school back in 1968. After a year running Tanners, he had also taken over the running of Coates, the farm Nick would have inherited had he remained in Scotland.

Nick had an agreement with James that he would one day return and takeover. He was always interested in how well things were going north of the border and wished James would take some of his advice, but, coming from his younger brother he felt James' pride would force him to stick firmly to what he believed to be right. Although James was quite different to Nick, both brothers had always got on with each other.

James had become a strong man who liked to enjoy himself. He would work hard, no one could deny it, and, following his long days on the land he liked a few drinks at night.

In the summer of 1972 James had married his long term girlfriend, Jill, a tall well-spoken Edinburgh girl who was as different from James as one could imagine. People often pondered over what had brought this unlikely pair together; if you'd been given a line-up to pick James' wife from, you'd have picked one of the others.

The wedding was another family gathering where all the relatives who rarely spoke could try and remember each other's names. Nick and Sarah had driven up from York.

Sarah was six months pregnant and found the journey quite arduous, however, they both enjoyed the wedding. Nick particularly liked catching up with some of his old friends and acquaintances. He regretted not getting back home more often.

A couple of years after the marriage, the first of two new additions made herself known. Hannah was a quiet baby who slept through the night from an early age, much to the relief of her hard working parents.

Becoming a parent can be something of a shock to the system, but Jill took to it like a duck to water. William and Florence were thrilled to have a grandchild living next door.

They already had two grandchildren, Georgia and Alan, who they adored; the trouble was that living in York meant they rarely saw them. Jill didn't have to struggle to find a babysitter, Florence was happy to look after Hannah at any opportunity. As Hannah passed her second birthday she acquired a little brother, Danny.

He didn't stay little for long, soon turning into a stocky toddler who was a tough little lad. He looked like a mini version of James. Although James had done his bit to try and renovate the old farmhouse it still showed its age. It was badly insulated and generally not very comfortable. It was cold in the winter and hot in the summer. It wasn't big by any means, but they were all quite happy living there just as it was, after all, it was home.

James never seemed to have quite enough funds to make the improvements they would have liked and always believed the next year was bound to be better. Surely their time would be just round the next corner.

Living in the countryside, well away from any main roads made life as a child an adventure. As they got a bit older, they would play outside from dawn 'till dusk and, as long as they kept away from any dangerous machinery, they'd be fine. Their minds were filled with imaginary worlds they'd conjure up, from wizards and witches to soldiers and secret agents.

The lure of freshly stacked straw bales was too much for any child to ignore, they looked so inviting. One of their favourite games was building dens or castles by re-stacking the bales. They could climb right up into the rafters of the Dutch barns and hide away; James didn't mind, he'd done the same as a boy, but Jill was always worrying there'd be an accident. Luckily it never materialised.

As they grew older, Hannah turned into a bit of a 'tomboy'. She, like her brother was quite happy playing out in the cold and wasn't averse to coming home covered in mud from head to toe, much to Jill's irritation.

Her old Bendix washing machine seemed to be running round the clock. Usually the British weather wasn't worth writing home about, but the summer of 1976 was exceptionally hot, with a full on heatwave between the middle of June and end of July, even in Scotland.

The whole family found the farmhouse uncomfortable, hot and muggy. Even sleeping with the windows wide open, was difficult.

The unrelenting heat, however, was only half the story. Rainfall had been below average since the spring of 1975 becoming increasingly sparse right through the summer of 1976.

Dorset and Devon were among the driest areas, with no rain falling for 45 days in some places. The lack of water led the government to pass the Drought Act with water rationing and use of standpipes.

The conditions were terrible for agriculture with millions of pounds worth of crops destroyed, resulting in soaring food prices.

All three farms on the Scottish estate suffered. Just as in Yorkshire, keeping the livestock fed was difficult with the grass turning brown and barely growing. The crops, particularly wheat and barley produced a very low yield that year.

Things recovered in the next few years with the typical wet and windy weather returning. As 1982 had arrived, James and Nick made a new deal with one of the larger supermarkets, TayMarts, whose name now adorned shops that were sprouting up in towns across the country.

They were constructed more like industrial warehouses rather than the old high street shops of yesterday's grocers and butchers.

The contract with TayMarts had seemed the only way they could guarantee a regular income from a reliable source. Regular but certainly priced in favour of the supermarket.

Nick and James worked through the contractual details with their joint solicitor, a Mr Kay whose offices were in a large double fronted Victorian building close to the centre of Edinburgh.

Mr Kay, a man in his mid-thirties, always appeared smartly dressed in hand made suits and well-polished shoes. He sat behind a massive double sided desk with two portraits, one of his father, the other his grandfather, looking down on him from the days when they too had dispensed legal advice from the same building.

He behaved in a pompous but authoritative manner more akin to someone in their fifties. He knew his stuff and had a strong reputation for being right, he had become the firms youngest ever partner at the age of 32.

There were two contracts, one covered 'produce' produced in Scotland by the three farms trading as Woodside Tanners & Coates Produce Ltd (WTCP Ltd).

The other contract was between Nick and TayMarts for his farm in Yorkshire.

WTCP had been set up in 1963, the shares owned by William and his sons, James and Nick. It was through the company that the three farms distributed their products to market.

William still held the largest percentage of shares, 50%, and also owned Woodside Farm outright, although he'd retired from full time work a few years earlier, he was quite happy for his sons to look after things.

James was Managing Director and the eldest and only remaining Brown family member farming in Scotland. He held 35% of the shares, these covered his output from Tanners along with a proportion for running Coates, which Nick still owned.

Nick, living in Yorkshire left the day-to-day running of his Scottish farm to his brother but still received a 15% stake in lieu of rent.

As Peter Kay studied the contracts James had laid out on the desk between them, he furrowed his brow. He didn't like the terms and pointed out that in both cases the supermarkets could force the farmers to reduce their price per item at any time to aid them with any special offers they were promoting in their stores.

Rather than them make a loss on an item, the farmers would have to take the hit. They also had the right to cancel orders at a moment's notice and various other benefits in favour of the buyer, were listed.

The three of them spent a good hour discussing the many pitfalls that lay before them. Nick and James weren't stupid, they could see that Mr Kay was legally correct in his analysis of the points listed in the contracts.

The Brown brothers understood the offer on the table and appreciated their solicitor's views. On balance though, they felt pushed into a corner, with the supermarkets they could end up being squeezed out of business, without them they would almost certainly suffer the same fate.

The contract for WTCP Ltd to supply TayMarts for the next 5 years had already been signed by Nigel Jones of TayMarts and now just awaited the Browns' signatures. After a final hesitation, it was duly signed and witnessed.

After the meeting, the boys headed into Edinburgh for a drink to celebrate what they hoped would be a good business deal that would secure the future of the farms they were running.

Their father was happy enough with the deal, he'd been lucky over the years but could see that times were changing and thought he would have probably done the same thing.

CHAPTER 13

I t was midsummer, 1985 when Nick received the news that his father had collapsed and died whilst out walking his two black Labradors. The dogs had returned home alone and barked for long enough to convince Ted, one of William's long-term farm workers, to follow them.

Ted had discovered William lying on the headland of a large field of wheat.

He was lying at an unnatural angle with his head resting half in a muddy puddle, he was clearly dead. It was later reported that he'd suffered a massive heart attack which would have ended his life so fast that he probably never knew anything about it.

At 73 years of age, William had left his mark as a successful farmer but had died never knowing what had happened to his youngest son, Jack. He'd never really come to terms with it, always believing he was dead but never having the chance to grieve.

The death hit Florence hard, she'd had William around for as long as she could remember. Florence was now 67 years of age and struggling with her mobility. She'd suffered from arthritis since her mid 50's and was now battling with the stairs and even short walks.

She'd relied on William and thought he'd be around forever. He'd seemed as fit as a fiddle, yes, he smoked too much and liked a drink, but it never slowed him down.

Even though he'd taken a back seat in the day to day running of the farm, when needed, he could work for longer and harder than a man of half his age.

The funeral was organised for the following week at the Aberlady Parish Church. There'd been a church on the site since the 12th century and the current one had stood for over a hundred years.

Behind the church was a golf course which also stood on the banks of the Forth. It was a pleasant setting although the wind cut through you as it raced unhindered across the open Scottish countryside.

The church was full and a handful of mourners had to stand at the back. After a short service, William was buried in the north east corner of the churchyard in a plot he'd reserved for his family as and when required.

Since the hot summer of 1976, Bill Prest, a middle-aged man who'd been in William's employment since he'd left school at 15 years of age had effectively been running Woodside Farm. He'd lived in a farm cottage at the end of the drive whilst William and Florence had remained in the farmhouse.

Now with William gone it was time for a change. There was no way that Florence would be able to manage for much longer on her own, she would need help.

The family knew she needed to move and so did she, although she'd be damned to admit it. The thought of being stuck in an old people's home all day didn't agree with the 'outdoors' life she'd always known.

She'd hoped that maybe she could live with James and Jill, but like many families, they weren't really that keen on having the burden of a partially disabled pensioner landed on them, family or not. Obviously, they didn't say as much but found plenty of good reasons why she'd be better off in a good retirement home. James, being the eldest son and living on the adjacent farm took control of the situation.

He took his mother to see a few of these establishments in the surrounding area. Some were downright awful, they looked more like prisons and their occupants looked like they would tunnel out given half a chance.

Much as she still disliked the idea, Florence agreed to move into The Manor House Retirement home located in Haddington, just a few miles from the farm.

She'd managed just over six months on her own which she found hard going and lonely, a move seemed like her only option. The

Manor House was quite new and had large windows with nice views over some open fields and woodland, grey pebble dashed walls supported a slate roof.

Around 30 residents were cared for by 10 well trained staff. Luckily, they had a vacant room. their residents tended to depart with little if any notice and one had recently moved on from this world, leaving a nice cosy room on the ground floor close to the front entrance.

On 16th January 1986, Florence moved to her new home. She had a few of her favourite items of furniture and ornaments brought in to personalise it. A handful of pictures stood on the mantelpiece, some of the family at various ages and one faded black and white picture of Jack taken just a couple of days before he'd disappeared 36 years earlier.

Despite these homely additions, the smell of the place, a strange mixture of old people, warm stale air and cleaning fluids was a permanent reminder that she wasn't at home.

Florence knew a couple of the residents who'd lived locally and soon made a few new friends. She whiled away the hours reading or playing 'Bridge', a game she was good at. It drove her fellow players mad that she won nearly every game.

Rare outings were arranged for her by James, but they became harder as she found it more difficult to get about at all. By the age of 72 she was virtually confined to The Manor House, wheel chair bound and only getting taken out at Christmas.

Eventually, all the days seemed to blend into one. Boredom seemed to consume many hours of her day and she often tried to bribe her visitors into bringing her a bottle of sherry or brandy, so she could get drunk and pretend she was somewhere else.

On more than one occasion she'd managed to get a glass of something alcoholic only to knock it to the floor in her feeble attempt to get hold of it, the arthritis in her hands making even the simplest of tasks difficult. She'd curse, and a tear would fall from her eye as she remembered how life had been not that long ago.

CHAPTER 14

Simon Elliott had joined TayMarts supermarket as a shelf stacker at the age of 17. It wasn't his dream job, but it was a job nevertheless.

Simon's father Alex was in the army and so moving from one country to another had become a part of life. Simon didn't find this strange as both him and his brother Ralph had known nothing else.

They were brought up in Greece before subsequently moving to Hamburg, followed by Northern Ireland and finally ending up in the south of England.

From the age of 5, the boys had attended an 'ex-pat' school for the sons and daughters of the servicemen based in Athens. Simon was an intelligent boy, some would say gifted, who had liked school and worked hard at his studies.

Granted, at times he found it difficult to get on with his father who was quite stern and a stickler for discipline but Simon put this down to his father's army training. Many of his peers felt the same way. When Simon had done well at school his father would say 'well done' but didn't seem that interested. His mother however was more supportive.

Simon wasn't really bothered, even at an early age he felt that he wanted to do things for himself. He wanted to get somewhere in life and wasn't interested in anyone else's opinions.

By 1959 the family had settled in Salisbury and Simon and his brother were both attending the local grammar school, Bishop Wordsworth's.

They were both used to the 'trying to fit in' phase, most of the other pupils had been together since primary school and knew each other well. In an odd way it helped to be 'the new faces', other children were interested in them and before long they'd both found new circles of friends.

Simon took his 'O' levels a couple of years later, he'd worked hard and made a concerted effort to revise well. It paid off with a good set of results – 4 'A's, 4 'B's and a 'C'.

Simon had wanted to go to college or university but, much to his frustration, he soon realised he had no chance, his father certainly wasn't going to pay for that, he believed Simon should be following in his footsteps with a career in the army and was quite determined to push him in this direction.

He went on and on about it, constantly using expressions such as "When Simon's in the regiment he won't be doing this and that…" or "When Simon's on leave from the army he'll be able to do x or y," so much so that eventually Simon had made the decision to leave home; he couldn't take it for one more day.

He hated the idea of army life, there was nothing he could think of that he would like less. He had waited until his parents were on a weekend away, they'd left him and his brother at home, which wasn't unusual and headed off.

He had it worked out in his mind weeks before they went; he swore Ralph to secrecy, packed his limited possessions and left home. On their return his parents reacted differently. His mother, Louise was quite shocked that he'd just vanished without a word, although she suspected it was because he would have been afraid to tell his father.

His father Alex was less surprised and didn't show much concern.

"He'll show up sooner or later. He's 19 years old, that's sufficiently old enough to look after himself, I was in the army at that age and I managed alright."

"I'm not interested in the bloody army. It's always the bloody army. We need to find him." said Louise. She started to think that Simon may have been murdered and was all ready to initiate a full Police search. Ralph decided he'd better come clean and tell his mother the truth once it became apparent, she wasn't going to let the matter rest.

Alex calmed her down and talked her out of searching for him, telling her he probably needed some space. And so Simon found his way to London blagging his way into the exciting world of supermarket shelf stacking.

He'd even had to lie about having a proper address or he wouldn't have got a job at all. Fortunately, he had met a young man called Steve on the train from Bournemouth who had agreed to let him sleep on his sofa for a couple of weeks.

Steve was a strange looking character with long blonde hair entwined with bits of material and ribbons. An untidy ponytail emerged from the back.

His ears carried an array of silver jewellery and he wore a dark brown afghan coat which had some red trim around the sleeves and thick fur collars that ran down the entire length of the coat.

His hands were suntanned and emerged from the matching fur around the cuffs.

On the luggage rack above his head Steve had stowed an old tartan suitcase that he'd taken on his weekend's partying, amid the mainly retired population of Bournemouth.

Simon, sitting opposite Steve and wearing a small pair of jeans and a corduroy jacket couldn't have looked more different.

Whilst trying not to stare, Simon had cautiously surveyed the character that sat in front of him.

"Alright cock?" Steve piped out cheerfully. This seemed a strange introduction.

Simon wasn't sure if this was a common form of address or intended as an insult, he'd been called some names in his time. Looking at the cheerful expression on his face, Simon deduced it was meant in a friendly way.

"Yes, thanks. Do you live in London or are you just visiting, like me?" Simon asked curiously.

The ice now broken, the two soon started to chat easily. They could have known each other for years. They talked of where they'd been and where they were heading. Simon told of his escape from Salisbury and had expressed his concern about finding somewhere to stay when he reached the capital, he hadn't many savings and knew he couldn't afford a hotel for a long stay.

"You can bunk down at mine if you like, it's a bit of a free for all, people come and they go, I like a bit of company." chirped Steve.

Simon was surprised that Steve would make such an offer when they'd only just met and just as surprised that he'd have his own house. He didn't look much older than himself, perhaps in his early twenties but not much more.

"Is it your own house? I don't want to be a nuisance," said Simon.

"It's fine, honestly. I inherited the old place when my Gran died a couple of years ago. It needs a bit of work on it but it's okay for me. It's down a nice little road, Isabella Street, just south of the river, not far from Waterloo," answered Steve.

He continued, "She left me all the furniture too. It was funny, the things I found when I went through all the drawers.

Every year, for Christmas we'd buy her that '*Oil of Olay*' stuff, we thought she loved it; she certainly looked pleased when she opened her presents.

In one of the wardrobes I must have found thirty packets of it that she'd never opened. I wonder what the poor old dear must have thought each year when the next lot arrived. Anyway, the room's there if you want it, and the Oil of Ulay too," he said laughing.

"Sounds great, that'd be really kind of you, I would be happy to pay my way," said Simon thankfully.

"That's settled then," said Steve. "We'll have a ball!"

Simon knew this wasn't going to be a good long term plan and that he'd have to make it a priority to find a more permanent place to live.

He'd got a few savings stashed away which he hoped would help towards a deposit, but he knew that even the cheapest rental properties in the area would merit a couple of month's rent in advance. He needed a job!

Steve's house bore all the hallmarks of a bachelor pad, it was jammed full of objects d'art or 'junk' with barely room to sit down.

Just making the journey from the front door to the living room was something of a challenge.

The curtains seemed to be stuck in a state of limbo, neither fully open nor fully closed.

A collection of fine antique furniture seemed out of place amongst the plates and mugs that stood in various stages of consumption, some with mould growing round their edges.

Many empty alcohol bottles adorned the window sills and mantelpiece along with a selection of overflowing ashtrays. A worn carpet that displayed the faded remains of a paisley pattern revealed itself between the 'mess' strewn across the floor.

This place had certainly seen some serious partying. Simon had been brought up in a house that displayed all the order of a military outpost. He had learned to be tidy and organised in everything he did. Even as a teenager he'd not been allowed to have any mess in his bedroom.

He didn't like living like one of his father's squaddies, however, as his eyes flicked around this tip, he wasn't sure how he would cope staying in this devastation.

So began an interesting first weekend in London where Steve showed him the sights and sounds along with some places that probably wouldn't be on the average tourist's itinerary.

As he lay on his bed that Sunday night he thought about the route he needed to take. It would have been easy to just slob about and fall into this hippy lifestyle of partying and sleeping, but he knew that wasn't for him, he wanted to better himself.

He knew that the very next morning he would get himself up and out to find some gainful employment. Surely someone would recognise he had potential?

Following a few hours walking up and down streets, looking in shop windows, occasionally asking if there was any work going, he'd spotted a sign in a supermarket window - 'STAFF NEEDED – APPLY WITHIN'.

He walked into the shop and was directed to the manager's office. A very short discussion later and he was on the payroll.

"You'll be on the night shift but we'd best see what you can do. You can start right away." The manager said, passing him a long white coat. Ten minutes later he was moving boxes round a cramped storeroom.

'*That was easy*', he thought to himself.

The job he'd landed meant working through the night from 10 p.m. until 6:30 a.m. 5 days a week.

This had 'pros' and 'cons'. On the one hand Simon could spend the day looking for something else to do, but on the other he wasn't good at handling the anti-social hours.

It made little difference though as when he did work a day shift, he couldn't sleep at night as Steve and his other mates insisted on partying right though until morning. For all his hard work at school and his grand ideas, here he was stacking shelves, not really what he'd envisaged when he'd set off a few weeks earlier.

Although far from being Simon's dream job, he always tried his hardest to do everything right. He would often study the way people went about choosing their shopping and think of ways he'd do things differently to boost sales.

He could see from the start a battle of wits, savvy customers would know to dig further back onto the shelves where the goods with later '*sell by dates*' were lurking.

Simon would ensure that items in need of selling cunningly concealed all that lay behind. It intrigued him as to the way a customer's mind might work when walking around the store.

After a couple of months Simon approached the manager and talked his way onto the daytime check-outs. This was like heaven after all those long quiet nights.

Although he hadn't progressed to higher education, Simon was quite switched on and soon moved through the junior ranks of the company.

After a stint on the cash registers, which he didn't really enjoy, he moved into the stock rooms behind the store where he helped in organising the distribution of products.

Simon had been very grateful to Steve for 'renting' him the small bedroom in Isabella Street, but, after three months of living in this strange world of hippies and vagrants he needed to move on.

With a job he now had an income, of sorts, it wasn't much but it was enough to find his own place. He hunted around and soon found a small bedsit flat not two streets from the store where he worked.

It was a tiny place with a lounge, small bedroom, bathroom and a kitchen. The kitchen, described as a 'galley' measured 3ft x 6ft and barely had room to accommodate the cooker, sink and two cupboards that had been shoe horned in.

Simon wasn't bothered, the place offered him somewhere to call home and the chance of some peace and quiet.

Simon was keen on keeping fit and liked exercise. Most mornings, when he'd been working all night, he liked to come home and change into his running gear. His work colleagues couldn't believe that rather than going to bed at the end of his shift he'd go on a five mile run.

Four months after having left home Simon finally decided it was time to call his parents. He'd felt very guilty about leaving and the stress he'd caused his mother, it was his father that he couldn't put up with.

His parents had known where he'd been, as he'd rung his Brother soon after arriving in London and every couple of weeks since to let him know where he was and that he was okay.

Ralph had passed these messages on to his mother and father who were still somewhat mystified as to why Simon had disappeared in the first place. They knew he was a resilient man now and was going to do his own thing, they were happy to know he was okay and getting on.

It was a wet Tuesday evening when Simon finally plucked up enough courage to call his mother.

He found himself slouched in his favourite reclining arm chair with the phone clamped between his shoulder and jaw, listening to the distant rings sounding out in his earpiece. After about ten rings, he was ready to put the phone down. '*Maybe they were out, what would he say? Maybe it would be better to wait…*'

"Hello?" The sudden change to the sound of a familiar voice startled Simon.

He sat forward on the edge of his chair and clasped the phone tightly in his slightly sweaty palm.

"Mum, it's me, Simon." There was a moment's silence. Was she still there?

"Oh, my word," she gasped. "Well this is a surprise."

Simon half expected her to tear a strip off him, but she didn't. She was certainly surprised, but she didn't show much emotion in her voice.

"Yes, I'm sorry Mum," said Simon. "I wanted to tell you I was leaving, but I just couldn't find the words, so I just…"

"Yes, I know… It's okay, as long as you're alright?"

Simon said he was fine and proceeded to tell her about his journey and enquired into his father's reaction to his disappearance.

"Oh, you know what he's like, he was a bit cross at first but he's got used to the idea now. He's out tonight but you must call him later and talk, you know it's for the best. *He,* well *we,* couldn't understand why you just ran off."

"I knew he wouldn't understand Mum, but it was the army. I just couldn't face it and I knew he wouldn't hear of me not joining up. I felt it was the only way out," explained Simon.

After a good twenty minutes, Simon had said all he could, as the call finished he felt better for having got this off his chest. He took a few long gulps of wine and relaxed back into his chair. That had gone much better than he'd expected. He now wondered why he'd put it off for so long.

Thinking about the conversation he'd just had, Simon thought about the direction his life seemed to be heading.

He'd had such grand ideas for his future and the thought of working in a supermarket had never been on his *to do* list. He couldn't remember sitting in school and daydreaming about working in a supermarket!

Strangely though, as the months had passed, he began to feel this fast moving retail world sucking him in, it seemed to be in his blood. He soon realised that he'd stopped looking for anything else.

This was 1965 and although the store wasn't large, small local businesses that traded in its shadow thought of it as a threat. Butchers, greengrocers and bakers were not happy to see new stores applying for planning permission to open anywhere near them, often they would try and rally up a protest to push them elsewhere, the old, '*not in my backyard*' adage.

Simon called his mother a couple of times during the autumn and following these he made the decision to go back home at Christmas to see his brother Ralph and his father, and hopefully smooth things out between them.

Simon was somewhat nervous as he sat on the train heading back to the family home almost a year after he'd upped sticks and left.

The carriage was busy, it was the 23rd of December and everyone seemed to be heading somewhere for the Christmas period. Simon wasn't sure what reception he'd get. His parents knew he was coming and had encouraged him to stay for a few nights over Christmas.

Simon was something of a loner but even he could get a bit depressed sitting alone at night with nothing but a bottle of wine and a television for company. He didn't fancy the idea of sitting alone on Christmas Day feeling sorry for himself.

The train from London's Waterloo station arrived on Platform 2 of Salisbury station an hour and a half after having set off.

Simon left the train and headed straight for the taxi rank. There were only a couple of people waiting in front of him and he was soon heading towards his family home in Downton Road.

Simon knocked on the door and opened it at the same time, he didn't feel that he would need to wait in the garden, this was his home – well it used to be anyway.

"Only me," he shouted. His brother appeared from the kitchen

"Hello Bro," he beamed. "Ma and Pa are in the front room. Come on, they'll be pleased to see you."

"Perhaps," Simon said half under his breath. To Simon's surprise his father stood up and smiled as he came in.

"Ah, you're still alive then?" He said in a playful way.

They gave each other a loose hug. Simon turned to his mother who nearly squashed him she held him so tightly.

"Easy there, the boy will pass out." His father said.

"Sit yourself down and tell us what you've been up to."

Simon was surprised, he'd expected grief for disappearing, but they all carried on as if it had never happened.

Simon recounted his journey to London and the job he'd got. His father's face purveyed his feelings on Simon's choice of career. He apologised for leaving so suddenly, "I'm really sorry for leaving so abruptly, I didn't think you would approve, I just didn't know how to tell you."

His father wasn't very impressed with his Son now working in a supermarket, however, he realised that Simon wanted to do his own thing and he didn't want to fall out with him over the issue.

The weekend went well enough, with plenty of food and drinks all round.

Simon had explained that he needed to catch a train on Boxing Day back to London as, although most of the country had a Bank Holiday on Monday 27th December, the supermarket was open and he was on the rota. Alex insisted in driving Simon to the station.

"You don't need a taxi, I'm taking you. Okay?"

"Thanks Dad that would be great." He didn't want to argue.

At the station he said his farewells and promised to keep in touch and come back when he got the chance. He told his father that if he was ever up in London, to give him a call.

As the years passed, Simon had worked his way up through half a dozen branches of the TayMarts supermarkets and was now ready to take on his first post as store manager.

This had been quite a feat against the competition of University graduates trained in the fine art of management, but he had worked hard and knew every aspect of the business from the ground floor up; unlike most junior managers who were fast tracked straight to the first floor.

Simon had quickly worked his way up to the ranks of management, from trainee in 1969 through to a deputy by the summer of 1970.

September 1971 witnessed Simon's appointment as the companies' youngest ever store manager at the newly opened TayMart store on the outskirts of London. This 10,000 square foot construction of concrete and steel cladding was the latest addition to TayMart's ever increasing empire.

CHAPTER 15

The store was located in the heavily populated West London suburb of Feltham, standing alongside the perimeter of Heathrow Airport. The area wasn't particularly attractive and seemed to be made up of post war urban sprawl and dreary industrial estates, none of which bothered Simon one jot, he was thrilled to have landed such a prestigious new post.

Simon had moved to a bland looking three bedroomed semi-detached house a short distance away in Hounslow. The property had a front porch that looked like an afterthought, a large bay window with triangular gable above that had been designed to look Tudor in origin…it failed.

The small front garden was so overgrown when he first arrived it looked like an experimental habitat for urban wildlife. The best thing going for the place was the cheap rent. The area was home to a largely Asian community and was generally an okay place to live, if not very exciting.

The peace and quiet was broken every few minutes by the constant stream of planes flying over the houses on their final approach into Heathrow Airport. Thankfully this stopped at night.

There was a small parade of local shops about 500 yards away which included a pizza take away, a second hand shop, an estate agents and a small convenience store that stocked just about anything you might run out of late at night. The final shop was a greengrocers.

Every morning they would lay up a massive outdoor display of every type of fruit and vegetable you could imagine in every possible colour. It must have taken hours to create this magnificent display and hours to clear it away at the end of the day.

Simon made a mental note of how appealing it all looked; maybe it was something he could introduce at TayMarts. Located at the western end of the Piccadilly tube line, Hounslow was only about three quarters of an hour from Central London, which suited Simon well.

He was awake early on Monday 13th September 1971 and following a quick shower, slice of toast and strong black coffee, Simon was ready for work. He believed in being early! You're either early or your late, there's no such thing as being *on time*. At 7:30 a.m. he arrived and headed towards the staff entrance, the car park being more or less deserted. Although the store wouldn't welcome its first customers for another week, there would be a lot of hard work needed to get the staff ready for the opening.

The office allocated to TayMart's newest manager was nothing flash, a small room about ten feet by twelve feet with a row of grey filing cabinets and a tall double doored stationary cabinet against one wall.

A plain Formica topped desk, unimpressive yet functional, harboured a high backed, grey clothed director's chair, from which was a view over the corrugated tin roof of the loading bay at the back of the store. The simple fact that the door carried an 8-inch sign introducing the room's occupant as MANAGER was enough to cause a gentle smile to spread across Simons face.

He pushed open the door and waited for the fluorescent tube to crack into life. A pile of letters lay on the desk waiting to be opened. After a moment's hesitation, it dawned on him that they were indeed for him - he was the boss now.

This wasn't Simon's first visit to the Feltham store, a couple of weeks before he'd been shown every last corner by John Snow, a well presented man in his mid-forties. He had been responsible for managing the store from its conception three months earlier through the shop fitting and preparation processes until it's handover that was to take place on the 13th.

He'd performed this duty on previous new builds and was pleased with the role he'd played. He had proudly talked Simon through the carefully designed systems that would now let this store spring into life. All the latest ideas in stock control and distribution had been incorporated.

New lighting ideas fast flow checkouts and now there was a week to get all the staff up to speed and the store ready for its Grand Opening in just one week's time.

As the staff had begun to arrive and find where they needed to be, the previously silent shell of a store began to breathe with a new feeling of life. The hustle and bustle of people meeting new work colleagues, possibly future friends, was just the beginning for what would become a community within itself.

Simon had gathered the entire team, consisting of two day shifts and a smaller night crew who would replenish and clean the store through the nights. With a tingle of anticipation, he stood upon a couple of stacked pallets which formed a make shift stage and welcomed them to TayMart's new flagship store. Following a short pep talk and a few American styled self-appreciating applauses and cheers, Simon sent them off to get the store ready for battle. Although they didn't know it then, a battle it was going to be!

Within hours the first of many articulated trucks had reversed into the loading bay to deliver pallets laden with canned and none perishable goods. Fresh produce would only be delivered in the 48 hours before the store's opening to the public, making the last two days by far the most hectic.

The week passed and everyone from Simon down settled into their new roles. A couple of staff left within the first few days as they just didn't fit in, but all in all most of them were getting on just fine.

There were a couple of hitches as with any new venture. Power failures in the freezer units caused some concern; there was a very limited shelf life for frozen goods when left in a rapidly thawing freezer. Luckily, after about an hour, the cause, a dripping pipe from a radiator in one of the upstairs offices was found and soon remedied.

A forklift truck backed into a fourteen-foot-high set of steel shelving, wrecking it, which didn't help, but, as no one was hurt it was put down to experience.

Waking on the morning of the 20th September, Simon took a few minutes to gather his thoughts. *'Could it really have been a week ago that he'd set off to work in his new job? It felt like a month.'*
Today would be the big day, it had to go well for Simon. He arrived early, parked his Volvo estate car in his own personal space at the rear of the store and walked through the staff entrance, picking up a stray crisp packet as he went.

He tutted to himself, he hated litter!

After he'd spent about an hour going through his paperwork, the dark green phone in front of him let out a sharp ring.

"Elliott," he answered abruptly. "What? Where?"

Simon banged the phone down and headed down the stairs and across the store to meet up with Willie, the senior security guard who'd just called him.

"Have you seen this bloody lot? What the hell's going on? What do these people think they're doing Mr. Elliott? They say they're protesting. What are we gonna do?"

Simon looked outside to see a group of people with banners, waving placards and shouting.

"Protesting about what for God's sake? We haven't even opened the bloody doors yet." He said angrily.

Around twenty people were picketing the front of his grand new store, chanting and waving an array of homemade banners. Most were either old sheets tied between pairs of poles or large bits of cardboard including the slogans...

'TayMart Out' and *'Save Our Shops'*

The general theme was easy enough to grasp, these people weren't that keen on a shiny new supermarket on their doorstep. Simon marched straight back inside and found the nearest telephone, he called the local police.

"What do you mean there's nothing you can do? We'll move them if you can't. They're on private property," he threatened. Following a short discussion with the police in which he was strongly advised not to take the law into his own hands, they agreed to come down and try to move them onto the street outside. After that, under British law, they were quite within their rights to protest peacefully.

This was all Simon needed on this big day for both him and his company. Having been back out and had a discussion with a couple of the ring leaders, it turned out the protestors were either local shop keepers or their acquaintances.

They had apparently fought against the store getting planning permission when it was first proposed. One protestor implied TayMart had won by bribing local officials. The fact that they'd got planning and built the store wasn't going to stop them making their opposition known now.

The store opened at 9 a.m. as planned. A local dignitary, who no one seemed to know, came along to cut a shiny blue ribbon and amidst shouting and 'boos' from the gateway he pronounced the store '*OPEN*' and the first customers filed through the doors.

There was no shortage of locals keen to see what this new-fangled shop could offer them; the rabble at the gates didn't seem to deter them either. Many had said they were just taking a look and wouldn't be abandoning their local butchers, bakers and greengrocers that they loved in favour of this corporate giant. They would definitely support their local traders. Well, time would tell.

Simon finally left the store at around 10 p.m. having ensured the overnight shift knew exactly what needed to be done. They would have everything back in position, stock replenished and cleaning complete before the doors opened again the next morning. Having spent many nights doing this very job Simon was more than happy to be heading home – he'd never really taken to staying awake all night.

Simon was one of those people who could arrive home looking unruffled even at the end of a hard day's work. His suit looked well pressed and his shoes polished. His hair still looked neatly combed although his face wore the creases and strains that revealed the hard day he'd won through. He still liked going for his daily run, he'd changed from mornings to evenings when he'd moved to Hounslow. This particular day, he just didn't have the energy.

As the cork slowly popped from a bottle of Bordeaux, Simon sunk into his favourite arm chair and re-ran the day's events through his mind, contemplating what may need to be done differently the following day. The bottle soon ran dry, four easily drained glasses.

The next morning Simon arrived to find two of the large front store windows had the tell-tale cobweb patterns, radiating from the point at which a brick had been thrown at them. More than likely delivered by the unhappy mob that had gathered yesterday, not that they'd ever get caught.

Neither window had been breached but would still need changing as soon as possible. As Simon passed Willie in the corridors he called after him.

"Willie, you're not busy are you?" He didn't expect an answer.

"Those broken windows, get them fixed as soon as you can." Said Simon abruptly.

"Where do I get them from?" Inquired the perplexed looking security guard.

"Just use some common sense. Grab a copy of yellow Pages, find a commercial glazier and tell them we need them now. If you get any problems, let me know, okay?" shouted Simon as Willie scuttled off on his mission.

The Feltham store settled down into its predefined routine. The protestors hung around for the first four days but by the start of the second week they had grown so disillusioned standing in the pouring rain that most had gone back to work.

Simon ran a very tight ship; he always paid a great deal of attention to detail. He couldn't stand anything out of place be it on the shop floor, in the store rooms or office areas.

The place was kept absolutely spotless and the staff always looked well turned out and tidy, woe betide staff that turned up in unapproved clothing.

The entire TayMart group followed the stores operational instructions which were like a bible to the store managers. This dictated the way every function of the operation had to be carried out, from the roles each staff member performed to the exact layout of the shop floor.

The store's owners had laid down the rules, who'd originally made them wasn't clear, although they probably came from a concoction of board room decisions. Where everything was stacked and how many of each items were to be on display was documented along with a hundred and one other instructions.

It wasn't long however before Simon decided he wanted to try and move things around a bit, convinced he could find a better way.

Having worked his way through the lower ranks he had spent the last few years watching how people went about their shopping, what sold best at what time of the year and what didn't move at all.

Now, looking down over his own store he couldn't resist trying a few things out, he was sure he could boost his stores turnover. This would be a risky undertaking as although he was the store's new manager, he was fully aware that he was expected to play entirely by the company's rules.

Simon was amazed that no one had realised certain key positions within the store were premium locations.

Items stacked at eye line were better movers than those on the shelves above or below, and not forgetting the child's eye height, ideal for getting the children involved in the shopping process.

Strategically placed displays at the end of aisles could distract the unwary shopper. The longer the customers could be persuaded to stay in the store the more they could spend.

As a trial Simon had decided to test a handful of items. The first was boxes of apple pies!

In order to maximise profits, the supermarkets had started to get their own home brand products made to compete with the big household names.

His company had very slyly created many items that were presented in packaging whose style and colours closely resembled that of the big household names.

This had caused something of a stir amongst these big brands, however, with the choice of taking legal action against the supermarkets, which would certainly have led to the removal of their own products from their shelves, or shutting up and selling their own products alongside, they took the weak option of keeping quiet.

Simon's first experiment was to place their own TayMart branded apple pies at eye level whilst demoting the original big brand pies in their similar dark and light green boxes to the bottom shelf.

Sure enough, the home branded pies sold four times more than the originals purely because of their new location. Most customers didn't seem to notice the switch, if they wanted apple pies, they got apple pies.

The same results were found with similar experiments consisting of branded and unbranded bleach, toilet rolls and sugar. Certain items didn't work as well it seemed that where the brand was very strong, such as with tomato sauce or coffee, the customers would search more carefully for their preferred choice.

Simon was well aware that he was playing a risky game, he would be in breach of his contract if found using this store as his own private test lab.

He shouldn't really take it on himself to rearrange the whole shop without authorisation. He believed in his convictions and made the decision to contact his area manager to explain what he'd tried, the results he'd had, and see if he could make further changes to the standard systems currently in place.

Bruce Stanniford, who was Simon's immediate boss looked shocked when the subject was first brought up. He thought Simon was being a bit naive to have dived into such an experiment without getting permission first; it wouldn't even dawn on any of the other managers to deviate from the rule book.

"If Head Office knew what you were doing you'd be for the high jump," he told him.

Bruce was in his late forties and carried more pounds than his frame was designed to take. His chin seemed to have long since merged with his neck.

Under his arms, damp patches gave away his uncomfortably high body temperature. He grabbed the knot of his tie and tugged at it as if to relieve the tension of the stress he was feeling.

Once Bruce had looked through the figures and Simon had explained it to him, he agreed it did seem like a good idea. He said that he'd recommend Feltham try a store wide test when he met the rest of the senior managers at the next meeting.

"I can't promise anything, they don't like having their boat rocked," he said.

Two weeks later Bruce telephoned Simon to give him the good news that he could use this store to try some new ideas - within reason. Everything was to be documented and accurately monitored. Simon was only too happy and agreed to their conditions. With this latest experiment he'd started to make a name for himself as a bit of a *maverick*.

After a fair amount of planning, Simon began implementing new strategies to get sales pushed up.

Initially the placement of products was his first concern. He had realised that not only were the positions on the shelves important but the order that customers would come across them during their shop would also affect their buying decisions.

It was well known that most people set off shopping with a list. Generally this includes bread, eggs, milk, fruits and vegetables along with a few other essentials.

The customer would find it easy to avoid buying things they didn't need if all these items were grouped in a nice heap near the entrance.

To avoid the customer making a quick getaway, Simon ensured that the essentials were spread out into the furthest extremities of the store. At Feltham the fruit was located right within the shop entrance.

A healthy, colourful display based on ideas he'd borrowed from the local greengrocers near his house. This impressive show of natural goodness would get the shopper feeling better about themselves. After making all these healthy choices surely they'd deserve a few treats!

The eggs, milk and butter were placed in the furthest aisle. The higher profit items such as fish, meat, cheese and other deli items sold better when laid out around the perimeter of the store. Packaged and branded items did better from the inner aisles. End of aisle displays could narrow the customer's path and slow them down. These positions proved particularly good at increasing sales without even needing price reductions. Part of the effectiveness of these 'endcaps' as they became known is that they're located away from the competing brands.

A shopper who selects from one of these end of aisle displays will usually not look at the normal store displays. These ideas were quickly proven to make a marked difference in the levels of sales and, following careful documentation by Simon and his close management team, were included in the rewritten procedure manual to be followed by all branches of TayMarts.

In the coming months, Simon initiated other ideas including the use of subtle music that played in the background, management of the temperature within the store and the hanging of bags of sweets within easy reach of children waiting patiently in the checkout queues, something parents would find highly irritating. Another idea, which had been tried in many other stores, was that of drawing shoppers in with 'loss leaders'.

Special offers on essential items would be advertised and emblazoned across the shop windows. Once drawn in, the shoppers would be side tracked into making all sorts of impulse purchases.

On the store's first anniversary, Simon had suggested they run a 'supermarket trolley dash,' something the Americans had introduced. This would be a good opportunity for free publicity in the local rag. The store would pick a winner – as it happened they chose the first customer to walk through the doors on the morning of their anniversary.

Simon was slightly worried in case it turned out to be a ninety year old granny, but it wasn't, it was Nicola Choudray, a young mum who turned out to be quite a fast mover.

She was told that she'd won as much shopping as she could get in her trolley in 90 seconds.

Anything in the alcohol aisle was not allowed as, firstly it would cost the store too much if the winner just piled up bottles of whiskey or vodka, but secondly it wouldn't look good in the pictures Simon was arranging for the local papers. Nicola was thrilled to bits. The rules were explained to her and she got herself ready by the store entrance.

The ninety seconds felt much less to Nicola. She tore down the aisles scooping armfuls of stuff into the trolley. In the few minutes she'd had, she'd actually worked out the things she really wanted and, being a regular at TayMarts, knew exactly where to find everything. It's fair to say that as the bell rang to tell her to stop, she couldn't have got anything else in the trolley. It was over flowing.

The photographers took more pictures of her standing with her haul alongside Simon, under the TayMarts banner. She loved it, not only saving a fortune, but had become something of a local celebrity too. Simon could see the benefits of free advertising far outweighed the free goods being given away.

What he couldn't do with was the increasing problem of shoplifters. The bigger the stores had become, the easier it seemed to be for certain unscrupulous customers to hide items about their person to avoid paying. Particularly common were bottles of wine and spirits, although it never ceased to amaze him the things people got caught with.

The store's security guards did their best but it was a difficult job. The store needed to clamp down on the thieves without falsely accusing honest customers, a certain way to lose a good customer for good.

Simon had protested to Head Office that the measures they were taking to cut theft were insufficient. He told them they needed a proper CCTV system which he believed would pay for itself in weeks.

A few of the other stores were in the process of installing cameras and a system for the Feltham branch was quickly commissioned. The state of the art system installed covered every aisle and exit around the store. New security guards were hired to monitor the bank of nine black and white monitors that now filled the wall of the security office located behind the cigarette counter at the side of the store.

The screens showed alternate images from different cameras and were watched whenever the shop was open, pictures were recorded in case evidence was needed, which it often was.

TayMarts were going from strength to strength with new stores opening all over the country. The company had been pursuing a policy of taking over smaller chains with anywhere from 30 to 100 of their own stores and amalgamating them into the TayMart family. They'd also bought larger open sites and created warehouse size shops that dwarfed many of their original stores.

Simon remained the manager of the Feltham store through the early 1970's during which time the store continued to increase its turnover and profit.

The hardest time was during 1973/74 when the country, and for that matter much of the world, was facing a new economic crisis, all stemming from the high price of oil.

The Arab states refused to supply the US with oil for supporting Israel in the 'Yom Kippur' war leading to an increase in crude oil prices from around $3 to $12 a barrel by early 1974.

The knock-on effect of rocketing petrol prices in Britain included a stock market crash, soaring inflation and high unemployment. The government were close to the reintroduction of rationing using coupons left over from the Second World War.

During the end of 1973 and early 1974 a three-day working week was introduced. The supermarket was allowed to trade for five days a week but suffered many losses due to thawing food when electricity powering the fridges and freezers went off.

Rolling power cuts couldn't be avoided and the store didn't have the benefit of generator back up, something Simon later recommended for any future occurrence. The trade unions fought for higher wages to keep up with rising prices of food and utilities, but the government dug their heels in saying the cupboard was bare.

This led to confrontation with the miners, the introduction of a three-day week and the fall of the Conservative government in the general election of February 1974.

By running a tight ship and watching all his costs very carefully, Simon kept the store on an upward path when a few of their rivals closed for good. It was late in 1974, some three years after taking on his position at Feltham that Simon was summoned to Head Office to discuss his next move.

The work he'd been doing was highly regarded by the Board and they wanted to move him into an area that would benefit the company on a bigger level.

The position Simon was asked to take was that of a Senior Manager in the buying division that organised all purchases for the entire chain, now comprising over 400 stores across the UK. It was felt that with his grasp for the business and the ideas he'd already instigated, he could use his talents better by working in a more senior management position.

CHAPTER 16

S imon was pleased to be getting out of Feltham, much as he'd enjoyed building the store up, he wasn't over impressed with life in Hounslow... he was ready for a move. He handed over the reins to his replacement in February 1975.

The new position he'd been given was based at TayMarts Head Office which wasn't that far from his last job. Simon decided it would be easier to keep living in Hounslow for now it was only a short hop down the A4 although he'd be keeping his eyes open for something closer to central London. The buyer department of a supermarket chain like TayMarts wielded a lot of bargaining power. Simon was keen to get his teeth into this work and already had a few ideas up his sleeve

The tall modern building clad in steel and glass stood in the shadows of a tangle of stilted motorways that streamed traffic in and out of central London. Located amongst three matching buildings, one belonging to an electrical wholesaler and the other a finance house, the building stood in the corner of a brand new business park in Hammersmith, West London.

As he pushed his way through the heavy revolving front door and stepped into the black marbled foyer, although he'd visited twice before, it still felt as though he was entering another world. From the ceiling hung a giant gold chandelier looking overly glitzy and somewhat out of place. Seated on a swivel chair amidst a circular reception desk sat an auburn haired girl with blue rimmed oval spectacles.

Before her lay a bank of telephones and a pair of television screens. Largely deserted, his footsteps echoed from the large bare walls that rose to meet the ceiling some thirty feet above. The large modern artworks and artificial Ficus trees that tried to break the monotony did nothing to dampen the acoustics.

"Good morning, can I help you?" She said through a pleasant if somewhat artificial smile.

"Yes, thank you, I believe you have an office for me, I'm Simon Elliott, the new…"

"Oh yes, Mr Elliott," she interrupted. "We've been expecting you," she said, sounding like a character from a James Bond movie.

"Mr. Mitchell will show you to your desk," she said.

As he followed his guide into the lift, seeing his reflection in the mirrored wall, Simon expanded his chest and reacquired his confident stance.

He felt good and it showed!

On the fourth floor they emerged into a smart open plan office space with desks distributed neatly in herringbone fashion.

"Would you mind taking a seat here?" Mr. Mitchell asked politely.

Simon sat at the empty desk at the end of the room and was about to open his briefcase when a young lady suddenly appeared, tapped him on his arm and asked, "Mr Elliott, would you care to follow me?"

"I thought this was my desk." Simon replied.

"Oh, no," she let out a little giggle. "You'd better follow me."

Simon snapped shut the catches on his brief case. Along each side of this open workspace were rows of four doors. The girl headed towards the end door which she pushed open to reveal a smart office that must have been about fifteen foot square.

"This is your office Mr Elliott, your secretary will be along in a moment." Simon scanned the room and digested its offerings.

It was smart but fairly bland. Functional oak finished cupboards filled one wall. A large oak finished desk with black leather, high backed director's chair was placed ready to receive its new occupant.

The window opposite gave a clear view over the converging roads below that carried the never ending queue of cars on their way through a forest of traffic lights.

Three sharp taps on the open door brought Simon's attention back into the room. The girl who had stepped in looked to be in her mid-twenties with long blonde hair that hung straight to a couple of inches below her shoulders.

"Hello," she smiled. "I'm Liz, your new secretary."

"Well hello, it's very nice to meet you," he remarked. "I didn't realise I'd get my very own secretary."

"Of course, and here I am. My office is right opposite. If you need me dial Extension 122 or better still, I suppose you could just shout."

Liz pulled open one of the filing cabinets in Simon's new office and started flicking through until she found the pink document wallet she needed.

"I'll go through these files with you when you're ready Mr Elliott, show you what's where," she said as she clunked the large drawer shut.

"Yes, that would be helpful. I'd better learn how things work around here before I turn them all upside down," he said with a slightly mischievous look.

Liz was not only to prove to be a very useful secretary but also became good friends with Simon. Although he didn't think relationships between work colleagues were a good idea, often leading to problems that interfered with productivity, he had quite an eye for his new secretary.

Simon was now one of six senior managers overseeing a group of around twenty staff who would spend an 'eye watering' annual budget on an ever growing range of merchandise, from produce to books. They ensured that all the stores in the chain had everything they needed - all the time. Simon's new boss was a man called Nigel Jones Purchasing Director. He sat on the board and along with his fellow directors, had his office on the exclusive fifth floor.

The large open plan office outside his had twenty desks in two rows of ten, each with its own small screen to provide its owner with a small amount of privacy as well as doubling up as a handy area for pinning notices and reminders.

At least five girls were hammering away at their typewriters creating quite a din.

A handful of Yucca plants attempted to make the office look a nicer environment. Simon was to work with this team of buyers whose jobs were to keep up to date finding the right products at the right price, to fill the vast number of shelves for their chain of shops.

A month into the job and Simon had found his feet. He'd studied the current filing systems in place and promptly recommended introducing an easier to use, index card system. There was no argument from the fifth floor where the directors and the executive board room was situated. Simon had already proved he could deliver results.

Simon received a note that he was expected in the Board Room at 10 a.m. the following morning. Always confident, he didn't give it much thought; he assumed they wanted an update. The next morning he made his way up to the fifth floor, he didn't bother with the elevator as he preferred walking rather than waiting.

The Directors had their own receptionist who was perched at a large desk outside the Boardroom's double entrance doors.

"Ah, Mr Elliott, they're waiting for you." She stood up and opened the right hand door for him.

"This way please," she gestured.

At the head of the table sat Mike Wilson, the Managing Director. He'd been with the company for twenty five years and been MD for five. He had the demeanour of an intelligent man and spoke with a strong Lancashire accent that gave away his roots.

"Sit yourself down Simon. You know everyone I believe?"

"Yes, thanks. Good morning everyone," he said pulling a chair away from the table.

There were five other men sitting on tall leather backed chairs around the oak boardroom table, they all acknowledged him with a nod of the head or a mumbled greeting.

Richard Webster, Marketing Director, sat to Mike's right, appropriate as he was generally considered to be his right hand man.

Opposite him was Vic Mountjoy, Sales Director, who sat next to Simon's immediate boss, Nigel Jones. Phil Aston was the Finance Director, a quiet man, who when spoke had a slight stutter and seemed to fidget constantly. Whenever Simon had come across him before he always seemed to be peering through his round rimmed spectacles at the calculator that rarely left his hand.

The final Director present was Miles Hartley, the youngest of the team, who looked after the companies staffing requirements, which were not inconsiderable.

"How's it going Simon? We're all very impressed with the work you did at Feltham," said Mike.

"Very well, thanks," Simon replied. "I'm just getting to grips with operations in the buying department. I hope my presence can make a difference."

"Well I'm sure I speak for all of us here," Vic looked around the table. "We will give you all the support you need, just let us know if there's anything that we can do."

The meeting was an easy going affair, mainly aimed at making Simon feel comfortable in his new role and giving him the confidence to make his mark on the department.

Although Hounslow wasn't far from his new office, Simon had seen a nice semi-detached house only about five minutes' walk away, and the thought of not battling his way down the A4 twice a day was very appealing.

The house in Caithness Road had been occupied by an elderly lady who'd passed away a couple of months before. It was a nice sized house, three bedrooms and a reasonably sized bathroom. It certainly needed some major renovation, the windows were rotten and the decor was overly floral.

Simon could see the house had potential and his first offer was accepted. Being busy at work Simon didn't have the time or inclination for any 'do it yourself' building work – he was much happier to pay the professionals to sort the job out.

Three months of building and decorating left the house looking great. With its new avocado coloured bathroom suite and fitted kitchen with bright orange cupboard doors, the place looked bang up to date.

He got a couple of friends to help him on the day of the move. Whittle and Clark, a well-known removals firm had handled 95% of the work, Simon just needed help with some of the smaller items and a bit of re-arranging when things were brought in.

Once moved in, he literally had to walk down the road, across Brook Green and down Shepherd's Bush Road to get to the office.

Simon had now got round to taking Liz out for more than just a drink in the corner pub. She'd agreed to go for dinner and a film to follow.

"Well its home time for me," Liz said poking her head round Simon's office door. "See you later."

"I'll pick you up about seven if that's OK?" Simon called back.

Liz lived a couple of miles away in Maida Vale where she lodged with a friend of hers who was a secretary for a firm of estate agents. Simon was there on time. He asked the taxi driver to wait whilst he went to the front door and rang the bell.

A moment later the door opened to reveal Liz looking absolutely stunning.

He'd never seen her with her hair down, wearing non-work attire. A blue laced blouse with an off the shoulder neck line and pair of high-waisted jeans with wide, flared legs made her look very slender.

"You look great," he smiled. "Your chauffer awaits," he gestured towards the waiting cab. Simon did have a car but found driving round London a bit of a bore, the traffic was usually bad and parking was a nightmare.

On a night out like this he wanted to be able to have a few drinks – they'd help steady the nerves.

"Leicester Square please," he instructed the driver.

The pair of them relaxed and chatted, they seemed quite easy together as the taxi pushed its way in and out of the traffic on the Edgeware Road.

They reached Marble Arch and down Park Lane, past The Grosvenor House Hotel, The Dorchester and the tall modern looking Hilton that overlooked most of London.

They'd soon gone down Piccadilly to the Circus at the end with its imposing neon hoardings that delivered their adverts to passers-by then into Leicester Square.

"This'll do fine, thanks," Simon said to the driver through the sliding glass window that separated the drivers cab from the passengers.

"Do you like steak? I hope so." Simon didn't wait for an answer. "I thought we could go to the Aberdeen Steak House before the film."

"That sounds lovely," answered Liz.

They crossed the square and went into a large red fronted restaurant. The place was large and laid out with booths to seat four, each constructed from high backed, red leather benches with smaller individual tables over the central floor space.

"This way please," said the waiter as he led them towards the rear. Seeing an empty booth by the front window, Simon butted in.

"Can we have that one?" He said, pointing to a secluded corner table. The waiter tutted under his breath and then relented.

"Can I get you a drink?" He asked as they took their seats. "Bottle of your house red please," said Simon.

"What about you Liz, what would you like?"

"G and T please, with ice and a slice," she replied.

The waiter acknowledged he'd understood the coded message and scuttled off to the bar.

"What would you like to eat then?" Asked Simon perusing the leather bound menus. "I'm just having a steak with some chips." Simon's tastes were very plain; he hated anything in fancy sauces or dishes that bore complicated names. His favourites were mince and mashed potato and steak and chips. "I love steak too," replied Liz.

The waiter returned, holding his small paper notepad.

"Have you decided?" He said as he pulled a pen from behind his ear and tapped the end on his pad.

"Madam, what can we cook for you?"

"I'll have the 8oz fillet steak, medium cooked with a side salad please, Liz replied."

"And Sir, what can I get you?"

"I'll have the 12oz sirloin, very well done please, with plenty of chips."

"No problem," replied the waiter.

"Oh, and a bottle of tommy sauce please."

Liz didn't think that was the sort of thing a sensible business man like Simon would ask for, although she didn't comment.

"I thought we might go and see the new Steven Spielberg film, 'Jaws', what do you think?"

"I've heard about it, something to do with a big shark."

"That's it, a giant, man-eating great white shark that tries to devour everyone around a small American island. It's meant to be very good."

"Sounds like fun!" Liz smiled at Simon.

The evening went really well, with lots of conversation, laughter and now and again talks about work.

They finished their meal and crossed the square again. The film was designed to keep the audience in suspense and make them jump when needed. It worked!

They found it quite amusing when they'd both nearly leapt out of their seats when a dead body popped up from under a boat.

On arriving back at Liz's, Simon politely refused the offer of coffee, not wanting to rush things. He thanked her and headed home.

Next day while on his way to a meeting with six of TayMarts London area store managers, Simon had been stuck in traffic on the North Circular, a congested route that was meant to speed you round the top side of London. As he crawled past a Burmah petrol station and saw cars queuing for fuel he had a brain wave.

Petrol, he thought. *I should have thought of this before. All those cars coming to our supermarkets, I wonder how much profit there is in a gallon of petrol.*

As the taxi crawled on he got out his pocket notebook and began scribbling some rough notes.

Like everything else they sold, volume would be the key. Surely if they could buy enough fuel they'd be able to get a better deal than independent retailers, it was common sense.

He didn't mention his idea in his meeting – he would do his research and if viable, present his plan to the Board of Directors. He'd done this with other ideas and knew that unless his proposals were backed up by proper figures, they wouldn't want to know. Simon didn't delegate jobs like this, he just got on with them.

He was soon sitting at his desk with a pile of phone books and yellow pages stacked in front of him.

Where would someone starting a petrol station begin? he thought. He leafed through the pages. *Here we are – Fuel, Fuel Oil, see Oil Fuel Distributors & Suppliers.*

He quickly began to look through the listings. He'd soon found a couple of well-known fuel brands and decided that must be the way to go. He was right. After calling two names on the list, he'd discovered that buying fuel in bulk was no harder than buying anything else.

The big distributors were as keen to sell as much as they could and, assuming the purchaser met their account criteria, they would be able to supply as much petrol as needed. Opening an account when you were TayMarts wasn't going to be a problem, companies would fall over backwards to have them as customers.

Getting accurate quotes was impossible as he hadn't a clue how much fuel a large forecourt would get through in a day, never mind a month. At this point Simon had realised that he would need to know how the planning authorities would react to proposals for fuel forecourts within the various stores' boundaries.

A quick call to the local planning department sorted this out. Simon spent a couple of weeks getting the rough details and costs into a business plan and then booked himself an appointment with the Company's Directors.

They were all impressed with the idea and found it hard to believe that neither they, or any of their competitors had thought of it before, it could be a real winner.

They agreed to take the discussions to the next level and see which stores may be suitable for a trial run. Getting planning permission would take quite a while, as for building the forecourts, there were various companies that specialised in building these sites and the turnaround time wasn't too bad. Simon, as the head buyer, was given the job of securing the best deal with one of the larger oil companies.

Nigel Jones was surprised and a little annoyed that the first he'd heard of this idea was from Simon in front of all the other Directors. He knew damn well why he'd done it, to avoid any chance that he'd claim the idea as his own.

He'd come up with a few reasons he felt it wouldn't work but was outvoted. To the other Directors this was another feather in Simon's cap. In June 1976, right in the middle of a heat wave, the first half dozen TayMart Petrol stations opened for business. Like groceries they would try and undercut their local competitors, by going for quantity they could afford to make a very small profit per gallon and still win.

Simon continued to date Liz over the coming months, often heading into London in search of entertainment. Liz had even persuaded Simon to travel by tube as it was far more economical than his beloved taxis.

He would take the Hammersmith and City Line to Paddington where he'd jump off and meet Liz before they both continued on the Bakerloo line, usually getting off at either Oxford or Piccadilly Circus in the heart of London.

Simon liked hanging round with Liz; he'd lived in London for a decade but finally learning his way round the underground made him feel more like a real Londoner.

Over the next couple of years Liz introduced Simon to her circle of friends and he even met her Mum and Dad. She thought it a bit sad that Simon didn't see more of his family; he'd explained that it was just the way things had turned out.

He called his mother from time to time and his brother Ralph would call and see him when he had cause to be in London. His father had never been to see him in London, but they did still speak occasionally on the phone.

In February 1978, whilst out at a restaurant in Hammersmith, Simon asked Liz 'out of the blue', if she fancied moving in with him.

"I've been stuck in Caithness Road for three years on my own, which is okay, but I could do with someone to keep it tidy. How are you fixed?" He asked with a mischievous grin on his face.

"I take it that's some sort of invitation is it? Do you want a cleaner, or a live-in maid?" she said sarcastically.

"A live-in maid sounds good. Do you cook?" Simon replied.

"You've got a bloody nerve. If I didn't know you this well I'd give you a slap round the face. If you want me to move in with you you'd better think about asking properly, I'm not some little skivvy," she answered.

"My dear, how would you like the idea of moving into my residence in Caithness Road? I would very much like the honour of your company," said Simon pompously.

"That's a bit better. I suppose I could. People in the office would talk though. But everybody knows we're seeing each other anyway and to be honest they can say what they like; it's none of their business. I think it could be fun - why not?" she smiled.

"Great! That calls for another drink." Simon waved the waiter back over. "A bottle of your house champagne please."

"You don't have to go doing that, I'm fine," Liz uttered.

"No, we're having a drink and that's that," he replied, smiling at having got his own way.

"You can be quite forceful, can't you?" Liz answered.

"Always, when there's something I want," he grinned confidently.

Simon, in reality was a very particular man, some may even say pernickety. He had lived on his own for a long time and liked everything just the way he liked it, neat and tidy. Everything had its own place and order, from clothes in drawers to the arrangement of crockery in his cupboards.

The following week Liz had moved all her belongings in and straight away she was rearranging things.

She had a totally different way of going about things; she believed a house was for living in, not keeping in show home condition. She liked things clean but she had a tendency to put her stuff down and just leave it.

Initially, Simon wasn't bothered, he was happy just to have a bit of company. He'd liked living alone but from time to time, it could be a lonely existence. In addition to the extra space, Liz loved the fact that Simon had a large colour TV, she'd been used to watching everything in black and white in her rented room.

Work at the office was always busy with Simon continually pushing to increase TayMarts profit margin. He spent many hours identifying new products that he thought their customers would buy and many more hammering down the prices they paid for everything else.

As the number of households that owned a freezer had begun to grow, so did the choice of new frozen products. Freezers changed the way people shopped, they could afford to go less often and buy more in one go leading to the introduction of bigger shopping trolleys.

TayMarts wasn't about to stand still and expansion continued despite the wider problems.

The economy in the late seventies was in a bad state. James Callaghan's labour government had a big challenge. The rate of inflation was too high, and it had hit over 25% in the mid-seventies. They'd managed to halve that rate by 1978 but were still concerned. The Government had already been limiting private and public sector wage rises to 6% per year and now reduced this to 5%.

The Trade Union Congress weren't at all happy. In September James Callaghan announced that an expected General Election was not going to happen, instead he had chosen to hold it in 1979 to give the economy time to stabilise. In September 1978 the workers at the Ford motor company were offered a 5% pay rise in line with the government's orders and rejected it. Over 70,000 workers went on strike.

They wanted 25% and, after much arguing ended up with 17%. The government then struggled to enforce its 5% policy leading to many other industries following suit. Tanker drivers were demanding 40% and when they didn't get it, they called a strike, causing petrol stations to run out of fuel.

This caused no end of problems for TayMarts, they now had twenty four petrol stations across the country that had been doing very nicely until suddenly they were running out of fuel.

Nearly all their store deliveries were made by road and they just weren't getting through. The shelves were not getting replenished and profits were struggling. During the winter of 1978 through to 1979 many public sector workers joined the strikes.

They weren't happy that the private sector workers were to get better pay deals than themselves. The winter would become known as *'The winter of discontent.'*

January 22nd 1979 saw the largest strike to hit the country since the general strike of 1926. The strike included railway workers, firemen, teachers, airport workers and even nurses who usually carried on regardless. With the dustbin men on strike, rubbish was piling up in the street, all in all not very nice. The chaos didn't end until agreements were reached on Valentine's Day 1979.

TayMarts rate of expansion was slowed by these turbulent times but not halted. They continued to develop more and more new stores across the country. Three years after arriving at Head Office, Simon received a note inviting him to another Board Room meeting. This wasn't unusual. As he arrived in the room he was invited, like a long-lost friend, to sit at the big table.

"Sit yourself down Simon," said Mike as he ushered him to the seat on his left.

"As I'm sure you know, we appreciate the work you've done for TayMarts, it certainly hasn't gone unnoticed."

A chorus of "here, here," was murmured from the other Directors.

"I'll cut to the chase," continued Mike. "We have decided to offer you a job on the Board as the new Purchasing Director."

Simon wasn't sure what to say. "That's great, thank you."

He couldn't help but smile as he remembered that the young boy stacking shelves on the night shift so many years ago, would now sit at the Board Room table.

"What about Nigel?" Simon asked, wondering where his boss, who wasn't at the meeting, would go.

It turned out that Simon's predecessor had been offered a 'sideways' move over to the Accounts Department where he could tap on his calculator to his heart's content. He'd never been very happy negotiating with suppliers, he didn't like confrontation. He'd remain a Director though and was apparently quite happy to move on.

Simon's only request was that he could stay in his existing office. He liked to work closely with his team and didn't want to be three floors above them stuck at the end of a corridor.

The other Directors thought this was a strange request, they all liked being out of the way, and it was nice and peaceful upstairs, one of the perks of the position.

"Well that's fine with me," said Mike. "But you'll get your office up here as well, maybe you can use it for important meetings, or special occasions," he laughed.

"Thank you, that would be great," said Simon.

As he arrived back downstairs he felt he should make an announcement to his colleagues. He wasn't sure how they'd take it, but they were fine.

Most of them had known the time would come, Simon was clearly streets ahead with all his clever ideas.

Simon and Liz had got on well enough for the first year, but slowly, things became less rosy. Simon worked long hours, he'd head off to work at 7 a.m. whilst Liz was still in bed and sometimes, he wouldn't return until 10.30 p.m. at night.

He'd see Liz during the day but had to treat her like the rest of the staff to avoid disruption in the work place, Liz couldn't quite see why.

At home he'd spend his life putting things back how he liked them and continually moaning about the mess Liz left in her wake. After two years of living under the same roof, she became more and more disillusioned and friction between the pair naturally escalated.

Simon realised why he had liked living on his own and Liz was beginning to see the same thing.

She thought he was suffering from Obsessive Compulsive Disorder!

Things came to a head one Sunday afternoon early in 1980. Liz had wanted her mother to visit and stay for a couple of days. Simon wasn't keen, he just didn't like other people in his private space, especially sharing his bathroom. He knew it was silly but that's the way he was.

He didn't refuse Liz's request but moaned about it enough that she finally snapped.

"To be honest Simon, you're impossible to live with. All you care about is keeping your damn house neat and tidy."

"I like things tidy, it's not that unnatural," he snapped back.

"Well I'll tell you what, why don't you keep it tidy on your own. I've had enough," said Liz slamming the bedroom door. The conversation or bickering as it had become, carried on until both of them could see they were digging themselves a hole they couldn't get out of.

An hour later Liz had packed a suitcase and called one of her friends to come and pick her up.

Simon was somewhere between being upset and wound up. He'd had some good times with Liz but not for some time. Somehow, he'd half expected this and when it came it was really a bit of a relief. Maybe she'd be back in a couple of days, maybe not. In a way he hoped she wouldn't.

The next day at work Liz pretty well worked to rule, ignoring all but direct instructions from her boss and former boyfriend. The only proper conversation they had was when Liz arranged to come around that evening to collect the rest of her belongings.

'That was the end of that then,' thought Simon.

"No problem," said Simon. "It's probably for the best."

"You can be such a pompous pig sometimes," yelled Liz as she ran from his office, tears forming in her eyes.

Simon didn't bother to run after her, he was keen to have the whole affair over with.

Liz remained as Simon's secretary for the next couple of weeks before asking for a transfer to another department. Simon agreed it was for the best and found her a role in the Human Resources Department where he rarely saw her again.

Cathy, a well-dressed lady in her late forties took over Liz's duties. She'd been with the firm for over twenty years and knew almost everything about everyone. Simon liked her. She came across a bit like a school teacher, but she got things done and kept his office organised with military precision.

CHAPTER 17

Simon had lived in his house since starting work at TayMarts Head Office a decade ago. Now he'd done well for himself and decided to move to somewhere a bit more glamorous. The house he'd seen was a beautiful white fronted terrace in Ovington Mews, close to Brompton Road, quite close to the world famous Harrods department store.

Compared to his house in Caithness Road, this four storey building was a world apart. Two large Roman style pillars held up an open porch front. A row of fine balustrades ran from one property to another at first floor level creating an elegant frontage.

The place was impeccably decorated and had been fitted with the finest hand-crafted kitchen and two marble tiled bathrooms. Simon had accumulated quite a few possessions over the years, but they looked lost when transferred to his new address.

Whenever he had a Saturday off work, he loved to walk down to Harrods and wander around the home furnishings departments, finding things he thought would help make his new house a home. There was no shortage of choice and luckily Simon, a bachelor with no children, could afford almost whatever he wanted.

Tuesday 28th January 1986 had been pretty much the same as any other working day. That afternoon he'd been at his desk until 5:00 p.m. when he'd given up trying to work, he just couldn't concentrate as his lower back was aching too much. Having been playing squash with a friend at the weekend, Simon thought he'd maybe just pulled a muscle.

On getting home he'd taken a couple of painkillers which helped for a while. The date stuck in Simon's memory due to the disaster he watched on the BBC news whilst trying to get comfortable on his sofa.

NASA's space shuttle 'Challenger' had disintegrated whilst trying to get into orbit, killing all 7 astronauts on board!

The next morning he didn't feel too bad and headed back to the office to face the usual heavy work schedule he'd grown used to. As the day had gone on he slowly noticed the same pain coming back, he wanted to get on and this was proving irritating.

Over the next couple of weeks the problem kept reoccurring with the pain starting out as a mere twinge in the morning and getting worse as each day progressed.

Simon was tired, he was having trouble sleeping, the pain was nagging away at him and, as if that wasn't enough, he found he had to visit the loo a couple of times every night, something he'd never had trouble with before. Simon was sure he'd picked up some sort of infection on his kidneys.

When it didn't clear up he decided he'd better pay his GP a visit. Not being keen on medical matters Simon had managed to avoid visiting the local surgery for years. His last trip had been about three years before when he'd suffered from a bout of tonsillitis that wouldn't go.

Sitting in the stifled atmosphere of the doctors' waiting room never appealed to Simon – having to mingle with all those sick people. He leant forward and picked up a magazine, all those gleaming celebrities full of their own self-importance.

Flicking through the well-read pages was more of a cover whilst he quietly surveyed the sorry looking crowd that were seated around him. He wondered what might be wrong with them.

The walls were adorned with posters advocating the benefits of exercise, the woes that would betide you should you decided to keep smoking or the terminal damage you'll cause by consuming more than 21 units of alcohol per week…

"Simon Elliott please," a voice called.

Simon threw his magazine onto the untidy pile and moved towards the relevant door.

"What can I do for you today?" The doctor enquired politely.

He was a stout gentleman of about 45 years old wearing round framed spectacles and an awful orange and pink striped tie.

"It's typical," said Simon "I really didn't feel well yesterday. As soon as I get in here today I feel fine," he said letting out a lame laugh.

"It's my back, I keep getting this nagging pain that keeps coming and going - has done for a good two weeks. It feels like it's in my kidneys. When it's there I'm finding it hard to sleep," he said trying to describe it to the best of his ability.

"I'd better take a look at you. Can you take your shirt off and sit down on the bed please?" the doctor asked politely.

He pointed at the trolley bed with its blue paper towel running the full length.

The cold end of the stethoscope on his back made Simon wince.

"Breathe in please. Okay. Out and in again. Okay."

The doctor took his otoscope and poked it into Simons left ear, then the right, then peered through it into the back of Simons eyes.

"Can you lay down please? I just want to feel your abdomen."

Various questions about the frequency of his trips to the toilet, how much alcohol he drank and how he felt in general accompanied the investigation.

Following a good bit of pushing and prodding the doctor declared the examination over.

"Right Mr Elliott, you can put your shirt back on now."

He looked again at Simon's medical notes he'd extracted from the cardboard file in front of him and began scribbling some notes.

He then picked up his prescription book and again started writing.

"Well I think you've picked up a dose of Nephritis, an inflammatory disease of the kidney which we should be able to clear up with a course of antibiotics.

I'm going to prescribe a course of Trimethoprim. Take three a day with food, you may feel nauseous to start with but that's quite normal.

If it doesn't pass you'd better come back and see me. Try and lay off the alcohol for a few days too."

Simon said, 'thank you' and headed back to his office. He felt better already; the fact that he'd collected a box of pills from the chemist had dissolved his anxiety.

After a week, Simon was sure the worst was behind him. He was getting the odd twinge of pain at night but not as bad as the month before. Another week went by and although Simon felt the odd twinge he got used to it and carried on with life. He threw himself back into work with 100% vigour; he'd got new deals to strike in order that he could hit his own performance targets.

Over the months that followed he kept getting aching pains and seemed to be in and out of the toilet quite frequently but he put that down to the amount of water he was drinking which helped the pains go away.

Deep down he knew something still wasn't right, but he was a busy man and he hadn't got the time for being ill.

Over the next couple of years, Simon had split his people into teams, each one concentrating on different areas of purchasing such as processed foods, cleaning products, others on things like alcohol or cordials.

The bigger areas included produce from overseas suppliers and farm contracts, an area that Simon had decided to focus his own efforts on.

Simon wasn't slow in reeling in the farmers who wanted to deal with TayMarts. He knew they needed his outlets and made sure they were getting paid as little as he could get away with. Simon was very hands on and made it his job to know everything that went on. It was the spring of 1989 when the price war between the supermarket chains took on a different pace. Simon wasn't prepared to lose. Some bosses would just sit back and let their staff get on with the day to day business, but not him, he insisted in dealing with many manufacturers and farmers on a one to one basis.

"George, get yourself in here," Simon beckoned through his open office door. "We've got a problem."

George dropped what he was doing and headed in.

"What's the matter boss?" he asked.

"Have you seen what Harrisons are doing with their bread and potato prices? They're trying to get the run on us."

Simon passed George an open newspaper with a massive double spread advert by one of their biggest competitors.

"They can't sell them for that price, we pay twice that for Trade, said George angrily.

"It's quite clever," replied Simon. They've made a couple of everyday essentials into 'loss leaders' they're just trying to get everyone through their door."

Simon stepped towards the window and looked out.

"Well they won't beat us, not on my watch. Get Paul and come up with some ideas – fast."

"Okay boss." George was already half through the door as Simon turned to head back to his desk.

An hour later Simon was calling from his office again, he wanted an answer now. George and Paul were summoned back in.

"Any ideas?" He asked.

"Well we could…" George started only to be interrupted by Simon.

"I've been having a think myself, how about we half the price of the entire fresh vegetable range?"

"How can we do that?" asked Paul "There just isn't the margin in it."

"Don't forget, we have the power to force our suppliers to take the pain with this one, we'll just tell them we're halving the price we're willing to pay, or they can stick their produce," a wry smile crossed Simon's face.

"By the way, what were you two proposing?"

George, who knew they hadn't really got a sensible solution thought quickly.

"Something very similar," he said as he glanced across at a sheepish looking Paul.

"You'd better work out our costings and start calling the suppliers, they're not going to be best pleased," replied Simon.

"Meanwhile I'll get onto Marketing and tell them our idea, see what they can come up with, they'll jump quickly when I tell them."

Simon's team had begun calling their suppliers of fruit and vegetables, mainly private farmers, and letting them know about Simon's 50% price cut.

Needless to say, most were not happy, some were quite adamant that they wouldn't accept a halving of their payment without a fight. Simon himself called some of them, one of which was a James Brown on a Scottish farm he'd never heard of.

Woodside Tanners & Coates Produce Ltd had been signed up by his former boss, Nigel seven years earlier. They'd subsequently renewed their contract and surely knew the way things worked. As far as Simon was concerned, James Brown was just another name on a spread sheet.

Following his statement about the forthcoming price reduction, Simon had been forced to hold the phone away from his ear as a whole range of expletives were fired at him.

He was somewhat surprised as he hadn't expected it. He hadn't understood much of the 'F'ing and 'Blinding' delivered with a sharp Scottish accent, but he'd got the gist of it. Before he could explain his side of the story the phone went dead. Back in Scotland, James' short fuse had blown and he'd smashed the receiver down in rage.

Simon, standing in his office doorway called out. "Have any of you dealt with the Browns of Haddington?"

Mark Howton, another of his team called back.

"I have. They were one of Nige's clients. They're quite big farmers – I mean they've quite a lot of land.

They've about 1500 acres in Scotland and the brother, Mick, or is it Nick had another two or three hundred acres in Yorkshire.

They're okay really, but that James can be a bit fiery if you rub him up the wrong way."

"I think I just did - he didn't like my suggestion," said Simon smiling as if not really bothered.

"You might have to call him back yourself when he's cooled down, I don't think he's talking to me at the moment." Simon switched his attention and got on with ringing the next name on the list.

By 1990 Simon's health wasn't getting any better and had decided he couldn't avoid the doctors any longer. He was suffering from itchy skin and severe tiredness, it was affecting his work.

In the mirror he could see that he didn't look as young and fit as he used to, he'd bloated up a bit which he put down to too much fine living.

Sitting in the waiting room once again he could remember why he didn't like coming here, all these sick people around spreading their horrible diseases. He hoped it would be a quick fix, a few pills and he'd be back to normal, free of this place.

Simon sat down in front of Doctor Woodbridge waiting for the interrogation to begin...

"Looking at your notes I see you saw my colleague four years ago with some form of kidney infection. How's that been? Any more problems?"

"Well, if I'm honest it's been coming and going ever since. Sometimes it's fine for a few days then I get the pains again. A few pain killers and its okay for a while," he replied.

He described his itchy skin and how tired he'd been feeling. The doctor gave him a thorough look over before scribbling more notes onto his medical record.

"I think this is all kidney related," he said, "I'm going to recommend you go into hospital for a few more tests. They'll do an ultra sound on you, a blood test and may do a biopsy of your kidneys. Now that won't be as bad as it sounds, it just needs a local anaesthetic and tiny incision. They then use a special needle to get a sample. It's a simple enough process."

"What will that tell us?" Asked Simon.

"Renal biopsy is the best test for kidney disease. It may be something else, but I would like to rule that out first. It could be kidney stones but I don't think you'd have lasted this long without seeing me, the pain would have been excruciating. Now I'll sort out an appointment for you and we'll call you with the details, okay?"

"Yes thanks. Will I have to stay in hospital?"

"It's carried out in the out-patient clinic so no need for an overnight stay. They tend to keep you lying still for 4 to 6 hours just to check there's no bleeding, then they'll let you go, you should feel just fine."

Simon headed home, he'd taken the afternoon off which he rarely did as he hated missing work, but he didn't feel in the mood for it. As promised, a couple of days later Simon had a call from the surgery informing him that he was booked in at his local hospital for the tests that Friday.

The instructions were for him to be there by 8:30 a.m. and to take a dressing gown. *Nice*, thought Simon. That Friday he had booked another day away from the office, although he didn't tell his team why. He decided to walk to the Royal Brompton Hospital, it was less than a mile away and it was a nice enough day.

After reporting to reception, he was shown to a bed in Ward 14, a day ward on the first floor.

He changed into an ill-fitting hospital gown that barely met round his back, not very fetching, and then waited a couple of hours before a porter came to collect him.

He was soon on his way to the maternity unit which he found a bit strange. This was where he'd have his ultrasound to pinpoint the exact location of his kidney before his biopsy.

With the ultrasound complete, Simon now decorated with various felt tip pen marks, was taken back to his ward to wait for his turn in the operating theatre.

Half an hour later he was off again, wheeled along the supposedly sterile corridors to the lifts.

On his first outing for his ultrasound scan he'd been taken in a wheelchair, for this journey he didn't even have to get out of bed. The porter skilfully manoeuvred him round a couple of tight corners and into the elevator.

On reaching the ground floor it was about 50 yards to the operating theatre. A nurse reassured him that all the equipment looked much more frightening than it was. He was to undergo a fairly simple procedure under a local anaesthetic.

"We only need to perform this biopsy in here to avoid any chance of infection, cleanest room in the house," the first nurse smiled.

"If you want to know what's going on, you only have to ask, not that I want you chattering away all the way through," said the other nurse.

Simon lay on his front as instructed. Following an injection of anaesthetic there was a short wait before the consultant arrived to take the sample.

"Now, I'm going to make a small incision. Can you feel that?"

"No, have you begun?" Simon answered nervously.

"That's fine, I've finished that," replied the consultant.

Simon was very pleased that he couldn't feel anything going on.

"Now I'm going to take the samples. It's very important that you lay absolutely still – no movement please."

It only took about five more minutes for the consultant to take the samples, two from each kidney, all about the same diameter as the lead out of a pencil and about half an inch long.

"That's it. All over thank you. You'll have to stay here for about an hour before we send you back to the ward, and I'm sorry, but no moving. You must stay on your front for now."

"Thanks," said Simon. The consultant headed off to his next job.

"Now, no moving," commanded one of the nurses.

"I suppose a cup of tea's out of the question then?" Simon asked cheekily.

"I'd love to get you one but you wouldn't be able to drink it in that position. Now lie still," she said firmly.

Simon was finally allowed to lie on his back again and wheeled back to his ward where he was instructed to remain.

After finally being allowed to move, Simon was given a cup of tea, which seemed like heaven. At 5:30 p.m. Simon was relieved to hear that he could go home. He had a week to wait for the results. The following Friday he was back in his favourite waiting room hoping Doctor Woodbridge wouldn't take too long to call him.

"Well Mr Elliott, I have the results here." He peered through his reading glasses that were half way down his nose and scanned the notes in front of him.

"I'm afraid it's not good news. The results show you have quite advanced kidney disease. Now I realise that's not what anyone wants to hear, however, there are things we can do to keep you living an active life."

"What sort of things?" Replied Simon

"I'm not an expert in this area and I don't want to mislead you in any way." He flicked through the rolodex on his desk.

"I'm going to make an appointment with Doctor Collinson for you. She *is* an expert in this field. She's based at The Royal London Hospital, Whitechapel. I'll write to her now and you should get an appointment quite soon."

"Thanks, I'll wait to hear then," said Simon with an air of concern.

"Sorry I can't offer you more information. Meanwhile try not to worry. As I say there are plenty of things that can be done to make life easier for you," said Doctor Woodbridge reassuringly.

Simon left feeling quite anxious, he'd assumed that he might need a quick course of antibiotics and it would all be sorted out, it seemed that was not the case. He was worried about having to wait weeks to be seen, however by Monday the hospital had already contacted him.

The speed of their response asking him to come in the following day at 10 a.m. was somewhat alarming.

He set off on what was to become a regular journey across London. As he left the station at Whitechapel it was only a few yards down Court Street to the Whitechapel Road.

At the junction, looking right, Simon could see the NatWest tower in the distance; it loomed over the smaller city buildings beneath. Over the road, to his left a clock labelled in roman numerals was centred in the large brick gable beneath which 'The Royal London Hospital' was clearly identified in foot high gilt lettering.

Simon made his way up the steps at the front and reported his arrival to the dark haired lady who manned the desk.

"If you could wait in waiting room 'C' please, someone will call you shortly," she told him, pointing down the corridor as she spoke. Simon sat along with four others awaiting their turn. Around five minutes later a nice looking woman in her mid-40's arrived at the door.

"Do we have a Simon Elliott here?" She called out.

"Yes, that's me," said Simon, standing up to follow her, "I'm here to see Doctor Collinson."

"Well, you're in luck then. That's me." She smiled as she led the way into her surgery. She was a kindly looking lady with dark, slightly curly hair and hazel eyes.

"I've had a chat with Doctor Woodbridge; he's sent me the results from your tests. As you're no doubt aware, you have kidney disease. Do you know anything about it?"

"No, just that it's making me feel quite unwell – I'm always tired."

"That's quite usual. The disease can progress quite slowly. Looking at your records, I think this must have started four or more years ago. Unfortunately, your body won't be able to cope on its own for much longer. The kidneys, as I'm sure you're aware are needed to clean the blood. When they stop functioning we need to replace their action with dialysis. Haemodialysis to be precise."

"That doesn't sound good – I don't know if I can do that, I hate the sight of blood. There must be another way," said Simon with an air of despondency.

"No, I'm sorry there isn't one that's suitable. I know you might not think it now, but you'll be fine, once you're used to it, it'll become second nature"

"Where do I go for this…"

"Haemodialysis," she finished the sentence for him.

"Yes, where do I go for it and how often will I need it?"

"The best place to have it done is right here. We have all the facilities in our renal department. You'll have to come down here three times a week for a few hours."

"Three times a week! You're kidding me," he gasped.

"Sadly not, we don't make jokes like that in here," she said sternly.

Simon's mind was flitting between his health problems and his job. He was usually calm and could see the answer in front of him. Today he couldn't. He didn't have time for three trips a week to the hospital. He just couldn't!

"How long will I need this dialysis for?" He asked.

"The rest of your life I'm afraid. Unless," Dr Collinson paused...

"Unless what?" asked Simon.

"Unless we get you a transplant at some point, but we're not at that stage yet."

This hadn't even crossed Simon's mind – the seriousness of his situation gradually beginning to dawn on him.

"You need to get going with treatment as soon as possible. I'm going to book you in for next Monday. You need to have a simple surgical procedure to create a couple of access points, probably in your forearm. Then, we'll wait a week before we begin the treatment."

"Can you make 9:00 a.m. on Monday?" Doctor Collinson said as she began sifting through the paperwork.

"I don't suppose I've got much choice," Simon groaned.

"Not really. It's got to be done. Here's some information I want you to read," she said passing him a booklet titled;
'WHAT IS HAEMODIALYSIS?'

"Thanks. I suppose I'll see you on Monday," Simon said as he stood up to leave.

Simon didn't really remember getting home. He'd been in something of a daze the whole way as his mind had mulled things over. Once at home he'd had to call Cathy in the office to explain that he needed some hospital treatment and wouldn't be in on Monday. "I'll be back on Tuesday, can you manage without me?"

"I guess we'll have to. Just get yourself sorted out," she said in a caring voice, Simon wondered whether she really meant it.

A week later, with two access points created, he was heading across London for his first session of dialysis. He was apprehensive to say the least, the thought of going all the way to Whitechapel three times a week was hard enough to bear, even before the dialysis. Once he got there he was shown to a bed that was curtained off to provide privacy.

A complex looking machine stood waiting for its patient to be connected.

The nurses in the renal department were very kind and did their best to put Simon at ease. They explained how everything would be done and that there really was nothing to worry about. All he would have to do is sit and read a book or watch the TV for a few hours whilst the machine did its important work.

"How long will it take?" Asked Simon.

"About four hours – a nice rest for you," the nurse replied.

Simon lay there watching the discs on the machine turn slowly, and his blood disappearing and returning, a sight he didn't like. He decided it would be best to focus his mind on something else. He tried reading but kept having to re-read the same page as his mind was really elsewhere.

He was trying to work out how he could live his life now he needed to be missing for the best part of three days every week. Surely, he couldn't keep up his high level position at TayMarts, his wasn't a part-time job.

The four hours were soon gone and, on reflection, Simon felt the procedure wasn't as bad as he'd been expecting.

"We'll see you on Wednesday then, Mr Elliott. You'll get to like it here, we're like one big happy family," the nurse said.

Simon wasn't so sure about the 'enjoying it' bit.

"Thanks for all you've done," said Simon and made his way back to the tube.

That Monday evening, Simon contemplated his next move. He had no choice but to tell his fellow Directors at TayMarts of his medical condition.

Over the years he'd worked hard for them and was one of the company's top employees.

Even though he wasn't well, he liked his job and he had no desire to retire and sit around at home. He wanted to know if they'd be happy for him to have a reduced schedule and work a good portion of his time from home.

He'd already worked out that if he went over to the hospital for the 7:00a.m. sessions three days a week, he could work Monday, Wednesday and Friday afternoons along with all of Tuesdays and Thursdays. He didn't mind working Saturdays either. He'd be able to read through reports whilst hooked up to his infernal machine.

On arriving at work Simon arranged a meeting with his fellow Directors. They all seemed genuinely sorry to hear about Simon's predicament, he hadn't thought it worth trying to brush over as they'd find out sooner or later.

They needed Simon and hoped he stay on as Purchasing Director for as long as he could. They said they'd do everything they could to make things easier for him.

Simon politely declined the offer of another secretary and assured them that he'd be just fine – Cathy did the work of two people already.

Deep down he hoped he wouldn't let them down.

CHAPTER 18

The battles between the supermarkets were as fiercely fought as ever. Every week one would come up with a new idea that would force the others into a countermove. Simon liked the pressure of this industry wide battle, it took his mind off the fact that he usually felt ill and made him feel like he had a purpose.

Six months after Simon had caused ructions amongst his farming suppliers with his 'half price payments', he was at it again.

TayMarts had spent a long time building up a massive customer base and weren't about to let their customers, whose loyalty was quite fickle, walk down the street and into their rivals who were slashing prices left, right and centre.

All the farmers had fallen into line and taken the 'hit' that helped keep TayMarts in the number one position for a few more months.

Even James Brown, who'd unleashed his verbal abuse on Simon, had in the end played ball. He knew that he had little choice; everyone was in the same boat.

All Simon looked at was the present and future performance of his company, a list of weekly figures that dictated his every move.

It was obvious to him that everyone needed to buy certain key items every week. The staples, including bread, milk, eggs, fruit and vegetables were the essentials where people compared the prices. If these were cheaper than their rivals, they would get the customers into the stores, where they'd then fill their trolleys with packaged products, which were the real money makers. To do this on a consistent basis meant that the farmers would have to reduce their prices, not for a quick promotion, but forever! Simon's instructions were clear enough, negotiate with them until they accept the terms or dump them.

Regardless of his illness, Simon hadn't softened up when it came to business, although even he occasionally wondered at what level the prices would bottom out.

With every supermarket playing the same game, it couldn't go on forever – prices could never reach zero. As usual, Simon liked to be involved in the discussions. He didn't go out of his way to upset people but his policies managed to do that on their own.

Straight away the farmers were arguing back that the costs of production from fuel and fertilisers, to labour, had been pushed up by inflation, making price drops unviable. One by one they were brought into line - their margins cut again and again.

Simon decided he'd better talk to James Brown himself after the trouble it caused the last time, he wasn't bothered by this sort of chastising – to him it was business, nothing more. As he dialled the number he was ready for the fight ahead.

The unmistakable Scottish tones of James answered.

"Hello James, its Simon Elliott from TayMarts. How are you?"

As soon as James heard Simon's voice he wanted to go on the offensive but bit his tongue. "Not bad thanks, but we're struggling a bit up here."

He was quite calm and didn't want to admit they were more than struggling; they were fighting to stay afloat. "What can I do for you today?" said James as Simon went through a bit of cheerful banter before steering his conversation in the inevitable direction of price cuts.

"The thing is this, James, we're all going to have to reduce our prices further or we won't have a market to sell to."

"You've got to be joking," said James, now sounding more irritated.

"We're already selling you the stuff for less than it costs us to grow."

Simon gave a brief summary of what the other supermarket chains were doing and explained that in his view, why they had no choice but to join in.

"I really don't think we can do this." Protested James.

"Well you'll have to think about it, so I'll get back to you in a day or two," said Simon before wishing him a good afternoon.

"How did that go?" Asked Mike, one of Simon's team who happened to be working on another file across the desk from him.

"Better than last time. He didn't say yes, but then again, he didn't say no either.

A couple of days later Simon called back only to be met by an unanswered phone. James spent many hours of his day tractor driving and it was two days before Simon finally managed to have another conversation with him.

Reluctantly he'd had to accept the new pricing structure which he thought would finish the business off.

Sadly, there just weren't any other places wanting to buy the quantities of produce that WTCP would be saddled with. James had found business harder and harder, struggling to make enough money to keep his farms going.

He was running Tanners and Coates as one large farm, and although Bill was still looking after Woodside, the three farms together were in reality one large company.

In their heyday these farms had produced a massive amount of income for their owners. Woodside had been in the family since the late nineteenth century and had made William, James's father a wealthy man.

The two newer farms had been acquired at a discount price by William in 1942 just before the war. William had died before the big stock market crash of 1987, which, in itself was quite a short-lived event.

Unfortunately this was the start of another downturn with the economy taking a turn for the worse before the 1990's even got underway.

The productivity on all three farms had remained good, although James did choose some crops that weren't as profitable as others. The boys' original deal with TayMarts hadn't been great but it had given the farms a consistent market to sell to. This led them to renew their contract for a further five years, due to expire in 1992.

The trouble was that as the economy turned at the end of the eighties, the supermarkets had suddenly found that not only did they have more competition than ever, their customers hadn't got the same amount of cash to spend – they wanted the best deal.

As consumers disposable incomes had fallen they had become very price conscious and paid much more attention to prices.

Simon Elliott had slashed the prices being offered to the Browns, he'd argued that they would have no choice but to comply. They hadn't anywhere else to sell the quantities they needed to sell.

If they didn't 'play ball' with TayMarts, they would possibly face penalty fines for Breach of Contract or even have their contracts terminated.

Without warning, the prices being offered were cut – again and again – often halved at a moment's notice.

It wasn't just TayMarts, all the big chains were doing the same. Because James and Nick were tied to TayMarts, they unsurprisingly blamed their worsening circumstances on them.

Out of the blue in June that year, Simon Elliot's half-price sale had involved forcing their supplying farms to back their *'buy one get one free'* offers. The balance was entirely one sided. The farms were expected, under the terms of their contract to supply twice the amount of produce for the same price.

"They can't do this to us, they're robbing us blind," James told Nick on one of his phone calls.

Nick wasn't in as much financial trouble but the same pricing policies were hitting him in much the same way.

"We signed the renewal contract so we're stuck with it. At least until I can come up with a better plan," Nick had responded.

"The farm's really going to struggle, it'll hit you next, what the hell are we going to do?" James was now getting more and more agitated.

"Listen James, we're fighting these bastards, we're not going to be beaten by a gang of bloody cut-price greengrocers."

The prices were driven down again and again as the economy worsened. Only a fortnight later James was on the phone again and sounding more annoyed than ever.

"You won't believe what that bloody Simon Elliot's gone and done now. Reneged on my order for green beans – they say that demand's dropped and they can't shift them. I've got 150 acres of the bloody things. I'll be left with more beans than you've ever seen."

"They can't do that, they agreed to them," said Nick in disbelief.

"Well he says he's not interested and if we check the small print we'll see there's nothing we can do. This'll bloody well finish me off." James was furious.

Nick understood his brother's irritation "Not bloody interested! Unbelievable!" Said Nick, "They need to be interested, without us they haven't got a business."

A third of the land around Tanners and Woodside had been turned over to green beans under the promise of a reasonable price per ton, not high but better than they would have got for other crops that year. Now James had nowhere to sell this hard earned produce. In the end he managed to sell a proportion to local wholesalers at half the price it was worth, and the rest was sent away for adding to animal feed.

The next couple of years were a real struggle for James. He could never find enough money to get on top of the debts. He'd re-mortgaged Tanners to raise cash, but that had soon been consumed.

With the capital and interest now added to the ever increasing mountain of debt combined with the ever decreasing income from the supermarkets, he was finding it a hard juggling act to keep going.

The Brown family had built their little empire over many years, and now, under James' watch it was starting to crumble.

James was always convinced that sooner or later something would turn up to sort the situation out, but as each day came and went with things evidently getting worse, it didn't.

To be fair on James, he was a master at juggling debt about, he could even fool himself about the severity of the situation. He would borrow on one credit card to pay off another – take out new loans, each one bigger than the last. The banks loved customers like him, he borrowed money and paid it back, at least that's the way he made it look.

The trouble was that at some point he would run out of places to go for the next move.

Jill could see the strain showing on James, he'd always been an easy going sort of guy but as the months went by, James's mood became more irritable.

It didn't take much from Jill or one of the children to cause him to snap back. He hated getting cross with his family. These were the people he loved but he just couldn't help himself.

At night he'd become quiet and needed a drink to just relax a bit. As time progressed one drink became two and gradually he felt it pointless to leave the last couple of mouthfuls in an otherwise empty bottle.

He didn't like the postman coming; he knew it only brought bad news. Inside he felt sick whenever he opened another letter, often he just stacked them up and hoped they'd just vanish.

The bank's letters, always recognisable by the small black crest on the top left of the envelope, were like a never ending stream of photocopies, always delivering the same repetitive message;

'You're on or over your limit… there weren't enough funds in your account to make the payments requested.'

James couldn't understand the logic in sending the same letter day after day, surely once a week would suffice. The fact that he never opened them made it seem all the more pointless.

The stress was hard to take; he couldn't bring himself to tell Jill how bad things really were. As each day went by James almost got used to feeling sick to the stomach.

This didn't help as the worse he felt the less he was able to accomplish. It's hard to focus on ways to make money or sort problems out when you're being hounded by your creditors and you feel too sick to sit in one place for more than five minutes.

He hated the bank for its total lack of interest in his circumstances. They showed no pity. To them he was just a name on a balance sheet. He hated TayMarts more. They'd been the architects of his failure and his despair. Bills were piling up higher and higher and the bank account was empty.

The clank of the letterbox signalled the arrival of yet another tedious message from his favourite bank.

He'd assumed it would be the latest in a long line of... "Payment to x has been *'referred to drawer,'* there weren't enough funds...bla bla..."

This time it wasn't. Unusually, he actually bothered to open the envelope. He was punch drunk from the constant battering, but wasn't prepared for the cruel message that was carried by the letter in his hands.

The words had hit him like a sledge hammer, one at a time. The message was clear:

Despite previous reminders the amount required to bring your account up to date remains unpaid.

If you do not bring your loan up to date within 7 days of the date of this letter, we will demand the entire balance outstanding under the terms of your loan agreement.

This amount includes, but is not limited to, the principal and interest and all other outstanding charges and legal costs.

Your bank overdraft will also become due for immediate repayment. We will start legal action to foreclose on the loan, which if not settled, will result in the sale of the property that you used to guarantee the loan.

Under the terms of your Personal Guarantee we also have the right to seek a judgment against you for any deficiency after the property is sold.

You have the right to bring your loan current after legal action has begun. You also have the right to assert in the foreclosure proceeding the nonexistence of the default or any other defence to our legal action and sale of the property. Payment must be received at this office on or before noon on Monday 16th March. You are advised to seek immediate legal advice. No further correspondence will be entered into.'

As he dropped the letter onto the hall table, the phone burst into life, its shrill ringing snapping James out of his trance. He picked up the receiver, "Yes," he bleated abruptly into the mouthpiece.

"Good morning. Simon Elliot here. Is that James Brown?"

'That's all I need', thought James.

"Yes, although I don't know about the good," quipped James.

"Sorry?" Replied Simon.

167

"Never mind. What do TayMarts want today? The shirt off my back?" James retorted.

"Well, I hate to be the bearer of bad news, but it's with regard to our order for potatoes. The markets have moved against us and we're going to have to cut the price offered for the coming crop."

"Forget it. You can't do this to us again, it's just not on. How big a cut are we talking?" Continued James.

"I'm sorry but we've little choice, we're looking at a further 50% cut. I've put the details in writing you should have them in a couple of days."

As James stood listening, and with the letter from the Bank lying on the table in front of him, reality suddenly dawned. He'd come to the end of the line, the remaining balls in the air were about to land at his feet. He didn't argue further with Simon Elliott, he didn't even wait for the goodbyes. With Simon still talking he just slowly put the receiver down and walked away.

For the next few days James had pretty much given up hope of a reprieve, he spent quite a long time sitting with his head in his hands, staring out over the fields.

He tried to come to terms with his predicament and fathom a way out, but he knew there was no way. Something was going to have to give.

On March 16th, 1992, the day of the Bank's deadline, James had woken feeling strangely calm.

He smiled. He knew everything would be ok now.

He'd realised he didn't need to fight this any longer, there was another way.

After calmly washing, shaving and getting dressed he walked along the landing and removed his Twelve Bore Shotgun from the gun cupboard that hid behind a ruffled, worn curtain.

Jill had left early, and the house was quiet and deserted. After sitting at the kitchen table to write a short note, he headed calmly towards the strip of woodland that lay behind the house, and without hesitation put the gun's barrels into his mouth.

'This seemed remarkably easy,' he thought and in a moment, he knew all his troubles would be gone. He squeezed the trigger. Then there was nothing more.

For James, the nightmare ended that instant.

For his family it was just beginning.

CHAPTER 19

J ill returned from her shopping trip at around 11:30 a.m. that morning and entered the house. She found her husband's neatly written letter on the kitchen table carrying his apology for what he'd just done. It instructed her not to go into the woods where he could now be found. She didn't want to believe the words she'd read. Maybe he was having a sick joke. Deep down she knew the answer, but it was human nature that made her go and see for herself.

Sure enough there was her husband's lifeless body lying amongst a beautiful carpet of flowering blue bells.

Lying on his back and looking up at the sky through his still open eyes, Jill was spared the sight of the back of his head, most of which was now gone.

She must have passed out for a few minutes before she struggled to her feet and headed back to the farmhouse.

If her world had been made of glass, someone had just smashed it into a thousand pieces.

Suicide is a cruel ending, not for the selfish participant but for the ones left behind to pick up the pieces.

James had loved his wife and his two children, both now teenagers. He knew they'd be hit hard by his decision but he'd lost the will to carry on and nothing really mattered any more. Logic had upped and left. Hannah, his elder daughter was distraught and just couldn't understand.

Danny seemed to bottle his feelings up and, although looking miserable, insisted on going back to school the following Monday.

Unsurprisingly he was finding it hard to pay attention and ended up in trouble due to his short fuse. Hannah made it clear she didn't want to do anything ever again. Jill's sister had come straight over from her home in North Berwick. She would stay with her sister for the next couple of weeks.

When Nick had been told of his brother's death, he couldn't believe it.

He knew his brother was struggling – he'd spoken to him regularly about the price cuts that were destroying not only themselves, but many of their friends in the farming community. As thoughts had flown round his head he tried to weigh up the situation, surely it couldn't have been bad enough for 'that'?

'Why would he do that? How could he do that to Jill and the kids? To him?'

For some time his feelings leapt between sadness for the brother he loved and hatred for what he'd just done to his nearest and dearest.

It was Bill Prest, who lived at Woodside that had telephoned the news through. Nick had insisted on knowing the facts.

"Have you told my Mother yet?" Asked Nick once he'd composed himself.

"No, just you. I'm going up there next. Not looking forward to that."

"Thanks Bill, try and break it to her as gently as you can, she's not going to take it well. I'd best give Liz a ring and tell her. Not easy is it," said Nick. "I'll be up to Scotland as soon as I can."

After the initial call to tell Sarah the news, it took another hour and a large glass of malt whiskey before Nick felt capable of ringing his little Sister down in London.

Upon hearing the news, she too was inconsolable. Sadly there was no way to make any of this easier on anyone, they just had to find their own ways to get through it as best they could.

The destiny of the Scottish farms was not Nick's priority but he knew this and other down to earth business matters would need sorting, sooner rather than later.

For the meanwhile he would get himself up to Scotland to help Jill's sister with the funeral arrangements. Sarah would come too.

They drove up two days after the horrific incident had taken place, hardly speaking on the four hour journey. Sometimes they used to cross from the A19, above Middlesbrough, to the A1 which ran parallel a few miles to the west. Today they carried on up, past a large sign that welcomed them to County Durham 'Land of The Prince Bishops', 'whoever they were', heading towards the eastern side of Newcastle. Here they began the decline into the mile long Tyne Tunnel that ran 40 feet under the wide river that crossed above, this had been under construction when Nick first moved south, now, for a small toll, it cut about half an hour off their journey north.

The A19 re-joined the A1 a few miles below Morpeth. They passed Alnwick and Berwick upon Tweed, then, close to the Scottish border, a pub that bore a large sign declaring it, 'THE FIRST AND LAST PUB IN ENGLAND!

An hour after entering Scotland they pulled into the yard at Tanners. Nick could see that things weren't as neat and tidy as they'd looked on his last visit just four months before. It was Christmas back then and maybe that had helped James hide his depression, he'd been in a party mood and looked quite content. With all the children running about and the quantities of alcohol the grownups were quaffing, maybe he'd put his worries away for the festive season.

Now it looked as though James had just given up – which of course he obviously had, Jill was standing in the doorway as if waiting for them.

"I'm so sorry," said Nick as he hugged Jill tightly. "I can't believe it. I just don't know why…"

He fought to hold his tears back. He didn't like to cry.

"I found this on the kitchen table," sobbed Jill, passing the bank's letter to Nick.

"Bloody hell. Why didn't he just talk to me – anyone, about this? We could have…" His words tailed off. The pain etched across his face revealed his feelings.

"And this, you'd better see this." Jill passed another letter across the table "This arrived this morning."

Nick unfolded it, immediately recognising the TayMart's letterhead. It was from Simon Elliott and more details of the latest price cuts and the conversation that had taken place the morning before James had taken his own life.

"I don't believe this," Nick said as he slammed the letter onto the table.

"It wasn't just the Bank, these bastards were as bad – they put the final nail in the coffin. I'm going to have it out with that bloody man once and for all!"

"Not now, please Nick," Sarah pleaded, then held onto Jill. They were both crying, neither capable of getting a full sentence out.

An elderly sheep dog lay in front of the stove and looked at the pair with his head tilted curiously to one side, he wasn't really sure what to make of the performance.

Within twenty minutes, things were calmer and the three of them were joined by Jill's sister Anne.

Jill put the kettle on and made four mugs of tea. As she removed the teabags and tossed them into the open bin, she accidently dropped one that splatted on the tile floor.

"Bloody hell," she cursed and burst into tears. Everyone was on edge.

"Will you please sit down and let me do that?" Anne said physically placing Jill back in her seat. Jill sat with her elbows on the table and her hands supporting her tired head.

"I just don't know where to start - what are we going to do?" She started to sob a bit more although she felt she was pretty much all cried out.

"Don't worry Jill, we'll get through this," said Nick staring down at the coffee mug stains that over the years had marked the well-worn kitchen table.

"I'd better get over to Woodside and talk to Bill and decide what's for the best."

Nick slipped his boots back on and pulled the door shut behind him.

CHAPTER 20

As he walked through the trees towards Woodside, thoughts of his childhood flooded back to him, playing soldiers or hide and seek in these very woods with James and Liz.

For a brief moment he remembered little Jack but his memory of him was now very vague. A pheasant, startled from within some bracken, burst into flight only a couple of feet in front of Nick's face and brought him back to the present with a start.

Emerging from the woods onto the sparsely gravelled drive in front of Woodside, he could see a solitary light burning in the kitchen window to the right side of the glazed rear entrance porch.

As Nick's final knock echoed round the open room, festooned with a multitude of coats and boots, the back door swung open.

Bill had been expecting Nick's visit and was pleased to see him despite the circumstances – in happier times he'd been like another brother to the Brown boys.

He was a friendly man with a weather - worn face that always carried a trace of stubble but never a beard. He was shorter than Nick and stockily built, his hard, callous hands gave away the years of manual labour he'd undertaken.

It was Bill that had had to make the difficult journey to break the news of James' death to Florence who still resided in her Haddington nursing home.

Arthritis had left her virtually immobile but her mind was quite active, and the news had hit her hard. Although she never talked about it, she had never got over the loss of her first son Jack, and now she'd lost another. It wasn't right for a parent to outlive their own children.

Bill had been looking after Woodside for the last fourteen years and had lived in the farmhouse there since Florence was pensioned off to her nursing home seven years earlier.

Woodside was the largest of the farms and Bill had become used to rattling round in this big old farmhouse, it was home to him now and he didn't much like the thought of 'upping sticks.' Like everyone else he wasn't sure what would become of anything now.

Nick was baffled as to why James hadn't stuck it out and wanted to hear Bill's view on the subject. Surely James could have seen there would be a way out of this – it seemed not.

James must have believed that if TayMarts didn't finish them off, then the bank would have done. After exchanging their condolences, Bill led Nick through to the office.

The office for the whole farming operation had always been in Woodside, in what was years ago, William's grand study. One wall had fitted mahogany book shelves that covered the full width and height of the room.

Half of these still housed William's old book collection, the remainder were stocked full of files and heaps of documents. The large desk stood on a traditional, hand crafted Afghan rug which had seen better days. A couple of leather armchairs and an old brass standard lamp were the room's only other adornments. Although Bill had been living here, it was still James that had looked after the office.

"Where the hell do we start with this lot?" Nick stood surveying piles of paperwork stacked in heaps that didn't adhere to any particular system. Ever since his school days James hadn't been a fan of paperwork. There were a lot of red letters and more unopened post stuffed amongst them.

"Maybe if James had sorted this mess out he'd not be in as much trouble as he thought," remarked Nick.

Following a brief look through the open files on the desk, Nick turned to the business in hand...

"This isn't easy Bill, but we're going to have to get to the bottom of these accounts, they're in a right mess. Sadly I don't think my brother really had his full attention on them."

"Aye, well I did leave it all to him, paperwork was never my strong point, I'm more of an outdoor man," replied Bill.

"I think he was too. Anyhow, we're going to have to go through it and you're going to have to help, you're running this farm now, I'm not sure what we do about Tanners, responded Nick as he found more invoices and letters."

"I wouldn't know where to start after looking at all this lot," sighed Bill.

"That's as may be. I don't like this any more than you. I've just lost my brother, but life's got to go on. As soon as we've got the funeral out of the way we're going to get this sorted out, you're going to help, Nick re-affirmed."

"I understand Nick, I'll do what I can," said Bill reassuringly. Nick wished his father was still around; he wouldn't have let it get to this. He'd have put these bullying supermarkets in their place.

Nick and Sarah stayed in Woodside that night but had to travel back to York the next day as they couldn't leave Chestnut Farm unattended.

Jill's sister stayed with her at Tanners to comfort her until they all returned a week later for the funeral. The week dragged by for all concerned, it was an anguishing time.

As the day of the funeral arrived, fortunately the rain had stopped. It was still damp and a grey fog hung in the air. Florence had one of her now rare excursions from her home that she now viewed more as a prison.

Bill pushed her wheelchair which fought against the pea gravelled pathways of Aberlady church yard – bringing back haunting memories of William's funeral seven years before.

Liz and Mike had travelled up from London the day before and were staying a couple of nights at Woodside.

Liz now walked down the path beside Jill. The two children, Danny and Hannah walked behind.

They seemed quite composed considering the trauma they were all going through. Following a solemn service attended by a good crowd of about eighty mourners, James was buried in a plot alongside his father. A lone piper played as the coffin was carried from the church and then lowered into the open grave – the sound of the pipes seeming to echo eerily in the fog.

"He'd be turning in his grave," Nick had looked sadly towards his father's grave, "If he could see this."

Everyone was invited back to Woodside for the wake, a tradition that was still practiced to celebrate the life of the one that was lost.

A good buffet was provided by a competent firm of local outside caterers along with plenty of beer, wine and of course the mandatory single malt whiskey.

It was one of those occasions where distant relatives caught up with the dramas that had taken place since the last family gathering. Like many families, these people would only see each other when one of them married or died, a few new children would usually be in tow.

People would look around and be surprised how much weight someone had gained, or lost, or how old they now looked with grey hair that wasn't there at the last family gathering. By early evening, the buffet had been reduced to crumbs and the remnants of pork pie and sausage rolls were left punctuating the now empty platters.

Bill had returned Florence to her room at the Manor House where she was sure she'd remain for the rest of her life, unless there was another death or marriage. Births didn't buy her an excursion; the new arrivals would just be presented to her where she sat. The last of the stragglers had made their way out and only the direct family, remained seated around the embers of the log fire in the living room.

A week later, Nick and Bill were sitting in James's small office which was by now looking much more organised. They'd spent the previous two days ploughing through the mountain of paperwork strewn across the room, opening letters, filing some and binning plenty of others.

Two large bags of unnecessary correspondence and envelopes waited to be burnt. Nick had been worrying about what Jill and the children would do next.

They were still in the house but the bank had a court hearing the following week in which they were fighting for possession of the farm. They stood a good chance of winning and would be evicting the family within days unless the debts were paid, and even Nick didn't have that sort of money sitting around.

'Jill says that James had a life insurance policy, that's got to be worth a few quid,' thought Nick. It was then that another terrible thought crossed his mind, *'They won't pay out for suicide – I don't think, I'm sure they don't.'*

Fortunately, having somewhere to live wasn't really an issue for Jill and her children, the Browns still owned two farms with houses, Coates, which belonged to Nick and Woodside, which was still owned by Florence. Coates was sitting empty and had been for six months since its last tenants had left.

What Jill was going to live on would be another matter, she had no savings and James's debts would mean there was nothing left.

The phone on the desk rang and Nick picked it up.

It was Simon Elliott!

His timing wasn't good. Nick had spoken to him many times before and had tried to remain polite despite the increasing pressures he'd put on James and himself.

"I'm sorry to hear about your Brother. Very sad. Unfortunately business carries on and we're going to have to re-examine our contract with his estate."

Nick couldn't hold back any longer. Inside him his anger was rising and he finally let it go like a pressure valve releasing steam.

"You bastard!

His body's hardly cold and you're having another go.

You killed him. You may not have pulled the trigger but you may as well have done. I don't know how you have the nerve to even pick up that bloody phone. What do you want? Me to end up in the ground like my brother? Well it's not going to happen. You can go to hell."

After a brief silence Simon answered back.

"There's no need to be like that, we've always tried to help your family and many others find a market for their produce."

"Aye, at a price that you decide. Sod the farmers; if one disappears there'll always be another crying out for help. My brother's dead! DEAD! You've been squeezing us tighter and tighter ever since we got tied in with you. We're all getting less per ton than we were a decade ago. Sooner or later it's all going to collapse. What'll you do then? When the last ones gone what are you going to do?" Nick yelled.

"You're blowing this out of proportion," said Simon.

"As I say, I'm sorry about your Brother but we're just a business and the whole point of business is profit. If our competitors drop their prices we have to fight back, and, if we have to fight then so do you." Simon seemed to be completely ignoring the delicacy of the situation.

"I'm not in the mood to argue with you now, but I'll tell you this, you're going to pay for what you've done.

You've not heard the last of this!" Nick didn't wait for a response – he didn't want a response. He banged the receiver back onto its cradle with such force it nearly shattered. It was a wonder that phone still worked it had been thrown down so many times.

Nick turned to Bill. "We'd best get on with this, it won't sort itself, we've got a battle to fight!"

"I'll drink to that," quipped Bill.

Simon by comparison was left standing by his desk in London, wondering what had just gone on. He placed his telephone down in a matter of fact way and opened the next file.

Nick and Bill quickly got to work. By the end of the day the pair of men had scrutinised the rest of the farm's accounts.

They had made out a rough spreadsheet that showed the position of the three farms. Nick hoped they could sell Tanners to clear the mortgage that James had taken out against it, along with the majority of another large business loan that he'd defaulted on.

With the money that was left, all the creditors owed by the other two farms could be paid.

There wouldn't be anything left but at least they could try and make a clean start. It all depended on what the Bank would let them do, time had already run out.

The trouble was that Nick farmed in York and Bill, for all his help wasn't really a businessman. Nick needed to come up with a workable plan.

It was either that or sell up! Throwing away the Brown's family heritage, something he wasn't keen on doing.

He talked to Sarah about the idea of moving back to Scotland, but, unsurprisingly, Sarah wasn't keen. Her whole life had been spent in York – her family were there, in short she liked it and in fairness, so did Nick.

When William had died he'd left Woodside to Florence, which eventually would be handed down to the surviving children. He had wanted the original farm to be passed to the next generation with explicit instruction that they should farm it and pass it on to their children with similar ties.

Ever since he was at school, Nick had found himself a natural leader. He would always take control of the situation, whatever it may be.

Whilst driving back to York, Nick's mind was awash with ideas, flicking through his mind like an unedited movie. How could he help sort out this sorry mess?

Then it dawned on him, if he could set up some form of 'co-operative,' bringing as many farms as possible together, he could negotiate with their customers, namely the supermarkets.

Most of them needed to stem the continual drop in prices that was slowly killing the farming community. Surely, if he could get enough of them together they could wield much greater buying power than they ever could on their own.

The death of James had confirmed to him what he'd known for some time. The farmers weren't going to survive unless something changed.

Time was fast running out!

Left on their own each farmer was more or less powerless and the supermarket buyers, like Elliott, knew it.

Shoppers had deserted local shops in favour of the supermarkets and created these 'cash rich giants' that now had their suppliers by the balls. If Nick could change the balance of power, it would surely make a difference.

Nick was excited about his idea, he knew there had been co-operatives before but he pictured something much more powerful – an association that would, like a union, fight for the rights of its members.

The Co-operative Wholesale Society (CWS) had bought its first farm in Shropshire in 1896, with the primary purpose of growing potatoes and other crops for the local co-operative society food stores. They'd gone on to acquire many farms covering thousands of acres but still worked pretty much to provide produce and milk for their own shops.

Nick pictured a similar idea; however, independent farmers would be represented by a common organisation that would operate as one big supplier. Sarah listened tentatively as Nick explained his concept.

"Sounds great in theory, but it's not going to sort out the immediate cash problems. I think it's more about revenge," she said, "and how are you going to persuade other farmers to join you? It could take years to get enough support to get anywhere and besides, you've got *our* farm to deal with."

"I don't think any of us have any choice. If we don't do something there'll be nothing left." Nick quietly sighed to himself.

As the car pulled onto the familiar gravelled drive, the couple were glad to be arriving back at Chestnut Farm after the previous stressful week.

They'd made the arduous journey to near Edinburgh twice in just over a week. Now the funeral was over they felt a weight had lifted from their shoulders.

Still, there was more to do now than ever, the Scottish farms needed a resolution to their predicament and Nick had his new visions of transforming the way farm pricing was calculated in North Yorkshire, maybe even across the country.

That evening Sarah headed up to bed quite early, tired out after the long trek home. Nick 'shooed' the cat from his favourite old armchair, a tatty yet well cushioned wingback covered with an old tartan picnic rug and slouched into it. The log fire burned and crackled at his feet.

He rattled the ice in his whiskey glass as he tilted it from side to side and began to plan the way ahead. A small notebook on the arm of his chair soon began to fill with ideas as he scratched away with the blunt pencil in his right hand.

It was well into the early hours before Nick realised how long he'd been sitting there, he'd have to be up soon! He checked the fireguard was in place, picked the cat up and gently tossed her out into the dark night slamming the back door behind.

Back in Scotland Jill had received notification that a Court Hearing had been set for Friday 7th May where the Bank would apply to take possession. Unsurprisingly, they'd won.

The selling of Tanners was taken out of her hands. The fact that most of the Bankers' legal team, Solicitors and Barrister seemed to be well acquainted surely was not inconsequential to the decision.

Jill had been given seven days to leave before the locks would be changed, leaving her the painful task of moving house with her husband only just buried. The Bank was unforgiving and showed an amazing lack of compassion.

James may have taken his life but that didn't change the fact that they wanted their money. The Courts had ruled in their favour and they were going to collect. Nick had agreed that Bill should move into the empty Coates farmhouse as he, and Sarah wouldn't need it. Jill would then move into Woodside.

Bill had got a couple of the farm hands to help load Jill's furniture and possessions into the old Bedford horsebox that still started but wasn't roadworthy. It was ideal for moving the few hundred yards to Woodside.

The job needed three trips — it seemed mind-boggling how much junk they'd accumulated in the last twenty or so years. The lads were quite adept at getting heavy wardrobes down stairs and through tight openings.

Bill liked Woodside but he hadn't minded when it was suggested he move into the empty Coates farmhouse, which was only half the size of Woodside. Living on his own he'd always felt a bit out of place in the sprawling Woodside family home, it would be much more suitable for a household of three.

Danny and Hannah weren't happy about any of it. They were struggling with the loss of their father and couldn't understand why all this upheaval was necessary. They'd been quite happy where they were. Jill however, was happy to be moving, she'd found living in her marital home without James very difficult, everywhere she looked, brought back painful memories.

Following a final walk round for old time's sake, Jill headed out of the house and passed the locksmith who was hovering impatiently by the back door. "Sorry 'bout this Ma'am, just doing my job," he said looking down and tugging at the front of his cap.

"You do what you have to," sniffled Jill as she dabbed a tear from her eye. As she headed across the wood she'd barely gone twenty yards when she could hear the man's drill whining into life. *These people certainly didn't hang around,* she thought to herself.

Knowing Jill had moved over to Woodside, Nick called her that night to check she was okay.

"Sarah and I have been talking. We're worried about you but we wanted to let you know that we'll make sure you're alright. If there's anything you need, just give us a shout."

"Thanks Nick, I don't want to be a charity case, we'll manage," she replied quietly.

"It's not charity, its family," responded Nick.

"I said we'll manage," repeated Jill. "But thanks all the same."

Tanner's farm had been sold at public auction a month after repossession.

Thankfully the funds were enough to cover all the outstanding debts with a small surplus which was returned to James' estate. Jill looked at the cheque she received –'*not much*, she thought, *for all that work and heartbreak*'.

A couple of weeks later, back in Yorkshire, Nick had arranged a meeting with seven farmers from around the local area.

They were to meet in The George Hotel, Easingwold, an old coaching inn located in the centre of the small market town, situated only about six miles west of Chestnut Farm. They were a mixed bunch covering two generations.

It had taken a few phone calls to persuade some of these gentlemen to come to a meeting. Most of them were used to doing their own thing and didn't like the idea of someone else poking their nose in their business.

They only agreed because Nick was a farmer, although, the fact that he spoke with a distinctly Scottish accent didn't help – it made him seem an outsider. A certain amount of bribery under the guise of free drinks had finally won over the last couple of moaners.

The meeting had been organised for 8:00 p.m. on a Thursday night, although it was half past before everyone was in attendance and had their drinks sorted. Nick stood up and surveyed his audience through a cloud of cigar smoke being generated by a couple of men sitting on his left. He banged his pint glass on the table. Slowly the room came to attention.

"Thanks very much for taking the time to come down here tonight, I appreciate you're all busy," he said looking around him.

"Anything for a free drink," one of them heckled from the back, causing a ripple of laughter to radiate around the room.

"Now, as most of you are aware, I invited you here tonight to talk about the dismal prices we're being paid for our produce. I'm assuming no one thinks they're being paid too much?" Said Nick amusingly.

Various moans and grunts rose around the room.

"Well it's time we did something about it." Said Nick.

"Here, here," someone piped up with a few joining in agreement.

"And exactly what d'you want us to do?" Asked one.

"I don't know how many of you have contracts with supermarkets. Most of you I suspect, and these supermarkets are so busy fighting each other they're not bothered about anyone else. They'll keep forcing our profit, what little there is, down and down until we're all finished." Answered Nick, grimly.

"Then where will they go?" Asked Bill Tanner who farmed over in Brandsby, a small local village set on the edge of a steep hill.

"I don't know," replied Nick "I don't think that's crossed their minds. All I know is it can't go on. We've got to draw a line. We have to take a stand whilst we still can."

"Hell Nick," said Ben Dawson, a stern looking character in his mid-fifties, "there are only eight of us – they're not going to give a sod about us, they'll laugh us out the room."

"I'm not planning on stopping with us few; I want to get everyone involved, well as many of us as I can. This is just the start but I need your help," replied Nick.

"Why don't we just go on strike, I mean we could picket their depot's, that'd throw a spanner in their works" shouted Paul Lansdon.

"Well it's a thought," said Nick. "But we all know what happened in the miners' strike they wasted most of 1984 and where did it get them? Most of them to the dole office. I think we'd just be shooting ourselves in the foot."

Nick laid out his plans for the 'Amalgamated Farms Association'. Farmers would pay a membership fee to cover the running costs, initially a non-profit making organisation just operating as a 'go-between' for the farmers versus supermarket negotiations. He figured that initially it would have little impact, however, if he could get the number of members to a critical level, the tables could turn.

Many of the men in the room were somewhat sceptical. Surely if this simple idea could work, someone would have already done it. The National Farmers' Union had been negotiating the farmers' subsidies with the Department of Agriculture since the end of rationing in the 50's, but had been no help with farmers trying to negotiate better deals on the open market.

The discussion went on until near closing time with plenty of lively discussion on the pros and cons and how this could work. By the end of the night Nick was pleased with the outcome, all the men present had agreed to give it a go, realising they had little left to lose.

The night had cost him many rounds of drinks but he felt pleased – his message seemed to have hit home. Nick realised was going to have to get the structure properly set-up.

He'd already 'sweet-talked' Sarah into the bookkeeping and having run his business single handed for over twenty five years, had a good grasp of what was needed.

Nick's next call was to a long-time friend of his, Jason Dixon, a partner in 'Hague, Hampshire and Dixon,' the firm of solicitors Nick had used for his legal requirements since arriving in Yorkshire. Jason was the son of one of the founding partners, hence the Dixon in the name that hung over their office door.

Their premises in York were situated in a small yard reached by a 'snickleway' off Stonegate, close to the Old Star Inne. This was where Nick had chosen to eat the night he first came to York over a quarter of a century ago, the night his appendicitis had made itself known.

A meeting was arranged where Nick would lay out the basis of a Contract to bind these unlikely group of farmers into a workable group.

"Good to see you Nick," said Jason, shaking Nick's hand firmly. "What are you up to now?" He said cheekily.

Jason was every inch the solicitor; he wore a smart three piece suit with a fine pin stripe pattern, along with a well-polished pair of brown Brogues.

Now in his mid-forties he still looked young with his dark brown hair, although if you looked closely you could see the first wisps of grey beginning to show through.

Over a cup of coffee Nick explained his ideas and his determination not to become another statistic at the hands of TayMarts.

He wanted to fight back as much for himself as for his late brother. Nick wasn't looking to get rich from his 'AFA' – he just wanted it to generate enough money to make the whole operation feasible. Jason agreed to draw up some draft agreements over the next couple of weeks and reconvene in order to check them through.

"I'll call you when I've got something ready."

"Thanks for your time, always good to see you," Nick said as he headed out into the typically wet June afternoon.

Holding a newspaper over his head in a half-hearted attempt at keeping it dry, his pace was somewhere between a fast walk and slow run as he made his way back to the car park on Bootham Row.

Back at Stillington, the work on the farm never ceased. Terry was Nick's farm manager and he knew his stuff, he was more than capable of running things in his absence, something he'd become more accustomed to over the last few months.

Over the years, especially after the war, all farms were striving to increase production year on year. This was another factor that had contributed to the falling prices that were now the downfall of many farms.

Due to the ever expanding mountains of grain and other produce, the EEC introduced the idea of 'set-aside', giving farmers the ability to leave some fields fallow and receive a payment for doing so.

The subsidy wasn't full compensation for the crops that could be grown, however, they were guaranteed income; it didn't matter whether you had a good year or bad, an empty field would still be just that - an empty field.

In general, the subsidies and grants were still far too low to help many of the struggling farmers; the majority of the benefits were swallowed up by the larger landowners.

Nick didn't like leaving empty fields but used the system to help let certain fields 'recover' after their soil had been exhausted of nutrients.

Two weeks after having visited Jason Dixon he received a message to say the Draft Contracts were ready for his inspection. Jason had drawn up agreements that each farmer would sign if they wanted to join the AFA. These would enable the association to negotiate with the supermarkets on their behalf whilst they would retain overall control of their own farming businesses.

The farmers would be able to leave the association but only after giving a notice of three months. Jason had done a good job, the contracts were straight forward, clear and concise. He'd also done all the paperwork to make the Association legal. Getting this small group of farmers to join him was only the first step of what was going to be a difficult journey.

Not only did Nick need to get a much bigger group together, but those that he'd hooked already had their own problems to overcome. Many had binding contracts with various supermarkets and other purchasers; they couldn't just stop what they were doing and start afresh. Those with contracts would wait until expiry and just not renew, they'd switch allegiance to the AFA.

Nick was undeterred by the challenge that lay ahead.

The death of his brother due to the unforgiving buying (and bullying) tactics of TayMarts had set his blood boiling. He wanted to hurt them – no, he wanted revenge!

Deep down he knew it was unlikely they'd even notice him, certainly not yet, but at least he could be an irritation.

CHAPTER 21

By the end of July, Nick had managed to get a bit more interest with around 20 farmers confirming their support for the plan. Twelve of them had signed up properly and the other eight had got their contracts but hadn't gone further yet. Nick decided that he'd need to get more publicity amongst the farming community and decided to give a talk at the annual Great Yorkshire Show held in Harrogate.

The organisers, the 'Yorkshire Agricultural Society', were quite supportive and designated a session on the Wednesday afternoon for Nick in one of the members' marquees.

One of the old pole tents constructed from well-worn canvas was laid out in 'theatre style' and used for everything from 'demonstrations in cookery' through to sheep shearing.

Nick's speech had been advertised in the show's programme and with word spreading in the tight-knit farming community, he was hopeful of a good turnout.

The audience had filed in and were seated on wooden folding chairs that creaked at every movement. Nick, peering around the curtain that hung behind the stage, was amazed to see nearly every seat occupied. He guessed there must have been 150 people waiting, either to hear what he'd come to say or to get out of the steady drizzle that had continued monotonously all day. Sarah held his forearm.

"You'll be fine, just stick to the script you've practiced," she said encouragingly. Nick stepped up onto the stage and walked confidently to the oak lectern that awaited him.

He tapped the top of the microphone and heard the reassuring boom coming back through the speakers confirming it was live.

He gave an artificial cough through the microphone to get the attention of the crowd who were all chattering away amongst themselves. Slowly their combined volume was reduced until the final lone voices petered out as they waited for Nick to start.

With a slow and deliberate voice, Nick spent the next hour laying out the situation as he saw it, and then proposing a way to try and get each of them a better deal.

"If we work as a team, become one large organisation, then we can negotiate much better terms with all of these supermarkets, they need us as much as we need them, they just haven't realised it.

At the moment, when we refuse their prices they know they can just move on to the next victim," he said passionately, urging those present to join him.

Nick continued, "I'd like to thank you for taking the time to listen to me today. I know some of you are dubious but I honestly believe that together we can do this. If you want to be a part of this, please can you add your name and contact details to the forms that my wife's laid out near the exit, and we'll let you know how we're going to proceed."

There was a steady round of applause as people stood up and began to leave. Nick wasn't sure what would happen – was anyone genuinely interested? He was pleased to see that nearly all the farmers that had listened, stopped and queued up to leave their names. There was a general buzz of chatter as they all discussed the idea amongst themselves.

Nick and Sarah gathered up all the forms and headed back out into the rain. They marched across to the member's pavilion.

"I could do with a stiffener," said Nick heading to the bar, "what would you like?"

"A Pimm's Cocktail please," Sarah replied, as she settled at an empty table.

Nick came back with the drinks, Pimm's and a pint of bitter for himself.

"I don't know how you can drink that stuff, it looks more like a fruit salad with all those leaves," Nick said jokingly.

"It's mint, adds to the flavour. You just stick to your beer and keep your nose out," Sarah answered back.

"I will. Anyway, how did we do?" Asked Nick seeing that Sarah was counting the lists of names.

"Ninety eight. Hell, that's more than I thought you'd get," Sarah said surprised.

"I'm glad you've got confidence in me," Nick huffed, in a friendly fashion. The pair of them decided to spend the last couple of hours of the afternoon looking around the show; after all, they were 'paid up' annual members and wanted to make the most of their free tickets. The show had been held on this 250 acre site in Harrogate since 1950. Around the main grandstand and show-ring were cattle sheds along with sheep, pigs, horses and even hounds.

There were hundreds of exhibitors selling all manner of country products. There was easily enough to encourage many visitors to come for two or even all three days. Nick enjoyed looking at the newest tractors and latest farm implements.

Sarah felt they all looked much the same, she preferred the various outdoor clothing stands and homeware.

After hearing of his meeting, Nick was thrilled by the number of people who approached him with messages of support. At 6 p.m. they finally returned to their car and attempted to get back to the road. The wet grass didn't help with cars getting stuck as everyone fought to get through the same exits.

Luckily Nick and Sarah had the benefit of owning a Range Rover that made light work of the slippery conditions. The unlucky drivers had to wait their turn as the half dozen tractors towed them onto the tarmac one by one. Traffic control had been handed over to the police who, unsurprisingly, had made a pig's ear of it.

A week later Nick had arranged to meet one of his neighbouring farmers, John Horner, who agreed to work with him to get the association professionally set up.

John was a similar age to Nick and like most farmers had also felt the ever tightening squeeze on prices being pushed ever downwards by the growing power of the supermarkets.

John had already signed a contract to join the Amalgamated Farms Association and was excited at the idea of a fight.

Now, he had stepped up to be Deputy Chairman, in effect, Nick's right hand man. John was a big man whose whole demeanour aired a quiet confidence and authority that always commanded attention.

He liked Nick's ideas and would be a great ambassador for the association, drumming up support from further afield.

By September, even though the AFA had managed to get a fair few members, Nick and John hadn't actually had the opportunity to try and negotiate a better deal for any of them. They faced all sorts of problems that hadn't really been factored in at the start.

The most common one was that the supermarkets already had contracts in place and wouldn't recognise the AFA's authority to negotiate prices.

As the months rolled on things began to change.
The number of members grew quite quickly and, as their individual contracts came up for renewal, they became fully integrated with the AFA.

Instead of getting a price directly from the supermarkets, they basically sold through the AFA who would haggle for the best price for all their members.

The supermarkets were initially not that concerned, this small association was just that - small.

The prices they were offered were the same as those the individual farmers were achieving. They told the AFA representatives that 'if the prices weren't satisfactory, they could always sell elsewhere.'

Nick and John knew that for the balance to tip in their favour they would need to increase their numbers, something they were determined to achieve.

By September 1992 the membership had grown at a steady pace and finally hit the magical 100 mark. John Horner had pushed hard – he'd manned a stand at most of the country shows through the late summer and autumn. His big boost came when he managed to persuade the National Farmers Union to get behind the scheme.

They'd been representing the farming community since being founded in 1908 and were already concerned with the prices farmers were receiving.

Despite their representations to parliament, they couldn't control market prices, the supermarkets weren't really doing anything wrong; they were operating in a free market and were just trying to maximise their profits and market share.

The NFU could see that if the supermarkets kept getting bigger and bigger, the farmers would be on an ever downwards spiral unless they could find a way to tip the balance of power.

It was the end of November when Nick and John arranged to meet one of the senior buyers from RightBuys, another large chain of supermarkets.

They were based in Nottingham and had over 200 branches across the northern half of the UK. Nick and John had driven down to Nottingham, a couple of hours down the M1.

The RightBuys Head Office was a modern, drab looking building on a sprawling industrial estate located to the south east of the city. Its concrete pillars with brick in-fills and aluminium framed windows looked suitable for the purpose but uninspiring. Their slogan was spelt out on a garish sign that hung over the front entrance.

'More in your basket, more left in your pocket'

The lady they were meeting was called Joyce Healey, a stern looking woman in her late forties. It was rare to find a lady haggling with farmers, but she had a fearful reputation – she generally gave her offer and walked away with the deal. It never crossed her mind that anyone would refuse them.

She wore copper framed glasses that sat just above wrinkle lines that bracketed her mouth – in her dark pin striped suit she looked like she meant business.

John had come across her once before and had discussed with Nick the best strategy to get the upper hand. He had no intention of being hoodwinked by this woman.

The pair had arranged the meeting to discuss the prices they wanted for fourteen farmers from across North Yorkshire who were ready to commit to the production of the next year's pea supply.

Eyebrows had been raised when Nick had called Joyce Healey to arrange a meeting. He'd informed her that future negotiations with certain farmers that sold to RightBuys, would now need to be carried out through the AFA, who now had full legal authority to enter into new sales contracts if they saw fit.

Joyce had always liked dealing with solitary farmers who usually had few other options open to them – if they couldn't sell their produce, they were in trouble. She didn't like the sound of this at all. However, she was keen to find out what these men were up to and agreed to meet.

They made their way in and were shown to a small Board Room where Joyce was already waiting. John had agreed to let Nick take the lead in the conversation, after all it was his baby. Nick knew that steaming in, all guns blazing would create a confrontation that would be less than helpful. He wanted to sell the benefits of the AFA, they would be fighting for the farmers, but he felt he could persuade the buyers there were advantages to be had for both sides.

They took their seats around the board room table which would easily have accommodated 16 people.

The two men sat in the middle of one side with Joyce Healey directly opposite. She peered through her glasses at the daunting looking pile of computer printouts in front of her that bore a multitude of figures. '*They must mean something to her, unless she just thinks it makes her look intelligent,*' John thought.

Nick explained to Joyce that the AFA members couldn't afford to have their prices cut time and time again.

"That's all well and good Nick, but we are in a very competitive marketplace and need to react quickly against our competitors when they price-drop, so if we can't buy at the right price then I'm sorry, we won't be buying at all!" She said slapping her hand on the papers in front of her.

"With all due respect Joyce, if the farmers can't make a small profit on their produce, they will end up going out of business, and the supermarkets won't have anything left to sell, and a supermarket with no produce wouldn't be so 'super' after all would it?" Nick said countering the argument.

Both sides' arguments held water but one side had to give. Although Nick had only a small percentage of the farmers on board, he knew that more were joining weekly and, within a couple of years, there could be thousands.

The supplies from the 14 farmers being represented by John and Nick supplied a large chunk of this supermarket's pea requirements and, already Joyce knew she couldn't just send them packing; it would make her job much harder having to find new suppliers who hadn't succumbed to the AFA's marketing tactics.

As expected she'd started her bidding lower than the previous year as she knew she'd be pushed up. As in all negotiations, Nick and John had started way above what they thought they could get. Their only real goal, a goal they had to hit if the AFA was to grow, was to get better prices for all these individual farmers than *they* thought they could achieve on their own.

The main selling price wasn't the only thing that concerned Nick and John. The rights of the buyers to suddenly cut the prices paid when they decided to venture into another price-war was almost more important. The contracts needed to have this stipulation removed – the farmers needed to know the price they'd get before they began, after all, how were they to calculate the profit and loss from a selling price that sometimes halved at a moment's notice.

After an hour or so, they finally agreed on a few key points. Joyce had spent much of the meeting punching numbers into her calculator and scanning up and down her lists of figures. Finally, she'd agreed to a price 5% higher than last year.

This wasn't much, but, the fact she signed away the supermarkets right to ask for a reduction, was a great result for the AFA. The farmers represented would receive the agreed 'fixed' price whether the market price rose or fell.

Nick did wonder if she was going to let them have this result only for the sale of peas (not one of their most competitive items). Maybe taking the view that she'd fight harder over some of the more important items later.

Never the less, the pair left with a positive result. The meeting went reasonably well, in Nick's eyes anyway.

They headed north, Nick feeling quite good about the outcome. The association had grown from an image in his mind to a real, working organisation that had their first meeting and left with a decent result.

Nick knew that he could build on this and, the more members they could entice to join, the easier it should become to get results.

Traffic flowed better for their return journey, other than a bit of congestion round Nottingham. They wanted to get back to the office and phone the farmers they'd been representing to give them the good news. At least they hoped they'd see it as good news.

As they pulled back into the yard at Chestnut Farm, Nick lowered his window to give a quick update to Sarah who was leading two muddy dogs back from their walk.

"How did it go boys?" She called out

"Not bad thanks, I think we got a result," Nick responded.

"The dragon didn't eat you alive then?" Sarah said smiling.

"Well we're still here; she wasn't as bad as we'd been told."

"Do you have time for a cuppa?" she asked, snapping the lead to stop the dogs jumping up at the car door.

"No thanks," replied Nick, "we've got a few calls to make. Our members will want to know the outcome. I'll be back in about an hour."

The farm driveway led round to the back of the farm buildings where they parked up. Nick had converted an old granary behind the fold yard into an office. It had worked out well.

The room was about 40 feet long, accessed via an old external set of stone steps that lacked a hand rail – great except when it was icy! The vaulted ceiling was supported by massive oak beams and joists which had been cleaned up and stained, now forming quite a feature.

Two old mahogany tables, a set that didn't quite match, were pushed together at one end of the room with nine dining chairs, all with well-worn burgundy leather seat pads, forming a perfectly adequate place for 'board meetings'.

Two old mahogany desks purchased from a local auction house sat in line along the longer wall and a double fronted sideboard completed the furnishings. The office was something of a work in progress and would have welcomed a few extra pieces of furniture. The old fabric of the building was complimented with a run of Italian designer track lighting that threaded through the roof beams. The next couple of hours were spent contacting the farmers whose corner they'd been fighting; the general response was positive which left Nick and John feeling more optimistic about the future.

"I'll tell you what Nick, if that's the work and time needed to deal with one order for just over a dozen farmers, we're going to need more help," said John looking at his watch.

"Aye, you're right," Nick replied. "I've been thinking about that. I know who might be up to the job."

"Who's that?" John asked curiously.

"Richard Locker, do you know him?" Answered Nick

"Can't say I do," replied John

"Nice bloke, quite sporty. A man's man. Been in the army and just got his voluntary redundancy.

He's in his late forties and he's looking for something to do. He was a Captain, so he should be able to take charge of a few farmers." Nick chuckled.

"Never come across him. He sounds okay though. Do you think we can afford to pay someone full time? I mean he's not going to want to do it for free is he Nick?"

"We'll have to do a few calculations," replied Nick. "But I reckon, if the numbers keep growing, we won't have any choice, we're going to need help.

"What did he do in the army? Will it be any help to us?" John asked as he flicked through his diary.

"I believe he flew helicopters," Said Nick.

They both agreed that Nick should give him a call to see if Richard would be interested in coming on board. After dinner that evening, Nick gave Richard Locker a call.

"Good Evening Captain, its Brown here, I hope I'm not disturbing you."

"No, not at all Nick," he replied. "Just watching the box, what's up?" Nick went on to tell him how well the AFA was going and that its numbers were increasing rapidly, necessitating the requirement for a full time pair of hands in the office.

"It's strange you've rang, I've been looking for something to get my teeth into, my only concern is that I would still need to be able to carry out my Private Piloting." Richard explained that he flew a 'Squirrel' as and when required for a wealthy Lancastrian land owner.

"Squirrel?" Nick sounded bemused.

"It's a helicopter Nick, AS350 Ecureuil, don't you know your choppers," joked Richard.

"Not much call for them round here, I know more about tractors," Nick replied. Nick couldn't see his part-time flying being a problem; after all, they didn't have anyone at the moment.

"Okay, that's great Richard, why don't you pop down in the morning to discuss the idea further," said Nick hopefully.

The following morning a rather dirty Vauxhall Cavalier pulled into the yard, one hub cap missing and what looked like scratched hieroglyphics across the passenger door.

"What happened there?" Asked Nick looking over the marks.

"Oh yes, that was Toby, my son, thought it would be nice to write his name with a stone from the drive."

"I bet he was popular," chuckled Nick.

"Luckily it's just a run about," smiled Richard, clearly not bothered. On the back seat, sitting on a ruffled tartan blanket was a rather old and somewhat overweight, black Labrador dog. "I'd best leave her in the car," said Richard "Don't want her causing trouble with yours."

He could see Nick's two dogs heading their way. As they walked off in the direction of the office, they could hear Richards dog barking from the partly open car window. Nicks dogs were responding loudly. Nick spent half an hour explaining to Richard how the AFA had come about and why it was so necessary.

"We need someone to 'man the fort' on a day to day basis, whilst John and I are out in the field, so to speak, trying to get more members. We need someone to take the calls and manage the office; do you think you could help?"

"Well I am looking for something to do, I need to generate some income," replied Richard.

"We would definitely be paying you," replied Nick. "We need someone who's switched on."

They talked through the day-to-day workings and were soon shaking hands. Richard seemed quite happy to be taking on the role of office manager, he'd not found anything else and this looked like an interesting change in direction.

Being from a military background he liked the idea of taking on the might of the big supermarket chains, he'd enjoy being on the side of the under-dogs and what's more, he didn't like to lose!

Richard soon settled into his new job, he worked three full days a week and spent the other two flying wealthy racehorse owners and business men up and down the country. Nick soon found that Richards flying had major advantages for the AFA's business.

When he had a meeting in London he could hitch a ride down if Richard was on his way to collect someone – then, he'd either wait for a ride back or jump on a train.

Flying was far preferable to the slog of driving. You could fly from York to London in an hour and a quarter, no traffic jams, no fighting for seats on trains, it was marvellous.

Ever the practical joker, Richard would enjoy putting the wind up first time flyers.

On one occasion, he'd been asked to go to Manchester Airport to collect a group of four businessmen who needed to get to London. He had arranged to take over from another pilot who was flying in from Glasgow.

Richard had learnt to fly in the army and had initially flown the massive Sea King and then the Lynx helicopters, he could fly pretty much anything.

This particular morning though was his first flight in a twin engine Sikorsky S-76, a sophisticated aircraft with retractable landing gear. Had things gone to plan he'd have had an hour to be briefed by the incoming pilot before taking off with his passengers. Due to the inbound flight arriving late and Richard being stuck in traffic, they missed meeting altogether.

Richard wasn't particularly concerned, he could find his way round an instrument panel and the fundamentals were the same for all these modern twin engine machines.

As he arrived, the four business men were already waiting. "Hi, I'm your pilot for today," said Richard as he introduced himself. The men had all greeted him, when one came forward.

"John here hasn't flown before, he's a bit nervous but quite excited about the experience, any chance he could ride up front?"

"No problem" said Richard loading the hand luggage.

"Sit him in the front."

The men got strapped in and ready. Up front, Richard handed John a pair of headphones with an attached microphone to allow them to communicate over the din of the engines.

"This is my first time flying in one of these," said John, looking somewhat apprehensive.

"Mine too," said Richard cheerfully studying his notes, not really thinking about how that came across. That wasn't what John had wanted to hear!

Richard ran through his pre-flight checks. The controls were all familiar to Richard and he was happy to get going, he just couldn't initially find one particular button.

"Can you see a start button anywhere?" He said, looking over the myriad of switches. John turned a shade whiter and his grip on the seat tightened.

Within a couple of minutes Richard had got his clearance from Air Traffic Control and was climbing smoothly up over the southern edge of Manchester.

He was an experienced pilot and it showed – John's nerves were calmed – for a while at any rate. Normally when flying into London in the single engine 'Squirrel', he would be required to fly along the path of the Thames, in case of engine failure.

Apparently he could just ditch it into the river! In the twin engine 'Sikorsky' he could fly directly to Battersea where he'd have to make a difficult landing at the London Heliport. A jetty protruded into the river from which an aircraft could take off or land, then manoeuvre its way into one of the four parking spaces.

There wasn't any room for error. As they descended towards the London Heliport, Richard came across a problem. As he'd tried to lower the landing gear, he was expecting three green lights to show that all the wheels were down and locked in place, but, he was only getting two, the third remaining red.

He didn't want to alarm his passengers however he felt he had to advise them of the situation. In the end he came in close to the Control Tower to allow them to make a visual check - it was the only way to know what was happening beneath the aircraft.

They advised him that all three wheels looked to be properly in place and that he could attempt to land. As it turned out, they were fine, it was just an instrument malfunction, but whether poor John would ever want to take to the air in another helicopter was another matter.

Nick, John and Richard worked well together and over the coming months the membership numbers of the AFA began to snowball, initially they were mainly Yorkshire farmers, but as word spread, they came from much further afield.

Richard had the gift of the gab and seemed to be able to persuade any 'undecided' to join the association. He was one of those people who seemed to have more than their fair share of energy, he just couldn't sit still.

CHAPTER 22

Simon Elliott was now in the office of Doctor Collinson, a Specialist in the field of Chronic Kidney Disease; she'd worked at the Royal London Hospital's specialist renal centre for the last five years, today she was issuing her verdict. "As you know Simon, your condition is deteriorating. You need a kidney transplant as soon as possible or, well... you know what the outcome will be.

We need to see what options are open to you. The rejection rate for organ transplant can be quite high consequently your best chance for long term success is a family member. Do you have any brothers or sisters?" She asked, studying the laptop screen on her desk.

"Yes I do," he replied. "I have a brother Ralph who lives in Brighton. He's a couple of years younger than me."

"Well I'm afraid this isn't going to be easy for you. We really need to find you a replacement kidney and this could be your best chance of finding a successful match," Doctor Collinson answered.

"What do you mean? Take one of his? You might find he's using them," said Simon sarcastically, trying to lighten the mood. The doctor ignored Simon's remark and continued to explain the general procedure in layman's terms.

"If you can persuade your Brother to help you, he'll need to be verified to check whether his organ will definitely be compatible.

The human body can function perfectly well on one kidney," she explained. "The other is obsolete really, more of a back-up."

"Yes, it might be," replied Simon, "but it's a hell of a big ask. What if my Brother did donate one to me and then gets ill himself? He could get this same rotten disease."

"That is a possibility, and one of the risks he's going to have to weigh-up. Obviously we carry out tests to check whether he's likely to have any unforeseen problems," she said reassuringly.

"We were always quite close when we were younger, but I'm not sure he'll want to be donating one of his major organs, he's quite squeamish. I remember the panic when he had to have an in-growing toe nail removed," said Simon.

"I don't want to cause you more stress, but, you need this operation within the next 6 weeks or I'm afraid it may be too late," she said closing her laptop.

"I'd best get on the phone to Ralph then," Simon replied. Then he deliberated for a moment. "No, I can't ask him over the phone, I'll have to make an excuse and go and see him." He stood up to leave and went to shake Doctor Collinson's hand.

"Well thanks Doc, I'll let you know what happens, and if he says *no*, well I'll pop in and say goodbye."

"Now come on, I'm sure we'll get you sorted out," she said with a half-smile.

Simon left the hospital and headed back to Ovington Mews; he was supposed to be on full-time sick leave but couldn't keep away from the office for more than a couple of days at a time.

As he ambled along he thought of a hundred ways he could broach the subject with his brother. *'It's not every day you have to ruin someone else's life to save your own.'*

Simon fretted for a couple of days, often getting close to phoning Ralph, but each time backing out at the last moment. Finally three days after seeing Dr Collinson he plucked up the courage to do it.

He knew time was running out. He grabbed his pocket diary which contained names, addresses and phone numbers of all his friends and contacts and ran his finger down to Ralph Elliott's number. Normally undeterred by anything, Simon felt the confidence slowly drain out of him. He hadn't spoken to Ralph for three months. As the phone began to ring he was still trying to think of the right words to say.

"Hello," said Ralph.

"Hi Ralph, it's me, Simon," he blurted.

"You okay?" Ralph responded. You don't sound very happy."

"No, I'm not. I need to see you urgently, are you by any chance in Brighton this weekend?" Simon replied.

"Yes. Why? What's up? You haven't run out of money have you?" Ralph laughed.

"No, it's nothing like that. I can't tell you over the phone, I need to speak to you in person," Simon said quietly.

"Simon, you've got me worried now. Let me know when you'll be arriving and I'll pick you up at the train station."

"Thanks Ralph. I'll call you in a day or two. And don't worry. I'll explain everything when I see you," Simon said reassuringly.

By Friday Simon had booked himself a train ticket and called Ralph back to say that he'd be there at 12 noon the next day. Saturday morning, 10 o'clock and the taxi was waiting outside Simon's house.

"Victoria Station please," he asked opening the rear door.

"Okay guv," chirped the driver.

They headed down a couple of back streets and crossed Cadogan Place then turned into Elizabeth Street, crossing Eccleston Square. Simon knew they would be at the station in a couple of minutes. The whole journey only took about five minutes.

Victoria Station boasted an Edwardian baroque façade in brick and stone topped off with a station clock which indicated he still had a few minutes to buy himself a newspaper and survey the Departures Board.

Thankfully his train was on time. Simon took his seat in the First-Class carriage towards the front of the train. The Guard blew his whistle and immediately the train pulled away and headed south crossing over the Thames on Grosvenor Bridge.

As he leaned back in the comfort of the blue upholstered seat, he admired the massive brick built Battersea Power Station that had long since ceased to produce any power. The four mighty towers that defined this landmark were now seemingly only good for adorning music album covers.

The train wound its way through the suburbs of London heading out towards Gatwick Airport. Beyond there the line passed through

Haywards Heath and through tunnels and cuttings carved through the chalk of the Downs.

Just over an hour later, the train was slowing for the end of its journey. Brighton station is set high above the town which was, for a long time, Britain's most fashionable resort. Ever since The Prince of Wales built his eccentric Royal Pavilion in 1783, tourists have admired its exotic oriental architecture.

Simon was relieved to see his brother Ralph standing close to the ticket office with a coffee cup in his hand, and a rolled up newspaper tucked under his arm. His ginger hair had always been quite bushy and from a distance it looked like he was wearing a woolly hat. As Simon got near, Ralph instinctively looked up.

"Hello Simon," Ralph called out.

"Hello Ralph, it's good to see you. Thanks for collecting me," said Simon giving his brother half a bear hug, trying hard not to knock the coffee out of his hand.

"What's up with you then? I don't normally get requests to meet up," inquired Ralph as they turned towards the station's exit.

"Get me a drink and I'll tell you," Simon replied cheekily.

"You still like a drink then. Okay, let's go to the Lord Nelson, it's just around the corner, nice and quiet and we can talk," said Ralph giving Simon a knowing smile.

"It's not one of those tourist pubs full of loud mouthed day trippers," he said as they neared the entrance.

They were soon seated on a couple of low stools with a pint of lager each in front of them. Simon had a good gulp from his glass hoping it might steady his nerves, it didn't make much difference. After a couple more, he felt as ready as he could be to broach his problem.

"You remember I told you I was ill a few years ago? All that backache I had experienced. Well it turned out to be a serious kidney infection," said Simon.

"Yes, I remember you had some time off work," replied Ralph.

"Well, I've been having more time off recently. It never really went away. It's got worse and worse," explained Simon.

"Can they sort you out?" Ralph said, looking concerned.

"Umm, that's the problem. It's quite serious, in fact it's life-threatening," Simon looked away.

"I've been having dialysis for a few months and now I need a kidney transplant or its curtains," Simon blurted out.

Ralph paused before answering.

"You might have told me… Months?"

"Yes, a few months, that's all I've got," murmured Simon.

"My god, that's awful," moaned Ralph.

"I know. Both my kidneys are *shot*. I need a new one to stand any chance," said Simon looking Ralph straight in the eye.

"When? I mean do you have to go on a waiting list or something?" Ralph replied wanting to get more of a picture.

"No, that's the problem. There are only certain people that can help me; my best chance is a blood relative with the matching blood group." Simon said hoping Ralph would cotton on to what he was suggesting.

Ralph took a long slug of lager and banged his glass back onto its allocated beer mat. The situation was beginning to register.

"You mean *me*, don't you?" Replied Ralph, his mouth hung partially open.

"I'm really sorry. I have to ask you. The doctor says that *brothers* or *sisters* are the best chance of success and you're all I've got," said Simon persuasively.

"Bloody hell Simon, you know how to liven up someone's afternoon," said Ralph abruptly.

"Believe me I didn't want to," answered Simon. "I know how hard this will be for you and if you don't want to do it, I'd understand. I don't know if I could do it if things were the other way around."

"I know you're in desperate trouble, but don't I need them myself? I mean, that's why I'm okay and you're not," said Ralph trying to get his head around it all.

"The doctor says we all have two kidneys, but the body can function perfectly well with just one, the other's more of a backup," explained Simon trying to placate his brother.

"That's fine, until the remaining one gives up like yours." Ralph replied struggling to weigh up the situation. "Look, I'm not saying I *won't* do it, I just need a bit of time to think about it. How long have we got?"

"I need to get it done quite soon Ralph. At the moment I'm alright having dialysis, it's not nice but it keeps me alive." Simon answered feeling very unsure about his brother's decision.

"I suppose I'd have to have a few weeks off work, which isn't necessarily a bad thing," smiled Ralph, trying to give a positive slant to the situation. "But you'll have to give me time to mull it over Simon. Somehow I've lost my appetite, shall we go? Why not come round to my place for a coffee?"

"That would be good, I'm not heading back until tonight," answered Simon, greatly relieved that the first major hurdle on the face of it, had been overcome.

"Do you want to stay for dinner?" Ralph asked as he poured Simon a large cup of black coffee.

"That's very kind, but I can't. I've got to be in the hospital first thing in the morning for my treatment," replied Simon.

"How often do you have that?" Ralph asked curiously.

"I'm there three times a week, four hours each session. It's tiring, but I'm used to it now. Simon replied. "One more thing Ralph, please don't tell Mum and Dad yet, I don't want them worrying. Have you seen them recently?"

"Yes I have. I went up to Salisbury about a fortnight ago they're both fine, just the same as normal. Don't worry I won't tell them. Hurry up and drink your coffee and I'll take you back to the station," said Ralph.

As the two brothers stood on the platform waiting for the arrival of the train, Ralph knew he would have to make the sacrifice, he just needed more time to think. How could he let his only brother die when he had the power to save him? He knew Simon would have done it for him.

The following evening, as Simon sat reading all the literature that Doctor Collinson had given him, the phone rang. It was Ralph. "I'm ready when you are Simon."

"What? Are you going to do it?" Simon sounded shocked and somewhat surprised.

"Of course I am you daft sod. I can't sit by and watch you *kick the bucket*," Ralph said, trying to make a joke of it.

"Well, I wasn't sure you'd do it. How can I thank you?" Simon replied in dis-belief.

"You don't need to. I'm sure you'd do the same for me," answered Ralph.

"Of course I would, you know that. But we still need some tests carried out to make sure you're a match; however the doctor says that siblings normally are," said Simon feeling hopeful.

"What do I need to do now then?" Ralph replied.

"We need to get you booked in at my clinic. The Royal London Hospital, Whitechapel. You'll be able to come and stay with me if you need to," replied Simon.

"Don't forget, I've got a job. I'll have to see what the company says. I'm sure they'll help, they're very good like that," said Ralph.

"I can't thank you enough little Brother, I'll make the call tomorrow and let you know when they can fit you in," said Simon eagerly.

"Okay, I'll leave it with you. Ring me when you know more," said Ralph, breathing a sigh of relief having made the decision. Simon replaced the handset and relaxed back into his chair; he felt a weight had been lifted from his overworked mind. He poured himself a small glass of wine something he'd been told to avoid, however he didn't think one more would make any difference.

As soon as the weekend was over, Simon made an appointment for Ralph to have his blood test. If this proved okay he would be summoned for a full medical examination.

His entire body would then be investigated to check whether he was fit enough to undergo the complex surgery of the transplant, and that he would be fine with only the one remaining kidney.

This would be a fairly straightforward but serious operation and the surgeons wouldn't perform it unless they were 100% happy. Three days later Ralph made the journey from Brighton for his blood test. The whole thing only took an hour; he had a cannula fitted so they could take multiple samples without making him look like a pin cushion and by that evening, Ralph was back at home.

The next day Simon received a phone call requesting him to return to the hospital the following Monday to meet with Dr Collinson to discuss the way forward. What he was about to learn would turn his life upside down!

As he sat in the waiting room, he hoped the news would be good. If Ralph's test had been okay, he could soon have a proper future, well some sort of future at any rate. Across the crackly intercom, Simon heard his call to action; "Simon Elliott to Surgery D17 please."

As Simon walked into Doctor Collinson's office he detected a less than confident look of worry across her face.

"What is it?" Simon asked. "Judging by your look it's not what I want to hear."

"I'm afraid not, Simon. I think you'd better sit down," she replied with a concerned tone to her voice.

"Well it can't be that bad, even if Ralph's not a perfect match, he's got to be a better choice than a random member of the public," replied Simon trying to keep upbeat.

"That's just it," Doctor Collinson replied.

"What do you mean, that's just it?" Said Simon nervously.

"I'm not sure how to ask you this, but there isn't an easy way, so I'm just going to say it.

Are you sure Ralph's your brother?" Doctor Collinson's question was completely out of the blue.

"*What?* What the hell are you talking about? Of course he's my Brother. I think I'd know. I bloody well grew up with him!" Simon was furious.

"Is it possible you could have been adopted?" Questioned Doctor Collinson.

Simon was leaning forward in his chair about to jump up and leave, upset and rattled by Doctor Collinson's remark.

"Of course, I wasn't adopted – what the hell are you talking about? Don't you think I'd have mentioned it?" He said, through gritted teeth.

"Well I'm sorry, this isn't easy. We've checked and double checked the results. There is no way he can be your Brother. We've even done a full DNA comparison. Maybe your Brother was adopted?" Doctor Collinson asked nervously.

"No, that's impossible. It's not right. You must have made a mistake, I've heard about things like this happening. Your team have got the files muddled up or the labs must have buggered up the results," Simon said angrily.

"Please, calm down and let me explain," said Doctor Collinson trying to quieten Simon down. She paused as he reluctantly leant back into his chair.

"We use the DNA profile test to find the number of shared genetic markers between two people, to analyse the amount of shared DNA. The test can determine the probability of a biological relationship existing between you. The stronger the commonality of the DNA shared means the greater the probability of a biological relationship.

Full siblings by definition have *two* biological parents in common, the Mother and Father, whereas half siblings have only one parent in common, *either* the Mother *or* the Father. Full siblings have more shared genetic markers than half siblings. When they sent the original results back I requested a re-test. I'm afraid that in your case there are none. There is absolutely no chance that Ralph is your biological brother. I'm sorry," said Doctor Collinson.

"No, you're wrong! I don't know what's happening here but you're wrong." Simon said adamantly, refusing to listen. For a moment he had forgotten all about the reason for the tests in the first place. He'd forgotten about his failing kidneys, all that was chasing round his confused mind now were the words he'd just heard.

"But how? How can that be right? He's my Brother; he's always been my Brother," questioned Simon. Then the next horrible conclusion began to dawn on him.

"If he's not my Brother either my Mum and Dad aren't his… or, *no!* It's impossible, it couldn't be! *They aren't mine,"* said. Simon slumping back in his chair.

"I'm sorry but you're right," Dr Collinson said calmly, as she touched his forearm trying to put him more at ease.

"The only way to know about your parents is to get blood tests from them, or you could…" she paused.

"Could what?" Repeated Simon.

"Well, it might be easier if you just asked them. They must know why the results are the way they are," Doctor Collinson answered back. Simon was shell shocked. His entire world had been torn in two.

"I know this isn't the time Simon, but we still need to find you a transplant. We need to know if you have any suitable relatives," she continued.

"My God, yes we need to know!" Simon said echoing her words. *"I need to know what the hell's going on!"*

It felt like he was in a terrifying nightmare. Simon expected to wake up in a cold sweat any second. He prayed he'd wake up, but he didn't. He left the hospital and wandered down the road aimlessly.

It was a bright sunny morning although it went un-noticed as Simon tried to work out what he should do now. Normally the most confident man you could find was now left like a lost, bewildered child, asking himself a question. *Who the hell am I?*

He finally decided to head home. He couldn't face the hustle and bustle of the underground and waved down a black cab. The driver seemed to want to chat, Simon didn't. He stared out of the window and finally when the driver realised his audience wasn't listening, gave up. Once safely home, Simon sat and thought for a bit.

'Did he ring his brother Ralph and tell him he wasn't his brother? No, he couldn't do that, he still wasn't certain the hospital hadn't made a mistake. On the other hand they were adamant they were right and they wouldn't have told someone this news unless they'd checked and double checked.

If he did ring Ralph, what would he say? He still didn't know if it was him or Ralph that wasn't the real family member. No. He'd have to ring his parents.

He didn't want to upset his mother. No, he'd have to speak to his father – it was the only avenue.'

Simon picked up the phone at least half a dozen times but couldn't go through with it. He needed to get his head straight first. He spent the whole weekend trying to decide the best approach. By Sunday night he was no closer to making the call than he had been on Friday night.

The words flying round his head just seemed to get more and more complicated and confused. Back at the hospital on Monday morning, Simon headed to his usual room for his normal dialysis session.

Things were the same as ever, he said his 'hello's' and got connected to his machine. The nurses were always friendly and Simon was now quite used to sitting, reading or doing some work whilst the machine whirred away next to him. This particular Monday he didn't read, he just sat staring out of the window thinking.

Four hours later, still sitting on the bed, he was rolling his sleeve down having just been released from the tether of the dialysis machine, another session finished, when he was surprised to see Doctor Collinson appear in the doorway.

"Hello Simon. I hoped I'd catch you. I must talk to you."

"That sounds serious," laughed Simon as he continued…

"I haven't rung my family yet, I'll do it today, and I know I should have but I just couldn't find the right words. When I'm finished here, I'm going straight home to get it over with."

"That's good, you must." She paused and her serious look didn't lighten. "But I have more news for you."

"More news? Well it can't get any worse," smiled Simon.

Dr Collinson's look said otherwise.

"After Friday's news how bad can it be? You'd best hit me with it," Simon continued.

"Well, since I last saw you, and Ralph's results being as they were, I decided to do some research. I'm not really supposed to, but I've got a friend in the DNA database department and he owed me a favour."

She moved closer into the room and sat on the edge of Simon's bed. "I thought I'd see if I could find any matches for you on the register."

"And how did it go?" Simon asked anxiously.

"They found a match, but I'm afraid it's not good news."

"Why? That sounds like good news to me." Simon was puzzled.

"There's a good match on the system, but I'm sorry, the DNA is from a dead man."

"Dead?" Said Simon curiously.

"Yes, I'm sorry, it gets worse." Doctor Collinson replied.

"What do you mean?" Asked Simon, trying to figure it out.

"There's a 90% chance this man *was* your full brother," replied Doctor Collinson.

"Are you serious?" Simon replied. By the look on her face, he knew she was.

"Let me explain," said Doctor Collinson. "The DNA tests calculate the probability that two people are full siblings or half siblings. The test analyses 16 genetic locations on the DNA strand. The allele gene at each location is identified by a number.

The test shows that the two samples, one from you and the other from this other man had 14 matches, giving a 90% chance that you are full brothers, i.e. you have the same Mother and Father."

"Who was he?" Simon asked, not expecting her to know the name.

"He was a man from Scotland," her eyes scanned down the document she was holding. "According to my records his name was James Brown," she continued.

Simon was sure he hadn't heard her right. "That's impossible. You can't be right," said Simon. "I knew a James Brown from Scotland."

"Well I'm sure there's more than one James Brown; it's not that uncommon a name. Maybe there are more details here. Let's have a look through this file," she said flicking through the papers of a pink folder on her knee.

"What does it say?" Simon asked nervously.

"James Brown, Farmer from East Lothian.

Suicide 14th April 1992.

Shooting. DNA taken by police who wanted to rule out foul play."

Doctor Collinson read the notes from the files and looked up to see Simon had turned as white as a sheet.

CHAPTER 23

"imon, are you okay?" Doctor Collinson looked concerned at Simon's reaction. He was leaning back on his pillow, white as a sheet with his hands over his eyes. He didn't respond. He just sat there.

"What is it Simon?" Said Doctor Collinson. "I know it must be hard to take."

"You don't understand," uttered Simon.

"Understand what? What is it?" Dr Collinson was confused.

"He *killed* himself." Simon blurted.

"Yes, suicide. It's here in the files," replied Doctor Collinson.

"I know because I caused it. He killed himself because of me or at least the rest of his family blame me for it," Simon insisted.

Doctor Collinson was now the one to have turned a shade paler.

"You're not serious," she replied. "How could you possibly know him?"

"I am serious. But how can he be my Brother? That's just not..." He stopped mid -sentence and sat up.

"Oh my God. I feel sick!" Cried Simon. He's got a brother, I mean... oh God what do I mean? He's got a brother called Nick. And he really doesn't like me." The reality was dawning on him by the second and becoming clearer, so much clearer.

"'I've got a brother Nick who hates me!

Simon was sure he was just enduring the worst nightmare and that he would wake up at any moment. He had to wake up. *PLEASE WAKE ME UP!'*

The voice was screaming inside his head. "None of this makes any sense. I'm Simon Elliott. I know where I came from, and now you're trying to tell me it's all wrong and that somehow, I'm related to a family at the other end of the country.

In a different country, for that, and out of all the families in the world you could have named it's THAT family. I've never even been to bloody Scotland.

And, if they're my family, how the hell could I live to be 48 years old with the wrong family? It's just not possible. You must be wrong. Someone's playing a sick joke on me. They must be," Simon was enraged!

"Now try and calm down, somehow we'll sort it out," said Doctor Collinson trying her best to calm him.

"How are we going to do that? I need to go," said Simon as he stood up ready to leave. "I was confused before I came in here, now I don't know what I am, or who I am."

As Simon stood up, he stumbled forward feeling dizzy and sick. He reached out and steadied himself on the end of the bed somehow managing to avoid falling to the floor.

"Are you sure you should go? Why don't you stay here and have a cup of tea?" Pleaded Doctor Collinson.

"I don't want more bloody tea. Sorry. I didn't mean..." Simon regained his composure and stood upright again. "You've been very kind but I need to get home," said Simon reaching for his clothes so he could get dressed.

Simon stepped outside into the bright sunlight. He put his hand up to shield his eyes feeling somewhat lost in the wide open space around him. Still feeling a bit groggy, he asked the hospital porter to summon him a cab. As the cab wound through the busy London streets Simon's mind was trying to make sense of the latest news to rock his world.

Once safely back at Ovington Mews, he poured himself a stiff drink of neat single malt – something that was well and truly off his approved consumption list.

His body wouldn't like this poison, but he was past caring, he needed a drink.

Sitting in his front room, Simon contemplated his next move. He'd made countless difficult business decisions over the years, but this was a whole new level.

The one thing he was sure of was that one of these people, the family he thought he was part of, knew the truth. They knew more than he did, and he had to find out what that was.

When he'd had to ring Ralph to ask him for his help, that was hard but this was a whole lot worse.

'What would Ralph think? He clearly didn't know or he wouldn't have bothered coming for the tests in the first place. What about his Mother and Father, they knew Ralph was going for the tests, or did they? If they had, it must have dawned on them that the truth would out, whatever the truth was.'

Having spent the whole weekend trying to summon up the courage to ask his parents whether it was Ralph or himself that was the 'misfit', the goal posts had now moved.

Now he'd have to ask how he'd ended up in the ranks of the wrong family for as long as he could recollect. After a further couple of hours fretting about phoning his father, he'd had a couple of glasses of malt and was ready to make the call. He'd made up his mind!

He needed to know the truth and wanted to know now. He picked up the phone and dialled. The phone rang about eight times, each ring seeming louder than the preceding one. The wait for an answer felt like an eternity. His mother answered in a quiet tone.

"Hello Mum," he said trying to sound calm. "Is my Father there?" He found the sentence hard to say, after all, he evidently wasn't his father.

"Yes, he's here, how are you?" She replied.

"I'll talk to you in a moment, but I need to talk to Dad first," said Simon taking a deep breath.

"Okay, hang on... Alex, Alex. Simon's on the phone and he wants to speak to you." Simon could hear her shout in the background.

"Hello?" The distinctive sound of his father's voice came down the line.

Simon felt his heart beating hard. He didn't want to get into any small talk that he couldn't easily move away from. This conversation was difficult enough, so he decided to cut straight to the point.

"I need to know who I am," Simon blurted.

There was a moments silence as Alex tried to weigh up the question. "Sorry, what are you asking? Have you been drinking?" Alex Replied.

"No, well, not enough. Ralph and I have had blood tests taken. He might be your son but the hospital tell me I'm not. I wondered if you had anything to add to that," said Simon in a matter of fact way.

"Oh my god I see," said Alex. There was a long pause.

"I knew this day might come. I hoped you'd never have to know." Alex slumped onto his armchair and rested his head on his free hand.

"It's true then?" Asked Simon. Even though he was expecting it, the answer that came back was a kick in the teeth. He took a deep breath to try and overcome the numbness washing over him.

"I can't believe you wouldn't have thought to mention it. You know that I'm not actually your son, and Mother, well I don't know what to say to her," exclaimed Simon.

"If you hadn't needed Ralph to have that test... you'd never have needed to know," replied Alex.

"Know What? That I was adopted?" Shouted Simon.

"You weren't exactly adopted," Alex said sheepishly.

"Weren't adopted! What the bloody hell are you telling me? I don't understand what's going on," Simon hollered.

"I think I need to see you to explain." Alex sounded defenceless now, not his normal bullish military self.

"Never mind see me," said Simon. "I want the truth and I want it now – I've waited over forty years."

"I'm so sorry you had to find out like this. I... we... never meant to hurt you. We've always loved you. We treated you as our own child. You were our child – you still are," muttered Alex.

"I want to know how things ended up like this," Simon demanded.

"Well, it's not easy. This will sound worse than it was but, we *bought* you," Alex sighed.

"What? Bought me! Do you mean you *'paid'* for me? Was I cheap?" There was a mixture of upset and anger in Simon's voice now.

"No, no, it wasn't like that. When we were first married we tried for a baby for a long time, and, well it just didn't happen. We really wanted a family. Your Mother was so upset, she really thought she could never have children," explained Alex.

"Yes, so what happened?" Simon pushed for the answer.

"Do you want the long version or the short version?" Replied Alex trying to sound composed.

"I just want a bloody version that makes some sense," Simon shouted back.

"Okay, okay. An opportunity arose. I was stationed in Cyprus, working at the Internment Camp in Famagusta. We were there for three years. There was all sorts went on in those camps. There was lots of comings and goings with local Cypriots working there. Doctors, nurses – all sorts. The conditions weren't good and food was in short supply. However there was a surprisingly vibrant community with marriages, illness, deaths, and celebrations."

"I don't need a bloody history lesson," cursed Simon. "I just want to know where I came from."

"Yes, I know, I'm trying to tell you, it's not easy. Anyway there were lots of children in the camp; pregnancy helped move the families up on the Palestine waiting list.

One day a young Jewish couple turned up with a young boy who clearly wasn't theirs. They looked like chalk and cheese. I told them that I knew he was stolen and took the boy from them.

I told them that I wouldn't have them arrested if they gave me the child and offered them some money. They didn't bother fighting it; they knew their chances of getting away with a young Caucasian was virtually nil. Initially I had every intention of handing the boy over to the authorities but then the idea came to me. I knew it was wrong, but the more I thought about it, the more sense it made.

I mean, we'd never track this boy's family down, they could have been anywhere, and where we lived no one would even notice we'd got a child that perhaps wasn't around before. It was all too easy," said Alex trying his best to explain the circumstances.

"And what about Mum?" Quizzed Simon.

"She was desperate for a child. She wanted to give the boy, you, a good home. And we did, didn't we?" Alex asked.

"So you just kept me. You just took me. No, abducted me," snapped Simon.

"*We* didn't really abduct you; *they* abducted you, we just wanted to look after you," Alex said correcting him.

"What about my real family, do you know who they are?" Asked Simon bluntly.

"We weren't sure at first, but yes, later, we did suspect. The papers reported a family who'd lost a boy in Limassol on the south coast, but we didn't want to give you back, so we sort of convinced ourselves you weren't the same boy and kept quiet," murmured Alex.

"Absolutely unbelievable!" Said Simon.

"Life was different then. There were families, children, coming and going daily, moving from Europe to Cyprus, to Palestine. There were tens of thousands of displaced people with no real homes. You were just another – one of many," said Alex trying to make the situation sound sensible.

"But you stole my life from me." Simon was quieter now, but his anger still there was surpassed by his sadness.

"We didn't steal it, not really, we just gave you a different life," pleaded Alex.

"I'm going now, I've heard enough," replied Simon irritably upset.

"Wait, Simon, your Mother wants to talk to you, please," begged Alex.

Simon could hear her sobbing in the background.

"Not now, I can't." Simon put the phone down and for the first time in years, he cried.

That night he couldn't sleep or think clearly. His mind was a jumble as he struggled to separate reality from the lies he'd lived for the last 45 years. He racked his brains for distant memories of the family he'd lost, but it was so long ago.

He thought about James and Nick Brown but couldn't believe they could be his brothers, he just couldn't see it. Surely, he'd remember them.

Who were his real parents, and what were they like?

He just couldn't remember any of it. From thinking he knew everything; he'd been thrown into a world where he knew nothing.

That night seemed the longest in his life, He didn't sleep.

He just tossed around with thoughts and ideas fighting for space in his now chaotic mind. He finally woke around nine o'clock the next morning. He couldn't eat breakfast but managed to drink a couple of mugs of coffee whilst sitting in his armchair, just thinking. He just sat in his dressing gown, right through the whole day.

At around lunch time he decided he'd better call Ralph – he didn't suppose his 'surrogate' parents would have taken the initiative. Sure enough, when he got hold of Ralph he was as much in the dark as Simon.

He thought Simon had lost his marbles, maybe had too much of his medication.

Once Simon had got his message across, Ralph was also left trying to make sense of a lifetime's misconception. Simon left it to him to confront Alex and Louise with what he'd just discovered.

Luckily Simon slept better the following night which helped, as the next day he had no choice but to get up – his dialysis would need carrying out whether he was having a personal crisis or not.

He opted to go to the hospital by tube as it was still the quickest way. Only 48 hours after he'd last been sitting on his regular bed at the Royal London, he was back again.

The nurses soon had him hooked up to the machine that relentlessly whirred away, removing the poisons from his blood. As he sat there he tried to work out how he was going to approach Nick Brown and break the news to him that he was his brother. How would he react?

How would anyone react when hit with such unbelievable news?

Simon was sure he wouldn't believe him, and if he did, where did that leave them? Nick had made it quite clear that he blamed Simon for James's death. And what about his need for a kidney donation – Nick was now the best, no, possibly the only hope, of supplying a compatible organ. Well, that was that. It wouldn't even be worth asking – obviously Nick wouldn't do it.

The trouble was, time was running out for Simon. Without this transplant he may only last a few months. *'Maybe that was for the best,'* he thought for a moment.

No - he hadn't time for procrastinating. He now had to tell Nick who he was and somehow ask for his help. *'The chances of him agreeing must be verging on zero,'* he thought, and yet he knew he still had no choice but to try.

Simon never believed in quitting, he also knew that this wasn't something for the telephone – you don't just ring someone after all those years, tell them you're their brother and ask them to become an organ donor.

He would have to get himself to Yorkshire. Simon didn't want to turn up out of the blue and decided he'd have to phone first to make an appointment – he didn't want to risk getting all the way to York for Nick to be out.

With his dialysis appointments every other day, he had to get there and back in a day or two at the most. Simon made his mind up to call Nick as soon as he got back home and see if he could meet him the next day.

The treatment was soon over for another day and Simon made his way back to West Brompton. As he walked the last few hundred yards home, he was already feeling nervous about the call.

Doubts had once again raced through his mind – *'how was he going to pull this off?'* He hung his coat up and headed into the room he used as his home office. His briefcase lay open on the desk with his faithful Filofax on top – essential notes and contacts pushed it to the point of bursting. Simon picked it up, undid the small leather tagged button that kept it under control and thumbed his way through to the letter 'B'.

There they were. James Brown's name and phone number with a casual black line deleting it. He'd done it when he'd heard of James's death. He paused for a moment and thought as a twinge of guilt washed over him.

'*My brother dies, and I just cross him out with little more than a cursory glance.*' Below James's name was Nick Brown's number and address. It was the first time Simon had really looked at the address – he'd known he lived in Yorkshire, but little more. '*York,*' he thought, '*nice place.*'

His hand hovered over the phone before he forced himself to pick it up. He punched the numbers into the keypad.

"Hello?" The distinct Scottish accent was strong in his ear.

"Hello, Is that Nick Brown?"

"Aye!"

"It's Simon Elliott from TayMarts."

"Aye, I know who you are. After what you did to my Brother I don't know how you have the bloody nerve to ring me."

"I know, I am sorry about that, but I didn't..." Simon was cut short.

"I don't want to hear it," Nick interrupted abruptly. "What are you after now? I suppose you're calling about the AFA?"

"No, it's not that. I need to meet you to discuss another matter," replied Simon nervously.

"I'm too busy for your games now or any time..."said Nick.

"It really is important or I wouldn't ask. I need to meet you in the next couple of days. I'll come to you, insisted Simon."

"What is it that's so important you'd come all the way to York for?" Nick quizzed.

"I need to talk to you face to face. Please, I realise I'm not flavour of the month but this is important," Simon begged.

"Well I don't like it, but if we must! I can't do tomorrow, or Wednesday. I could just about manage Thursday morning, and I'll tell you this, you'd better have a bloody good reason for coming up here after all you've done, or it'll be the last thing you ever do," shouted Nick.

"I have," replied Simon, "I could be there by eleven o'clock, is that okay with you?"

"That'll do," snapped Nick. Do you know where we are?"

"Yes thank you. I've got your address, I'll be getting a taxi from York station," answered Simon.

Simon put the phone down and breathed a huge sigh of relief that he'd got the call over with. He flicked the kettle on.

He would have rather had a proper drink but it just made him feel lousy. Now he'd got two days to wait before he met with Nick. He knew he had an uphill battle to face after that awkward conversation, and not only that, he was about to shatter the lives of the Brown family in the same way his had been the week before, if they'd actually listen to him.

Trying to relax as he spread himself across his sofa, thoughts crossed Simon's mind... *'There's no way Nick could know who I am, could he? Had his parents, MY parents ever said anything? Would he even know that there'd been another brother? If I knew nothing about all this, then there's a strong possibility that he wouldn't either. Why the hell did my real parents have to get rid of me in the first place? They probably won't want me back, but it's gone too far now. I'm going back.'*

Simon returned to his office on Tuesday but found it hard to focus on work, he wasn't his usual upbeat self. He got his secretary to bring him the file on the Brown family which he spent an hour looking through.

Perhaps as a company, TayMarts had been hard on them, but no more so than they had to any of the other farmers. TayMarts were in business to make money after all. He turned page after page, reacquainting himself with all the transactions. Then he turned another page and was hit like a hammer blow by the words that stared back at him. The father's name was William Brown, below were added the words – 'DECEASED'.

CHAPTER 24

As he scanned further down the page it became clear that William had owned the biggest of the three farms and was the major shareholder in Woodside Tanners & Coates Produce Ltd.

Having died in 1985 he left the business to his two sons James and Nick. Simon sat for some time staring out through the window. He was ill enough as it was, without being hit by blow after blow. Only hours before he'd been thinking about the conversation he'd have with his real father, now he knew he'd never meet his real father again.

Would his mother be alive?

He hoped she would, it was certainly possible. However, there was no mention of her in the work's file.

Simon finally shut the file and put it in his briefcase. There was a pile of correspondence to attend to in his 'in tray' which he proceeded to trawl through.

Feeling decidedly ill and with a head swimming with thoughts, he tried his best to concentrate on his regular work. He began checking and signing letters and made a few straight forward business calls along the way.

His attitude was that he might as well feel ill at work rather than feeling sorry for himself at home. Come six o'clock, he was ready to go home. He tired easily and he'd had enough for one day.

Simon's Jaguar was parked in its usual space close to the front door, along with the other Executive's cars.

Driving in London always required a certain amount of confidence, the timid could spend hours getting nowhere. As the traffic built up, Simon was in no mood for hovering and to a blast of horns, pushed his car's nose into the busy stream of traffic.

For the first half mile he travelled under the massive concrete roadway that carried the A4 overhead, finally, the two queues merged as they pushed towards the city centre. As he'd emerged from under the covered roadway he noticed that it had started to rain, quite hard.

The four mile journey was soon over for another day as Simon shoehorned the Jaguar into the remaining resident's parking space outside his front door.

Wednesday morning dragged by with the usual trek to Whitechapel and back.

That afternoon he tried to occupy his mind with the latest edition of 'The Grocer', essential reading for anyone and everyone in the retail food business.

With his train leaving early for York the next morning, he didn't sleep much that night. All he could think about was his meeting with Nick. What the hell do you say to a brother you've never met?

The next morning Simon's taxi arrived at Kings Cross in plenty of time for his train. He meandered around the station concourse, bought a take-away coffee and The Times newspaper.

There was hardly any seating around the station so he leant on a pillar and sipped his coffee. In no time at all the message on the departures board changed from 'on time' to 'boarding'.

The train to Edinburgh was sitting on platform 7, waiting to take Simon on the next part of his journey. He made his way to coach H First Class, immediately behind the engine a dirty Intercity 225 locomotive. Simon managed to fill the couple of hour's journey between London and York by reading his paper and staring at the countryside passing by.

At York he had a long walk to the bridge that crossed to the station's exit, he was unimpressed to find the queue for the taxi rank snaked into the distance. He had no option but to take his place and wait. He hated queuing. It was about twenty minutes before he was climbing into the front seat of a silver coloured Ford Mondeo, giving the rotund driver his destination.

"I need to get to a farm near Stillington please," he asked.

"Ok? No problem," answered the driver. The car pulled away, heading under the city walls and over Lendal Bridge that crossed the River Ouse.

"That's impressive," said Simon, looking towards York Minster, framed by the car's windscreen.

"Aye sure is. I drive by that often, I don't really notice it anymore," said the driver.

"I suppose that's often the case," said Simon. "When you live somewhere you just ignore all the tourist attractions. It's like that for me in London. There's loads of places I've never even been."

Simon wasn't really in the mood for small talk but was keen to keep his mind off the encounter ahead.

A mile or so further on, Simon looked across at a massive factory on his right that seemed to go on for as far as the eye could see.

"Is that chocolate I can smell?" He asked.

"Aye, Chocolate. That's Rowntree's. You can always smell it, more so when the weather's warm. They say you can eat as much as you like when you work there," replied the driver smiling.

"That must cost them a fortune," said Simon imagining how profits would fall if his own staff helped themselves.

"No. They say that after eating as much chocolate as you like for a week, you never want to touch it again. They found it was the best way to prevent staff from helping themselves," he laughed.

Simon envisaged it taking longer to get to Stillington, but fifteen minutes later they were there.

"Now where do you want to be?" The driver asked.

"I don't really know," admitted Simon. "The address is Chestnut Farm, apparently it's on the Easingwold Road."

"Ok, we'll have a look," said the taxi driver as they headed out of the village. After a mile they'd passed two farm entrances and stopped at each to try and read the signs, then, they came to the third on the right.

The brick gateposts bore a smart black wrought iron sign bearing the name *'Chestnut Farm'* in gold leaf with a chestnut tree painted in its centre. "This must be it," said Simon. The driver pulled onto the long, gravelled driveway that led up towards the farmhouse.

As the house and farmyard came into view, Simon was quite impressed with the place. He thanked and paid the driver, taking a business card from him so that he could summon him back when he was ready.

Simon took a deep breath. He didn't want to look nervous but on the inside butterflies filled his stomach.

As he stepped out of the car he saw a man emerging from a farm building across the yard. Surely that couldn't be Nick Brown?

"Can I help you?" the man called out in a strong Yorkshire accent.

"I'm looking for Nick Brown," replied Simon. The man turned back to face the building he'd just come from and shouted. "Nick, there's a fella here to see yer." Ten seconds later another figure emerged. *'That's him,'* thought Simon.

"Morning, are you Simon Elliott by any chance?" Nick asked, as he strode across the yard, not sounding particularly excited about the idea.

"Yes, hello." Simon held out his hand. Nick kept his hands in his coat pockets. Simon lowered his.

"I don't know what's so important you'd trek all the way up here but you'd best get on with it, I've got work to do," said Nick.

"Yes, this is difficult. Is there somewhere private where we can talk?" Simon asked, not relishing the idea of anyone overhearing the conversation.

"Aye, I suppose so. This way." Nick led Simon over to the house. He walked into the kitchen with his wellington boots still on. He picked up the kettle and began to fill it.

"Don't worry about your shoes in here," Nick said. "We're in and out all day. You'd best sit down." He said gesturing towards a gnarled old kitchen chair.

"Is coffee okay for you?" Nick said as he poured the hot water over the instant granules.

"That would be great," smiled Simon trying to be as friendly as possible. "I know you have a strong dislike for TayMarts which, looking at it from your side of the fence, I completely understand."

"Dislike?" Nick questioned. "That's an understatement! You've spent years trying to grind us into the ground.

Your tight-fisted approach resulted in my Brother taking his own life, that's something that's *not* going to be forgotten."

"Look, can we just put that behind us for just a minute? I've got something to tell you that's going to be very difficult for me to say and you to understand," said Simon bluntly.

"If you think you can walk all over me with your bullying tactics you can think again. From now on, the AFA's the one that's going to call the shots," argued Nick.

"Please, this is very difficult for me; just forget about TayMarts and farming for a moment," Simon pleaded.

"Forget about it!" You must be crazy, replied Nick staring Simon in the face.

"Yes, please. What I'm about to tell you, you're going to find hard to believe. I'm finding it hard to grasp myself," replied Simon.

"Well. What the hell is it?" Nick asked. "Come on, spit it out."

"I don't know how to say this, I really don't," said Simon faltering.

"Just bloody say it. I haven't got all day," urged Nick.

"Ok." Simon paused. "I'M YOUR BROTHER!"

There was a moment's silence. Then Nick laughed hysterically. "You must be a brave man to make jokes like that. I'm not sure I get it," he said.

"I'm not trying to make jokes. I am your brother, I don't know how else to tell you," replied Simon earnestly.

"Don't be so bloody silly. You did just say what I think you said, didn't you? If you've come all the way here to play some daft joke on me you can get out now, my brother's dead, as you know." Nick was losing his temper now.

"I'm absolutely serious. I am your brother. I know it sounds ridiculous, but it's true." Simon reiterated. "Will you just listen, please, I only found out myself on Monday," he went on, trying to appease Nick.

"I haven't time for this, you're talking utter rubbish." Nick made to leave.

"I'm sorry, but you need to listen to what I have to say, now sit down. Please," said Simon grabbing hold of Nick's arm.

Nick reluctantly sat down and drew a cigarette from the gold packet in his jacket's top pocket. He lit it with a cheap plastic lighter and leant on the table.

"Get on with it then, I'm a busy man."

Simon began. "I haven't been very well for a few years but recently it got much worse. I've got chronic kidney disease."

"That's a shame," said Nick sarcastically.

"A week ago, I believed I had a family in Salisbury, including a brother called Ralph. The doctors tested Ralph to see whether he'd be able to donate a kidney to me.

He was supposed to be the best choice, being my brother, or so we thought. Trouble is, when the results came back, he was unsuitable, because he wasn't my brother."

"So where do I fit into all this?" Asked Nick, who had now calmed down a bit.

"The hospital checked the DNA database to try and find me a match, and they found it. A perfect match with someone else, your brother James," spluttered Simon.

"Well he can't save you, you've killed him already. Ironic really isn't it?" The relationship between them still hadn't clicked in Nick's mind.

"I never killed him," replied Simon. Anyway, don't you see what I'm saying? If he was my brother, so are you."

Nick paused for a moment as the meaning behind these words began to dawn on him. He'd begun to realise that Simon couldn't possibly be making all this up, he wouldn't dare.

"I can't get my head round this," said Nick. "How can you be sure? Knowing the NHS, they've probably messed up the tests."

"They explained it to me, they reckon there's a 90% chance we're full siblings. They don't like to say 100%, but listen, enough of that for a minute. What I can't understand is this, if I *am* your brother, how come no one knows about it? Surely you'd know if you had a missing brother?"

Nick looked decidedly shaken. "My God - you must be Jack! But you couldn't be. No you just couldn't be."

"I'm Simon, who the hell's Jack?" asked Simon. Nick paced slowly up and down in deep thought.

"Nick, answer me. I said who's Jack?"

"He was our brother," Nick replied. Little Jack, we lost him a long time ago."

"What do you mean, you *lost* him?" Exclaimed Simon.

Now it was Nick's turn to sit down and explain things.

"How old are you?" Said Nick curiously.

"I'm 48 years old," replied Simon.

"Aye, that'd work. Jack was a couple of years younger than me and I'm 50 now. Back in 1949 we all went on a holiday, a cruise round the Mediterranean. We stopped at various places, one of which was Limassol in Cyprus. Jack disappeared from the market place and was never seen again. That was 45 years ago," explained Nick.

"This week, my Father, or the man I thought was my Father told me he found me in Cyprus," said Simon.

"*Found* you? What do you mean found you?" Quizzed Nick.

"I haven't had the nerve to visit my so-called Father yet for the full story, I've only had a short telephone conversation with him, so I only know the rough facts," replied Simon.

"I told you it was important that I met with you," he added.

Nick took out another cigarette and offered one to Simon.

"No thanks, I don't smoke," he said, wondering if now might be a good time to start the conversation around the possibility of Nick becoming a donor. Hearing a car pull up on the gravel outside they both looked out.

"It's my wife, Sarah." Nick paused. "Well, this'll be interesting."

The door opened, and Sarah glanced around.

"Hello," she said. "Business meeting is it?"

"No," said Nick.

"You shouldn't be smoking in here" she said to Nick. "You know the children don't like it." Nick wasn't really listening. He was deciding on his next choice of words.

"This is my wife Sarah. Sarah, this is Simon Elliott from TayMarts." Sarah's smile left her face as she reluctantly shook his hand.

"And what do TayMarts want with us now? Surely you've done enough damage," she said scornfully.

Simon and Nick looked at each other both struggling with the uncomfortable atmosphere in the room.

"I have found something out that's been a bit of a shock, taken the wind out of my sails so to speak. Turns out Simon here is my brother," said Nick.

"Yeah right," said Sarah looking bemused. "Either of you want another cup of tea?"

"Did you hear what I just said? Simon is my *brother*, your brother-in-law!" Nick said at the top of his voice.

"What on earth are you talking about? Have you two been smoking something you shouldn't?" Sarah replied flippantly.

For a moment she wasn't sure whether to smile or not. Simon stepped in and broke the silence.

"It's true Sarah. I'm afraid, it turns out I'm a Brown."

"And how have you come to that ridiculous conclusion?" Sarah said arrogantly.

"I think you'd better sit down," said Simon as he began to repeat the same conversation he'd had with Nick only a few minutes earlier.

When it was over, Sarah was speechless.

"Unbelievable," she said, talking directly to Nick. "I mean really. Are you trying to tell me that your brother could go missing years ago and then end up, with you as one of his customers? I mean, it's a bit farfetched, don't you think? Not forgetting he just happens to be working for a supermarket at the other end of the country, that co-incidentally wants to hammer us into the ground and close us down."

"I am still in the room," Simon interjected. He was starting to feel a bit irritated and it showed. "I know it sounds utterly improbable, but that's the way it is and we're all going to have to deal with it one way or another. It's not just going to go away."

"Mother always said Jack would come back," said Nick in a much calmer voice. "And God knows what Father would have thought if he'd known you were the one trying to put us out of business.

"I didn't take this job just to spite you and it was never to 'put you out of business' as you say. We were just doing what every business does, trying to maximise our profit. The more competition that appears, the more our prices need to be competitive. Let's face it I'm not exactly thrilled with the situation myself. I've had most of my life stolen from me and I want to find out the truth," said Simon as he rinsed out his coffee cup.

"Simon, I mean 'Jack's' right. We all need to try and get on now, if he really is your brother," said Sarah trying to make sense of the situation.

"It's *Simon*," he said correcting her. "I don't think I could get used to being called Jack at my age."

"Get on with each other that's a laugh, after all that's happened with James and everything. You can't just brush it all under the carpet. I'm still finding all this hard to take in," said Nick grimly as he turned towards Simon. "I need time to get my head round it, work out what the hell we do now. Our Mother's still alive – did you know," said Nick.

"No I didn't. I'd read that Father had died. God, it feels strange even saying it. Where is Mother?" enquired Simon.

"She's been stuck in a nursing home in Haddington since Father's death," Nick replied.

"It's about 20 miles from Edinburgh, that's where we originate from. That's where you're from too. You don't even remember, do you though?" Nick replied.

"I know quite a bit about your farms. It's funny to think I'm actually Scottish, I always thought I was a born a Greek, not quite the same is it," Simon answered back.

"And there's Liz to take into account. She'll need to know about this," said Sarah butting in.

"Who's Liz?" Simon asked curiously.

"My sister, sorry I mean *our* sister," said Nick. "She's the youngest. She's a couple of years younger than you. Don't you remember anything?"

"No. I sometimes had fleeting memories of being on a big ship, but I couldn't place it. I just thought it was with my family. I mean, the Elliot's. Maybe that was a different ship, I just don't know anymore. I can't believe you're telling me I've got a sister as well. Is Liz in Scotland too?" Simon said curiously.

"No. She moved years ago. She lives in the middle of London," replied Nick.

"I could have been living round the corner from her. I've lived in London since I was 19. Anyway, I've got to get back there tonight, I have to be at the hospital first thing in the morning," Simon said wearily.

"Why?" asked Sarah. Simon then had to explain how he needed dialysis three times a week just to keep going until a suitable donor could be found. Nick listened intently to Simon's story again as he explained it to Sarah.

Nick had been bowled over with everything he'd just found out. The fact that Simon needed a kidney transplant and that *he* may be a perfect donor hadn't even crossed his mind yet. He was so confused, for years he'd often dreamt that his brother Jack would just walk in. In the back of his mind he'd long since resigned himself to the fact that Jack was dead.

It seemed ironic that for the last few years he'd battled with Simon Elliott and TayMarts supermarket and following James death, really grown to dislike Simon. Now he wanted to celebrate the fact that Jack was back, but how could he get over the fact that Jack, or *Simon* as he now was, had driven James to his death? Nick knew he was going to have to deal with the situation, however uncomfortable it felt. If Simon really *was* his brother Jack, he needed to sort his confused feelings out, but it wouldn't be instant. Could he even do it at all? He just didn't know.

"I'll call a taxi," said Simon, "I'd better be on my way and give you both time to take all this in."

"No, there's no need for a taxi, I'll drive you back to town." said Nick willingly.

"Why don't you stay for a bite to eat?" Sarah asked, trying to bring a bit of sociability into the situation.

"That's very kind," said Simon. "But I need to catch the 5.30 train back to London. I've time for another drink though, if you're offering."

"Aye," said Nick. "This time I need something a bit stronger. Do you fancy a glass of malt? You are Scottish, after all."

"I wondered why I always had a liking for the stuff. My doctor wouldn't approve. But go on then; I suppose a small one wouldn't hurt," replied Simon.

"How we're going to tell Mother I really don't know," said Nick "It could finish her off."

"Maybe when the time comes," said Simon, "we could go together. If I just turned up alone I don't think she'd believe me."

"Aye, well we'll see. Now, we'd best get you back to the station," said Nick draining the last drops of whisky from his glass.

"Well, if you're sure Nick," Simon replied.

"Yes, it's funny, I didn't want anything to do with you or bloody TayMarts before you arrived. Now I haven't any choice. I've got to get used to the fact you're my brother. I haven't forgotten what you did to James though... It's going to take time," said Nick solemnly.

"Don't you think I wish I could have handled things differently too? I don't think you can blame me entirely for his death, I was just running a business," said Simon. "I'm sure the banks played a large part in it. Anyway, can we please leave all that for now? We've all got a lot more things to think about?"

"Alright, let's get going. I'll get the car," said Nick reaching for his car keys.

As they drove back to the station the atmosphere in the car had been thick with unspoken tension. Both men had had their lives turned upside down and their future paths were uncertain. They were both pleased the journey was nearly over.

Once at the station, they attempted a forced hand shake and agreed they'd talk in a couple of days after they'd all had time to come to terms with their new circumstances. Nick pulled away from the station feeling remarkably calm, which surprised him. He'd thought that if he'd ever met this Simon Elliott, he'd kill him, and, if he ever found Jack it would be the best day in his life. Now he'd met them both and never in his wildest dreams could have believed they'd be one and the same.

Back at Chestnut Farm, Nick found Sarah sitting in the kitchen where he'd left her. "I've been sat here mulling the situation over and over. What are we going to do?" She asked as Nick appeared in the open doorway.

"What do you mean, what are we going to do? What else is there to do? We're going to get on! Life's thrown us a curved ball and we're going to straighten ourselves out and get on," said Nick emphatically.

"What about the Association? You're going to find it difficult to fight TayMart's over prices when your brother's one of their top men," said Sarah worriedly.

"I think he's taking a back seat from all that. He doesn't seem too well," replied Nick.

"You'll have to ring Liz as soon as possible. She ought to be told," said Sarah.

"I know I'm going to call her tonight. Just give me time to get my thoughts together," said Nick kicking his shoes off.

"Maybe my alarm will ring in a minute and I'll wake up from this nightmare!" Nick pulled his wellingtons on and headed out to the fold yard. He spent the next half an hour helping Terry shovel mud from the shed's entrance whilst explaining the story of his lost brother who'd just shown up on the doorstep. Terry, unsurprisingly, found it all hard to believe.

Simon didn't have long to wait at York Station, which he was glad about, the wind certainly could blow down the open ended platform.

Relaxing in his window seat, Simon rested his head on the Antimacassar cloth that was placed over the back of the seat and closed his eyes.

His mind was awhirl going through the things he'd learnt in the last couple of weeks. Not only had he got a mother to see he never knew he had, he'd now have to go down to Salisbury and see the family he thought were his, how would that be? Not comfortable, that was for sure.

As the train pulled into Kings Cross Station Simon stood up, took his jacket from the luggage rack above and pulled it on. He made his way to the doors with the train still a few hundred yards from the platform. Over the years he'd learnt that by getting off first, with the First Class coach at the front of the train, he had a good head start to the taxi rank.

Any hanging about and the queue for cars rapidly grew as hundreds of like-minded passengers would head the same way. A few moments delay in getting there quickly could lead to a half hour wait.

Simon was soon climbing the steps to his front door and felt ready to put his feet up. The following morning, as he stood in his bathroom brushing his teeth, he stared at the man looking back at him from the bathroom mirror, not really sure who he was, it was a strange feeling.

He pondered the string of events that had unwound before him. Meeting Nick and Sarah and finding out that he also had a sister was far too much to take in on top of having to continue with his treatment.

Today meant another tedious trip to the hospital to lie in that bed hooked up to that infernal machine that whined on hour after hour. Each appointment felt like he'd just got unhooked from it and here he was again heading back.

By the time he'd had a couple of cups of coffee he'd managed to get a grip of himself and fell easily into his usual routine.

CHAPTER 25

O nce again lying on his hospital bed, his head was swimming with thoughts that he just couldn't compartmentalise into any sensible order. Simon wanted to clear his mind and focus on some sort of plan he always prided himself in having a good reliable plan for every occasion. But this was different.

Focus, for god's sake, you know you need to, he told himself. By the time his session was over he'd decided that he needed to go south and talk to his 'adopted father', he didn't know what else to call him. He needed some answers before he contemplated meeting his real mother. An old woman who'd probably given up hope of seeing her son after nearly half a century, it would be a major shock.

Everything Simon did would have to be done fast. This wasn't just his way of going about things but down to the fact he was no longer a well man. He needed to fit everything in between his dialysis sessions and even then, he never felt good these days. Without a transplant he knew he didn't have long to live. Having met Nick he'd tried to put the problem to the back of his mind, he hadn't the first idea how he could even broach the subject of asking him for help, and it just seemed an impossible situation. At least Nick hadn't disowned him completely, Simon knew he'd had good reason to.

That weekend Simon had made the journey back down to Salisbury to have it out with his parents face to face. He wanted to know what the hell they had been were thinking.

They'd known he'd be coming ever since his call had shattered their normally uneventful lives. Simon's taxi pulled into the horseshoe driveway that had once looked pristine, but now bore cracks and scars where weeds had fought their way through the joints, towards the light. The car stopped right outside the front door. Simon thanked the driver and handed over a twenty pound note.

"Keep the change," he said briskly.

As he was about to knock on the front door of the house he took in a deep breath, he wasn't looking forward to this meeting, and he wasn't alone. The atmosphere inside the house was heavy. Ralph had gone out and left Alex and Louise fretting alone. Alex looked different, the usual authoritative look of a Major had been replaced by a sheepish look that barely hid the worries he'd got bubbling up inside. Louise hovered behind in the hallway.

"Come in son, please," she uttered quietly.

"Do you want a cup of tea?" Enquired Louise, whatever the occasion, somehow the English always felt a cup of tea would help the situation along.

"Might as well," replied Simon abruptly. The three of them moved through to the conservatory at the back of the house and took their seats as though a formal presentation was about to be unleashed upon them.

"Well," said Simon. "I'm not sure where to make a start."

"I think I should set the record straight," Alex said in a hushed tone. "I know you must be feeling very angry Simon but we never set out to cause all these problems. It just sort of happened. One thing led to another and, well, here we are."

"I want to know what happened," demanded Simon. "I know you've told me on the phone, but I want to hear it face to face. I mean you don't just go out and come back with someone else's child. Normal people don't do that sort of thing."

"It wasn't really like that," replied Alex trying to find the strength within him. "If you give me a few minutes I'll try and explain. After the war I was stationed in Malta for a couple of years, 1946 to 1948, your Mother," he paused, "Louise and I married in 1945 and she didn't want to be left alone in England for two years whilst I was living overseas, so she joined me. We wanted children and kept trying, but, no luck. Then, in March 1948, I got the message that I was to be moved to Cyprus.

There were Internment Camps on the island and they were growing in size by the week, they needed to bolster the forces there. So off we went. Got a little two bedroom apartment near the camp at Famagusta. The place was massive, there were thousands of British and allied soldiers there, it was incredible.

The British were intercepting Jews who were desperate to get to Palestine but the Brits would only let about 1,500 a week in, the rest remained in the camps. Anyway, as I told you, early in June 1949 this young couple turned up with a small boy. That would be you. They tried to pass you off as their own but you didn't fit in. They didn't have any papers either."

"You should have reported this to someone, surely there were procedures?" Simon questioned.

"We were going to, but... Your Mother."

Louise had hardly said a word, she looked drained and washed out. Clearly, she hadn't slept much in the preceding days finally she broke into the conversation.

"When your Father arrived home with you, you were crying. As soon as you sat on my knee you stopped, it just felt right. By the following morning I'd decided we should keep you. I know it sounds silly now, but at that moment it seemed the right thing to do. You couldn't help us find your real family, you didn't understand what had happened."

"Didn't I want to go home to my parents?" Simon said quietly.

"To be honest, by the second day you seemed happy enough with us. It made it all the easier. Louise was happy which made me happy," interrupted Alex.

"What happened next?" Simon was feeling edgy.

"The next year we were moved again, to Athens this time. By now it was just normal; we were another happy family. No one ever questioned it," explained Alex.

Simon was hungry for information; he wanted to know everything there was to know. The three of them talked for another hour with Simon asking countless questions as if interrogating a couple of criminals. Alex and Louise were trying to explain the circumstances in as much detail as they could.

"I've got to decide what to do now," Simon said, having heard enough. "Really, I should tell the authorities and walk away, but I can't, you've seen to that. The trouble is, to me, you're all I really know as family, I'm not sure I'd feel better if you were both locked up."

"I know it's going to be hard," said Alex "But we'll do whatever we can to make things right. We love you and we don't want to lose touch with you. Your brother Ralph would be devastated if you were to just go. If you want me to go to the police, I will, if it helps," pleaded Alex.

"What's the point? It's too late now anyway." said Simon.

"I know it was wrong, but we can't turn back the clock. We've told Ralph what happened and he's shell shocked too, that's why he's not here. He wanted to see you on your own, a bit later," explained Alex.

More apologies followed before Simon decided it was time to head back to London.

"I hope we'll see you later," said Alex.

"We'll see..." Simon left it at that.

Back home Simon needed to get his head together before he could face visiting his real mother, a lady he hadn't seen for 45 years.

Back in Yorkshire Nick and Sarah had been trying to get used to the idea that Simon was 'Jack' and how it would change their lives. Nick had telephoned Liz the same night to reveal the news. It was one of those difficult calls, Nick had thought of many ways to tell her but there was no use rehearsing, he would just have to dive in and see where the conversation headed.

Liz had answered the phone after three rings, an efficient office habit she'd become used to.

"Hello."

"Hi Liz, its Nick, have you got a minute?"

They exchanged the usual rally of greetings before Nick threw his 'bombshell' into the ring...

"Your brother Jack's turned up."

"Sorry, Nick I don't think I heard you right, Jack who?" Liz replied.

"Our brother, Jack, he's turned up."

"Don't play games Nick; it's not the sort of thing you should joke about. It's not funny at all," she replied.

"I'm serious Liz; he's been here today, sitting in my kitchen not two foot from me," Nick blurted.

"Bloody hell Nick he can't be. Surely he's dead."

Liz was shocked, she was too young at the time to remember Jack at all, but she'd grown up knowing that her brother had vanished. Like the rest of the family she'd assumed he must be dead. She, like Nick never thought he'd be back and now, wasn't sure what emotions were flooding through her.

"I thought he was dead too, but if this guy's right, he says he's our brother. His story's pretty convincing. He's called Simon Elliott and lives in London, like you," Nick said.

"My god, I can't believe it," Liz replied.

"It gets worse, we know this man," added Nick.

"You're confusing me now, what do you mean you know him?" replied Liz.

"He works for TayMarts, the supermarket that we supply. He's one of the ones that drove James to his death," Nick said harshly. After a long and involved conversation trying to explain who was who, and what was what, Nick replaced the receiver and lit yet another cigarette.

The week was only going to get harder. Nick had agreed with Sarah the night before that he would drive to Scotland and see his mother, alone.

He couldn't risk phoning her with the news as he didn't know how she'd take it. He finished the mug of black coffee that was his only breakfast and picked up his small canvas overnight bag and threw a few essentials in. He knew that even if he didn't need to stay and look after Florence, he'd probably have to stick around for Jill who would also need to know the news.

Sarah waved him off on this trip that he'd made so many times before but this time it was for a different reason. As he headed up the A19 towards Thirsk, he looked over towards Sutton Bank where the giant chalk white horse stared back at him.

It had stood silently on the same hillside surveying the Vale of York since the mid nineteenth century. It was mid-afternoon when Nick swept into the driveway of Woodside, the gravel scattering as he turned sharper than he probably should have.

Jill had seen the car approach and peered out of her kitchen to see who the visitor was. She was somewhat surprised to see her brother-in-law stepping out and immediately worry crossed her mind.

'Why would Nick turn up unannounced unless there was bad news?' She thought to herself. By the time she got the back door open, Nick was almost there. The look on his face was expressionless which in itself gave him a look of concern.

"Hello Jill, how are you? Are you managing ok?" He gave her a gentle hug and kissed her cheek.

"I'm fine thanks, what's up? Someone hasn't died have they?" She asked curiously.

"What sort of a welcome is that? No, they haven't, quite the opposite actually. Can I come in?" Nick replied.

"Yes, I'm sorry. I just thought, seeing you here, there must be something up. Not that I'm not pleased to see you. Do you want a cuppa?" She said filling the kettle.

"Aye, that'd be great. I do have some news as it happens, I think you'd best sit down," he said warning her.

"What is it?" She said as she carried on making the tea.

"I'll let you make the tea first." Nick changed the subject to the usual 'How are the children doing and how's the farm,' until she'd finished brewing up and sat at the kitchen table opposite him.

Since Nick had last seen Jill, she seemed to have aged a lot. The stress of losing her husband had certainly hit her, and the children hard. Nick knew his news would rock the boat again and would rather not have had to tell her but he knew he had to.

"Come on then. Spill the beans." She smiled, hoping that the news might be good for once.

"I'm not sure how to put this, and before we start, no I'm not making it up," said Nick.

"What is it? You're worrying me now," said Jill.

"It's my brother Jack. He's turned up," blurted Nick.

"Whose brother Jack?" Jill replied nervy.

"My brother Jack your brother–in–law. The same brother Jack that disappeared in 1949 on our Mediterranean cruise."

"No, I don't believe it," Jill muttered.

"Well I can't say I did at first, but his story stacks up but that's the easy bit. You won't believe who it is." Nick had stood up now and was slowly pacing up and down the long Woodside kitchen.

"What do you mean, *who it is*? You've just told me it's Jack." Jill was more curious than ever now.

"Yes, but Jack has another name now, the one and only Simon Elliott from TayMarts."

"Jack is Simon Elliott! They're one and the same person," Nick blurted out.

"No. He can't be. No. Not him. I don't believe you," said Jill frantically.

"That's what we all said." Nick was agitated at having to go over it all again.

"I won't let it be him," Jill was angry. "Why was he so horrible to James and you, if he knew you were his brothers?"

"That's just it. He didn't. He's as shocked as we all are, he had no idea, or at least he says he had no idea. He never even knew his parents weren't his real parents. He turned up a couple of days ago and told us the story. I couldn't ring you, I had to come and tell you, and Mother," Nick replied.

"Have you seen her yet?" Jill asked anxiously.

"No. I thought I'd better come here first. I'm going there next." Nick looked more worried as the full impact of what he still had to do was brought once again to the forefront of his mind.

"I don't know what to think. But for your poor Mother to find her son now, after a lifetime of thinking he was lost for good. That's awful," said Jill looking forlorn.

"It is and it isn't. At least she'll see her son again. She's bound to be relieved to know the truth. I just wish it hadn't been Simon Elliott, I hated that man. Why did it have to be him?" Nick said regrettably.

"You say 'hated', have your feelings changed somehow?" Jill asked curiously.

"They're going to have to. I still can't come to terms with it. I know he contributed to James' death, and I hate him for that, but he's my brother too. I just don't know what to think anymore. For years I just wanted Jack to come back, and now he has," said Nick gloomily.

"Well if I clap eyes on him he's going to wish he'd stayed away," said Jill harshly. She was unforgiving.

"I know this is hard Jill, but we've got to get round this, he's your brother-in-law too," said Nick trying to sound positive.

"Your Mother's going to need some support. Do you want me to come with you?" Jill asked hopefully.

"No, thanks, I'd best do this on my own. You're right though, she's not going to find this easy, but on the other hand it might do her good. She can finally put her mind at rest."

Nick then spent the next half an hour explaining to Jill all the details that Simon had told him, including the fact that he was unwell.

The whole situation was going to take some getting used to. They normally led lives that proceeded at a steady pace, with their ups and downs. Now the whole family had been shaken to the core.

Nick asked Jill if he could stay the night at Woodside as he didn't fancy tackling another four hour drive back to Yorkshire that night. He was tired from two nights lying awake and was worried he'd drop asleep at the wheel.

"Of course you can, you don't have to ask. I'll happily make up the spare bed for you. It'll be ready when you get back," said Jill.

It was only a ten minute drive to the Manor House nursing home on the edge of Haddington, long enough for Nick to smoke two more cigarettes whilst trying to keep calm and collected for the task that lay ahead.

The nursing home looked quite appealing on the outside, like an upmarket country house hotel. The grey walls were a bit dreary, but they always looked freshly painted.

The rolling gardens were well tended and a groundsman was energetically raking up leaves as Nick pulled through the gates. He parked under the overhanging branches of a beech tree, next to an old looking Vauxhall that had so many bird droppings on its roof, it had almost changed colour.

The reception desk was unmanned, and Nick had to ring the small hand bell to get some attention.

"Your Mother's in her room Mr Brown. She's just had a wee bit of supper," said the duty nurse.

"Is it ok if I go in?" Nick enquired.

"Yes, you go right ahead," she replied.

He always tried to visit two or three times a year. He knew it wasn't really enough, but living so far away it was all he could manage. He gave three sharp taps to the door and let himself in. He didn't really expect a reply.

"It's only me, Nick, are you decent?" He called as he opened the door. Florence was 76 years old and had been living in this room for nearly nine years. She could only walk a few steps with the aid of a Zimmer frame, any further and she needed her wheelchair. She was sitting up in bed. A smile formed on her pale face as the sight of Nick registered.

"Hello Mum." Nick leant over the bed and gave her a kiss on her wrinkled cheek.

"Well this is a surprise," she said. "I didn't expect to see you for a while. How are you son?"

"I'm fine thanks, fine, how about you?" He replied.

"I'm okay, nothing much changes round here. Anyway, what's happening, anything fresh?" She always asked whether there was anything 'fresh' to report.

"Well I have got some news, big news," Nick said trying to sound upbeat.

"I hope it's good. I need cheering up; I get fed up stuck in here day after day," Florence replied.

"I'm not sure what you'll think. Now, what I'm going to tell you is going to be hard to grasp." Nick paused for a moment as if to calculate the best choice of words.

"It's our Jack. He's alive," he said, holding her hand.

Florence slumped back into her pillow her face looked as though she'd just seen a ghost. She just sat there, unable to respond, except for a solitary, "No."

"It's true; I've sat and talked to him," Nick responded calmly.

As Florence didn't say anything, Nick thought he'd better elaborate and proceeded to tell her about the man, Simon, who'd turned up on his doorstep claiming to be Jack.

A minute or two passed and Florence hadn't cried or screamed she just sat there stunned and motionless.

"Well aren't you going to say something?" Nick asked, trying to take the edge off the atmosphere that filled the room.

"I don't know what to say. I've waited for years. I always knew that one day, Jack would walk back in. I often thought about what I'd say and how I'd feel when it happened. Now you've told me I just feel empty. I think I'm happy, I mean, I want to be happy but it's been so long."

"Where is he?" She asked.

"He's living in London and has no memory of Scotland." Nick replied quickly. He had spared her the story of Simon's role in TayMarts and his contribution to James death. For the time being at any rate.

"I wish your Father had lived to see the day," she said sadly. Nick wondered if his father would have been so pleased having been involved with the supermarkets relentless battles over produce prices, would he have got over it? Florence carried on…

"What will I say when I see him? It's not right, a Mother losing her child for so long," she sighed.

"He was only 3 years old when I last saw him, he must be…" she tried calculating his age in her mind.

"He's 49 years old now Mother," Nick interjected.

"Yes. 49. I won't even recognise him. He's lived a lifetime without me. I am pleased he's okay, of course, but the biggest thing is the relief. The pain of not knowing. It's weighed on my mind for all this time," she said.

Nick was pleased she'd remained quite calm he hadn't known how she'd react. She seemed to be okay.

"When do you think he'll come and see me? He will come and see me won't he?" Florence said hopefully.

"Of course he will. I'm sure it won't be long he's as shocked as the rest of us. I think he just needs to get used to the idea for a few days."

Nick got them both a cup of tea and, from his jacket inside pocket he produced a small hip flask containing a fine single malt. He smiled at his mother, "This'll help," he said as he unscrewed the lid and poured a wee dram into each cup.

"Aye, that'll be nice, have you anymore where that came from? They don't like us drinking in here. I don't know why," she chuckled, "there's nothing else to do."

He stayed for another hour as they chatted about Jack's return along with Nick updating her on everything else. He then bid her goodnight and headed back to Woodside, reliving the conversation he just had. He was glad that was over. His mind was confused with the ups and downs of the past couple of days.

He'd got to choose his path, should he let Simon into his life after the troubles he'd caused or not?

His old Range Rover glided down the long single-track road that led to the three farms, the overgrown hedges scratching against the car's paintwork with a terrible screeching.

Nick wasn't bothered, the vehicle was just another farm vehicle and it had suffered plenty of abuse whilst carrying out its duties over the years.

Back at Woodside Jill had prepared a hearty stew with mash and dumplings a meal that Nick hadn't eaten in a long while. Along with a pint of stout he felt content, sitting in the same kitchen he'd eaten in so many times as a boy. It brought back many memories.

After they'd eaten, he telephoned Sarah to tell her how his mission had gone so far, telling her he'd be setting off early to drive back to York. Nick and Jill spent the evening sitting in front of the log fire chatting about everything and nothing, the conversation frequently turning back to the subject of Jack's unexpected return.

As the night had gone on, Jill seemed to be coming to terms with the situation. Finally, they bid each other goodnight and headed their separate ways. Nick woke early the next morning with the sound of cattle being brought into the yard.

He pulled his watch from the bedside table and squinted his eyes to try and read the time – 5:30 a.m. Nothing changed round here. Nick showered and dressed then made his way down to the kitchen where he was surprised to see Jill already up and about.

"Morning Jill," he chirped.

"I hope you slept well?" She enquired.

"I slept just fine thanks, like a baby. That bed is really comfortable," he replied.

"Can I get you some breakfast?" Jill asked standing by the toaster with two slices of bread waiting to be toasted.

"No thanks, I'm fine. I need to get back to Yorkshire before lunchtime. A coffee would be great though," he replied.

The roads were quiet and Nick was rolling back into the yard at Chestnut Farm just before 11 a.m. Now at 50 years of age, Nick was generally a fit man, however, every time he climbed the stairs or stepped from his car after a long journey, he felt his knees creak and his legs ached. He was happy to take a stroll around the yard to get his blood flowing.

CHAPTER 26

Simon had been back to work for a couple of days, trying to catch up with the work that had piled up in his absence. He found the whole process strange now, having discovered that he would undoubtedly have been on the other side of the fence if things had gone the way they were meant to.

He would have been another of the farmers fighting for better prices rather than the one trying to cut them down. And now, knowing his true family lay at the end of the business decisions taken by him and his team at TayMarts, Simon wasn't sure where his future lay. The never ending battle had lost its sparkle.

With his illness not likely to improve, Simon knew he may not have long left and needed to make some important decisions. The first thing that was clear to him was the need to see his biological mother. Although he really had no recollection of his real parents, an instinct was rising up from within him, urging him to find her.

On his scheduled Friday visit to The Royal London Hospital, Whitechapel, Simon had asked Dr Collinson what could be done to enable him to stay away for a few more days, as he didn't fancy the thought of travelling from London to Scotland and back in a day, even leaving the night before wouldn't give him much time.

"Well, there's a couple of things I can do for you Simon," she said. Dr Collinson knew what he'd been through and was always keen to help.

Over the time she'd known Simon she'd actually become quite fond of him, although as a professional she tried hard not to let it show.

"If you watch what you're eating and drinking, an extra day without treatment won't kill you," she predicted.

"That's good to know," Simon smiled.

"Still, the best option would be for you to have a session in The Royal Infirmary of Edinburgh. I can get you booked in. It'll be a nice change of scenery for you," she said.

"Yes, great. I can look out of a different window for a few hours!" Simon remarked.

"Do I detect a touch of sarcasm there? And watch those potassium levels, how many times must you be told?" She scolded.

"Yes, yes doctor, you know me," replied Simon smiling.

"Yes, that's what worries me," she answered.

Simon asked Dr Collinson to make the necessary arrangements for the following week. He'd decided to head to Edinburgh on the Tuesday morning and come back on Thursday, this would hopefully give him enough time to see his mother, the farms and take a quick look round his 'home' country.

Simon had called Nick and asked if it would be possible to visit his mother on the Tuesday evening. He wanted to know if Nick would travel up with him as he thought that arriving on his own might be a bit much for her. He didn't want to give her heart failure before he could talk to her. Nick agreed that it would be for the best if they went together. "If you're going by train, I could join you at York, and ride up with you," he suggested.

"That would be good of you," said Simon. "I could do with the support and besides, I haven't much idea where I'd be going when I get up there."

Simon told Nick that he'd take the mid-morning train from Kings Cross, this would avoid the early morning commuters' rush. This train was also cheaper although it did take a bit longer, calling at Stevenage, Grantham and Retford, as well as its usual stops, arriving in York just after lunch time.

"I'll get the tickets, so if you just jump on at York. I'll be in the First Class coach right behind the dining car near the back of the train," said Simon.

"First class, eh?" Said Nick "Us farmers usually sit in the 'cattle' section."

"I used to, but now I'm not so well I like a bit of comfort, and besides, TayMarts will be paying," replied Simon.

"Well I'm not going to argue with that. It'll be nice to get a few pounds back out of them," quipped Nick.

"See you on Tuesday then." Simon put the phone down and leant back in his chair.

Well, that was sorted he'd soon be heading north to the place it had all begun. On Tuesday morning, half an hour before his train was due to depart; Simon perused the magazines in WH Smith, looking for something to occupy him for the next few hours. He immediately dismissed the chat magazines featuring celebrities, most of whom Simon hadn't heard of. He was always amazed that anyone could really care whether some glamour model had been for a night out with some overpaid footballer or fancy pop star. Simon generally went for something like Private Eye or maybe one of the broadsheet newspapers; occasionally he'd pick up a car magazine, as like most men he had a quiet passion for the latest supercars.

Checking the departure board he could see he still had a quarter of an hour to kill. He picked up a coffee from the open fronted shop next door, as always, the temperature held in this cardboard cup was so high that he had to keep swapping it from hand to hand. Getting the cup close to his lips he realised that drinking it wouldn't be an option for at least ten minutes. The time soon passed and he made his way to the platform, still juggling the hot coffee with his newspaper.

He was pleased to see that coach H was one of the nearest. He found his seat, a forward-facing airline style seat and made himself comfortable. He folded the tray down in front of him and wondered why he'd bothered buying the coffee he was still carrying, he still hadn't drunk it and now he could have free coffee in a proper cup and saucer. With a sharp jolt the train lurched forward, pulling slowly away from the platform. He did his best to read the paper and after flicking through most of it he gave up and chose to watch the scenery pass by whilst his mind pondered the strange path that life had led him down.

A couple of hours later the train was slowing through the suburbs of York, clearly indicated by a large display of flowers that had been planted in four massive letters that spelled out the name across the railway embankment.

As it pulled towards the platform, Simon looked out for Nick who he hoped would be waiting. Sure enough, there he was. He stood tall wearing smart country style clothing consisting of a pair of brogues, brown slacks and a tweed double breasted jacket. As the train slowed to walking pace Nick had spotted Simon, signalling to him and acknowledged him. Once he'd helped an elderly lady remove her oversized case from the carriage door, he climbed aboard, his canvas overnight bag hung casually over his right shoulder. Simon stood up and greeted him with a decent handshake. There was no repeat of Nick shunning the gesture. The table opposite had just been vacated by a group of four business men and looked inviting compared to the seat Simon currently occupied.

"Nice to see you again," said Simon "Shall we sit there? – there's a bit more room." Nick pushed his bag onto the overhead luggage rack and slid into his seat. It had only been a couple of weeks since the two of them had discovered their true relationship and here they were with neither of them knowing quite where they stood in relation to the other.

An uneasy pressure still created an atmosphere that neither could see but both could feel. Nick knew it would be hard to drop his dislike for Simon, the TayMart employee that had caused his family so much misery, yet he knew how much he wanted to be friends with his long lost brother Jack. The fact that they were one and the same person made the whole thing hard to grasp.

With a long journey ahead, Nick didn't want to make things any harder than they already were so he decided to try and get on with his lost brother as best he could.

"So how's it going Simon? Last time I saw you, you were going down to see your so-called parents," Nick asked.

"Yes, that's right. I did go down to Salisbury. I wanted to try and get some answers. Find out how I ended up living the wrong life all these years," Simon replied.

"And did you, find out exactly what happened? That's a story I'd like to hear," Nick said curiously.

"Do you want the long version or the short version?" Simon laughed.

"Best make it the long one, I'm not going anywhere," Nick replied. Simon spent the next half an hour telling him the story of his parents, Alex and Louise, and how they came to have a new son called Simon.

"That's certainly some story," said Nick as Simon finished. "Your parents, well I'm sorry but they want locking up. They abducted you plain and simple. If they hadn't taken you we'd have all been together all these years, rather than fighting and James might have still been here." Inside Nick couldn't avoid the feeling of resentment and anger.

"I know, but when you've spent your life believing they're your parents, it's not easy to just see them get locked up. I know you're right but I don't think I could do it" said Simon.

"If William, our Father, was still around, he'd have made mince-meat out of them. He wasn't a man to be messed with. Ruined his life it did. Although he rarely mentioned it, we all knew that inside he was suffering. He always blamed himself for not finding you. He did everything he could, even hired a man to stay out there, but it just wasn't enough," said Nick. As the two chatted the miles away, Nick thought he could see more of Jack reappearing and his old adversary, Simon, drifting further away.

"So how did you end up farming in York when the rest of the Browns were left in Scotland? Did you fall out or something?" Simon asked bringing the conversation around.

"No," laughed Nick, "It was nothing like that. I just wanted to make it on my own. I didn't like the idea of just being spoon fed. I mean no offence to James, God rest his soul, but he just moved into Tanners and cracked on. That was his choice and that's fine, but it's not the way I wanted to go."

"So why did you choose York?" Simon replied.

"That was just by chance. Our mother, Florence, came from Norfolk which is where I went to look for a farm, it just didn't work out, I couldn't find anything suitable."

"How's that then?" Simon was probing.

"I spent a few days looking round various farms, but they weren't what I was looking for, so I headed back," said Nick.

As he recounted the chance meeting of Sarah on the train, his stop-over in York and his episode of appendicitis, he thought it sounded farfetched, meeting this beautiful girl and later marrying her. But, like Simon, his story was real. The stories continued, both of them trying to stay away from the strains of recent years where the Browns and the AFA had been in a never ending battle with TayMarts.

"How do you think *your*, or should I say *our* Mother will take it, me turning up after all this time?" Simon asked.

"I'm not sure. She seemed okay when I came to see her last week. I thought I'd better forewarn her. She was shocked, I mean who wouldn't be? But it was like she'd always known you'd come back. Whereas we all thought you were dead."

"That's nice," said Simon with a sly smile.

"Don't get me wrong, we always wanted you to come home, but after all those years, you've got to admit, it did appear to be unlikely. All this still seems somewhat surreal. And to think that we've been cursing each other over the last few years and didn't even know we were brothers! It all seems so futile now," said Nick feeling a bit remorseful.

The train ground to a halt at Edinburgh Waverly station, the brakes letting out a horrendous screech that made most of the passengers' wince. Nick knew the station like the back of his hand and led Simon out onto Princes Street. Between them they'd decided they should go and see Jill first, much as Nick had done the week before. Simon was well aware that Jill still held him responsible, at least in part, for driving James to his death. Nick had told him he may be safer to keep out of the way for now, but Simon had made it clear, he wanted to try and straighten things out with her.

He wanted her, and the rest of the Brown clan to understand that he had no knowledge of his early years and abduction, which, after all, wasn't his fault. He knew Alex and Louise were to blame for putting him in his current position but he couldn't help feeling some anger towards his birth parents who'd let the situation happen in the first place, letting a boy of three wander off in a crowded market place.

"Woodside - is it far?" asked Simon as they climbed into the back of the taxi.

"No, about half an hour," Nick replied.

"Haddington, please, towards Aberlady." Nick directed the driver, who nodded obediently.

"It's funny, I suppose the last time I was there would be the day we left for that cruising holiday as a family," said Simon.

"Aye, bloody long holiday," laughed Nick. "We were only supposed to be going for a cruise round the Mediterranean; you've been gone for 46 years!"

The atmosphere between them had become more relaxed as the journey progressed, and to an outsider they may have been two brothers who'd never been apart.

"I need to attend Edinburgh Hospital tomorrow Nick, is it easy to get to?" Said Simon feeling more at ease.

"Aye, it's on Lauriston Place, a few streets over there," replied Nick pointing across the driver's head. The car made its way down York Place and onto the London Road. As they left Edinburgh behind, Nick pointed out some of the local landmarks. They passed the turning for Musselburgh Racecourse which had been like their father's second home. Nick told Simon about William's passion for betting. As they got near to Woodside, Simon began to feel somewhat uncomfortable, a feeling that lay somewhere between excitement and nervousness. Would he have any memory of the place after all these years? Consciously he couldn't recollect any of it.

The A1 led down to Haddington. Nick leant forward and signalled the driver to turn towards Aberlady. "Left here please, and just stop for a moment, will you?"

Turning into a narrow country lane bordered by shoulder high hawthorn hedges, the taxi pulled up half onto the grass verge. Simon could see the corn fields that fell away down to three separate farms with the wide waters of the Firth of Forth beyond.

"These are the three family farms," indicated Nick. "The one to the left is Coates. That one, just visible beyond those trees is Tanners, James's farm but that's gone now of course." He didn't look directly at Simon as he made his point, "And there, in the centre is Woodside! What d'ya think?" He said proudly.

Simon wasn't really sure, his emotions were confused. "All this land," he gestured. "Is this all the Brown's?"

"Well, it was once, before TayMarts had their way," Nick said with menace in his voice.

"Can we leave that for now?" Asked Simon.

"Sorry, yes. Everything you see was once the Brown's land right down to the Firth. We lost around 300 acres when the banks foreclosed on Tanners after James' death. Woodside is still owned by Mother." Nick replied, looking out at the rolling landscape.

"Ok," Nick said to the driver, who slowly pulled back onto the road. "We need to be down to that farm in the middle."

A few minutes later, the car was pulling up outside this old farmhouse which had obviously seen better days. To Simon there was a definite familiarity to the place, even though he couldn't consciously recall being there. The slate roof overhung the walls that were now heavily overgrown with ivy.

The front door had been painted in black gloss which was now flaking away, and the two stone pillars either side that supported an open porch had moss covering their northern faces.

Woodside had been home to Jill and the children since they'd had to leave Tanners. It looked a good sized building but the grey pebble dashed rendering looked uninviting and in need of a fresh coat of paint.

Nick paid the taxi driver and swung the door shut behind him. The two brothers made their way over the thick gravel which made walking feel more like paddling through sand as it crunched beneath each step.

Nick pushed the front door open at the same time as knocking and calling out, "Jill, it's only me."

"This way Simon," he said as he made his way into the kitchen. Jill was there leaning over the sink, washing some pots left from lunch time.

"Hello Jill," said Nick. "This is Simon…"

She turned to face the pair who were making their way in. Nick barely managed to get his next sentence finished before the bowl she was holding whistled past his left ear, narrowly missing Simon who'd instinctively ducked down to his right. It smashed against the door frame leaving a gash in the paintwork.

No sooner had Jill let go of the bowl, she was then flying across the kitchen towards Simon who was still regaining his balance.

"You bastard!" She shouted. By now she was right in front of him with her hands hitting and thumping Simon's upper body which he was trying to protect with his arms shielding his face.

"How could you? How could you?" Her rage was swallowed up by her own crying that was pouring from deep within her soul.

Nick had quickly pulled her off Simon, her arms still flailing around. She slumped exhausted onto a kitchen chair with her head falling into her hands.

"Come on now Jill, calm down," said Nick.

"I'm sorry," said Simon. "Do you want me to leave?"

"Yes, get out!" Sobbed Jill.

"No," interrupted Nick. "This isn't going to go away. You're staying and Jill, you need to calm down. I'll put the kettle on."

Nick sat next to Jill who very slowly regained some composure.

"I'm sorry," said Simon again "I know you don't want to hear what I've got to say after all that's happened, but I want to try and make things better."

"How can they ever be better? James isn't coming back. You've seen to that," Jill shouted angrily.

"I know everyone blames me and yes, perhaps I didn't help matters but I never meant for him to, well, to do what he did. I was just doing my job. And now, now I know who he was I feel worse than I can ever describe. He was your husband, but he was also my brother," said Simon.

For the first time Jill raised her head from her hands and looked at him.

"Sorry for throwing a bowl at you," she murmured.

"That's ok, I'd probably have done the same thing, he replied."

"No, I'm sorry because it was one of my favourite bowls, and I missed." A whisper of a smile briefly crossed her face.

"I was joking. Nick, you'd best make that pot of tea," she said calmly. "I'm still shaking."

"I will if you promise to sit quietly and not throw anything else," replied Nick.

"Mm, now that I look at you I can see a bit of James in you, in your eyes," Jill said, looking back at Simon.

"Nick told me your story, all seemed a bit unlikely to me, you know, a bit farfetched," said Jill.

"I know, I didn't make this up, as far as I know, it's true, I am Jack, not that I remember him any more than you."

"What do we do now? None of this is right; I mean it's just not right," said Jill.

"I know Jill," replied Nick. "It's not the sort of thing you can prepare for we're just going to have to find a way to get on with things. First thing is I'm going to have to take Simon to see Mother – she's expecting us. God knows how she's going to react. She seemed fairly calm when I came up last week, I think if she's had time to think about it, she'll be alright."

Nick stood up, the chair letting out a screech as he pushed it under the table, pulled his jacket back on and suggested that they should be leaving.

"Do you mind if we use the Land Rover?" Asked Nick.

"No, you help yourself. The keys are in the usual place," Jill replied.

Nick opened one of the kitchen cupboard doors that had various bunches of keys hanging on the inside. He instinctively knew which was which and fished a set out.

Simon followed him as they headed on their way, Jill remaining alone, empty tea cup still cradled in her hands, staring into the distance in something of a trance.

The old Land Rover was parked under an open lean-too with a rusty tin roof, alongside an old tractor trailer laden with sawn logs.

"I'm not sure how well this old thing will go, if at all, it's been here as long as I can remember," said Nick.

He put in the key and turned the ignition. A couple of turns of the old diesel engine and it spluttered into life. There seemed to be enough straw in the foot well to fill an entire stable.

"This really is a taste of the country," smiled Simon.

"Aye even smells like it," laughed Nick. They headed off back up the drive, the old suspension revealing every pothole along the route. Luckily it wasn't far to the Manor House nursing home.

"Is this it then?" Simon asked as they pulled in. His nerves were turning his stomach. Even though he had little recollection of his mother or father, only flashbacks that had come to him in the last few weeks, he knew this was going to be a strange feeling for him and her.

"Come on," said Nick. "Let's get this over with. We might all feel better when you've talked to Florence."

Inside they were greeted by Staff Nurse Hart, one of the nurses on duty.

"Your Mother's waiting for you," she said smiling at Nick. "She's not eaten all day, not herself today. I've never seen her so on edge," she continued.

"Well, we're here now, can we go in?" Asked Nick.

"Aye, go on in," she replied.

Nick gave a couple of sharp knocks on the door at the same time as pushing it open.

"Only us," he said as if the pair of them visited every other day. Simon followed him in to be confronted by an old woman sitting in a high-backed armchair by the window.

"Hello Mother, I've brought Jack to see you."

"Hello," said Simon quietly.

Florence didn't reply straight away, just looked him up and down as though searching for a sign of familiarity to the little boy she'd last seen nearly half a century ago.

"Well step a bit closer Jack, let me take a look at you, my eyes aren't what they used to be." Simon moved closer. Both of them examined each other.

"Yes, Jack, you've grown a bit, but it's you alright. Aren't you going to give your Mother a hug after all this time?"

Something stirred deep in Simon's memory, he couldn't decide if he could remember her or whether there was just some natural magnetism, whatever it was he thought he knew her. Yes, this was his mother!

He leant forward and put his arm round her shoulders. He'd wondered if he'd cry or his mother would cry but it wasn't like that at all. The whole event was remarkably unemotional, probably due to the length of time that had passed. They may be mother and son but to all intents they were strangers.

"It's good to see you Mother, I bet you didn't think I'd be back," Simon said, trying to lighten the mood a little.

"I'm sorry Jack, I'm so sorry we left you behind, we never meant to, we just couldn't find you," Florence said quietly,

"I thought you'd come back, I always knew you were alive. I just wish your father had been here, he wouldn't have believed it. He thought you were… dead."

"Well I'm not, not yet anyway," said Simon light heartedly.

"If you don't mind, I'd like to know what you remember about that time. You see I don't remember it at all, I'd just like to know what happened," said Simon curiously.

Florence stared into the distance as she began to recount the story of their fateful summer holiday. Simon, or Jack as he was known to his family, sat on another chair and listened intently. Nick interjected with the odd comment when he'd remembered things. He was quite interested to hear the story which hadn't been told much over the years after all he was only 5 years old at the time. After about an hour, Florence had finished her tale which had left Simon feeling somewhat sorry for her. His parents had made a stupid mistake and spent the rest of their lives regretting and reliving it on a daily basis.

They weren't the criminals in all this - that was Alex and Louise. Florence had then wanted to know what had happened to Jack for the last 45 years, as any mother would. Simon explained that he couldn't remember much before he'd arrived in Athens. He gave Florence, and Nick, a quick run through where he'd been and how he'd ended up where he was now, leaving out some of the unfortunate interaction between him, James and Nick.

Half an hour later they were on their way, Simon had promised he'd be back to talk to his mother later, after all, they'd missed a lifetime together.

"Well I'm not going anywhere. It's rare I get to leave this Godforsaken room. Do you know how long I've been cooped up here?" She said in a matter of fact tone.

"No," said Simon.

"No, neither do I, but it's been a damned long time," she replied.

"You've been here since 1986 Mother, you said you liked it," said Nick.

"Well I might have done at first. But that was nearly 10 years ago," she snapped.

"Come on Simon, I mean Jack, we'd better be making tracks now, it's nearly tea time," said Nick.

As they made their way out of the room and along the corridor, Simon was the first one to speak.

"I'm glad I've got that over with," he said. "It's taken a weight off my chest."

"Aye, it went better than I thought it might," replied Nick.

That night they stayed at Woodside where, thankfully, Jill had calmed down. It was still going to take time for everyone to come to terms with things, Jill couldn't yet forgive Simon for his part in driving her husband to his death and Nick, although being civil, still had the same thoughts reverberating round his mind.

Simon had been thrown into a world he didn't really know and just felt like a fish out of water. That night he slept in the room he'd apparently had as a young boy. As he lay there he wasn't sure but thought just maybe, he remembered it.

By morning, looking around he was certain. Yes - he'd been here before! Simon explained that he didn't need breakfast but would welcome a lift into Edinburgh to attend his hospital appointment and maybe tomorrow pay one more visit to his mother before heading back down to London.

Nick borrowed Jill's car as he didn't fancy taking the rickety old Land Rover on a 40 mile round trip, he didn't think it was capable of getting there and back. He dropped Simon off outside the hospital, where he'd be for the next four hours.

Simon followed the signs through the hospital to the renal department, located on the first floor at the side of the building where he found a small curved reception desk and a waiting area. He was surprised that the nurse on duty seemed to know who he was.

"We don't get many new faces round here Mr Elliot," she said placing a tick by his name on her chart.

CHAPTER 27

Simon was shown into a ward with six beds, each separated by garish blue flowered curtains that formed individual cubicles, most of which were only partly closed revealing other patients being put through the same treatment that he'd grown so accustomed to.

"This is your bed," the nurse indicated. "Make yourself comfortable and we'll get you hooked up."

Simon hung his jacket over the back of the chair.

"I'll be back in a minute to get you sorted out," she said pulling the curtain shut behind her, the sound of her heels echoing across the room. Simon was soon hooked up to his machine and took the chance to mull over the events of the past couple of days. Circumstances had changed so fast he wasn't sure who he was, where he was going or what the future held for him, all he knew was that whatever had happened hadn't changed the underlying fact – he needed a kidney transplant, and soon. All this had begun in the search for a suitable donor, if he hadn't been ill, the truth would probably never have been discovered.

Now he knew he needed Nick's help but he still didn't know how he'd go about broaching the subject.

The two of them may now be on speaking terms but persuading him to donate a kidney was in a whole different league. He'd now met his one remaining brother, two sisters in law and his mother, the only member of his family he didn't know at all was his sister Liz who was in London.

'Maybe she'd be a suitable donor,' he thought to himself and then cursed himself for being so selfish.

'I've never even clapped eyes on her and I'm thinking like that, but maybe it's not my fault, the human mind is programmed for self-survival.' As thoughts

drifted in and out of his mind the time soon slipped away, and the day's dialysis was over.

Once he'd said his goodbyes he decided he'd like a look around Edinburgh, see a few of the sights. There was an almighty 'bang' just as he stepped through the front entrance.

"What the hell was that?" He asked a nurse who'd walked out beside him.

"Don't you know? It's the one o'clock gun – up at the castle."

"Do they do that all the time?" He asked.

"Every day, at one o'clock, except Sunday. You should go and take a look."

"Thanks, I think I'll do that," he replied. Simon could see the castle it didn't look far so he decided to walk it. It wasn't far but it was enough of a climb to leave Simon feeling as though he'd been on a marathon run, he wasn't as fit as he used to be.

He spent an hour looking around and learning a bit about the history. The gun he had heard had been fired daily at one o'clock since 1861 to provide ships in the Firth of Forth with an audible time signal to accompany the visual signal of the time-ball dropping at the top of the Nelson Monument. When he'd finished he wandered back down to the city centre and just took in some of the atmosphere, all the time trying to imagine living around these parts as a small boy.

By three o'clock he was ready to get back to Woodside and summoned himself a taxi. Nick and Jill were back at the house; Simon knocked on the door and waited for an answer. Jill appeared, dressed in black trousers, wellingtons and a Hunter jacket – she'd obviously been doing a few manual jobs around the farm.

"Ah, you're back. Best come in. Don't look so sheepish, I promise I won't throw any more pots at you," she smiled.

"That's a blessing," replied Simon, feeling that her mood was a bit better today. Nick was sitting in the kitchen with a Labrador at his feet with a mug of tea in one hand and a biscuit in the other.

"How did you get on then?" Nick asked.

Simon proceeded to give them both a quick summary of his 'day out' whilst sparing the medical details.

"I hope it'll be ok if I stay tonight. Will that be alright with you?" He said looking at Jill.

"Aye, it's fine. I'm getting more used to the fact that you're one of us now," she replied.

"Well that's very kind of you as I'd like to go and see Florence in the morning, before I go back south. I can call a taxi."

"No, I'll run you up there," said Nick. "I want to take a look at some of the fields on the south side of Coates."

"I'll cook supper for 8 o'clock, I hope you eat lamb?" Jill said rummaging about in the fridge.

"I like anything," said Simon "Although this bloody illness means I have to be very careful with some things."

"I'd like to have a walk round the farm if that's alright, see if it stirs any memories," he continued.

"You help yourself," said Nick. "Do you need a guided tour?"

"I don't want to be more of a pain than I already have been, but if you're not busy, that would be great," Simon replied.

"No, I've nothing much to do. Give me five minutes and I'll get my boots on. I'd better see if we've any to fit you, what size are you?" Asked Nick.

The two of them spent the next hour and a half wandering from Woodside to Tanners and Coates. Simon thought he recognised certain things but couldn't be sure. He'd only been young when he left but he did used to play round there. The old fold yard at Woodside surrounded by stables with their burgundy painted doors certainly seemed familiar. The rusty wrought iron metal work that held the roof up looked every bit as old as the hundred years Nick mentioned.

"There used to be two massive Dutch Barns over there," pointed Nick, "but they had to come down about ten years ago, they kept swaying every time the wind blew – slates were flying off left right and centre, we thought they'd have someone's head off!"

"I can't imagine how I'd have done as a farmer, it all seems so alien to me." Said Simon.

"You'd have been fine, if you'd grown up here like us," replied Nick.

"I guess you're right. Sadly it wasn't to be though, was it?" Answered Simon.

That evening they enjoyed a fairly civilised evening meal, Jill turned out to be a very good cook.

Simon was tired after a long day and turned in to bed at 10 p.m., falling asleep in a matter of minutes. The following morning, they woke up to a gale blowing, and the wind whistling through the badly fitting old farmhouse windows. Nick ran Simon back up to the nursing home where he had another good hour-long chat with his mother. They both felt quite comfortable in each other's company and were equally interested in how their lives had headed in separate directions.

Nick could tell that Simon wasn't well, even over the last couple of days he could see him struggling to battle on. Simon knew his days at TayMarts were numbered. His health was deteriorating week by week and his enthusiasm that had once been inexhaustible was now waning.

Ironically, had Simon not been the driving force behind the supermarkets onslaught on the price paid to farmers, James might not have died and Nick wouldn't have formed the AFA and the farmers wouldn't now be in such a good position for the future.

Nick had formed the AFA as a way to pull the farmers together and to halt the crushing effect the supermarkets were having on their industry. As it was growing its power was becoming a force to be reckoned with. The supermarkets could no longer call all the shots, if they wouldn't pay the price then they would struggle to get hold of the supplies they needed.

As the time for Simon to return to London approached, talk inevitably turned towards Simon's illness.

"I assume you're still needing that kidney transplant?" Nick said as though it was an everyday occurrence.

"Yes, I'm afraid I'm running out of time. Maybe it's for the best though, now all this history's come to light. At least everyone knows the truth now," he said.

"You say James would have been a suitable donor, had you not…" He stopped, realising the direction he was going in would just cause new aggravation. "I suppose I'm next on your shopping list?" Nick proclaimed. Simon was surprised Nick was so blunt.

"Technically, yes," said Simon "But there wouldn't be much point in me asking you. Not after all that's happened. No, I've had my time, not quite how I thought it would all work out but life deals us some strange hands."

"Oh no you don't Simon," said Nick abruptly.

"What?" Replied Simon.

"You're not getting out of all this that easily. You go disappearing for 45 years and cause no end of trouble – what with James and all the work I've had to do to fight bloody TayMarts. No, I think you need to stick around and help sort all this out," said Nick forcefully.

"What are you saying Nick?" Said Simon.

"I'm saying we'd best get me tested and see if my kidney's any good to you. It might have suffered a bit of alcohol damage over the years," he smiled.

"Are you serious? You'd help me with this?" Said Simon.

"Aye, but don't get all soppy on me, I'm just doing what I think is right. Anyway, it might not work out," replied Nick.

"I don't know what to say." Simon paused.

He couldn't believe what he was hearing, he was sure that Nick would never forgive him for what had happened. Maybe he wouldn't, but he didn't seem to want to see another brother die.

By the time they were in York Nick had agreed to let Simon sort out an appointment in the next week or so at York hospital and see whether they were indeed compatible. Nick left the train at York and headed off to tell his wife that he was considering donating one of his major organs to a man that, only a couple of weeks ago he'd have happily seen pushed under a bus.

As the train hauled its ten carriages out of the station on its final two hour run to London, Simon was feeling a new sense of optimism, maybe even happiness, something that he'd not felt in the last few months. He leaned back in his seat and hoped that perhaps, after all this time, the family that he'd once been a part of might at last pull itself back together.

Simon had one more reunion to make – with his sister Liz. He'd got her phone number from Nick and would call her once he was back in London. He knew nothing of Liz.

She'd been a baby when he disappeared, and although he'd come across his brothers by accident over the years, he'd no recollection of ever having seen Liz. Nick had given him a brief account of her moving to Leeds and subsequently London, other than that he didn't know much at all.

The next day, Friday, ushered in the usual trip across town for yet another dialysis session. When this was finished and Simon had arrived back at his London home, he picked up the phone and dialled Liz's number.

"Hello, is that Liz, Liz Brown?"

"It's Liz Aldrich, but yes, I was a Brown once. Who is this?" She said.

"Sorry, yes it's your brother Jack. I was a Brown once myself," he replied.

"My God. I can't believe you're really alive. I'd heard you'd shown up, Nick called me yesterday to say you might call. To be honest, I wasn't sure whether to believe him, after all you've been missing for close to half a century," Liz said still feeling curious.

"I thought that maybe we could meet up?" Simon held his breath waiting for Liz's answer. "We've a bit of time to make up."

"Of course we can, that would be nice. I can finally see who Jack is after all these years. How about tomorrow night?" Liz said excited at being reunited with her long lost brother.

"That would be good," said Simon "Where do you live?"

"We have a house just off Bayswater Road. How about you?" Liz replied.

"Well, it's hard to believe but I'm just off Brompton Road, over the other side of Hyde Park. I could meet you in the bar at the top of the Hilton if you'd like?" Said Simon.

"Great – how about 8 p.m.?" Liz answered.

"Do you want me to wear a carnation or something, so you'll recognise me?" said Simon smiling.

"Don't worry; I'll be able to spot you. If you're really a Brown, I'll recognise you," she said laughing.

That night, he could feel his stomach tighten with the nervous anticipation of the meeting he was about to have.

He hoped he'd be able to spot her. He got to the Hilton about a quarter of an hour early as he figured he'd rather be the one sitting with a drink than the one wandering in to a busy restaurant and trying to spot a stranger.

The 5* Hilton Hotel stood proudly towering above everything around it in the heart of Mayfair. The lift carried him swiftly to the 28th floor where the bar was already quite busy with a lively atmosphere created by the crowd within. Simon found himself a small table for two by the window and ordered himself a gin and tonic. From where he'd positioned himself he could keep a close eye on the entrance and try to spot his sister when she arrived. A young couple in their late twenties entered the bar followed by one old man with a grey beard and ears that quite impressed Simon – they were like bin lids!

Behind him came a lady who looked about the right age, displaying all the signs of someone looking for someone.

That's got to be her, thought Simon who rose to his feet and signalled with his arm towards her. She smiled and headed in his direction.

"Liz?" Asked Simon.

"Yes, Jack?" She replied.

"No, I mean yes. I'm still not used to being a Jack. I've been a Simon for as long as I can remember. It gets a bit confusing."

Liz gave him a loose, slightly formal hug and sat down opposite him.

"Well here we are," said Liz.

"Yes - strange isn't it? The sister I didn't know I had has been living on the opposite side of the park," said Simon.

The waiter walked over and asked Liz what she'd like. She ordered herself a white wine spritzer and turned back to Simon.

"It's all strange, let's be honest, you're supposed to be my Brother and in fairness you're a total stranger. You could be anyone, although I can see a bit of James in you."

"I'm not sure what to say to that," Simon quipped.

"Oh, sorry, I didn't mean that nastily, I just meant that we are, strangers that is. To me you were always just part of a family story," said Liz trying to correct herself.

"You're quite right, you don't remember me but I never even knew you all existed." He paused, "I love it up here, and the view is amazing. On a clear night like this you can just see for miles."

From where they were sitting they could indeed see for miles – across metropolitan London, towards Buckingham Palace and then the buildings that rolled relentlessly out towards the horizon.

"I know it's great. How long have you been in London? And for that matter, how did you end up here at all? You were lost in Cyprus. It's not exactly around the corner," said Liz. Simon had by now become quite used to recounting his side of the story and began reeling it off to Liz who, apart from the odd interruption, listened with interest.

"Amazing. They all thought you'd gone for good you know," she said.

"Well I'm back, I'm just not sure how I'll fit in with all this," he replied.

"You'll be ok now, I'm sure," she said smiling, and then proceeded to give him a brief summary of her progress down the country, from their home in Scotland, to Leeds and subsequently down to London.

Her career and her husband, Mike and after a couple of hours, a few more drinks and much story-telling, they headed home.

"You must come round and meet Mike sometime, I'm sure he'd like to meet you and we do only live across the park," said Liz.

"That'd be nice, I'll give you a call," he said as he closed Liz's taxi door. The weather that night was quite warm so Simon opted to take a casual stroll back home.

Simon was surprised to get a call from Nick on Sunday afternoon asking whether he'd made the appointment for him at the hospital. He almost sounded keen.

Simon had spoken to Dr Collinson whilst at the hospital on Friday and she'd promised him she'd get it sorted out which he relayed to Nick. He expected to know the following morning and said he'd confirm it when he got back.

"I can't believe you need to sit in a hospital for hours every other day," Nick remarked.

"I'm sort of stuck with it, could be worse, there's plenty of folk stuck in there permanently. At least I get some time at home. Anyway, I really appreciate you doing this it means such a lot. I'll call you tomorrow," said Simon enthusiastically.

Back at the hospital on Monday, Dr Collinson told Simon that York Hospital would do the test whenever Nick could get in – he just needed to give them a call. It was a simple blood test and a few health questions, nothing difficult. If this turned out to be a match, they'd need to act fast as Simon's health was deteriorating faster than before.

"If you get any worse, you may have to be admitted," the doctor said sternly.

"I don't think I'd like that," said Simon. "I was only saying to Nick yesterday at least I get to go home."

"We'll see how you go in the next couple of weeks, but unless you're very careful with your diet, I'll have no choice but to admit you. At least it sounds like this thing with your brother might work out okay, that's a good step in the right direction," she said.

Simon headed back home having been catapulted back into a state of worry and depression. He needed that operation or he knew his time was up. That night he called Nick and passed on the details of who to call and what needed to be done, also trying to express the need to get this done quickly without sounding pushy. Nick told him he'd get the tests done a.s.a.p. and report back. Simon hung up and sat staring into space, going over what had just been said, analysing the details of the conversation as he would the details in a business contract.

Two hundred miles away, Nick sat back in his armchair, took another mouthful of the whiskey he wasn't supposed to be drinking and reflected on the path he was about to take.

He would need a major operation and would be off work for weeks – maybe a couple of months. That wasn't good. Sarah didn't like it; she still couldn't come to terms with the idea that Nick would risk his life to help this man that had caused them so much misery.

"I'm surprised you're even thinking about helping this man, after all he's done to you. To us," Sarah said objectively.

"He's still my Brother for God's sake. I've got to try. I've got to know him a bit more and he's not a bad bloke. Admittedly his business ethics are a bit ruthless, but he just wanted to be the best at what he did, he thinks much like me, he just happened to be playing for the other side.

He didn't know he was fighting his own family. I've lost one brother and I don't think I could live with myself if I didn't try to help. I'm probably his only hope, unless Liz is a suitable donor and I don't want my sister put through that," said Nick trying his best to put his point across.

"I suppose, if it was my brother, I'd do the same. Unless you're put in that position you never really know what you'd do," Sarah replied.

"I'm calling the hospital tomorrow to find out what's to be done. For now, I think I'll have another glass of that 15-year-old Balvenie, it's going down a treat," said Nick.

"You're going to have to knock that on the head too," replied Sarah. "What do you mean?" Nick asked.

"If they were testing your blood tomorrow they'd find most of it was alcohol! If you do the operation I'm pretty sure they won't want you full of malt whiskey," she replied.

"It might not be in the best condition but at least it'll be sterile," Nick joked.

Nick arrived as requested on Wednesday morning where having made his way to the renal department, was shown into a small consultation room.

Dr Fisher sat there, reading through some notes. He peered over the top of the file as Nick entered.

"Take a seat young man."

Nick was called many things but at 50 years old he wasn't often referred to as young.

The doctor did look as though he was probably close to retirement age, his hair grey and thin on top, with hands trembling ever so slightly yet noticeably as he held the file in front of him. He laid it down and leant back in his chair.

"Mr Brown. Nice to meet you. Now I understand you're interested in donating a kidney to your brother."

"Yes," Nick replied. "It wouldn't be my first choice but he's not in a very good way. How do we go about it?"

"Firstly, I need to talk you through all the pros and cons, and then we take some blood and just check you're a good match, and then we'll come up with a time to perform the operation. Okay?"

"Yes, that sounds good, you'd best tell me what I'm letting myself in for," Nick replied.

The doctor went on to explain the process in detail.

"We'll take blood and urine samples. The donor must be either the same blood type as the recipient or blood type "O." If these look okay, we'll give you a general medical and finally a renal Arteriogram to check that both your kidneys are in good order. How many units of alcohol do you take a week?"

"Well I'm not really sure. I try and have my fair share" said Nick smiling.

Ignoring Nick's quick response, Doctor Fisher carried on asking questions.

"You could do to stop smoking and drinking, certainly for the time being. Is that going to be a problem?" he asked.

"No, I suppose not," replied Nick at the same time as thinking '*how the hell am I going to cope with that?*'

"How much pain will I be in and how long before I can get back to work?" He asked quickly.

"I won't lie to you. The first week to ten days after the operation will be very uncomfortable. We'll give you painkillers to help you through it. Generally we expect donors to be fully recovered in around two months," he replied.

"All sounds like good fun! We'd best get on with it then," said Nick.

"Are you sure you don't want to know a few more details? It's a big decision," said Doctor Fisher.

"No. If you keep talking I'll end up changing my mind. I've heard enough already, Nick replied. "As long as it's unlikely to kill me, I'll take my chances."

"It shouldn't kill you, but there's always a slight risk," uttered Doctor Fisher.

"You're not selling it to me – let's just get on," said Nick. His mind was definitely made up.

"I'll just need to listen to your heart. Can you slip your shirt off?" Asked Doctor Fisher.

Nick unbuttoned his shirt and sat on the edge of the bed. The doctor listened to Nick's chest and back. "I see you've had some surgery. Appendectomy?"

"Yes, long time ago," replied Nick.

"You'll get another scar, four to five inches just to the side there," he indicated.

"Won't bother me, I'm not planning on entering any beauty contests," Nick smiled.

The doctor explained there were a number of forms to be completed and once these were done, Nick would be given a bottle to hand a urine sample in before he left and then sent down to give blood.

The results would be known in around three working days.

Once back at Chestnut Farm, Nick had thrown himself into his work, he'd been away for quite a few days and he wanted to take his mind off the constant internal wrangling he was putting himself through.

Even though he no longer needed to fight with Simon at TayMarts, he still had hundreds of farmers relying on his Association to keep their sales prices at a decent level.

Richard Locker had been looking after things as usual and had a ton of messages to go through with Nick, all in all though, everything was going well. Richard's Labrador, Tess, had made a rug at the side of his desk her home – she could lay there undisturbed by everyone's comings and goings and had almost become a part of the furniture.

Richard had been following Nick's family history unfolding from close quarters and was surprised to learn of Nick's decision to donate one of his major body organs to the enemy, as he described TayMarts.

"I always said they wanted our blood," laughed Richard "Surely this is beyond the call of duty!"

He understood really and told Nick to take all the time he needed, he could keep the ship afloat. Sarah was taking a bit more convincing. She tried to see both sides but she only knew Simon as the man from TayMarts and she'd never known Nick's younger brother Jack who'd disappeared all those years ago.

She was mainly worried about the impact on Nick's health, it didn't seem a good idea, she liked him just the way he was, 100% complete well 98% if you counted the missing appendix.

That evening they had another long chat about it with Sarah voicing all her concerns. Nick though, was a forceful man and he'd made up his mind, whatever had gone before, he'd help his brother become a part of the family for whatever time he had left, which, without surgery, could only be weeks. Sarah had always loved Nick and promised to stand by his decision.

"Look at it this way; at least I'll have my own trained nurse on hand to look after me," he smiled.

"That's what worries me – you'll have me running around after you for months," joked Sarah. Exactly three days after Nick had had his tests he could wait no longer, he wasn't the most patient man, and he wanted to know the results.

He telephoned the hospital and asked to be put through to the renal department. Unfortunately the nurse on duty couldn't get hold of Dr Fisher and didn't know where to find the results; however she did promise that someone would call Nick back as soon as she had any information.

Nick had to carry on with his day but was having trouble concentrating on the job in hand, in his mind he couldn't decide if he'd be happier if the results were for, or against him making the donation.

After having replied to a handful of letters left on his desk, Dr Fisher finally called back. "We've got the results of the blood test and you're a perfect match.

We've a few more tests to do but it looks like you'll be a suitable donor for your brother."

"Thanks. That's good news. I'll give him a ring and see when he needs me," replied Nick.

Nick tried ringing Simon that night, but he couldn't get an answer. He tried a few times but to no avail – the phone just rang and rang.

"I thought he'd be at home, Sarah," said Nick pondering.

"I'm surprised he's got the energy to go out. I'll try again in the morning."

The following morning, Nick had done a few jobs around the farm and come back to the house for a coffee when the phone rang. It was Dr Collinson from the Royal London Hospital, Whitechapel. She informed Nick that Simon had taken a turn for the worse and had been admitted the morning before.

"How bad is it? Will he live?" Nick asked bluntly, never one to side step the issue.

"Well we hope so, but he's not well at all, without a transplant he's not got long. I'm so sorry."

"What do you mean by 'not well at all'?" Nick replied.

"Not good. He collapsed but luckily came round and called for an ambulance. He's in intensive care now in a stable condition," she said.

"I assume you know I've had the tests to be a donor?" Replied Nick.

"Yes, I've got the results here on my desk, that's why I took the liberty of phoning. If you're still prepared to help, we need to get on with it before Simon gets any weaker. He needs his remaining strength to get through the surgery."

"Yes, I'm going to help – just tell me what I need to do, and when," he asked.

"If possible I'd be looking at next week, I've just got to get authorisation and make a few arrangements. I'll call you as soon as I've got some firm news," she replied.

Nick was now quite shaken up. As he spoke he could feel his mouth had dried up as the reality hit home. He would be undergoing major surgery and it could be within days. It would probably be no worse than when he had his appendix out, the difference was that he didn't have time to worry about it then, one minute he was fine, the next he was in an operating theatre.

He had hoped the surgery could take place in York but Dr Collinson had advised him that this was out of the question. They needed the donor and recipient in the same hospital, in separate theatres at the same time and Simon was in no condition for trekking back up the country.

Nick would have to stay in hospital for five days to a week before he could be moved back to York.

"Are you doing the surgery?" He asked.

"No, it's a specialist procedure," Doctor Collinson replied.

"I hope this surgeon knows what he's doing," Nick said trying to sound humorous but was genuinely concerned.

"Mr Meedon is highly respected. He's been performing these transplant operations for over a decade with excellent results. You don't need to worry about that," she said affirming her conviction.

"Just like to know what I'm up against," said Nick.

The next few days were strange for Nick.

He found himself sorting out his affairs as though he was going away for a long holiday, which, in a way he was. Jobs on the farm needed organising and his desk needed clearing. Richard was used to running things in the office but still needed to be brought up to speed on a few of Nick's jobs. Terry, Nick's farm manager also knew how things worked but Nick still liked to make sure everything was going to be looked after whilst he was away.

CHAPTER 28

Simon had woken up in a hospital bed with an array of machines around him and a tube inserted into the back of his left hand. A bag of fluid hung on a stand next to him. He knew he was in hospital, but how the hell had he got there? Pain throbbed slowly and intensely through the back of his head and he felt weak.

Lifting his hand seemed an effort in itself. He lay staring at the white ceiling whilst racking his brains, hoping for an image of what had happened to pop into view.

He remembered sitting in his usual armchair, he had a light supper, chicken and brown rice and was going to watch a bit of television, but what then?

His mind was blank. In fact, he'd stood up to carry his tray through to the kitchen and just collapsed, falling across a small round side table sending the onyx table lamp smashing on to the floor along with his bowl and cutlery.

He'd remained there until luckily, he came around about half an hour later. He'd been able to get to a phone that was within reach and dial 999.

The operator had picked up enough of his mumblings to get the ambulance to the right address where the front door was thankfully unlocked. Back in the present, a nurse spotted that he appeared to be conscious, his eyes open and slowly surveying the room.

"Ah, you've decided to join us then?" She asked.

"Yes. How long have I been here?" Simon replied.

"Since yesterday evening, I'd best get the doctor to look you over." She thought he still looked a bit grey but at least he'd woken up.

Dr Collinson walked into the room and picked up the clipboard that hung at the end of Simon's bed. "You've picked a fine time to wake up - I was just leaving." She smiled.

"Sorry, I'll try and time it better next time," answered Simon.

"Now I've told you about watching what you eat and drink and I'd take a bet you've been up to no good. I know very well you've got a taste for whisky. Well that's it now, you've pushed it a step too far," she said in a matter of fact way.

"What do you mean that's it? Am I going to live?" asked Simon.

"I think so, you're not leaving here until you've got a kidney that works," she replied.

"What if my Brother won't help?" Said Simon.

"He will. I've already spoken to him," she said.

"He will? Are you sure? What did he say?"

"He seemed keen to help – I've told him we need to act fast and he's ok with that," she said smiling.

"Well he said he'd help but I wasn't sure he meant it – not after all that's happened," said Simon.

"Well for now you need to rest – you're not leaving that bed. You can have some water, maybe a cup of tea if you can manage it, but that's it for now," said Doctor Collinson.

The transplant was planned for the following Thursday and would be carried out right there at the Royal London Hospital.

Nick had made arrangements to travel down with Sarah on the Tuesday although he wouldn't be admitted until Thursday morning. Sarah would be staying at Cambridge Heath Hotel only a five minute walk from the hospital until Nick was fit to travel back home.

Simon hadn't moved far, only a few yards down the hall to a private room once he was fit enough to leave intensive care. Nick and Sarah visited him on the Wednesday morning to see how he was doing, which in itself seemed strange as had it been a month earlier, they wouldn't have cared less about his future.

Sarah would have liked to have gone out for a meal that night but firstly Nick wasn't allowed anything but water after 6 p.m. and secondly, he wouldn't have had the appetite for it anyway – he was wondering how he'd let himself in for this in the first place. As he sat there one thing kept going through his mind, he wanted justice for his family, for his brother and that were now dead. He was trying to rebuild his relationship with his lost brother through the most tricky of circumstances, but he was damned if the abductors of Jack were going to walk free.

Simon, even though feeling totally let down, had unavoidably built a bond between himself and his 'surrogate' family which was all he'd ever known, and now, couldn't bring himself to inform the police.

Nick was still angry and felt no such leniency. He knew his father would have wanted to see the full weight of the law come down on them – if he'd found them in his younger days he'd have dealt with them personally, which would have probably involved his favourite 12 bore shotgun.

Sarah wasn't sure that this was the best time to take action but Nick was having none of it, he was sure his operation would be fine, but what if it wasn't?

If he didn't make it through alive, unlikely but possible, these people would get away with what they'd done, and he wasn't going to let that happen.

As Simon lay in bed with a drip in his arm, Nick, back in his hotel room, had found the phone number for the Salisbury police station and called them. It took some explaining, but eventually he'd fully recounted the story of his brother's abduction nearly half a century before and the evidence that had now come to light.

The detective he spoke to explained that it would take some time to collate the details of the case which may not be logged in the current database, after which they would certainly follow up these new 'leads'.

Nick had hoped they'd fly down to the Elliott household and drag them off to the nearest police cell, but this seemed unlikely. Nick had no intention of telling Simon what he'd done, not until after the operation at any rate, he didn't want to make things worse at this juncture.

Thursday morning came, all too soon for Nick's liking.

He'd got a small bag of belongings ready and, having been escorted in by his wife, was soon being shown to a bed in the day admissions ward located in the west wing of the Royal London.

It was a small male-only ward with four other beds, each already harbouring a patient who wanted to keep himself to himself, as did Nick.

He'd had to dress in one of the unappealing blue gowns with half the back missing, after which he was left with just his newspaper for company. He lay there until 2 p.m. when he was wheeled off to the anaesthetic room adjacent to the theatre. He couldn't help but remember that cold night of 18th March 1966 when he'd been lying in a very similar room prior to the removal of his appendix.

Nick tried to persuade himself that this would be no worse. The operation would only take around two and a half hours to complete and Simon was already lying on the operating table down the corridor with a team of surgeons working away, getting ready for the insertion of a new kidney.

The surgeons were leaving the original kidneys in place and inserting the new one lower down in the abdomen, just above the groin. The transplant kidney would have its own artery vein and ureter.

Nick's operation went smoothly enough; it was quite a common procedure and had a good success rate. The surgeons had successfully removed his kidney and found nothing to cause concern. Nick was woken up around 6 p.m. by a friendly nurse.

"How are you feeling?" She asked. Nick seemed somewhat disorientated.

"Have you finished?" He replied dozily.

"I certainly hope so! You're in our little recovery room," she replied.

"I feel tired. Did you need to wake me up so soon?" Nick said.

"I'm afraid we did, we need to check your blood pressure.

You shouldn't feel much for the next few hours whilst the anaesthetic's still working. If you have any problems just give me a shout. We'll monitor you here for the next hour and then you'll be moved back to a ward."

"Do you know if the donation worked" Nick asked.

"Sorry, I couldn't tell you, they're still operating. I do know they retrieved your kidney without issue. I'll let you know if I hear anything," she said.

"Thanks," Nick replied. An hour later he was wheeled down to his new temporary home, another bed in a different ward. There was still no sign of Simon appearing in the recovery ward.

Nick felt uncomfortable but not in much pain, the anaesthetic that covered the trauma his body had undergone still left the majority of his midsection numb. Even though it didn't hurt he didn't think he should be moving around and did his best to lie still, he soon nodded off.

Simon had arrived in the recovery ward only about twenty minutes after Nick had been wheeled out and had remained unconscious for a further 30 minutes. Simon finally woke up and described his condition as 'like having been run over.' Unsurprising as he'd been in a bad way before he even went in.

"Did it work?" he mumbled to the nurse.

"Yes, Mr Elliott, I believe so. The doctor will be along to see you shortly, just try and stay still please."

"And my brother, Nick, how's he?"

"He's doing just fine; he's back in his ward, sleeping like a baby."

For half an hour Simon lay there looking at the ceiling. He studied the fine cracks in the plaster, the fluorescent light fittings and the little flashing light on the side of a smoke detector. How many others had stared at these mundane day to day objects that would normally go unnoticed, whilst lying on one of these beds? Hundreds probably. Finally, he heard the familiar voice of Dr Collinson drawing him out of the daydream he'd found himself in.

"How are you feeling Simon?"

"I can hear you so I must be alive. I can't feel much down there though. How did it go? Will I live?" He asked.

"Mr Meedon tells me that it went as planned and your new kidney is all connected although it'll be a few days before we know if it's working okay. Your Brother's fine, just resting now."

"Will I be able to see him?" Asked Simon.

"I think it's a case of him visiting you. He'll be up and about before you, but that could be a few days yet," she replied.

"Can you send my thanks to him?" Said Simon.

"I'll do that. Now you rest, I'm going to get you moved back to your room shortly. We'll be keeping a close eye on you."

For the next few days there they were, two brothers separated years ago now lying in separate rooms barely fifty feet apart, once bitter rivals and now the unlikeliest of donor partners. Sarah came to see Nick every day and sat with him for a couple of hours. Nick sent her down the corridor to see how Simon was doing. The nurse in his room had told her that he was recovering well, which she'd relayed to Nick.

Nick had found the first few days very uncomfortable and the pain from his abdomen was quite severe. Even with the painkillers supplied by the nurses, it was hard to avoid the constant aching which wouldn't disappear even if he lay on his back or his side.

On Friday morning, as the two brothers lay in hospital, the police in Salisbury had received all the files from Scotland that detailed the disappearance of one Jack Brown from the island of Cyprus in 1949. Further to Nick's information they'd contacted Dr Collinson who'd confirmed that DNA proved Simon Elliot was indeed the missing boy, Jack Brown. They decided that this was a serious accusation and they would bring Mr and Mrs Elliott in for questioning as soon as they could be located.

It was a normal quiet Saturday morning at the Elliot's' house, Alex sat in his conservatory reading the paper and Louise was in the kitchen ironing when their peace was broken by a loud knocking at the front door. Louise was surprised to see two police officers standing there.

"Mrs Elliot, Mrs Louise Elliot?" One of them said.

"Yes, that's me, has there been an accident?" She replied.

"No, nothing like that. Is your husband at home?" the elder officer enquired.

"Yes, he's through here." She led them through to the conservatory.

"Mr and Mrs Elliott, we're arresting you on suspicion of abduction. You do not have to say anything, but it may harm your defence if you do not mention when questioned something which you later rely on in court. Anything you do say may be given in evidence."

The words hit them with a sledge hammer blow. Louise clung to her husband who had stood up as the police had entered.

"Oh Alex, what are we going to do?" She shouted.

"Just keep calm Louise, don't say anything." There were no handcuffs, the Elliott's were just led out to the waiting police car and ushered into the back. The pair just sat quietly although they hadn't wanted to believe it, they'd always known that their past would probably catch up with them.

By Saturday morning, Nick felt well enough to get out of bed and have a wander round. As he stood up straight his mid-section felt very sore and it took him a couple of attempts to get fully upright. It reminded him again of having his appendix out.

The nurse on duty gave him directions to the room Simon was lying in further down the corridor, on the same floor.

He gave three sharp knocks on the door and poked his head through.

"Aye. Right room," he said as he peered inside. Simon was lying there with an array of monitors surrounding his bed.

"How're you doing Simon? You look like you're wired up to the national grid," Nick chirped.

"I'm good, thanks. You look well. They tell me it went okay," said Simon.

"Still bloody hurts," smiled Nick.

"At least you're up and about," laughed Simon.

"Yes. I was sick of lying looking at that ceiling," Nick laughed.

"When can you leave?" asked Simon.

"Hopefully by Monday, they just want to keep an eye on me before I jump back on the train to York. How about you Simon?"

"I'm not sure. They haven't told me yet, they just keep telling me we need to take it one day at a time," he replied.

"What will you do when you get out? Are you planning on going back to work?" Asked Nick.

"What, to fight with you again?" He gave a short chuckle. "No, I think my days at TayMarts are over. They're not really expecting me back, they've offered me a good pension," said Simon.

"You can't be pensioned off at fifty, you'll be bored to death," replied Nick.

"I know it's not really me. To tell you the truth, I've done a lot of thinking over the past few days, there's not much else to do in here," said Simon.

"And what was your verdict?" Replied Nick.

"I know we've had our differences," said Simon.

"That's something of an understatement," Nick interjected.

"Yes, well I do regret some of the things I've done, and, you know, what happened with James. How would you feel if I came and worked with you, swap sides so to speak?"

Nick couldn't believe what he was hearing.

"I'm sorry, my hearing must be going. I thought you just said you'd come and work with me!" Exclaimed Nick.

"That's exactly what I said," replied Simon.

Nick paused for a moment as the pair just looked at each other.

"That would mean you'd have to battle against your precious supermarkets? Are you serious?" Asked Nick.

"Well it would make a change. After all, it's where I would have been if things had worked out the way they should, and I do have a bit of insider knowledge. Might help make up for some of things that have happened, smooth things over a bit between us," Simon replied.

"I'm not sure. I'm still trying to get used to us being brothers, but, whether we could work together, well that's another matter," said Nick wistfully.

"Well get back to bed and think about it," Simon said with a wry smile on his face.

Back in his hospital bed, Nick did just that. He lay there just thinking about all that had happened and the prospect of his former business enemy working alongside him.

Since James had died, his whole focus had been on beating TayMarts and in particular their main man, Simon Elliot. How could this ever work?

He wasn't sure what to make of the idea but all the time he could picture young Jack, lost for all those years, just looking for someone to bring him back into the family.

What would his father have thought had he been here now? Just when life had dragged you down a road you couldn't have imagined, it always seemed to have a way of throwing up yet one more turn.

He stared at the vertical blinds that swayed backwards and forwards across the open window, the sound of the traffic below droning on and on – not something a country boy could ever get used to.

Nick's thoughts were only interrupted by a nurse who insisted on taking his temperature and blood pressure for what seemed like the tenth time that day.

"I'll be glad to get home to some peace and quiet," he said as she rolled up his sleeve.

"Won't be long now," said the nurse "The doctor says you might be okay to leave tomorrow." This cheered Nick up no end, a possible escape from the sights and smells of this hospital that he'd now seen quite enough of.

Sure enough the doctor gave Nick permission to leave the next morning, under strict conditions. He was to rest at home, no heavy lifting and no driving for at least ten days. He would also have to attend a couple of check-ups at the York hospital.

This was fine, Nick would be quite happy to rest for a few days, let Sarah run around after him, he was sure she'd be happy about that!

The train journey back to York wasn't too bad, the First Class seats being fairly comfortable. On the way he and Sarah discussed Simon's idea of working for them, an idea that was still hard to grasp.

The years that they'd spent fighting each other couldn't just be brushed under the carpet. To Simon it had just been work; he didn't seem to appreciate the damage he'd been causing to the Farms.

To Nick, with the death of James it had been very real, a deep anger and hatred that had been nurtured within him.

When Nick was at one of his lowest points, it was Nick's friend Matt that had helped him turn the corner.

He'd warned Nick of the utter futility of battling relentlessly in revenge for his brother. "The only person that you'll hurt in the end is yourself. When you're angry and you focus all your thoughts on your opponent, all you really do is damage yourself. You need to let it go, forgive them to save yourself."

Nick knew his obsession with beating TayMarts had taken its toll on him and he wanted to find a way out. It was this advice that helped him decide to donate a kidney to his long lost brother, a deed that had already made Nick feel better in himself. He'd come this far and now his brother, whilst showing remorse, was offering to leave his hard earned career behind him and side with the AFA.

Nick's mind became clearer. This was Simon's olive branch and Nick knew he must take it. The Brown family had been through enough heartache and now there was a chance to leave the pain behind.

By the time the train had arrived in York, Nick had decided to let Simon join the AFA and hoped that together they'd be able to make up for some of the years they'd lost.

As opponents they'd fought hard, who knows how much they could achieve working together.

Now Nick had made his peace with Simon, he didn't really have the same enthusiasm for fighting TayMarts, however, he still knew he must stand up for his members and secure better deals all round. Many farmers still had to sell up and lose their livelihoods because they just couldn't afford to sell at ever decreasing prices, and having seen his brother James destroyed, he didn't want to see others in the same boat.

With Simon's new-found knowledge of where he'd come from and the life he could have led, he seemed to see the other side of the story in a much clearer light, he had a compelling desire to help undo some of the damage he'd caused.

Simon remained in hospital for a full two weeks after the operation. As Nick tentatively started work again back in Yorkshire, Simon was only just heading to his London home which he'd left. A week after the operation, Ralph had visited Simon and broken the news to him that Alex and Louise had been arrested. Simon didn't need a degree in psychology to realise that Nick must have informed the authorities.

He couldn't blame him, not after all the heartache the Brown family had been through. In a way he wanted them to face the consequences of what they'd done, it was wrong and they'd always known it.

As soon as Simon arrived home, he called Nick to see how he was doing.

"They've let you out then?" Said Nick "I hope that kidney of mine's doing its job?"

"It's amazing, I already feel like a new man. I've got so much more energy I can hardly believe it. I can't thank you enough for standing by me. I heard that you'd called the police about my 'parents'. I just want you to know that I'd have done the same thing had the tables been

turned," said Simon.

"Sorry but I had no choice, I couldn't just let them carry on without consequence. I shouldn't think the punishment would be much after all these years.

Anyway, I'm pleased your operation's been a success; just see you behave yourself – no unhealthy eating or drinking now," said Nick.

"I wouldn't dare," Simon replied. "Have you given my job idea any more thought?"

"Yes, I've given it a lot of thought. If you're up for it, you can work with me. You'd have to pull your weight though, we've no room for lightweights round here," said Nick laughing.

"That's great news, I'm sure I can be of some help, and by the way, I'm no lightweight as you so delicately put it," replied Simon defending himself.

"Now there is one problem that strikes me. You live in the middle of London and we're based in York. That's a bit of a distance," said Nick.

"I suppose I could either work from home here, I'd be near the headquarters of many of the supermarkets, obviously, or, I'd have to move up to Yorkshire and work from your old barn," said Simon.

"Less of the old barn, that's our high tech nerve centre. It just looks like an old barn," remarked Nick.

"I'll give it some thought. There's not much keeping me in London. A change of scenery might be good for me," said Simon.

Back in Salisbury Alex and Louise were charged with child abduction and granted bail. Six weeks later, the Crown Court heard the full story.

They denied abduction claiming they'd found little Jack and were just looking after him, but the evidence was stacked against them. The jury of nine men and three women found both of them guilty of child abduction as detailed in the Child Abduction Act 1984 section two. It was a unanimous decision. The judge made it clear that, just because so many years had passed, it made the crime no less serious. Others must realise that they can't get away with such a crime just because they weren't found straight away. Alex and Louise had shown remorse and apologized for what they did.

The judge summed up by telling them that 'what they'd done to the Brown family was unforgiveable'.

He remained unmoved and sentenced the couple to seven years in prison each. They were completely shocked.!

Alex had remained stern faced; Louise had broken down in the dock and had to be carried out. Ralph who had sat through the whole trial was also shocked, although, like Simon and everyone else, he knew that what they'd done was wrong.

When Simon heard he wasn't surprised. He still had mixed feelings for his 'former' parents. He thought he might visit them in prison, but not for the time being.

It was two months before Simon was well enough to start work for the AFA. His new kidney seemed to be working well and every day he felt better, much more like his old self. Having felt lousy for so many years he'd forgotten what it felt like to be fit and well. The decline had been very steady. It was only now that the energy was returning that he felt ready to return to work.

He kept his house in London, for whatever reason, besides which he liked the old place. Nick had found him a nice cottage to rent not a mile from Chestnut Farm, his new place of work. Simon continued to recover and, although still needing regular hospital check-ups, was enjoying not having to be hooked up to the dialysis machine three times a week.

It wasn't long before he'd moved up to his new cottage, a far cry from the buzz of the city. Having been used to having shops that sold anything he could want within walking distance, this country living was going to take some getting used to.

The only thing within walking distance was a primitive local shop that doubled up as a post office. For anything else, he'd need to drive into York. The initial introductions to Richard and John in the office were slightly awkward; they'd all spoken before, usually arguing over produce prices. Now they'd have to work alongside each other.

Another antique desk had been found and brought in ready for Simon's arrival. Everything he'd need was present and correct. Simon settled into his new seat, took his diary from his brief case and opened it.

"Now, where should I start?" He asked, looking at Nick.

"Well you could telephone your former employers and get us a better deal for carrots, their offer's laughable. I don't know where they got the idea that we'd take that little?" Nick smirked. He threw a file onto Simon's desk that listed a group of farmers who were waiting for an outcome.

"I think I can handle that." Simon picked up the phone and dialled the number he knew all too well.

"Morning. Can I speak to Simon Elliot's replacement please?"

"It's Simon," he stopped mid-sentence. Simon looked across the room at Nick who was tapping the keys of his calculator.

"IT'S JACK…JACK BROWN!

ACKNOWLEDGEMENTS

I'd just like to acknowledge my mentor, Mandy Hildred of Action Coach for pushing me to get this book published and Daisa & Co for actually achieving it.